north

Book 1 of the Morningstar series

LJ FARROW

Text and Artwork Copyright © 2016 LJ Farrow

All rights reserved. No part(s) of this book may be reproduced, distributed or transmitted in any form, or by any means, or stored in a database or retrieval systems without prior express written permission of the author of this book.

ISBN: 9781535606127

*For MJW, who blessed us with a mother's love and an unfailing belief
in the talents of her children*

Contents

amaoke 13
nanatha 167
now 247
after 401
Acknowledgements 413
Glossary of Terms 415
About the Author 417

Amaoke paused on the ridge above the small house and rested his axe on one shoulder. His smile was small, but it did not measure his delight at returning; rather, it marked his amusement that in his mind, this place was still and only hers.

He marveled that after centuries of life, and centuries of change, his brain rejected the idea of personal ownership. His mother's people had no concept of private ownership; everything belonged to nature, to everyone who had a need, not to anyone in particular.

So the small house in the clearing, the garden, the sunflowers, the view of the setting sun – all were hers if he had to assign any ownership at all.

Amaoke paused here, as he did every time he returned, until he could catch her scent and feel her ownership settle upon his shoulders. She owned him, too – yet another departure from the traditions with which he had been raised. A person, it was believed, was owned only by him- or herself. One's unique life-force was a gift of the Great Spirits and was sacred and precious. But for the first and only period in his long, long life, Amaoke knew his person was wholly devoted to another human being. And the Beast inside him was now, mostly, quiet.

Murmuring a prayer as old as time, the words to which only he was left to remember, he started down toward the house. When he got close enough to be heard, he began to hum her favorite tune, and stepped purposefully and loudly on the dry branches under the trees, announcing his return.

His wife, Nanatha, opened the door when he was ten feet away, looking like an expectant child for all her eighty-odd years of life.

"Four nights gets longer every time," she exclaimed, as he set down the axe inside the back door.

Amaoke scooped her up as he always had, in one strong arm, nuzzling his face into her neck. She was still ticklish, and shrieked like the girl she had once been. "And that beard grows longer in four days, too, I would swear to it." She shook a finger at him as he set her gently on her feet, and, despite her protests, kissed her deeply.

"Ama," she scolded, "I'm too old for that."

He peered closely at her flushed cheeks and neck. "Since when?" And just for good measure, he kissed her again, tasting her sweetness, inhaling her crisp, clean scent mixed with earth from her garden, bread from the hearth, and a trace of his own scent because she was his mate. And then something else, something new, unfamiliar, and dark. Just a hint of something he couldn't place, like dead wet leaves at the end of the autumn, and then it was gone. Amaoke wanted to believe that he was imagining it, wanted to be uncertain that he had sensed it at all, but in a moment, his heart knew what it meant. She was fading, soon to be lost to time, like so many other things.

She fed him a hearty rabbit stew with winter vegetables, and before bedtime, she gathered up her scissors, his razor, and soap. Each time he returned, she shaved his beard. It amused him; she said she couldn't see enough of his face under it, and he told her a wife should be thankful for a beard on an ugly husband.

The shaving had become one of their intimate rituals, almost a celebration of his return, like a renewal as they picked up the rhythm of their lives each month. He suspected that his wife recognized how pleasurable the shave was for him and so he left it for her to do each month after he returned from the forest.

"Hmmm. Are you sure it was only for four days?" She smiled, stroking his beard.

"It felt like four hundred years," he remarked, putting his hands on her waist.

"Ama!" She ducked away, laughing. "What got into you out there?"

As she trimmed with her scissors, he closed his eyes. She said, "There's animal fur in this beard again. Ama, my goodness, what do you get up to out there?" He could hear her smile in her voice.

"I caught some rabbits for my supper," he murmured.

"In your teeth?!" she teased.

He opened one eye. "Well, ma'am, when I'm not burdened by your delicate sensibilities, I may not clean them as neatly as usual."

"And this looks like a white dog's hair over here. Just one," Nanatha remarked as she examined it carefully.

"Let me see," he requested, taking it from her and holding it out in the firelight. "Nope. Just getting grey hair. Sorry I'm such a mess."

"Fine with me if you want to carry all of that around in there like a Wildman," she laughed, then tried unsuccessfully to be stern. "As long as I never find a woman's hair in there," she warned.

"If you did, it'd be yours." Without opening his eyes, he bared his white teeth in a grin and patted her bottom. Then he gave up being patient altogether and stood up suddenly, taking her scissors away and swinging her into his arms.

"Ama!" she shrieked, protesting but laughing. "I'm not done!"

"You are now," he growled, snuffing her candles between his fingers and setting her gently on the bed. Her mild protests turned to sighs as he kissed her, then to soft moans as he reached beneath her nightgown and gently stroked her body. He kept his clothes on and pushed her hands lovingly away from his buttons. After decades of marriage, he knew where to touch her, and when she finally gave a soft, sweet cry, he pulled up the covers and held her until she slept.

amaoke

In the beginning, before the Beginning, the Ellam Yua, Great Spirit of the Universe, breathed life into the spirit world, sending forth beings of significant power and energy to set in motion a balanced order. These spirit totems were incapable of destruction; instead, they supported the creation of the natural world.

Among these, the spirits of the world, was one favored by Raven, the beloved, most beautiful Morningstar, whose songs and deeds exalted the works of the Great Spirit.

When the Raven created humans, with their frailty and their freedom, He asked the elemental beings of the earth to help and serve them, and show them the Way. The Morningstar could see that man was also beloved of Raven, and It was incensed when asked by Raven to serve man. Morningstar brought forth heat and ash from under the earth, and it shook, and it burned, and Morningstar cried out to Raven, saying that all-powerful fire could not be weakened enough for man to control it.

So Raven cast aside the Morningstar in favor of the other spirits and animal totems who showed a willingness to teach man the universal truths. As for the Morningstar, it kept with it the greater and lesser spirits of the darkness as Its helpmates, and was determined to make mischief about the earth. And these greater and lesser spirits lost the purity and knowledge bestowed upon them by the Great Spirit, and became mad, and developed new tastes, but bent themselves generally to evil purpose, bringing illness, death, and destruction, the antitheses to wholeness, health, and sacred creation.

It was the Morningstar who sent Bear Woman after her husband, making her jealous of the other wives, teaching her to murder her own kind, and causing the disastrous abandonment of her child. Her anger trapped her within the Bear, and the goodness of her motherhood and the family love of a wife were lost in the fire of her rage, destroying the natural order of these things.

The Morningstar turned the tribes of man one against the other; Its spirit energies confused their tongues so that they could no longer understand what their brethren spoke of, and this frustration separated them and generated mistrust.

As the path of men progressed, they took more of the land than was their own, and some of the ancient animal persons and their totems were lost forever, as was a belief in the natural order, and the desires of the Great Spirit were lost.

Men forgot which animals were sacred, and were tempted to eat of sacred flesh, and lost the respect for the natural world, no longer dancing and singing their thanks for gifts of sacrifice.

Men lost respect for men, and hunted, raped, and murdered one another, and poisoned one another with war, misusing the mysteries of plants and trees to weaken one another. Many were enslaved, and Raven could no longer walk with mischief among His people.

And it was still not enough, for the Morningstar knew that the spirits of the water, and of the earth, and of the air, and all the totems carried power in unity, and there were still enough who believed in this power to save the sacred Earth. The Morningstar saw the awesome power of the Great Spirit that still lived in the people, and It had a vision about the close of the world, in which It was defeated by the Ellam Yua, the all-knowing person of the universe, using the creative strength in nature to arm the people against evil.

The Morningstar sought a new way into the hearts of men to divide them and distract them from the creative force, and, determining that the downfall of Raven's beloved people was the purpose of the hunt, it sought to contaminate man with Its own evil spirit.

Using a pureflesh woman and a debased man, the Morningstar created a Beast, the first warrior chief of his kind, to instill genuine Fear into the people, and make them doubt the natural order, in an attempt to weaken the magic of the Great Spirit, and help evil prevail over the sacred.

1

NOKI FINISHED HER HEARTH CHORES and settled into bed alone. She hid herself under the many furs her husband's family had provided for their marriage bed. She did not remember falling asleep, but just as suddenly it seemed she was awake, because she sensed someone in the dwelling. Once she shook off the vestiges of a bad dream, she realized it was her husband's silhouette by the banked embers of the fire.

She suspected she was still asleep and dreaming, because Uqii was away on a hunting trip with the other young men from the village. They had set out from this late-winter hunting camp after relocating their families to the small sod houses in the shadow of the Kilbuck mountains. Here the trees were quiet with their mantles of snow, the blanketed forests damping the cries of the wind that lashed the tundra closer to the river. Wind's angry cries were not heard in this place, only the whispers of his children as they made their way across the treetops and played in the hollows, but this night was quieter than many another, and Noki wondered why she had not heard the approach of his sled.

Uqii appeared to be trying to warm up, just as he always did after a long sled trip or workday outdoors. Now she could feel the cold air clinging to his coat, and invading the dwelling, as if it wanted to displace all the heat preserved there. But there was something – she wasn't sure what — that was not quite right about his movements, as if he had been hurt.

Noki abandoned the blissful warmth of the bed and crossed to the doorway to look out on the night. The cold was bitter, and the full moon's light made the icy crust on the snow sparkle. Her husband's sled was there, and the dogs watching her from the shelter were his dogs, but they were eerily quiet; none of them spoke or called out. Nor did they sleep despite their late travel. It was far too early for his return, and an impractical distance to come for a short visit, but Noki smiled.

She and Uqii were still very newly married, and she knew he would brave the teasing of his brothers, cousins, and the other tribesmen in the hunting party to sneak away for a visit.

But still, Noki felt so drowsy that she could not shake the sense that she was dreaming, and she could not be convinced he was really there until she crept up behind him at the hearth and took a handful of the fur on his coat in her fist. Something flickered deep in his gaze as he turned to her, and she was briefly wary, but then she realized it was the reflected embers of the fire in his dark eyes. As soon as he opened his parka to pull her to him, she forgot any fear as his scent flooded her and his warmth surrounded her.

He did not speak, but this was not unusual. Uqii did not talk about things best expressed in other ways. His kiss conveyed all the love and longing that Noki herself was feeling. He stayed with her through the little hours of that long winter night. It seemed he could not get his fill of her, and sometime later, when the stars dimmed, they finally slept, Noki drifting off contentedly in Uqii's arms.

She woke suddenly from another dark dream and reached out for him, but the bed was empty and cold.

Noki went to the door and looked out upon a muted white morning. Snow fell in ragged white flakes from a sky of the same color, and the silence had a presence that sat upon the camp, absolute and pervasive. She noticed the sled tracks cut into the snow crust, both approaching and leaving the dwelling. The steady snow was filling the tracks, erasing them as she watched, but Noki smiled in spite of the sadness she felt.

It was then that she noticed the blood in the snow at her feet. A single bright crimson drop just outside the doorway that she couldn't explain. The snowflakes that landed there stained red as they settled, as if the blood were fresh. It was an ill omen.

2

SEVERAL DAYS PASSED. The weather was softening, and the music of the snowmelt was everywhere. Water dripped rhythmically from the branches of trees and shrubs, and the song of flowing water could be heard, softly at first, and then growing, becoming the roaring voice of the river, with the symphonic thunder of the breaking ice as it released its hold and was carried downriver to the sea. The women in the hunting camp knew spring was approaching and ventured out on the calmer days to gather berries from the previous harvest that had been preserved by winter's icy kiss. After the full moon's passage, the hunting party returned. Uqii was not with them.

Noki knew something was wrong when Anaq, the wife of Uqii's eldest brother, Unin, brought her a share of meat and fur. Anaq kept her eyes down while Noki formally accepted it, and said very little, which was unusual. Anaq was usually talkative, and she was proud of the honor of being the wife of the eldest son, so her silence was almost an assault, giving Noki reason to worry. Her fears escalated; usually, a husband would present the animals he had procured directly to his wife for ritual preparation.

It was Unin who brought her the news she awaited, that Uqii had been mauled by a bear, that they had not chased the animal off in time, but that Uqii had died a good, brave death. Which simply meant to Noki that he had suffered much from his wounds and did not ask his brothers to hasten his death. The men had observed the rituals for the dead, curtailing their hunting for the days it would take Uqii to travel to the land of the dead. They had performed his burial, leaving a totem memorial so that he was provisioned for the afterlife with his hunting weapons and other tools.

"When?" she wondered aloud, unable to help herself. She cast her eyes down, awaiting the rebuke for addressing Unin without permission.

But Unin was sorry for her, and he was kind. "The day of the full moon."

Noki thought he must be mistaken. That night she had seen Uqii alive. With profound sadness, she realized that the spirits had sent her an elaborate dream. Uqii had already gone on. But she remained silent, as custom dictated.

Unin touched her arm gently and said, "I will take you if you choose. Come to my woman, Anaq, and she will make a new place for you in the family dwelling with our mother and sisters and their children." Then he left her alone.

Noki felt very lucky. Unin could have expected her to come to him and submit to his desires like any other wife. He was giving her the choice. And by making her the offer, he was protecting her from the claims of other males in the family, including his brothers. Because he was the eldest son, he could waive the right. But once he offered it, even if he did not pursue the claim, and her, she was virtually free to remain a lifelong widow.

The only exception was his father, Atluq, who had three unmarried daughters, a wife, and several of his sons' wives and their children still living in the family dwelling. Atluq had the authority to supersede Unin's claim. Noki was fairly certain he was too old for such nonsense anyway. So she settled into a lonely life without her beloved husband, yet she was never alone.

When the hunting group returned to the village by the river, Noki mourned the loss of the hunting lodge where she had been allowed to live with her husband, the last place they had been together. She returned to her residence in the women's dwelling with her mother's cousins, as she would have even if Uqii had returned. He would have gone back to the *qasgiq*, the men's residence in the center of the village, where they would have picked up their lives of relative separation. She would have delivered his meals to him inside the men's dwelling, and he would have visited her in the evening for fellowship in the separate corner of the home that she shared with her mother's female relatives.

Village life was group life; it demanded her participation. Noki readily helped where she was needed, sewing hides and making clothing, working in the fish camp, and weaving grass mats and baskets with the other women, as yet oblivious to changes that had already been set in motion.

One afternoon, as Noki came up the path from the river, she felt lightheaded, so she kneeled to set her heavy burden on the ground. The basket of fish she carried was no different than others she had easily shouldered at this time of year, but it was still unseasonably cold, and both her sleep and appetite had been poor of late. She had thought it was her grief of Uqii's loss, but while she sat, she contemplated the time passage of two moons. She realized with astonishment that she was quick with child.

But Uqii's visit – it was impossible, he had been dying, if not already dead. And spirits couldn't – could they? Only then did Noki remember the initial strangeness of Uqii's movements that night. Only then was she truly afraid.

She sat there, among the pines, listening to the wind fray the tops of the trees. She sat for a long time, past when she knew she would be missed at home. Should she accept Unin's offer, and let him bed her as soon as possible? She shuddered, both at the thought of being close to anyone other than Uqii and at the thought of disgracing two families with such a lie.

Even though Noki knew the truth was even more unbelievable, she could not dishonor herself in such a way. She shouldered her burden, which felt heavier than ever, and made her way carefully home, knowing that the life of a disgraced woman could be forfeit. She wondered who was left to speak on her behalf, if it should come to pass that she was to answer the questions she knew were ahead.

Noki's parents were long dead, having been lost to exposure in a storm. They had gone out to secure existing food stores during a blizzard, and as the snow and wind became stronger, they were believed to have walked past the dwellings in the whiteout and onto the icy tundra beyond the village, to their certain death. Noki had no surviving brothers or sisters, but a maiden aunt that lived within the family dwelling had remained with Noki and raised her when it became clear that her parents would not return.

Her aunt, the elder sister of her mother, had been the one to agree upon Noki's marriage to Uqii, a treasured childhood friend, on behalf of her parents. Uqii had presented her as a possible wife to his own parents, who agreed that Noki would make a good wife.

Although Noki was imperfect due to a slight limp from a leg shortened from birth, the match was deemed favorable by Uqii's parents because she was respectful, in perfect observance of every ritual requirement when handling food and interacting with others. She was felt to be a prosperous partner for a young hunter. Noki's parents had had high standing among her people, and Uqii's family was known for producing strong sons who grew up to be excellent hunters. His cousin, Uqqak, was one of the *nukalpiat*; indeed, he was the most accomplished hunter and provider within the village. Sadly, Noki's aunt had died of a fever before the most recent winter festival, where Noki had danced the ritual dance to publicly acknowledge her marriage to Uqii. Noki decided there was no one for her to tell about the baby, so she remained quiet.

It was easy for her to disappear into the routine of her daily life, as those in mourning withdrew from much societal interaction during the year following the loss of a loved one. Noki had lost her aunt and her husband, and those with whom she shared a dwelling were still observing the mourning rituals for her aunt. She kept herself belted and covered, as befitted a widow in mourning for her husband, and when her daily chores were completed, she retired to her dwelling, remaining out of sight, as was also customary when in mourning, and waited for the summons that she knew was as sure to come as summer was to follow that fateful cold spring.

3

BY SUMMER'S END, HER BELLY grew too round to be ignored, and under a harvest moon, Noki was summoned before the elders. The villagers had been too proper to speak of it, but many had stopped talking directly to her, and the other women were suddenly unable to make eye contact with her during their chores. There had been none of the usual laughter and joking when performing shared tasks.

Noki presented herself at the *qasgiq* and came before the elders with her head high, and her eyes cast respectfully downward. In the long silence, she saw, out of the corner of her eye, that Unin had taken a position next to her. He, too, stood with her before the elders.

Finally, one of them spoke sharply, addressing Unin. "Have you brought the brother's woman to your bed? We did not know she came to your roof."

Unin paused, long enough that Noki knew he was afraid for her and perhaps considering a lie. But he would no sooner disgrace himself than would Noki. Nor would she allow him to do so on her behalf.

"No, I have not taken my brother's wife," Unin replied softly. He turned to Noki, and just as softly asked her, "Has another man lain with you without my permission?" Rape was unusual within their society, but men who would force their advantage with young widows were not unheard of.

Noki felt sadness for Unin, and love, too. If a man had so violated her, she knew that Unin would feel responsible. He would believe he had failed to protect her. He could face punishment from the elders. She could already sense his grief.

"No, big brother," she responded formally. The gasps of the council felt like slaps.

"Disgraceful woman!" one observed, the statement so quiet and yet so emphatic that its impact was worse than a blow to Noki.

Another, more gently, said, "Speak, child. You must tell us with whom you have been." Without raising her eyes to see who was speaking to her, Noki recognized the voice of the eldest member of the village. "This is a grave matter." He sounded weary and disappointed.

"Uqii fathered my child," Noki replied confidently.

"Do you disgrace us, and your family, with such untruth?" the elder asked. His voice was still kind, but stern as he continued, "Elder women report that you still bled after Uqii left the hunting camp. You are not far enough gone, child."

Noki took a deep breath. "I admit that is true, good fathers." She hesitated a moment then, but only a moment, considering all there was to be said.

Noki started again. "I believe Uqii is the father of my child," she repeated with confidence, this time claiming the child before she recounted the events that occurred on the night of Uqii's death. She told them how she believed it a dream after learning Uqii had died, but had no other explanation for her expectant state.

The elders were silent for a long time after Noki finished speaking. To her surprise, it was not one of the elders but Unin who spoke first.

"Fathers, we never found his sled or his dogs after he died. We thought they were frightened by the bear and then were lost."

The elder waved this away with a small gesture of his hands. "I can hear truth in what she says."

"It is the reason she asked me when Uqii had died," Unin murmured, perhaps to the elders, probably to no one in particular. He spoke up then, saying, "I will vouch for her."

"It is impossible!" another elder protested.

"Only if you have lost faith in the Great Spirit," the most senior elder replied. "Is it not possible that on his way to death, a great love allowed Uqii one last visit home? We will all think on this," the chief said. "But we will take care. Although great love is powerful and creates possibilities, so, too, are some spirits capable of great mischief."

Thus Noki was returned to village life, her judgment suspended, and she continued her everyday tasks as her people focused on the harvest. She knew that her life was still in danger, and that the fate of her unborn child was dependent on her survival.

She knew she would be allowed to give birth, and the child would immediately be taken from her to be examined by elder women who would then report to the council elders and the chief. There were many reasons to discredit her story, due both to timing and to superstition, and acceptance of such an anomaly was unheard of to Noki's knowledge. There was no one she could safely ask about it. If the elder women could not positively confirm that the child was Uqii's, Noki could be banished from the village, but it was also a possibility that she and the child would be executed to protect the rest of the group from spiritual harm.

4

AS HER BELLY GREW, NOKI'S dreams became more vivid. Her favorite and most frequent dream was of a blue-eyed Arctic wolf running through a snowy forest, or sometimes across the frozen tundra of her childhood. Sometimes she walked with the wolf; other times, it was as if she saw through the wolf's eyes. She awoke from these dreams to the vigorous kicks of the baby.

Some nights there were no dreams, and no sleep, as the child grew big and strong within her. The kicks distorted Noki's swollen belly. She was surprised at their strength.

As her pregnancy neared its end, her dreams became darker and more disjointed. She dreamed of Uqii; he was always frightened and bleeding, and she was following him through the forest but could never catch up to him. He would look back at her, but he never spoke.

Worst were the dreams of an enormous, dark, winged creature. Noki thought perhaps she was dreaming of Raven, but legends of Raven were almost always associated with levity and life. These dreams were vague, she was unable to see the creature entirely, and she would awaken abruptly, shaking and sweating, with the sound of beating wings still in her ears.

On an icy night in late fall, when the voice of Wind had already frosted the skin of the trees, and hardened the surface of the still water in the shallow inlets, and the sky threatened snow, Noki awoke suddenly but did not know why. She had not been dreaming, and the baby was still. With that thought, she inhaled sharply and nudged her enormous belly, and received a reassuring wiggle in response. Her hearth fire was completely extinguished, leaving the air braced with cold, and she could feel the heaviness of her breath as it clouded above her bed.

Noki went to the door of the dwelling and looked out. The air was still and silent. The night was holding; dawn was still hours away. Pulling her fur blanket around her, she stepped outside. There was a strange glow to the north, upriver, somewhere at the edge of the forest, but Noki could smell no smoke.

She suspected this was another dream, but she felt a pull that was more than an intense curiosity about the glow beyond the trees. She was unable to think further of sleep, entirely tempted by the need to investigate. She stopped a moment and listened, reassured that the village was asleep, and there was no one about to stop her.

Her feet had swollen, so she had taken to wearing an old pair of Uqii's mukluqs. They had been made by his mother; he had abandoned them in favor of a pair that Noki had fashioned for him out of rabbit fur and sealskin. She was grateful for his old boots now. She ducked back into the dwelling and pulled them on in haste. She shed the blanket but did not bother with a parka before going out into the night.

Once outside, Noki noticed a slight breeze that pulled her long hair across her face, but she did not feel cold despite wearing only a caribou-skin gown. She went carefully down the path to the river's edge to try to get a better look at where the light was coming from. It certainly looked like a massive fire, but she could see it no better from that vantage point than she'd been able to at her dwelling.

There were a number of *qayaq* and *umiaq* stored on the lesser bank, weighted or covered depending on their recent or more remote use. Noki pulled a *qayaq* to the water and climbed in. She lifted an oar and balanced in the middle of the small craft, mindful of her belly and her changed center of gravity. She said a humble prayer that her pregnant state would not negatively affect the man who owned the boat, singing softly to the *ellam yua* in supplication for her transgression, asking for him to be blessed with many catches.

The water near the village and for some miles upstream was slow-moving, especially as winter was still some days away, so Noki had little trouble as she headed out. The boat skimmed through the water effortlessly, and she steered it toward that eerie flickering light in the trees.

Visually, the gap had been deceiving, as many distances are when judged over water, and it took longer than Noki anticipated to get there. The woods next to the river were eerily quiet, even for the time of season, and she started to be afraid. There were no calls from the owls that hunted here at night, and the lesser sounds of the nocturnal scrambling of small animals were absent.

As Noki came ever closer to the light, she became steadily more convinced that it was a huge fire, but she was still unable to smell smoke. There did not appear to be any birds or other animals fleeing in the forest, as she would expect if a fire threatened their forest homes.

Finally, as she came around a jutting peninsula that extended into the river, creating a small bend in the water, she could see that there was indeed an enormous fire. It appeared to reach the heavens and swallowed a large clearing that Noki could not remember seeing before on this stretch of the riverbank. Sparks from the top of the fire appeared in a constant stream that was blowing upwards as if the blaze were a great volcano throwing the very stars into the night sky.

As Noki brought the *qayaq* up on the pebbled bank, she was struck by the fire's roaring voice and impossible heat. The child growing inside her began moving vigorously, and Noki had the absurd notion that the baby was trying to escape from that place. Noki placed a reassuring hand over her belly. "I feel it, too, little one," she murmured, acknowledging her sense of unease.

The fire had a bitter, metallic smell unlike that of any other fire she had known. Her initial impression was confirmed: for such a great blaze, there was very little smoke.

Then she felt and heard a rushing sound, and sensed rather than saw a darkness in a part of the sky that had previously been clear. Despite the warmth of the fire, Noki felt cold inside and out. Then she realized that the sound had abruptly changed. It had become the flapping of great wings, and she saw, on the far side of the fire, an enormous winged creature as tall as the trees, descending quickly and alighting with a thunderous crash, like a dark star out of the heavens. Noki gasped aloud, and her rushed intake of cold air felt like swallowed fire. This was the creature from her dreams.

It had some features of a man, with ears that were unnaturally pointed and the legs of some unnamable beast. Its torso and arms were those of an impossibly tall, well-formed man, but its wings were its most arresting feature. They were improbably large, perhaps three to four times the size of the creature's body, and covered in thousands of shiny black feathers.

Noki, in her astonishment, was mesmerized. She knew immediately that although this was the creature from her dreams, this was not Raven, the playful, revered god of her people, who loved humans so much that he sometimes appeared to them. Nor could it be Loon, whose white wings opposed those of his rival, Raven, and who was unlikely to present himself on the land, particularly during winter's inception. This figure was both terrible and beautiful to behold. It folded its wings very gracefully behind itself and appeared to be studying her carefully, tilting its head and watching her response.

Noki tried to convince herself that she could not be here, that she was dreaming, that her body was back in the village, slumbering away in her dwelling. The Great Spirit was sending her a vision. She became slightly less afraid, consoling herself with the assuredness that this could not be happening, that she was not really present in this place.

Before she could regain any focus on the figure at the other side of the fire, it had vanished. In its place stood a man. A very tall man with eyes like Noki had never seen before, very large, round, and shiny. It looked nothing like any person she had ever seen before. Its skin was ashen, almost luminous, the color of the full moon, and its hair was shoulder-length, wavy and dark. Its nose was long and narrow, like its angular face and chin. For all its strangeness, it was not unhandsome. And then it smiled, a terrible smile full of spiky sharp teeth, and Noki was terrified.

It began to laugh, and its laughter chilled Noki to her bones, but she was unable to move from the spot. Then the sound became louder, and the tone spiraled downward as its form shifted and expanded, and where before there had been a man, there was now a bear. A furious, unnaturally large Kodiak bear that reared up on its hind legs and roared. But the roar was not the voice of a bear; it was the cry of a thousand dying people. Noki felt screams echoing around her. She was immediately certain that this creature, this spirit, had taken her husband's life. When the bear dropped onto all four feet, fixing a hungry, wild look upon Noki, she turned to run.

Just as suddenly, the roar of the bear was gone, and Noki paused, not wanting to look back. She was immobilized with fear, listening for and expecting to feel the bear's breath on her hair, or the bear's teeth or claws in her back, and she felt every hair on her body stand on end. A single drop of sweat formed between her shoulder blades and slid, excruciatingly slowly, down the cleft of her back. There seemed to be no time, and her breath stopped, so great was her terror. Then Noki thought of her baby and was about to sprint back to the river, knowing it was impossible to outrun a bear, ignoring all the teachings she had ever been given: it is best not to run from a bear. But instead of an attack, she felt a firm hand on her arm.

She cried out, whirling around to fight, but stopped short with a raised fist. Uqii stood with her beside the fire, and the bear was gone. Dream or not, dead or not, she fell against him in relief. He felt cold, but she did not care. After leaning against him a short while, she realized he was wet. She stood apart from him then and noticed that his garments were dark in spots. There was wetness on her hands and in her hair, and Noki realized in horror that it was blood.

When she looked more closely at Uqii, she could see his wounds, the stigmata of his mauling. He was broken apart in so many places, with blood and fluids leaking out from every injury. He appeared to be bleeding everywhere. His face was sad, but he placed a gentle hand on her belly, and Noki could sense his spirit was near. The baby in her womb moved beneath his hand.

Noki placed her hand over his and looked up at him once more, but now Uqii was gone. In his place was the other, the handsome, terrible face of the evil that had taken her husband. Noki was dizzy, now hearing Uqii's screams once more as they mixed with her own. Then the darkness came down over her, and the world went black.

Noki awakened to a crimson dawn, gradually hearing the sounds of the winter birds and the river. She was on the ground, at the river's edge. The icy water lapped at her boots. She pushed herself up on her elbows, not ready yet to sit. She remained dizzy when she moved her head. She looked around. There was no fire, but the entire clearing was scorched bare and black. The ground was still warm, a bitter burnt smell hung in the air, and it was as if the cold was unable to penetrate the clearing. There was a single bloody handprint on the front of Noki's gown, over the biggest part of her belly. She put her head down on the smooth stones of the riverbank and wept.

It was sometime later that she made her way back downriver to her village. She managed to stow the *qayaq* and make it back to her dwelling without being noticed. Most of the villagers were just awakening, and the morning fishermen were already gone. She wondered if the *qayaq* she had taken belonged to one of them, and what they had thought to find it missing.

The knowledge that she was not alone and the familiar smell of the cooking fires along with the scent of pines and early snow was comforting to Noki. She sank gratefully into her bed and slept without dreaming.

When she awoke, the sun was low in the sky. She boiled water and tried to remove the stain from her dress. To her surprise, it was indelible; she couldn't even get it to smear or fade. The blood had dried black, leaving Uqii's handprint immortalized. Once the garment was dry, she found a hiding place for it among the blankets and furs of her bed.

Noki spent the next several days thinking about what had happened as she went about her daily chores. Were it not for the handprint, she knew she would believe it a fantastic dream. The handprint was a reminder, a proof. Noki felt very strongly that the message was Uqii's and not of that other, malign spirit. It felt like a warning, an omen, so she kept it hidden. She felt that her husband was trying to show her what had happened to him, and alert her to the reality that she faced. The child was his, but the circumstances of its conception had been influenced by other spiritual events.

She recalled the words of the elders; they were awaiting spiritual confirmation. Noki now knew that the spirit that had murdered Uqii was somehow implicated in her pregnancy. She feared for her baby but also feared what the baby could be, and she began to plan. She knew she could never let the child out of her sight, could never give it to the elder women, and if the worst happened, it would be she alone who would have to destroy it.

5

AS THE WINTER SOLSTICE APPROACHED, Noki dreamed only of the wolf. He rolled in the snow and was playfully jumping about her as she walked through the winter forest. He led her farther and farther from the village, running on ahead into the trees before circling back to make sure she followed him. Finally, the wolf disappeared over a ridge and didn't come back. Noki woke with a heavy feeling in her heart, thinking there was no way she would find him again. She had no name for him, no way to call him back.

But the next night, the wolf ran again through her dreams. His blue eyes seemed kind, rather than feral. And as he looked at her, she heard her own voice saying, "Ah-mah-o-kee." The wolf's ears lifted, and his tail wagged vigorously, and he looked strangely satisfied as if she knew him. His large pink tongue lolled out happily, and he rolled in the snow before letting out two or three joyous yips.

This time, when she awoke, she knew what must be done. She must be ready to leave the village, clandestinely if necessary, and she had to be prepared to travel some distance alone, perhaps with her baby. She had no hope of being accepted into another Inuit family, and had faith that she would receive signs from the ancestors that would show her where to go and when to stop. She prayed for wisdom in finding shelter when she burned the *ayuq* in her ritual fires. Sometimes she whispered her words aloud to Uqii because it gave her comfort. Her heart was sad but resolute.

Noki counted the fish in her salt cellar and wrapped dried meats and root vegetables. She collected some of her lighter fur blankets and heavy sealskins. She had sewn new deerskin clothes and swaddling blankets for the baby. She had five strong waterskins, and had finished a second pair of boots. She lined an elkskin wrap with fur and added a large hood for herself. It would be warm enough to sustain her through harsh temperatures, and the new parka was generous enough to accommodate either her gravid belly or her child.

The longest night of the year came and went. Still, she waited. She continued to help with the sewing and weaving that became the predominant tasks of the winter dwelling, as well as some basket weaving as she was able on the shortest days of the year. Her pregnancy proscribed her participation in the winter festivals, so she waited within the dwelling, knowing the time for her baby's arrival was very near.

And every few days, the elder women came, to fuss over her, and look at the whites of her eyes, and feel the hardness of her belly. They questioned her about her body habits and her diet and demanded she alert them immediately when the time came. They were perfunctory, wise, and also, she could see, suspicious. Perhaps a bit fearful, even. Noki could not blame them, but their demeanor made her sad. She was already on the outside of the tribe, just waiting for the final judgment.

6

THE THIRD EVENING AFTER THE solstice, she returned to her dwelling long after the last of the light faded in the west. Large snowflakes were softly falling, and the cold was settling over everything as winter began in earnest. Wind was howling down from the mountains, on his way out to the sea.

Her baby was moving somewhat less vigorously, which Noki knew meant the time was near for it to be born. There was no more room for the child to grow. Her ribs felt stretched as her belly had taken over her form, and even taking a deep breath was distressing.

She ate a light supper of dried fish and berries. She whispered a short prayer and spoke a few words to her enormous belly, singing, "Soon…soon…we will meet by the moon." It was an old song remembered from long ago, when Noki's mother had sung it to her. Then she banked her fire and went to sleep.

She woke suddenly sometime later and sat straight up in bed. Her legs and lower belly were wet, and she could feel an impossible amount of fluid coming out of her. A short time passed, and she felt the pressure in her bones increase. Her belly tensed and softened with her birth pains, and Noki knew it was time to call the elder women to help her, that her chosen course was unwise. She was afraid, and she knew she should have help. She had assisted at births in which the mother, the baby, or both did not survive.

But Noki was more afraid of what was to come, that which she could not predict. When the pains came faster, and harder, Noki placed a strap of dried elk skin between her teeth to stifle any of her cries, and puffed air in and out through her nose.

She waited many hours like this, taking only sips of water and pinches of salt as she sweated and cried. Daylight came and went. Noki began shaking as the pressure crescendoed into delirious agony.

She squatted next to her bed and reached down between her legs. She felt the wet dome of the baby's head and put her head down, determined as she began to push harder and harder. It was the hardest work she had yet done, and she felt the worst pain of all, nearly unbearable, then a moment of relief before the entire baby slid out and away from her.

She caught the baby up in her arms and turned it over. It was a very tall, healthy boy, but he was somewhat floppy and not crying. Noki wrapped him up and rubbed vigorously, and he began to shake his fists and his feet and cry. He cried out once, loudly, in protest, and Noki stopped rubbing and held him close, briefly.

She set him on the bed and swaddled him, then turned her attention to the cord. She looped two pull-through knots in it, the first close to him, and divided it with her *uluaq*, the filleting knife she used in the fish camp. Then she sat back on the bed with him and looked him over. He was very well-formed, robust, and longer than any baby she had ever seen. He opened his mouth again to yawn — and she noted that he had several erupting teeth! Noki could hardly believe what she was seeing, so she placed the tip of her finger into his mouth, and sure enough, the tiny teeth were like sharp river stones jutting up from his pink gums. To her surprise, he did not bite her finger but rather turned his head to her and started to suck on it.

"Oh!" Noki exclaimed, realizing he must be hungry, and instead offered him her breast. He latched on easily and suckled away. She watched him, enchanted, and he took hold of her finger. One eye fluttered open briefly to look up at her, the sky-blue color both startling and familiar, and she smiled.

"Welcome, Ah-mah-o-kee."

"Welcome, Ah-mah-o-kee."

7

NOKI WAITED UNTIL AMAOKE SLEPT soundly, and then recovered the supplies she had hidden beneath the extra furs near the wall of the dwelling, including a small runnerless sled she had fashioned from the hollowed bark of a fallen tree by reinforcing it with braided strips of caribou skin that crisscrossed the surface like a loose net. To this, she had sewn a harness of dried grass with a shoulder halter made from the pelt of a beaver that fit across the upper part of her shoulders and chest.

She loaded the sled with the waterskins, furs, and other provisions that she had prepared in anticipation of her journey. She worked quickly, as she sensed that morning was approaching, and with it, as the village awakened, her relatives and the elder women would be coming to her, as her absence of the day before was surely not unnoticed.

She wrapped the baby as warmly as she could, tucking him against her body inside her parka, with only his little face upturned to her. He wrinkled up his nose, but kept silent, happily fed for now, and she ducked out into the cold morning air. The stars were still bright, but she could smell the coming day and sensed the movements of the night creatures returning to their homes. There was the smoke of a new fire coming from the roof of the *qasgiq*, which signaled the awakening of the men ahead of their morning ice-fishing forays and early trapping trips.

Turning back to the doorway, she pulled the loaded sled through and carefully settled the halter across her body, ensuring that it would not put any pressure on the baby as she went. Then she leaned into the burden, pulling it along behind her into the woods, mindful of the fact that there was no snow to cover her tracks. She made her way along a familiar deer path before detouring to the water's edge and taking a few steps onto the ice, leaving a trail in the snow that ended at the riverbank.

Taking great care, she remained on the ice a few feet from the bank, pleased to see that her light sled left no track, and she made her way a few miles more. She could only hope that the elders would believe she had walked out onto the ice with her baby and perished in the frigid waters of the river. Noki kept slowly advancing until she felt it was safe to return to land, returning to the forest long after she was confident that she could not be followed, stopping only to offer the baby her breast in the freezing air.

She passed out of the trees onto the tundra, but kept the forest and the river on her left as she made her way northward and westward. At midday, the sun settled down on the horizon, and she stopped to rest in the shelter of a deadfall at the edge of the trees. She fed Amaoke once again, and changed his garments, despairing of his pitiful cries when she exposed him briefly to the cold.

The clouds were gathering above the Kilbuck mountains as she continued her journey, and by midafternoon they had spread out across the dome of the sky, and the cold was bitter and sharp, threatening snow. It started in earnest as the day darkened, and Noki pushed onward, keeping close to the trees so as not to get lost in the swirling storm out over the tundra.

The snowflakes came more quickly, driven by Wind as he rode down from the mountains, and Noki was forced to slow her progress as the wet weather pushed her roughly, and tugged the sled toward the trees. Amaoke slept, and Noki envied the baby, wishing she could stop, but she wanted to put more distance between them and the village if there was to be any chance of their survival.

As night deepened around her, she fell into an exhausted trance; her only focus the need to keep moving. She put one foot after the other, mindlessly pushing onward, practically asleep on her feet. She had been awake for nearly three nights and suspected that she was suffering from visions. She feared falling into the snow, succumbing to exhaustion, and surrendering both of their lives to the elements. She gradually became aware of shadowy movements at the periphery of her vision, dreamlike among the lazy drift of the snowflakes, making her unsure she was seeing anything at all.

But gradually, several figures emerged, separate from the trees and the tundra, their loping stride making her think of the sled dogs she had grown up with in the village. But these creatures were much larger, and their movements were stealthier. Unlike the sled dogs, they were as silent as the snow, shadowy beings that moved with her. She could feel their watchfulness, and with dawning horror, much, much too late, she realized they were stalking her.

Without stopping her methodical pace, she glanced around, taking stock of her situation, finally recognizing from their shape and movements what they were. The pattern emerged, revealing that she was now at the center of an advancing line of wolves, at least six large animals stalking her, assessing her level of weariness, and waiting for the right moment to attack. They had long since flanked her, and the pack was spread out evenly between the trees at the edge of the forest and the open tundra, leaving her no path to escape.

Drawn to her food stores, or the scent of her bleeding from childbirth, or the small cries of her newborn, they were patient, and she knew that she had made a terrible miscalculation by bringing Amaoke out into the wild alone, and that what she had feared would come from the village elders was now to be carried out by these beasts. She and the child could not avoid capture and sacrifice.

Nevertheless, as she walked, her maternal brain calculated an escape for her child, and she began to more closely examine the nearby trees, wondering if she could get high enough to place the infant out of reach of these wolves. Perhaps a hunter setting traps on a trail nearby would hear Amaoke's cries, and he could be saved. But the wolves were too close, and she was not assured that she could secure safety for the child in the trees.

The wolf formation was slowly collapsing inward, and now, despite the darkness, she could see the lightness of their coats, and in the absence of light, the dark voids where their eyes were. They remained silent as they dogged her footsteps at the edge of the trees and continued to close in.

Still, they made no menacing moves toward her, no rush to attack, and she was even more afraid when she realized that their behavior was not what she expected. She realized that she still harbored some small hope that she could save her child. She thought of everything, even considering changing course to head back toward the river, hoping to find a place where she could set the child afloat, knowing that the remaining slow current could carry him back to the villages along the delta of the Kuskokwim river, ignoring the fact that the elements would be insurmountable obstacles to his survival long before he was discovered by the people of those places. And once seen, would not his unusual appearance result in his abandonment?

She continued to fight her exhaustion and realized that she would be unable to deny sleep any longer. Finally, she was falling asleep on her feet. Her head pitched forward, and she jerked it upright, trying to remain awake and on her feet. She had to stay alert to what the wolves were doing. It was then that she felt a cold nose under her hand, and a furry body brushing against her leg as if helping her to keep going. It was a familiar gesture of friendliness employed by the dogs, an affectionate display to an owner, like a reminder that it was time to feed them or that they wanted to play. She recalled such behavior from her father's dogs during her childhood, and she realized that the entire wolf pack had now drawn in close to her, beside and behind her, seemingly guiding her onward, pushing against her when she stumbled.

They remained close to her as she pushed onward, and when it was next time to stop and feed Amaoke, they drew apart, leading her to a fallen tree where she could sit down and drink some water and eat some salted fish. They remained nearby, watching quietly but not disinterestedly as she fed her hungry baby, but made no aggressive moves until she was finished. When it appeared that she was contemplating not getting back up to continue her journey, they began yipping at her, individually at first, and then in a chorus that crescendoed into howls that bounced between the trees, escaping into the sky, persisting until she tucked the baby back into the folds of her parka and stood once more. Did they sense some danger that she could not perceive? Were the hunters from the village searching for her?

They resumed their positions near her legs, pushing her onward past dawn's light, when they melted back into the trees without a sound. In the daylight, it all seemed like a vision brought on by blood loss, cold, and exhaustion, but it was easier to continue walking. She thought about the animal spirits of legend that presented themselves to travelers. Her traditions had taught her that spirit guides existed, but she was afraid, because such guides were usually present to lead the living to the land of the dead. She was half delirious with fatigue, and wondered if, ironically, she had fallen into the snow, and the two of them had already frozen to death, and these wolves were their guides to the river of tears. If so, their deaths had been painless, and she was still with her baby, which was a blessing.

The forest was tranquil, and the snow had stopped, but Noki traveled onward, pausing as she needed to feed the baby and change his soiled clothing. She had passed through her initial exhaustion and had regained some small amount of energy but was by no means stronger, and as the day wore on, she knew she would have to find a place to stop. She needed shelter for herself and Amaoke; without it, the elements would take their lives.

As the day came to an end, and darkness crept back over the land, her wolf familiars returned, coalescing from between the trees, surrounding her once more, pushing her onward. At one point, she stumbled and fell to her knees in several inches of snow that had drifted up against the line of trees. She despaired of ever getting back to her feet, but the wolf closest to her whined insistently, which made Amaoke cry out, and she grabbed a fistful of the fur in its thick neck fold and pulled herself back onto her feet.

They kept her walking for another few hours, to the darkest part of the night, when the high clouds rolled back from a bright half-moon, revealing an S-shaped band of trees where the forest thinned across the path up ahead. The middle of the section was composed of a stand of trees marked by pines stretched four across to separate the open tundra between the forest and the mountains from a sheltered meadow next to the river. The wolves led her through the stand of pines and across the field to the north.

When she thought she couldn't take another step, her escorts stopped, too, and she peered ahead at a small clearing among the pines where a giant maple tree grew at an extreme angle, nearly parallel to the ground. Its trunk twisted backward, and it was the only deciduous tree among the stand of evergreens, which gave it the graceful appearance of a maiden reclining with her arms outstretched as if to a lover, its bare branches on a bed of eternal green. It was a beautiful sight, and Noki realized that the ancient tree also provided a shelter beneath the skyward-reaching branches.

The wolves climbed beneath the arching roof of branches, so dense that even the snow could not reach the ground, and they lay down in the space, waiting for Noki to follow, and she unwrapped her baby in the snug clearing created by the tree, where the wind was unable to reach them. She reclined among the warm bodies of the wolves, and offered her breast to Amaoke, slipping into her own dreamless sleep as he fed.

8

WHEN NOKI OPENED HER EYES, it took her a moment to remember where she was. Then she jerked awake, clutching at her chest and sighing her relief to find Amaoke asleep at her breast.

The sun was shining, shafts of light were filtering down through the branches of the maple, and the resulting glow gave the small space a magical appearance, which Noki took as a positive sign that she and the baby would be all right.

Covering herself, and wrapping the baby to ensure his warmth, she stepped out of the shelter, realizing that her wolf familiars had once again departed them. The clearing had a very different appearance in daylight; the snow sparkled on the snowy blanket that covered the small meadow, and she could see the tracks she had left from the stand of trees to the maple. She could see her breath in the air and pulled Amaoke closer. The river ran in an arc along the western edge of the meadow, and there was a familiar humped shape at the northern corner of the clearing, several lengths from the water's edge. *How?* Noki wondered, but smiled as she walked toward it, grateful to the wolves for their guidance. There were too many things that she was unable to explain in her recent life for her to be overly surprised by this turn of events.

As she neared it, the hump resolved itself into the reassuring silhouette of a small sod house, apparently an abandoned hunting lodge. She had been unable to see it in the darkness of their approach the night before; if her wolf guardians had known about it, they had avoided bringing her to the place. Perhaps, whether spirit guides or fleshly beasts, they were loath to approach human dwellings. She spent the next several minutes clearing snow and ice from the doorway, then went inside.

It was even larger than she had anticipated; whoever had constructed it had dug down into the soft soil a few feet and then built upward, using whalebone struts to reinforce the walls. It was a very sturdy little home, close to the water and multiple food sources, a very desirable outcome of her exodus from the safety of the village. There was a central firepit, long unused, and the space had been cleared of any personal items that would suggest that whoever had built the structure was planning to return. Snow was blocking the central hole in the roof, but Noki knew it would be a straightforward task to clear it so that she could build a fire.

She returned to the shelter behind the maple tree and retrieved her sled and provisions, transferring them to the sod house. She spread out several layers of furs to create a sleeping platform, then fed the baby, and once he was sleeping comfortably in their new bed, she went outside to address the smoke hole.

Clearing the roof of ice and snow, she pulled the last bit of ice capping the opening out of the way, doing her best to keep any snow from falling into the firepit. She climbed down from the roof of the dwelling and returned to the shelter of the maple, sinking down to sing prayers of gratefulness to the great tree, thanking it for shelter and provisions. Then she gathered up dead branches that had fallen into the clearing to use as her fire starter and returned to the house.

She continued prayers of blessing, placing four stones in the corners of the dwelling, and a fifth stone at the center, marking the house, nailing down the boundaries, creating a sacred place for herself and Amaoke. The largest stone was the fifth, placed directly under the smoke hole; it would anchor her hearth to the home.

She returned to the doorway, ensuring that the entryway was properly cleared as she had seen the boys in the village do it, neatening her earlier attempts at removing the snow and ice and making the entry more inviting.

It was not until these preparations were completed that she endeavored to start a fire, the first in the home she would share with her son. She left him sleeping as she went out into a clear afternoon and gathered stores of wood for their hearth, and refilled waterskins with fresh water she retrieved from the river after breaking a hole through the thin ice at the water's edge.

. . . . .

Over the next year, Noki taught herself to trap small animals for furs and meat, gathered berries and other edible plants, and built fish traps and nets to collect fish to dry and to set in their own oil for winter stores. She was disadvantaged as a hunter; hunting was the province of men, and among her people, women did not participate in the collection of the animals, only in the preparation afterward. Still, her natural curiosity had led her to ask Uqii about his hunting trips, and he had indulged her, sharing stories of the hunt at her hearth fire when he came to her dwelling for companionship. But women did help build traps sometimes, and she had set nets and prepared fish since she was a young girl working alongside her aunt and the other women in the fish camps. She had participated in building elk and caribou fences, and had helped with the rest of the families when the time came to corner the animals so that the men could capture them.

She chopped down dead trees and cached the firewood in the shelter of the maple tree. She stripped aspen bark and wrapped small branches to fashion snowshoes for herself, which aided her in traveling further abroad to set traps for winter hares and foxes.

She harvested fish oil and gathered river stones to use to sharpen her collection of tools. When it was too cold to hunt, she sewed clothes and boots for her rapidly growing baby. After only a few months, he was crawling across the floor of the dwelling with fantastic speed, and she was amused that he never put his knees down; instead, he scuttled about on all fours, hands and feet, in a graceless shuffle that reminded her of a walking bear and made her laugh to see his delight in his mobility.

His hair quickly grew long; before his ninth month, it was a river of darkness flowing down his back, and he was walking unaided. She said ritual prayers for his protection, burning wild celery and *ayuq* to purify him, and she made a small braid behind his left ear into which she sealed her prayers. Over the years, when she refreshed it, she would repeatedly tell him that he carried the magic of her love in that braid, sometimes wrapping it with thread she dyed red with the juice of spring berries.

Noki knew that Amaoke's birth could be seen as a violation of the order and custom of *Yup'Ik* ways, and because even she could not reconcile her suspicions about the unnatural conditions surrounding his conception, she knew it was most prudent to raise him away from the collective of village life. It was likely that the elders would have excluded him from the village family because his existence was not in harmony with accepted traditions. Noki, perhaps, would have been forced to choose between village justice or exclusion, but more likely would have had to forfeit her life, leaving the baby to die from exposure to the elements. Amaoke's appearance was such that no member of the tribe would accept that Uqii was his true father; indeed, his appearance would have led them to believe he was unnatural, an aberration.

She soon had to supplement his diet of breast milk with small pieces of dried fish and berries, because he was always hungry, and she felt it was becoming more challenging to keep up with his wants. As summer turned to fall, she continued to fish and trap, but was concerned that what she had put away might not be enough to see them through the winter. She needed to find a way to hunt larger game, but she was limited in the distances she was willing to travel while Amaoke was still so young, and was unsure how to keep him safe in a hunting camp while she sought her quarry.

One morning, while Amaoke still slept, Noki went down to the river to replenish her water stores and heard a distressed lowing cry coming from the stand of trees to the north of their home. She crept quietly along the riverbank and peered into the early morning gloom, but at first, the deep shadows of the forest concealed the source of the sound. She stepped into the trees to allow her eyes to adjust to the darkness and saw movement near a large deadfall within a group of older trees.

She stepped closer carefully, and saw that a female caribou was trapped; her antlers and forelegs had become entangled in the mass of downed branches, and she was crying out in her distress. When she saw Noki approaching, she renewed her struggles, thrashing with all her weight against the ensnaring growth and rolling her eyes wildly.

When Noki was close enough, she could see that the animal was severely injured, and that it had probably been chased into the trees and run up on the deadfall by a predator or something else that had spooked it. Its rear flanks were covered with deep gouges made either by sharp teeth or claws, and its hindquarters sagged to the ground, useless. From the angle they made with the rest of the animal's body, the spine was broken.

The trees just to the east of the deadfall also appeared broken, and the tops of a few of them were scattered in an artificial clearing, created when some of the larger trees had been downed by something substantial and weighty. Noki examined the trees nearby and realized that the damage was recent; the pine boughs that littered the ground were still alive, and the truncated branches on the remaining tree trunks were sticky with sap.

Noki wondered what could have done such damage, as no animal she could think of could down the trees in such a way. While she pondered this question, the pitiful cries of the caribou diverted her attention back to the unfortunate animal, and she pulled her *ulu* from her belt, stepping carefully to get in close by the animal's head.

Noki had no fear of the massive antlers, as they were mired in the branches of the deadfall, but she was still wary of the power in the neck and shoulders as she settled her footing. She spoke a soft prayer to the beautiful beast, thanking it for the gifts it had come to give her, and then quickly slit its throat, ending its misery and her dilemma about having meat for the coming winter. She almost cried in relief, curling her fingers into its soft coat, which had already thickened for the coming cold.

As the sun cleared the horizon, she noticed that whatever had damaged the trees appeared to have come from above, as the opening at the top of the clearing revealed significant damage to the surrounding treetops, and the pattern of breakage of branches and trunks followed a relatively straight trajectory that ended just short of the deadfall. As soon as she made the observation, a small breeze stirred the air, and she could smell a bitter scent that immediately reminded her of the great fire in the woods, the night she had learned the truth of Amaoke's conception.

She closed her eyes, suddenly afraid, and it was then that she heard the beating of enormous wings, and the earth shook as something massive landed near her in the clearing. She stood very still, and the scent grew stronger, until a strange voice that sounded more like many voices combined spoke to her in her own tongue. "Open your eyes and look upon the one who brings you this gift of meat."

Despite the early sunshine, her body felt cold, and she thought desperately of Amaoke, slumbering nearby. She opened her eyes slowly, fearfully, trembling uncontrollably, hoping that she could somehow protect the baby from this monster.

Its appearance was relatively benign; it had assumed the form of a man, but was dressed in a parka and boots that were similar in design to her own. Its unusual face was still striking, somewhat handsome, even, except for the dead eyes that were too shiny, reflecting the light like the surface of the river, alerting her that it was inhuman – but she already knew it to be unnatural.

It gestured at the caribou with hands that had too many fingers, fingers that ended in filthy bladelike fingernails, and Noki finally understood the marks on the poor animal's flank. It smiled at her, proudly; in some offhand manner, it made her think of the way Uqii smiled when he brought meat to her to prepare, but she pushed the thought away in disgust, not wanting the comparison in her mind.

As if it could sense her thoughts, it stepped toward her, placing that dirty hand on her body possessively, letting it travel from her neck to her hip, suggestively following her curves beneath the clothing she wore. Her flesh was cold where it touched her, and she shrank back but found she was unable to pull away, and she shuddered violently and involuntarily. It smiled, enjoying her reaction, its needle-like teeth stained with some dark substance she feared was blood.

It leaned in close enough to kiss her, but she turned her face away as it hissed in her ear, "It is not time for us to feed on you. Meat, a gift, for you and your child, until he is strong enough to hunt for it." Its breath stank of many dead things, and Noki could feel bile rising in her throat. She swallowed painfully, tasting the bitterness that she could smell, and closed her eyes tightly. She remained unable to move.

She could feel the monster studying her, but it was neither moving nor breathing. It spoke one last word in farewell, "Morningstar," and then it was gone, more abruptly than it had come, although the feel of its hand on her body lingered. When she opened her eyes, the clearing was gone, the trees were intact, and there was the dead caribou, run up on the deadfall, free of any defiling wounds, just waiting for her knife.

9

IN THE WINTER, THE SPIRIT of the mountain roared with power, and the wind howled down from the Kuskokwim peaks, its icy breath lethal to the exposed. Its howl was that of the wolf at harvest, and in the spring, its voice became a love song, almost a caress, chiming through the treetops. By summer, it was a conspiratorial whisper, a cool respite from the surprising days of high heat. In fall, the wind came mostly in sharp gusts, gone from the trees in the morning, but delivering cold air and fog as the days grew shorter.

The crisp chill that the spirits delivered on the wind to the inland grasslands near the river on that autumn day told Noki that a harsh winter was ahead, and she continued to repair her fishing nets with nimble, weather-worn fingers. The stiffness in her joints was also a response to the changing weather, although the sun still warmed the air and heated the crown of her head in a way that reminded her of childhood *qayaq* trips on the river with her father.

The early fall sunlight made every color in nature seem more vibrant, and this was Noki's favorite time of year. She glanced over at the riverbank, where her son fished for fat trout with his first handmade spear.

Now in his tenth year, he was uncharacteristically tall, already taller than any *Yup'Ik* tribesman she had ever known, including his father, Uqii, and there was no end in sight to his potential growth. He towered over Noki herself; indeed, he could lift his mother easily into his arms and swing her around with playful affection. The transition to manhood was still a few years in the future, but his stature suggested greater maturity.

His manner remained that of a carefree child. In warm weather, he disdained clothing, and his long limbs and torso were bronzed from the sun, making his blue eyes even more striking as they blazed out of that dark face. He looked nothing like any *Yup'Ik* person, but for all that his features were foreign to her, he was not unhandsome. His face was compelling, evincing intelligence, fearlessness, and wonder by turns.

The gusting mountain wind had raised gooseflesh on his wet skin, but he continued to concentrate on his task as he balanced on one of the slippery rocks just off the bank. He had attached the spear to his ankle with a leather thong so as not to lose it. Although neither the current nor the depth at this spot warranted the precaution, it was Amaoke's nature to prepare thoughtfully for any eventuality, a trait she attributed to a small gift of reincarnation from his father, Uqii.

She knew a fish had come near to his perch by the subtle change in his posture. Then quickly, oh so quick, was the release of the spear, and at such an awkward angle that Noki barely saw the flick of his wrist.

Just as swiftly, giving up balance for accuracy, he splashed into the water, unceremoniously losing his precarious perch. Moments later, he came up out of the water, spear and fish in hand, victorious as he leapt onto the bank.

As he always had, he shook himself off, water droplets spraying from his skin and in a fine cloud from his long black hair. Every time he did this, Noki was reminded of a dog shaking off water, so characteristic and expressive was the movement.

He bounded over to where Noki kneeled in the grass, tilting his head in another canine gesture, his face crisscrossed with wet strands of hair plastered to his cheeks and forehead. He bowed his head slightly and bumped his forehead into hers, stealthily pulling her *uluaq* from her belt before she was aware he had done it. Then he flopped down next to her and cleaned the fish, saying a small prayer of thanks before flinging the entrails overhand into the water.

Noki smiled to herself, thinking of the irony of his skill with her fish knife, traditionally a tool that mothers passed on to their daughters in the fish camps of her childhood. Amaoke was both son and daughter, learning all the skills he needed to survive, having only her as mother and father, and substitute for an entire village that would have provided his care and education otherwise. She was left with a silent yet pervasive regret that her son lacked the intricate and beautiful experience of growing up within the village family. She hoped that as an adult he would have the skills necessary to rejoin society and protect himself as he should in order to thrive within an Inuit family, and learn there what he had been unable to learn from her.

He pulled jerky from the pouch next to his abandoned elkskin clothing and began to eat, settling down on his back to rest at Noki's side and warm himself in the sunshine. She watched the flash of his white teeth, secretly relieved that as he'd developed, they had come in just fine, despite their jaggedness when he was born. They had been the even, straight teeth of any other child, and with the loss of his milk teeth, his canines had grown in somewhat more prominently, and they were sharper, interposed neatly top and bottom. Had he not possessed such an open, relaxed manner and ready laugh, his smile might have appeared more feral, or more menacing. But at most, it was a distinctive smile and suited him.

To her relief, the prominent eyeteeth did not impede his speech; he was well-spoken, and Noki hoped that would help with any associated social impediments they imposed. For Noki knew that although she had raised Amaoke away from the eyes of others, he would one day rejoin society, for if he could not, she felt he would have less than half a life. She hoped he would find some belonging, some acceptance in the world. Most importantly, she hoped, as any mother hopes, that he would find love, and be loved.

10

DESPITE NOKI'S CONCERN OVER HER inadequacies as a teacher, Amaoke proved to be a proficient and prolific hunter. During the warm months, it was not unusual for him to return from an afternoon roaming the woods carrying a brace of rabbits over his shoulder.

Noki knew from watching him that he had some unusually sharp senses, especially his sense of smell. He often could tell her what animals had passed along the deer path that wound through the woods to the north, which was used as a byway to the river's edge, and she frequently observed him exhibiting scenting behavior when he was performing other tasks with her.

Many times, while cleaning fish with her on the riverbank, she had observed his subtle head movements that reminded her of the sled dogs when they smelled another animal. He tilted his head, and his nostrils flared wide, and he would invariably tell her that a family of beavers was near, or that a hawk had captured a fox, as if this information constituted the routine observance of his surroundings. It was reported so innocently, in much the same way that the elders used to teach the children to observe weather patterns so they could predict the onset of storms or the likelihood of favorable weather for seal-hunting or fishing.

His hearing was excellent as well, and she learned not to be surprised when he would interrupt some activity, and, head tilted, creep across the meadow and dig down quickly into the soft soil, capturing mice or voles that were burrowing below. He also heard other sounds that she was unable to discern, and she would frequently see him standing alert, turning his head from side to side, putting first one ear and then the other forward while staring blankly into the distance. Amaoke rarely told her what he was listening to; she thought perhaps even he was unable to fully characterize the sounds he could hear, and thus he had no information to impart.

His eyesight was puzzling to her – although he clearly saw better in the dark than she could, it seemed that his far vision was somewhat limited. She attributed this to the physical differences in his eyes. His pupils were large and black, but the boundary between them and the colored irises was not as sharply defined as it should have been, the darkness seeming to bleed out into the blue a bit, having a softer edge than she would expect in another's eyes. Noki had no explanation for this, and she thought perhaps it was normal – after all, she had never known anyone to have blue eyes before her son. At night, next to the fire, his eyes reflected red, which she had likewise not seen before, but again, she attributed it to the difference in pigment rather than ascribe it to more farfetched theories.

In her deepest heart, she knew that these remarkable traits were more than unusual, but he was her beloved child, and his idiosyncrasies were made normal to her by familiarity, or were ignored in the way that only a mother would ignore them when faced with certain realities in her own child. Because she taught him all the rules and rituals of right-living that had been taught to her, and because he accepted them with a good-natured understanding, she saw no inherent threat in his exceptional, and occasionally strange, behaviors.

She was careful never to remark directly on the differences she observed in him that made him unlike any other person Noki had ever known, and she did nothing to circumscribe any of his natural tendencies, in an attempt to neutralize any inherent self-loathing that might arise in him from knowledge of such differences. If she expected him to have any future chance of surviving in the company of other people, hers or other Inuit, he needed to remain ignorant of the incongruity of his features as well as of the subtle departures from what was normal. The reactions of others would be enough of an education, she surmised, should he eventually come to live communally, as she suspected he must someday.

As he grew older, the day finally came when he asked about his father, and she gladly told him about Uqii, all the love she had felt, how much he would have wanted a wonderful son, and the ways in which Amaoke would have pleased him. She wanted to believe that Uqii could have accepted Amaoke as he was, but in her inner heart, she knew that the child's appearance would have created doubts about his paternity in any *Yup'Ik* father.

In a rare moment of honesty, or weakness, she wasn't sure which, she told him about her dreams, and the visions she'd had of the Morningstar, both before and after his birth. She suspected that weakness was the more likely reason, since it gave Noki a strange sense of relief to share the burden of the secret with someone, anyone, else. She left out any doubt about his paternity, explaining that no matter what the visions meant, Uqii was his true father.

But Amaoke was a thoughtful young man, and he had often challenged her stories of the spirits, particularly when the stories belied the expected motives of a particular individual. When she told him the story of the *Ungalek* appearing to the people and causing their deaths, and explained that it was believed that the *Ungalek* was actually Raven in another form, Amaoke rejected that belief. He told her that all the other stories of Raven suggested he loved people too much to harm them, and that the *Ungalek* seemed more a monster than anything else. He refused to blindly swallow the accepted interpretation of the story if it disagreed with an overwhelming strong belief he already held. She was concerned that this sort of wrong-thinking could bring him misfortune, and despaired that he had no elders to mentor him and explain these things better than she was able to.

In this instance, his uncanny reasoning was brought to bear on the subject of his birth, because he could smell her fear, she supposed, when she told him about the Morningstar. For days, he followed her every step, questioning her, demanding answers about why they lived alone and what had forced her to leave her village. She explained to him that even she did not have all the answers, but Amaoke knew she was leaving something out. His supernormal senses were keen enough for that.

She should have explained to him how different he was, but she still could not bring herself to tell him something that fundamental. She explained that the motives of the spirits were often suspect, difficult to interpret, and that she would have had no way to prove that the Morningstar's intervention was a positive one in the face of the superstitions of the elders.

He accepted that explanation for a time, but he was quietly unsatisfied, returning to her nearly a month later, asking her to tell him whether he was like Uqii, his father, wanting more information than she had given him. When she was confused by the question, he shook his head sadly and pointed out to her all the ways in which he was so very different from her. Noki realized that all the differences she quietly ignored he was painfully aware of — and looking for an explanation.

As gently as she could, she listed the traits that she knew came to him from his father, from those parts of his personality that were questioning and optimistic, to his meticulous approach to problem-solving, even some of his hunting prowess. Then she admitted how he differed from any other *Yup'Ik* person she had ever known, trying to reassure him that the universe may have intended these differences, even if they had not been seen before among her people.

What she didn't emphasize were her observations that he had some uncanny gifts that were reminiscent of the wolf she had dreamed of, the totem that she had freely assigned to him as his protector. She had often told him the story of the spirit wolves who'd guided her to this home that they shared on the banks of the river, the only home he had ever known.

She was confident that in her broad teachings about the spirit world, totems, and the stories of the *ircenrrat*, human-animal hybrids that were accepted among her people as a part of the natural order, that he could eventually find comfort in his differences. In fact, Noki suspected that his existence was best explained by his being like one of the *ircenrrat*. It had always been her belief that the spirit, the Morningstar, had somehow chosen her and Uqii to bring him sufficiently into the human world by birth, keeping him from slipping back into a spirit realm. She had little remaining fear that there was any evil design in motion; Amaoke was too good, too kind, too loving for that. The Morningstar's absence since that long-ago day had helped calm many of her other, less easily explained fears.

Noki had buried some of the memory even from herself, a denial that protected her emotionally as she faced the task of raising her son alone. She was hopeful that she was equipping him with everything he would need to survive when she was gone. She had all but forgotten that the Morningstar had spared her life until her son could survive on his own.

11

ONE LATE SUMMER MORNING, WHEN Amaoke was in his twelfth year, Noki woke to find him gone from the dwelling. It was not his usual habit to awaken early, despite her teachings of the importance of enthusiastically greeting the day. In their routine, Noki would arise before the sun and gather water or start a fire if the air was cold enough, then cajole him into getting up.

Once he was awake, however, he went directly outdoors to relieve himself and stretch, and he was meticulous about sweeping the doorway of the dwelling for her, because she had taught him it was a respectful gesture for a young man to make. It let the universe know that he was taking care of the small but essential details that influenced his standing with the other creatures and spirits of the earth. If he were industrious and neat, he would be rewarded with good fortune in the hunt and in life.

She was surprised and pleased to see that he had gathered water for her and prepared the hearth for a new fire. The doorway was swept clean, but there was no sign of him at the river's edge or in the nearby forest. When she called to him, her voice echoed back to her, but there was no answering call.

The morning passed, and most of the afternoon, and still, he did not return. Her concern grew, as much for the departure in his behavior as for the fact that he had not carried any food stores with him, and all of their water skins were in their usual places.

Noki crossed through the narrow stand of trees and scanned the open tundra and the foothills for any sign of him, but saw nothing. Her calls to him went unanswered, save for the responding screech of a golden eagle. She was interrupting its hunting, probably startling its prey with her cries.

Late in the afternoon, when the shadows of the trees huddled like silent giants over the land, she heard his voice calling to her, and he was very excited, more excited than usual. *"Aana! Aana!"* she heard him call out to her, and her heart was glad with relief that he had returned, and to sense the happiness in his voice.

She emerged from the house as he stepped out of the forest beside the reclining maiden, that tree at the edge of the clearing that she continued to associate with their deliverance by the wolf totems. His stature exceeded by half again that of the tallest *Yup'Ik* tribesman she had ever seen, and his growth was still incomplete. He had the musculature of a more mature man, but his face was still boyish. She gasped when she realized that he was carrying a porcupine caribou carcass, that of a large cow, draped over his shoulders. She was reminded of the other caribou from that long-ago encounter with the Morningstar. Although the females were somewhat smaller than the males, the animal had to weigh nearly twice Amaoke's weight, yet he carried her with ease.

She went across the meadow to meet him as he approached the dwelling, and as she got closer, she could see that it cost him only minimal effort to carry the animal. She realized, not for the first time, that she had no real understanding of what he was capable of, and that his abilities continually surprised her.

He stopped in front of her and bent over to touch noses with her before continuing to the dwelling. He did not bother to look back, assuming, correctly, that she was following. She wanted to scold him for disappearing, but his exuberance took away her desire to be cross with him. He was not yet a man, but behaving like one, and she couldn't bring herself to instill her baser fears in him. Life was hard enough.

He presented the animal to her so earnestly that she had to smile; his mannerisms recalled Uqii to her, and she was both saddened and grateful. Together, they anointed the animal, welcoming her and thanking her for the gifts she brought them. Working side by side, they removed the skin. Noki was pleased to see that he had returned with the liver; the heart he had eaten following the kill, and it was the only meal he'd had that day.

He helped her ready the meat for the night, and they would eat some of it and prepare much of it for storage by drying it and curing it in salt and oil. She finally asked him how he had managed to bring down the animal, but he merely shook his head slightly with a secret smile. "I have to *show* you, Aana."

She tugged gently at the small braid behind his left ear, laughing at his attempt to keep a secret and his teasing. He relented, telling her the story about how he had awakened during the night to a sound he hadn't heard before, a repeated clicking that confused him. He had gone outside, and thought it strange that the sound appeared to come from the foothills beyond the tundra, but he was unable to see anything. He could smell a musky scent that told him there were a large number of animals moving together, a herd of them.

Amaoke had done the morning chores that Noki always despaired of him doing, making sure she had wood for a new fire since the morning was cold despite the season. Then he had left, climbing into the foothills and tracking the animals back down into a valley to the north, where they had gone into the trees to feed. It was easy to follow them, both because he had their scent, and because of the clicking sound they made.

"Their feet make that sound, my son," she explained, and he looked at her in surprise, because he had assumed they made the sound with their voices somehow. "It is the joint, here," she explained, indicating her ankle, and continuing, "like the popping of your old mother's bones when the weather is cold."

"I will take you to them tomorrow," he promised, yawning and stretching out on the furs of the bed.

"They will be gone." Noki shook her head.

"No, Aana, there were so many, and I can find them again," he replied confidently and promptly fell asleep.

The following morning, in the still predawn darkness, Noki followed Amaoke from the dwelling into a soft, fresh rain. Old sealskin parkas that Noki had saved kept them dry, although Uqii's old parka was far too short in length to cover Amaoke fully. The summer humidity kept them from any real chill. Noki thought it poor weather for hunting, but Amaoke seemed pleased as he led her along the tree line facing the tundra.

They reached the foothills by midmorning, and after a short walk through scattered trees and low-lying brush, they descended into the forest proper. The lichen on the trees was spongy with moisture, and the sound of the rain had dulled to the soft dripping of water from the leaves. The soggy ground growth between the trees made their progress slow. After several minutes, Amaoke turned to Noki with a mischievous light in his eyes. He pointed, silently, at a place ahead where the ground was disturbed between the trees, and she could see that the small plants had been trampled, and the soil was marked with multiple hoof prints. She smiled at him; he had tracked not just a family but a whole herd!

Amaoke slowed his pace further, but she observed his determined manner as he watched the path created by the caribou. Occasionally, he paused to sip water from the leaves before continuing. It was nearly two hours later that he put a hand up to stay her step, and crouched down himself between two small aspen trees. Noki could neither see nor hear any new signs of the herd, but she stilled, crouching down and taking two short lunging strides to position herself at his back.

His eyes were closed, his dark thick eyebrows knit in concentration. He was sampling the air, nostrils flared, then softly blowing out each breath between his lips. Then he tilted his head in that canine manner he had, listening. Then, as if deciding, he nodded slowly, once, twice, and turned to look at her.

"Wait here, and watch," he said to her in a soft voice full of optimism. "Don't move. You smell nervous," he informed her, as an afterthought, surprising her, before he slipped off into the trees to their left, and before she could follow his progress, he had disappeared.

Noki tugged briskly on the hood of her parka, letting the excess water run off of it, and focused on a stand of white spruce where she expected her son to appear, but he did not emerge there on the path or anywhere else in her field of vision. She remained still and quiet, finally lowering her weight onto the moss beneath the trees and leaning against the trunk of one of them.

Nearly an hour later, she saw slow and purposeful movement near the spruce trees, and the top of Amaoke's head came into view. He was moving upward between the trees, and he had stripped handfuls of moss from some low-hanging branches. He planted first one boot and then the other on different trees, climbing with his body spread-eagled between the trunks, finally wedging himself in place with his legs once he had gotten several feet above the ground. He had removed his parka, and his chest and arms were bare. His head and shoulders were obscured from Noki's view by the lowest branches and leaf cover, and he was draping his naked torso with moss. He seemed to settle his weight against his outstretched legs and became impossibly still.

Noki suspected that it took an enormous amount of strength to remain still, and she had not seen anyone climb into the trees in such a way before. She was fascinated, and watched him for so long that his appearance in the trees became just another part of the landscape. Had she not witnessed his climb into position, she might not immediately see him there, so still and patient was he in his perch.

Sometime later, she noticed the rain had stopped, and she saw moving afternoon shadows deep in the forest. The shadows coalesced into forms, and finally, she recognized a small group of caribou, a bull leading three cows. The male led the group by several lengths, and as the animals came closer, the flat beams of his large antlers became more prominent.

Noki didn't move, and she dared not breathe, as the majestic animal neared Amaoke's hiding place. The bull paused, perhaps sensing that all was not entirely right in the forest, maybe even picking up Amaoke's scent, but he was unable to fully pinpoint the threat. The cows halted their progress as well, remaining several paces behind. After many moments, he must have ruled out an immediate threat, and she heard the click of his feet as he pranced in place before moving forward. His females did not immediately follow him, seemingly waiting to see what would happen before they moved.

As the caribou passed beneath him, Amaoke dropped silently from the trees. He curled his legs up to his body as he fell, landing on the inner face of the animal's near antler, reaching out to catch the other in his strong hands as he used his weight and momentum to pull the bull's head down and around, breaking its neck swiftly as he fell. Noki heard the crack of the bone as the neck twisted, and the three females scattered at the sound, bounding out of the area before the bull lost its balance and slumped to the forest floor.

Noki stood up, worried that Amaoke was hurt, thinking he could be caught beneath the animal as it fell, but he rolled to his feet seconds later, leaves and moss trapped in his long hair and a triumphant smile just for her on his face. She had never seen anything like it, a brilliant barehanded kill that required patience, cunning, strategy, and strength.

Then he bent reverently over the caribou, singing prayers of thanks for its gifts as she had taught him always to do. The top of his head briefly touched the velvety skin of its antlers, his hair obscuring his face and draping over its head. Then he stepped back and opened its torso, bleeding it and cleaning it. He passed the heart to Noki with a nod, leaving only the liver in place. Taking a bone needle from the pouch at his waist, he placed a cross-stitch of stretched gut across the opening in the caribou's belly.

Noki returned the heart to his hands, marveling at the efficiency with which his teeth dismantled it. He passed her the best parts, and when they had finished, wiped the blood from his lips and put on his parka.

Noki watched in amazement as he shouldered the impossible burden, and silently set out through the trees for home. It was then that she recalled the Morningstar's prophecy, and she realized that she had witnessed the success of a burgeoning hunter, as talented as any of the *nukalpiat*, but that it was also an omen of her demise.

12

AMAOKE AWOKE FROM A PARTICULARLY vivid dream. By the time he concluded the slow climb from sleep to full awareness, the details were fading, slippery as the small sardines that invariably escaped in the overflow of the fish net when it was pulled from the river, swimming away, lost to memory.

He half sat up, propping himself on his elbows, still sleepy and disoriented, and realized that the light seemed wrong; it was much later in the day than he usually got up. When more of the sleep cleared his head, he pulled on pants and boots and a warm parka, because the dwelling was cold enough that he could see his breath pluming upward from his face.

He stepped outside the dwelling to relieve himself. He felt the silence of that late fall day in his bones, and he cocked his head to listen to it. No birdsong. A meager sun lit a mostly gray sky that threatened neither precipitation nor clearing.

A thought presented itself, sudden and unwelcome. Amaoke wondered why his mother had not awakened him, as was her custom and habit.

He ducked back inside and surveyed their shared dwelling. The remains of the fire in the hearth were cold, evidence that there had been no morning fire. All of the water skins were full; the smallest was missing, as was the woven grass bag that his mother used to collect small plants and berries in the forest.

These were signs that she had started her morning routine as if she had planned the day to proceed like any other. She had carried water up from the river and gone out gathering, with the reasonable expectation that she would return shortly to make the fire at the hearth and pester Amaoke until he awakened.

Noki was an ordered being. Nearly every day of his life that he could remember, she'd kept a routine and stuck to it faithfully. He suspected it was her way of restoring order into a life derailed by the supernatural. He was the one who lost track of time, who wandered off without warning, who fell asleep in the woods and had to race back in the dark – she never did.

He was fully awake with that sobering observation, and for good reason, he was concerned. He stepped back outside and called to his mother. His voice echoed back to him, distorted by the landscape, but it was the only answer he received.

He tried to recall whether she had told him what she had planned to do. The answer was at the periphery of his memory; he had to admit that he did not always listen as carefully to her words as he could have in recent days.

While he pondered, he set off into the woods, slipping into the trees next to the reclining maiden. His feet carried him forward, the repetition of this trek as familiar as breathing to him. It came to him that she had been lamenting her inability to gather all the berries she wanted to before Wind brought the winter down upon them.

They had feasted on berries since late summer, as the harvest had been bountiful that year. Amaoke had not been concerned; he knew the first freeze would preserve many of the fruits until spring, when they could be readily picked at the first thaw. But Noki had insisted there was still time to bring in more before winter took hold, and perhaps this had been the latest morning chore.

He adjusted his path somewhat to intercept her in a small clearing a short walk from the dwelling where salmonberries had been abundant. There was a light dusting of snow that had fallen during the night. His heart leapt joyfully when he found that his mother's footprints had disturbed the ground ahead of him on the path. The clearing was not far ahead, so he called out to her again, but still, there was no answer.

A few more steps and the path through the trees widened slightly. Amaoke noticed the ground was disturbed ahead, snow and dirt churned together. A few feet beyond the disturbance brought the rank scent of a bear and something else to his nose, something unpleasant. He stopped, closing his eyes and concentrating on it.

The predominant scent that flooded his nose was fear, followed by blood, and finally, his mother's warm scent. It incorporated the hearth, the earthy scent of the pines, and a signature smell that was a unique blend of things for which he had no names; he just knew they were indelibly tied to his memories of her.

Amaoke gasped out a sob of fear and started to run, twisting his body between the trees as he left the path to take the most direct route into the clearing.

"Aana! Aana!" His cries were strangled screams of despair when his nose confirmed what he already knew, why she had not returned, why she could not return, and his eyes blurred with tears. He stumbled at the end of his run, and barely kept himself from falling when he made the final turn into the clearing.

The sun had gone. The dense gray sky had darkened, seemingly flattened over the earth. It was suffocating, oppressive to him as he surveyed the scene at his feet.

His beautiful mother had been violently rent by a bear. It was apparent that she had been caught unaware as she harvested berries, and her bag had been torn from her shoulder, spilling its precious fruits across the top of the snow. The berries lay scattered like singular bright pink treasures, their beauty entirely incongruous with the scene he now witnessed, helpless to shed the terrible image from his mind.

Noki had come to rest facedown near the largest of the bushes. He focused on the area devoid of color that she had created with her methodical picking in an effort to avoid seeing her broken skin and oddly settled limbs. Her eyes were open in a silent plea, and her fine shiny hair was even then moving in the light breeze, an imperfect and cruel mimicry of life. A single drop of blood was the only mark on her face; it punctuated the smooth, unblemished rosiness of her cheek, like a crimson tear falling from an unseeing eye.

His attention was drawn to a disturbance in the undergrowth at the far side of the clearing – one of the bushes was nearly split through the center, presumably marking the bear's path of egress. Amaoke was torn between tracking the animal down to exact revenge, with the knowledge that he would most likely forfeit his own life in the bargain, and the undeniable pull of his mother's remains.

He found that his legs had suddenly become curiously weak, and he sank to his knees beside Noki's prone form. His head pitched forward, pulling his torso down onto hers, abject with grief, wanting only to stay with her, wondering how long it would take for him to succumb to death here too, for the elements to rob him of life so that he could join her. At that moment, if he could have willed it, he would gladly have given up his own breath to restore hers, knowing that she would never forgive him such an indulgence. She had taught him to live, to survive against all odds, but until that moment, his young and naïve mind had not considered that to do so would involve such pain.

He recalled a fall he had taken when much younger, into a deadfall after he tripped and fell when running through the woods nearby. A thick skeletal branch had pierced the soft flesh of his side, and the physical pain had been unbearable, both at the time of the injury and later, when retained splinters of wood had festered out of the wound, but that was as nothing to this agony, which was equally physical, as strange as that seemed. He could feel it behind his eyes, threatening his reason, and deep within his chest, stealing his breath away, so overwhelming that he could not even make a sound.

He was unable to move for a very long time, his hair joining with hers and dancing in the breeze. It was full dark when he finally sat up, hearing the first soft calls of the night birds as they came out to hunt.

He shrugged out of his parka, numb to the cold, and lay her gently upon it. He settled his mother into the warm furs that she had so lovingly sewn together for him with her own hands. Heedless of the blood and other soilage, he gathered up her bag before setting out, knowing it had been one of her favorite things. Then he set out with her in his arms, returning her for the last time to their dwelling.

Amaoke took care to observe the rituals that she had worked so diligently to teach him, the period of rest, the repeated circling of the dwelling on foot in the direction of the travels of the sun and moon, the preparation of her shroud. He sewed her body into the hides himself, putting her few possessions and tools in with her, keeping for himself her prized *ulu* knife and one other token.

Before closing the shroud over her head, he sliced off one long lock of her hair. This hair he incorporated into the tiny ritual braid behind his left ear, into which she had told him she put so much of her own affection and love.

When the prescribed days of mourning came to an end, when he could believe her passage into the spirit world was assured, he placed her onto a simple platform and fashioned a pulley to transport her from the dwelling. Using his own power, and his prayers, he lifted her body out through the roof of the sod house, to ensure her proper exit from this world and her entry into the next, in a ritual observation she had taught him, and under a new winter sun, saw her off for the last time.

Finally, without plans or more provisions than he could carry on his person, he turned his back on the only home he had ever known. His own fate and the timing of any eventual return were unknown, as they must be, and he paused only long enough to place a hand on the trunk of the reclining maiden and bow his head a moment before disappearing into the trees.

13

WINTER FOUND AMAOKE TOO SOON, alone in the foothills, with too little food to survive the harsh season that Wind threatened as it roared down from the mountains. Cold settled on the land like a smothering blanket, followed by heavy snows that delivered deep powdery drifts between the trees.

Game was scarce, and Amaoke's efforts at trapping had only been marginally successful. His stomach was often complaining, and his sleep was poor, marked by frightening and vivid dreams that he was unable to recall during his waking hours.

He had created a shelter beneath an enormous half-dead Sitka spruce. The old tree appeared to have been struck by lightning halfway through its life; one half of it was stunted and crumbling, and the other half continued its angled path skyward. It leaned enough that its top had first merged with and then grown out through a neighboring pine's branches.

A small triangular space resulted between the lower needle skirts of the two trees, with the limbs touching the ground on one side. There was a generous opening opposite that Amaoke would have been able to walk into after the thaw. Still, it was usefully diminished by snow and the aftereffects of a late sleet storm that had flash-frozen a waterfall of icicles from the outer branches to the snow's crust.

Amaoke used other broken pine boughs to camouflage the entrance to the shelter further, and these maneuvers, plus the snowpack, insulated it sufficiently to protect him from the worst of the elements.

The shelter was also situated only several thousand paces downwind of a large cave. The cave was the dwelling of a bear Amaoke had tracked to the location several weeks earlier, the very bear who had taken Noki from him.

He knew that a confrontation with the animal was inevitable, although it was never entirely clear what he intended to accomplish other than get himself killed as well. Despite all the anger and pain he felt, he had no illusions about any of his special abilities placing him at advantage against a bear. But the animal had not emerged; it was likely to be truly hibernating, given the severe cold.

Hibernation did make the animal vulnerable, but that did not mean that Amaoke could just enter its den and dispatch it. For one thing, many bears could emerge from their torpor with the right stimulus or even a break in the weather. For another, the bear did deserve his respect, as it too was part of the cycle of life. He knew his mother's teachings well.

Yet his heart was hardened by his grief, and when he considered the beast's slaughter, he was comforted. Now he was starving, too, and increasingly concerned that he was ill, because he had lately been sweating at night in spite of the bitter cold.

He was also losing time, which he could not wholly understand. Occasionally he would sleep the day through and remain wakeful under the moon. Other times, when he was out hunting, he would somehow forget the time and would come to his senses many hours later, having wandered far afield.

Initially, he had worried about being so far from shelter, but the cold that winter seemed to be bothering him less and less. He would walk for hours in the bitter cold without noticeable adverse effect.

Some mornings he awakened within the shelter, not remembering when or how he had returned there, sure he'd been out hunting. Occasionally he discovered the remains of small game that he could not recall catching; once there was evidence that he had partially ingested the raw flesh of a snow hare – some of its fur and blood had dried upon his lips. His mind refused the thought of doing such a thing and having no recall of it; the upset of the moment caused his stomach to seize, and he rejected the meal shortly thereafter.

And there was the moon. It called to him in a way it never had before. Brother Moon, *Iraluk*, forever chasing his beloved sister, *Akerta*, the sun who warms us. Even as Amaoke lay wrapped in fur blankets in the shelter, the moon's light upon the earth outside was a presence he could feel, spiritually and physically. He found that on the nights closest to the full moon, he was most affected by these strange happenings. On more than one occasion, his blackouts ended with him awakening out in the open, under a night sky dominated by the cool bright orb.

As the dark of the year receded, marking another birth anniversary for him, Amaoke noticed that his stature and weight were increasing, in complete contradiction to the relative famine of the harsh conditions he was suffering. He was slightly faster, which helped his hunting somewhat, but this improvement was accompanied by an impatience and too-easy frustration that were equally detrimental to some of the same efforts.

The next full moon rose only a short distance above the trees before beginning its descent behind the mountains. The early cries of hunting owls marked the night. Somewhere in the foothills, a wolf cried out in song, its pack mates joining in, and Amaoke felt that song in his bones, his heart, his soul. He trembled at its simple beauty, he understood its sadness, and his tears flowed freely – for his mother and for himself. Without her, he had lost everything – love, companionship, and a home. Worst of all, he had lost his way, and he could feel his own descent into madness.

. . . . .

When the bear emerged for the first time the next spring, Amaoke was waiting for it. He witnessed its slow, shaky descent from the cave, noting its deceptively labored progress as it headed toward the nearby river. He allowed it to disappear into the forest, confident he could track and follow it if he needed to, sure he was safer keeping his distance.

His heart still cried out for revenge, but his mind was beginning to question the soundness of engaging the animal for any reason, and coming up against its internal resistance to death. When he finally moved from his hiding place, he was initially able to find its trail by observation and scent, but he decided that following it was unnecessary; it would return to its den.

The bear's spoor marked the entrance to the cave, and that scent alone should have deterred all intruders. Amaoke ventured into the cave, which stank of musk and the deep unpleasant odor of its many kills. The predominant odor was that of half-rotted fish, and all the smells taken together flooded his sensitive nose. It was simultaneously offensive and yet attractive to him in a way that he did not understand, and that made him even more uncomfortable on a deeper level.

There was a slight bend at the entrance to the actual den; the rock walls took a curve to the left from the opening. The deeper darkness inside, away from daylight, was deceptive; at first, he thought the cave extended several yards deeper into the earth. Once his eyes adjusted to the shadows, he saw that a sizeable hollowed-out space, an alcove, really, was the extent of the dwelling. The air was even more rank where the bear had bedded down; the small area had captured its body heat and the humidity from its breathing as it had slept.

Amaoke barely had time to register his disappointment with the space; it provided no place for him to position himself in ambush, although the shallow nature of the dead-end did leave the bear more exposed than he'd expected. Still, it would have been a life-or-death struggle in close quarters, with the bear at great advantage.

Apparently, the bear thought so, too. Its huffing grunt at the cave's entrance put a cold finger of fear on Amaoke's heart. It had scented him, or perhaps even decoyed him when it had left the cave, and that huffed breathing meant it was tasting the air to confirm he was trapped inside. Smart of it – he was easier prey than anything else it would have to hunt for and catch in its post-torpor debilitation, and compared with its other possible food sources, he was the slowest. He'd stupidly made it simpler by putting himself right where it wanted him.

He was bereft of any sharp weapons, and a quick survey of the back of the cave did not provide any ready items that would significantly increase his odds of survival.

He pressed himself up against the inner rock face at the start of the curve and rolled his head around it until he could see the animal at the cave's entrance. She was a full-grown female, but that added information did not provide any reassurance. His best strategy was to hope she would blindly charge around the curve, where he had a slight advantage in maneuverability and could potentially hug the inner curve of the rock wall and escape the cave.

But even her mad, sliding scramble to turn her bulk around and give chase would take less time than he would need to reach the trees, the only slim chance he would get to escape and possibly survive. Long before he got there, he would feel her claws in his back as her bulk dropped him to the ground, and then it would be quickly over.

But she was not likely to charge – she knew the back of the cave was shallow. She did not need to compromise her advantage; she did not even have to wait him out. She could either advance on him with all of her deadly weaponry, tooth and claw. If wary enough of his position, she could back into the cave and crush him into her bedding with her considerable weight, suffocating him handily.

His mind settled on these deadly certainties almost immediately, and then the bear spoke out with intent. She reared up on her hind legs and roared out a challenge from the cave entrance. Something in her scent changed subtly, bringing to him a new smell, aggression, and something dormant in Amaoke awakened for the first time in response to that challenge.

His body was moving involuntarily, his skin suddenly rippling over the deeper flesh, and a strange answering cry was forced from his throat, coming from deep within him. He felt himself pitching forward, as if he were preparing to run, but he could no longer stand upright, and his hands were thrown out onto the slick, mossy surface at the base of the wall.

His vocal register spiraled downward into an inhuman range, and he could hear the blood rushing past his ears and the nearby thunderous crashing that was the beating of his heart. A crushing pain in his chest was accompanied by the stark sounds of the cracking of bones as his ribcage compressed inward, and his breastbone arched forward, impossibly deepening, the pain of it arresting the feral growl that had started the process.

His breathing became notably louder and harsher, until he could hear it as much as he felt it. His limbs felt weak and floppy for what seemed an eternity, but in reality, could only have been several moments. Then his muscles pulled and hardened as sinuous changes racked them into new configurations, his arms pulled forward, his legs contorting, reversing their curvature. His feet elongated and narrowed, the long tendon at his heel tightening rapidly as it lifted off the ground, toes extending to grip the earth.

His abdomen and genitals drew inward and upward; while this was not as painful as the rest, neither was it pleasant. Worst was the impossible stretching of his face, which felt as if it must split open to relieve the stress; he watched as his nose flattened over his teeth and the middle of his face elongated, narrowing and stretching into a snout.

His tongue curled out of his mouth, and he drooled excessively as his gums broke open, his enlarging teeth erupting violently. He tried to scream, but the only sound echoing in his brain were agonized howls that could not possibly be coming from him. His teeth sharpened, aching and bleeding in their sockets, drawing further agony.

Then, almost as an afterthought and an annoyance, billions of needle pricks all over his body as constellations of hair follicles thickened, covering him with thick white fur and nearly completing the transformation. Last were the hands he could see splayed upon the ground, which still looked somewhat human, although his perspective was so skewed it was making him dizzy. The world had shifted downwards and sideways, and he was suddenly looking *up* at the bear from a bizarre angle.

She had stopped roaring, but still towered over him, and he caught a new scent from her; this time, it was fear. It inflamed him. A strange whine escaped him, and he growled, feeling his tongue against his teeth as his lips pulled back from them. He snapped his jaws angrily, once, twice, spraying saliva and his own blood as he bounded forward on powerful legs, sliding sideways before his sprouting tail righted his balance and he launched himself at the space between her legs, springing forward with one strange, half-human hand to defend himself. He watched as wickedly sharp claws extended outward from rapidly shortening fingers. He connected with the bear's soft belly, tearing her flesh, and he could smell her blood and the wet dead leaves at the cave entrance before he lost consciousness, hearing the bear's scream of pain and surprise.

. . . . .

Amaoke awakened sometime later and found that he was back in his makeshift shelter beneath the pines. He knew it was daytime due to the quality of the light penetrating the branches, but he was disoriented, sure that it was not the same day that he could last recall. He did not remember returning home; he could not remember much at all.

The rank smell of his body made him gag, but worse were the unwelcome tastes in his mouth. His tongue felt as though he had bitten it several times, and it was swollen and dry.

He looked around, seeing that the pine-needle floor was disturbed with leaves, mud, and flecks of bloody gore, all of which he had apparently dragged in on his person. His body was filthy, covered in dark splatters of what appeared to be blood, and there was prominent hair scattered across his chest, abdomen, and legs that had not been there before.

His fingernails were ragged and broken, clotted with dried blood and what looked like dark, thick fur. His face felt strange, so he put his hands up and discovered that his cheeks and chin were also covered with hair – there was a substantial new beard. He shivered, and looked around, also wondering what had happened to his clothing, struggling to remember, to put together any memory – no matter how sketchy. The details were out of reach.

His eye fell upon a half-full water skin, and he was suddenly thirstier than he felt he had ever been before. He crawled over to it and downed several refreshing gulps of water before his stomach cramped violently. He barely made it out of the shelter and stumbled to his knees, retching and regurgitating a seemingly endless stream of partially digested chunks of flesh, bile, and old blood.

He eyed the mess sickly, realizing that the quantity was much more food than his stomach could have accommodated under normal circumstances. As that realization settled upon him, he lost consciousness once more.

The next time he awoke, he was still filthy but felt better than he had before. His mouth didn't taste any better, though, and he was face down in the pine needles on the floor of his dwelling. He had dragged himself back inside, but could not recall it.

The air was appreciably warmer, and the sun was shining. He could hear more exaggerated flow from the river, which was suggestive of advancing spring thaw. He wandered toward the water, noticing that his bare feet were less affected by the twigs and roots in the undergrowth than they should have been, and his skin was less affected by the cold air.

When he reached the steep bank, he closed his eyes and turned his face up to the sun for a prolonged moment, savoring the pure pleasure of having its warmth on his face. Then the breeze brought him further evidence of his rankness, and with a resigned sigh, he plunged into the frigid water.

He noticed that as the filth was carried away, the body hair he'd acquired seemed to slough away, too, as he rubbed himself clean. It released its hold on his skin, leaving his face and body as smooth as it had been before the madness had begun. When it had all washed away, he climbed back up the riverbank.

Amaoke could hear a squawking commotion in the woods, so he followed the sounds of the crows and a partially obscured trail of carnage up the hill to the bear's den. The carrion birds scattered at his approach, revealing their grisly quarry.

The bear's carcass was several days old, with the unmistakable signs of predation. The hunter in him examined the scene at the mouth of the cave and concluded that the bear had been disemboweled in a fight with another large predator, which surprised him.

He examined the disturbed ground as the displaced birds complained about his interruption of their meal. They had retreated a short distance into the trees, where they could berate him in safety. Their dark eyes glittered with an unsettling intelligence and hungry, vicious greed.

The ground told a confusing tale — a single wolf had attacked her, surprising her from its hiding place within her den. Yet there were no other animal prints but the bear's leading into the cave. The other prints leading into the cave were unmistakably Amaoke's own, and there was no corresponding evidence of his departure from it.

He stepped into the cave proper, sensing no danger, and became dizzy and nauseous when he saw the rent remains of his clothing. There were set handprints in the mud by the cave wall, and he traced their progress and transformation three times before the dim, dark flashes of recollection once again threatened his consciousness.

He kneeled at the cave's opening with his head down, breathing deeply to fill his lungs with fresh air, but with the stench of the carcass there before him, he was denied relief. He forced himself to take another good look at the animal, and the damage done to it was more significant than the pickings of carrion; a larger, more robust creature with strong jaws and lethal claws had fed upon it. From the looks of the body, its killer had returned more than once to feed on the remains.

Amaoke stumbled to the edge of the clearing and placed both hands on a young aspen tree. Half-sliding and half-falling to his knees, he pressed his forehead against the papery bark with enough force to strip it and some of his skin, in an attempt to manage and distract himself from the waves of nausea that accompanied the realization that the monster that had done this was the monster that he had become.

He wept freely, grateful only for two things: the avenging of his mother's death, and the relief that she had not lived to see what he had become.

14

BROTHER MOON OWNED HIM, AND each month as *Iraluk* grew in size, he grew in strength, and Amaoke was powerless to deny his call.

He ran on four legs for the two days preceding and following the full moon, sometimes longer in those early years, when he discovered he had no control at all. Frighteningly often, he was unable to change back.

If he experienced any strong emotion, it threatened and sometimes triggered an unwanted change. All too often, in the time following that first change, these episodes were marked by variable losses of time and memory that left him disoriented, unbalanced, and adrift in the world.

Amaoke, the man, still sheltered beneath his Sitka spruce; Amaoke, the wolf, had taken over the den of the bear but refused to sleep in the alcove, preferring to lie across the opening several feet shy of the entrance. He watched the seasons pass; the leaves falling from the trees and the snow drifting down were equally soothing to his confused brain.

He had eventually harvested the bearskin following that first change and sewed new clothing from the hide. When in human form, he made a habit of caching furs and bone needles under the pine and sewed spare garments on his best days in preparation for the times he would awaken, naked and dirty, unaware and afraid of what had transpired in the lost time. He continued to learn that even as a man, his susceptibility to the elements had lessened, but his refined sensibilities were soothed when he could clothe himself.

When he was in his right mind, he scoured the walls of the cave for hiding places to keep his weapons and tools, and he found a small natural shelf scored high on the back wall that was perfect for his mother's *ulu*. He hid it there, in the hollow, where he knew he could put his hands upon it quickly if that were needed.

Amaoke, the man, never stopped searching for the answers to his dual existence, needing to find some meaning for it as a way to maintain even the most tenuous hold on the sanity he had left. The wolf just was, and the two parts of the whole were as far apart – nearly as far apart – as if they had been separate entities.

Amaoke recalled the stories that his mother had told him about the *ircenrrat*, dual beings that could take the form of either animal or human. But, he reasoned, such creatures were of the spiritual world, and he himself was flesh, blood, and bone, borne of his beloved human mother and father.

When the wolf robbed him of time, reason, and memory, it took longer to regain this line of thinking. It took years for him to remember that there was more to his origin story than he could recall. Something…something about the father that was lost…but his brain was too often trapped in the limbo imposed by the struggle between its dual natures. Clarity was impossible; he failed to make those memories materialize in any accessible form.

The wolf encountered other wolves but had been raised with human restraint. So early encounters with like beasts had engendered dominance disputes, for which Amaoke had the physical attributes he needed. Still, he lacked the appropriate instinctual responses required to perceive the hierarchy. He suffered significant battering in dominance displays with other males until he learned to categorize them by scent and display the proper outward signals of submission. His early fear and aggression were met with increasing force from more dominant males, and when he failed to properly submit, he was alternately savaged or run off by multiple members of a pack.

The scent signals of females enticed him like any other male, and the intricacies of mating and mated females cost him flesh on more than one occasion. Even more confusing were the invitations given by some of the mated females that lured him in for even more punishment.

But unlike in other wolves, his mutilated ears or a punctured belly would eventually heal completely. Serious bites did not fester, and his regenerative properties were extraordinary, even though the injuries were no less painful. The wolf's instincts were thus honed, his behavior schooled, long before the man could retain detailed memories of all that happened when on four legs.

He learned to roll over, to offer his throat and belly, and he was tolerated. He controlled his fear and damped down as much aggression as he could manage, and he was allowed to hunt and feed and sing with them.

Many more years would pass before Amaoke the man could consciously piece together the pattern of his days, and in some ways, this was a fresh hell. His human sensibilities were now exposed to the savage pragmatism of his animal self, and the wolf's existence was newly tempered by the man's conscience and complicated ethics. The internal struggle became, in some ways, even worse, even more disturbing than the gaps in memory had been.

But as his existence evolved into a seamless narrative, there was a reconciliation of time and place. Amaoke achieved better control and mastery of the change, recognizing the internal triggers that could call the wolf and trying to manage them. There were still some events that overwhelmed his control and swamped his senses, and no matter what else happened, he was an utter slave to the moon, but these subtle changes came with tangible benefits.

His memory improved; he grew more dominant naturally as he matured, and he learned to assert that dominance and accept the submission of lesser wolves without the need for excessive violence.

And while the unschooled wolf had been desperately anxious to mate, responding to pure scent and instinct, his burgeoning status in the pack hierarchy and his human awareness caused him to hold himself apart from such an eventuality. He was understandably concerned about the possible outcome of mating; his mind contemplated the possibility that his condition could affect any offspring he produced.

Eventually, he realized that such events would occur in due course. As a natural consequence of his dominance, willing females were attracted to him, and his performance protected some of them from crueler mates. Yet his still-fragile conscience, tenuously accepting of its more feral qualities, dreaded impregnating any of them.

Sometimes he succumbed to a form of despair that led to spending greater and greater amounts of time in wolf form. The more extended periods virtually ate time, and he would realize along the way that whole decades were passing. He inwardly cursed his own cowardice for avoiding his human life, but his wolf brother had a place in wolf society, and while he could never fully belong to them, he was also not physically alone.

One night he ran through the trees, half-heartedly chasing a snow hare and trying to swallow his guilt over the unfair advantage he had in this form. Despite the wolf's driving anticipation of the taste of its prey, Amaoke was jarred from his reverie by a memory unbidden.

Dawn was coming, and a falling star on the horizon grabbed his attention. Day. Morning. Star.

His mother's face in his mind, and the story of the being that had visited her. The creature that had been implicated in his very existence. The Morningstar.

His feet slowed, and there in the dewy dawn, he shed the wolf, shifting form slowly, until his limbs unfurled, and the man lay in the grass, running his tongue over receding teeth. He ran his fingers gratefully over his form, rejoicing in the fondly remembered function of human hands, tugging on his full beard that he knew would entirely fall out on its own in just a few days if he held the wolf at bay. Scratching a spot he could never properly reach with hindfoot or tooth, sighing his appreciation that there was another form to take. He lay quietly, several moments more, then slowly climbed onto shaky legs and took a few steps.

A sudden change in the air brought to him a bitter new scent, sulfurous, with notes of spent embers from an old fire, with the brackish smell of the river soil and sour decay. It was not a change in the wind, but rather a new downdraft associated with a darkening of the sky above him, and a loud flapping, like the amplified sound of the beating of the raven's wing.

Amaoke turned his face skyward and saw it, a creature with an impossible wingspan rapidly descending, heavily crashing through the forest canopy, splintering the tops of trees with unimaginable strength, then landing with a force that shook the very earth.

Despite its impressive wings, the being was unlike any creature that swam, crawled, or flew in the natural world. Its skin was smooth and dark, as if bathed in ash, but still somewhat luminous. Its form was vaguely humanized, save that its feet were grotesquely out of proportion, with elongated toes that were spanned by membranous webs, which were choked with dirt and which ended in triangular pointed and ridged toenails that curled into the earth beneath it.

Its torso was somewhat birdlike, with an exaggerated chest cavity and flat, hollowed abdomen over a pelvis that revealed no gender. Its shoulders were hunched but appeared strong, and its arms ended in hands that resembled the fragile fingerlike projections of a bat's wing. Its head was that of a smooth-faced man, fine-featured, with wavy dark hair that seemed to move independently of the breeze as if the strands were not subject to the laws of gravity. This last feature was, strangely, more unpleasant than the other aspects of it, and Amaoke had to look away from the writhing mass of its hair.

Its most arresting feature was its incredible wings, which fluttered gently before folding gracefully and flattening down to the creature's back. They were enormous and delicately covered with thousands of deep-black iridescent feathers.

"Firstborn, wolf-born, child of moon," it greeted him in a voice that seemed to come from somewhere inside Amaoke's brain, and although the language was foreign to him, he understood what it said. The sound of its voice was split, as if it was composed of several cries of unnatural pitch and impossible timbre all speaking in concert. It both hurt and pleased his ears, and he shook his head, trying to determine whether this was an elaborate vision, a new and terrible aspect of his madness.

Its motions remained birdlike, and it shuffled for several moments more, watching Amaoke closely. Then it shifted seamlessly into the form of a very tall man, keeping its fine-featured face and genderless appearance. Amaoke noted that there was no dimple in the abdomen. As its features changed, there was an accompanying rush of air, which crackled, charged like the anticipated threat of a lightning strike. The subtle scent of ozone and a single black feather that fluttered lazily to the ground were the only reminders of its prior form.

It strolled in a complete circle around Amaoke, examining him with open curiosity and obvious pleasure. It had manipulated its own enormous size, scaling its form to match Amaoke's stature, and when it made eye contact, he noticed the unnatural shine of its eyes, as if they cast off light that wasn't even there in the predawn dark.

Then its lips parted in a terrifying smile that revealed multiple rows of needle-like teeth, sharp and deadly. Its breath was redolent of every dead and rotting thing that Amaoke could imagine, and he thought he could hear a chorus of screams that sounded chillingly human coming from the depths of its throat.

Finally, it nodded and spoke once more. "Noki, your mother. So, so lovely. Our time with her was, alas, necessarily short. And you, the son, the one, fine of form and all that we intended you should be. Such a pity that she never saw you fully realized." Still, it used the odd yet understandable language.

Amaoke growled, and the change hovered nearby, the wolf returning, coming forward in answer to a perceived threat. This was the enemy, the Morningstar, the dread being that had interfered in his conception. If Amaoke was incensed to hear his mother's name on its lips, the wolf was murderous over it.

"You dare speak of her —" he gasped out, the statement registering as an uncontrolled growl, his body already fighting for control of the transformation.

The smile never left its face, and just when Amaoke realized he was too far gone and felt the shuddering, rippling motion of his flesh and the hair erupting across his back, the monster reached out to him. Just like that, the change abruptly stopped, leaving him slightly winded and still wholly human.

"Does the wolf even question its existence?" it asked knowingly, then answered its own question. "It does not. Yet you do. Human weakness. What if I told you that you seek what is not and can never be, as long as I exist here. Purpose, if you must have it, is mine and comes from me. Your existence is the product of my will, and your motivation shall be the gratification of your unique appetites because that will serve me.

"Your ever-growing power will be used as a weapon in the way of my naming, at a time of my choosing."

It waved one long arm to show Amaoke the simple, terrible truth. A vision slipped over him, robbing him of every other sense but the experience it created in the depths of his mind.

The eagle captured the salmon, pulled it struggling and dripping from the river where it labored upstream to propagate its kind and to die. In the work of carrying such a precious burden, the eagle was challenged by the wolf for its kill.

Though the magnificent bird defended its catch with talons wicked and sharp, the wolf prevailed, taking the fish and crippling the eagle such that she, too, became prey earned by the wolf, in addition to what was stolen from her. Thus the wolf fed on sea and sky.

The monster showed Amaoke this truth, that the eagle had fledgling eaglets in the nest near the top of a cottonwood tree.

It forced Amaoke to watch their slow starvation until the strongest remaining eaglet, with the vicious burden of hunger and survival, began to hunt and eat her brethren in the nest. The final sibling escapes the nest but not the crippling plunge to the dark earth, where it suffers pain in addition to its hunger, and fear, hearing the strong one's cries of anger and delayed gratification.

The truth. The only mercy found is in the injured eaglet's death before its sister's first flight, a controlled spiral descent to the ground to finally feast on her fallen nestmate.

Then the wind in his ears returned him to himself as the Morningstar flapped its mighty wings, and his rage at the senselessness that it advocated over the natural order of the universe was unleashed. He knew that its worldview could never be embraced if he meant to preserve his humanity, and Amaoke made himself the ridiculously naïve promise to do so as the change rolled over him. He welcomed it, body and soul, no turning back.

The monster before him was flesh, flesh that would satisfy, meat he wanted to rend with tooth and claw, recreating the order that Amaoke desired, which embraced all of the possibility for hope and justice in the universe.

But then he was snatched from the ground in powerful arms. The earth dropped away, impossibly far, and in the rushing wind, the sun broke over the mountain, and he was dropped, falling from a cruel and terrible height, his first object lesson from the master that Amaoke was made to be used up, and the futility of resistance of any kind.

Amaoke heard the cacophony and the chaos as he hurtled back to earth, and the Morningstar spoke to him, its voice both inside him and becoming ever more distant as he fell. "You have survived three hundred years. We shall see what the next three hundred will make of you."

As the final words faded, he arrived at his destination, and the ground welcomed him with catastrophic violence. His broken body became the only truth he knew for a long time, made worse by the added knowledge that there would be no respite waiting for him in an oft-wished-for death. Healing came at a terrible price, and more than once he screamed himself awake, having to chase the carrion from his own ruined body.

15

THE TRANSITION FROM BOY TO man and from man to wolf was far behind him, and Amaoke as he now existed was as different from the boy he had been as a wolf is from a man. His mature face was perpetually set in a scowl, and it displayed none of the laugh lines that it surely would have if the demeanor of his boyhood had survived the intervening centuries. He had a quiet, brooding presence unmodulated by interactions with other people, and other than the long-ago instruction by his mother, he possessed no contextual knowledge for interpersonal relationships. He had endured several human lifetimes outside of formal society and had interacted with only a few people, whether indirectly or accidentally.

He understood the need to spend equal time in human company as in lupine. It upheld the natural cycle no better to abandon human for animal than to deny entirely the wolf who was his counterpart. He also knew it was the human path his mother had prepared him to take.

Of late, cold weather prevailed; slowly, Amaoke noticed that winter crept in earlier, springs arrived later, and summers seemed to come not at all. He saw the southward migrations of larger game in more significant numbers than he could ever recall, and it was increasingly difficult to find enough small game to sustain himself between kills. The wolves sang infrequently, and he suspected most of the larger family packs had migrated south following the animals that they depended upon to survive. Amaoke, too, prepared to travel southward to find sustenance, but before he could go, something extraordinary happened across the river.

One late fall, a group of families traveled into his territory. They set up a hunting camp directly across the river from his hidden den, somewhat south of the location of his childhood home. He could watch them from a convenient vantage point beneath the reclining maiden; it provided cover for his wolf form, and the change of the riverbed over the intervening years had given him a clear view of the activity on the opposite bank. He could see many of their daily activities, and he was struck by their efficiency as a group. They were performing all of the daily chores that he had shared with his mother, but everyday tasks that had consumed the two of them were accomplished in a matter of hours with many hands working together.

There were many more mouths to feed, many more skins to process and sew, and more food to prepare. The other major difference Amaoke noticed was that there was strict separation of tasks by gender. He was somewhat surprised and secretly amused that many of his personal strengths were actually feminine chores. Amazed because of the way it changed his perspective of his childhood and amused because he thought of his mother, having to teach him everything and telling him nothing. Surely she had known and noticed those tasks at which he was most proficient, and she had the context that he had lacked until that moment.

As he watched the young members of the village at their chores, he decided that he would have been a very successful girl and only a marginally passable boy. The wolf huffed in disapproval, but the man still found it funny, and it might have prompted a rare smile had he been in human form when the observation was made.

It also gave him a newfound respect for his mother, who, by necessity, had raised him to do everything that was needed. From what he could presently observe, she had taught him most of what he needed to know to be a man without ever having directly learned those things herself!

But he could see that their hunters returned empty-handed, and there were not enough fish to sustain the villagers. That was terrible because he could see that they were hungry. What was worse was that more people were arriving every day, in what were apparently family groups of the same origin, as they shared a common language with that first group of settlers.

Although the words they used were not the same as the language spoken by his mother, the tongue was close enough that he understood most of it easily. But he did not need to speak their language to hear and see their increasing despair.

What touched him most was the occasional glimpses of a young mother carrying her infant strapped to her body while carrying out her chores. The child's eyes were exceedingly large in its hungry face, twin pools of dark want, haunted somehow by unmet needs. His heart ached, because he saw in those two a reflection of his past, as he imagined his lonely mother, his own unmet needs. The other children were also too thin, the adults drawn and tired, persevering, hoping for survival.

He wandered warily in the wake of the hunters, listening to their prayers, watching their rituals, seeing as they did the empty traps, and the hollowed-out clearings that betrayed no signs of sustaining game. He observed the elders study the sky, saw them reach the same conclusions that he had, that warmth would be long in coming if it arrived at all.

Amaoke himself built ritual fires, and burned the dried *tarvaq* he had saved, and prayed for blessings in the hunt as his mother had taught him. He purified his clothes and hair, bathing himself in the fumes in hopes that such spiritual observations would attract prey.

He awoke from a fitful sleep in the dark early morning after a new moon, his human form feeling weak and empty. He realized that a sound had reached his ears that the hunter in him recognized. It was a distant clicking sound, the sound of a wandering caribou. He listened again after leaving his dwelling, sure that it was a hunter's music carried in his mind, part of the patchwork of dreams he could never remember, the ones that plagued him as his hunger plagued him.

But he heard the sound again, unmistakable. It was far off, south, in the trailing end of the foothills before they flattened out into low tundra marshes that would stretch along the massive river delta to the faraway sea that he had never seen.

In spite of his many years, the change was still challenging to force with his own will when the moon was absent, but it came on him slowly, because he let thoughts of food and prey dominate him until his mouth watered with the promise of meat. Then the feral instincts came forth; those and the strength of hunger and desperation instructed his form, and the wolf ran down through the trees to find its prey.

It took him the better part of the day, running steadily onward as briskly as his weakened state would allow, to pick up the trail. It was nearing dusk when he sighted the animal, which was all the worse for having persisted in the northern woods when its brethren had migrated. He could see its skin hanging, and its rib rack and hip bones were more prominent than any he had ever seen. He briefly wondered if it was afflicted by some madness or other illness, but when the wind brought the animal's scent to him, there was no sickness that he could detect. It was dying the slow death of starvation, as the snowpack provided ample water.

Amaoke easily brought it to ground, suffocating it quickly. His hunger was interfering with his reason; the wolf had no allegiance to those camped on the river, only to itself. After opening the abdomen with sharp claws, he reluctantly shifted back to human form. Despite his nakedness, he had been in wolf form so frequently over the previous weeks that he maintained some extra body and facial hair covering, but it was still freezing. Some focused work was needed to clean the entrails from the carcass, and he assuaged the beast inside by eating the heart. It was more optimism than strength that he called upon to lift the body high enough into a tree to cache it; in this way, it was protected until he could return, fully dressed, on two legs. Winter's deep freeze would preserve it.

When he returned the following day to retrieve it, he was still hungry and tired, and the weather had worsened. Snow was spit out of low clouds in large rags, and a wet cold penetrated him to the bone. It took Amaoke longer than expected to disentangle the caribou from the branches he had balanced it upon, and by the time he had knocked it to the ground, darkness had fallen, and the snow and wind were worsening.

He slung the animal's body across his shoulders and started the long walk back, but he had only gotten a few steps into his journey when his nose told him he was not alone. Moments later, he saw the shifting shapes of three wolves, shadowing his progress through the snowy woods. Two skinny females and a male, looking to challenge him for his kill. He suspected that the only reason they had not just immediately attacked him was that their noses were telling them something that their eyes could not.

Amaoke, at his advanced age, knew that he was dominant to most other wolves, even though he had, over his many years, submitted to some of them in order to be allowed to live peacefully among them. Dominance was part of a ritual, a set of behaviors that humans rarely exhibited in a way that would translate to their animal brethren. So he stopped walking, and without putting down his prey, relieved himself at the nearest large tree to convey the message more succinctly, and continued his journey.

Although the threesome dropped even further back, they kept on coming, the desperation of their hunger overriding their acknowledgement of his dominance. Amaoke knew he could change, face them down, and chase them off, but that would use up precious strength that he needed to preserve. He was about to face a new challenge, one in which he could not predict the outcome, so he was conservative with his energy for now.

The wolves trailed him back to his cave, where they took up whining and yipping at him because they knew he would understand. The females' scents had changed, both of them, suggesting they viewed him as alpha and preferable to the male they were following, which wasn't a surprise – after all, he was the more dominant male in their presence, and he had a cache of meat.

He relented somewhat, as he had known he would, for the sake of all; if there was to be enduring survival in this persistent cold, it would be achieved in concert with others, not alone. He tore the liver out of the carcass and pulled it apart, delivering the chunks to the starving wolves, then chased them away from his den with the most menacing growl he could muster, making it clear that his generosity had reached its limit. They scattered like birds, each taking a different route back the way they had come, slipping like shadows into the deeper forest.

He built a fire and spent the better part of the night thinking and praying. He knew he could leave the meat at the hunting camp, but that would only feed them once, and it gave him no useful way of alerting them to the diminishing presence of game that he had personally observed over the previous seasons. To do so might inadvertently give them false hope that there was enough food to sustain them here, and they would surely starve.

Additionally, they were reasonably experienced hunters, and it was altogether possible that they were capable of tracking him back to his home, which was an undesirable outcome. He considered the possibility of making the gift of meat and then leaving the area, striking out southward to the sea, and looking for better food resources. Still, he was as likely to encounter other people in those travels as if he remained with this group. He also suspected that the Morningstar would have preferred he stay solitary, apart from humanity, and Amaoke knew that all of his mother's teachings had been undertaken with the opposite aim. She had tried to prepare him to be a man among other men, not a man apart.

By the time the sky was lightening the next morning, he was across the river and approaching the hunting encampment on foot. Across his shoulders, he bore the caribou carcass, and he carried no visible weaponry.

The first person to see him approaching was a young man doing what dutiful young men have done for centuries, clearing the doorway of a dwelling. The boy paused, fearful of the stranger, but equally curious and pleased to see the game he carried into the camp. He acknowledged Amaoke with a nod and then ran off, down one of the central pathways between the dwellings. Amaoke assumed, correctly, that the young man was off to seek help and guidance, so he stopped where he stood, and schooled himself to stillness, hoping his temporarily bearded face was not alarming.

Before the young man returned, however, his frantic scramble through the camp seemed to have set in motion the entire population. By the time he returned with several other mature men, two of which were likely the elders of the group, Amaoke was surrounded by a separate group of women and children of all ages, many of whom peered out at him from behind their mothers' legs. Amaoke had no way to gauge his appearance to them; he was much taller than the tallest man who emerged ahead of a group of men that came to greet him officially, and their faces were smooth, their eyes large and dark and questioning.

The men came to him, and he recognized the scents of some of the hunters he had followed through the woods. A few carried hunting spears, but they looked more curious than menacing.

Amaoke made eye contact with as many of the people in the group as he could, before kneeling to make himself shorter than they were. He bowed his head slightly to lift the caribou from his shoulders, and some of the villagers gasped at this display of strength. When no one spoke, he laid the carcass reverently on the ground, and said in his own tongue, "I am alone. I offer meat to share with you."

Some of the youngest men looked slightly confused, but the eldest among them nodded his understanding. When he answered,

Amaoke was able to hear enough of his language in theirs to make out what was said.

"We have nothing to offer in return," the old man told him. "We will accept the gift you bring and can only offer to share the meal with you."

"I am grateful," Amaoke replied with sincerity, feeling the scrutiny of all of them directed at him. It was a weighty thing, all that attention, all those eyes. Some of them were afraid; he could smell their fear but thought he could ignore it so far from the inexorable demands of the full moon.

As if he could read Amaoke's thoughts, the older man spoke a few words, seemingly into the air, and the entire group dispersed, some returning to abandoned chores and some back into their dwellings. A group of women came forward to accept the meat, and he saw that one of them was the young mother with her baby strapped to her chest. The child openly examined Amaoke and opened its mouth in a toothless grin, giving a small surprised sound of delight. Its mother cast her eyes downward respectfully, but Amaoke could feel the eyes of the older women look upon him with surprise. He remained kneeling, both out of respect and because he desired not to be viewed a threat while they took the animal away for preparation.

The men gathered loosely about him as the women withdrew, and he returned to his feet, standing at full height once again. The tallest among them had to crane his face upward to make eye contact, and making eye contact with Amaoke seemed to give each of them difficulty. The elder who had previously spoken stepped forward. He had no problem maintaining eye contact, and with a small shake of his head, he indicated that Amaoke should follow him.

The escort of armed men accompanied them, and other men joined the procession, which led to a central dwelling in the camp. Inside, there was a hearth in the middle of the space with banked embers, to which one of the youngest men added wood as they entered, even though the dwelling was still warm from the presence of many bodies. There was evidence that this was where most, if not all, of the men spent their time when they were not hunting, trapping, or fishing. Various personal effects such as water skins, knives, and spears were present along the outer wall, either hanging above or stowed beneath a long bench that ran along the perimeter of the space. Ceremonial items and dried plants were suspended more centrally, near the smoke hole, which was the primary source of light on that gray morning. There were fish-oil lamps hung at intervals along the walls, but Amaoke identified them by smell, as they were not presently lit. As he had in his mother's dwelling, he was obliged to duck his head down, unable to stand fully upright.

The dwelling continued to fill as one by one, each male in the village entered, in order of whatever seniority was afforded them: first the two elders, then the group of armed men whose ages varied, who were most likely the most accomplished hunters for the group or the heads of households. These were followed by younger men, some old enough to be married and some likely unmarried hunters, then those of adolescence down to boys of only a handful of years. There was hardly space to accommodate them all, but they entered nonetheless, all engaged with his presence, all present to witness whatever was to come next, all likely to participate in deciding his fate.

The elder sat down at the place nearest the entrance and offered Amaoke the seat beside him. Amaoke demurred, saying, "No, good father, I have not earned the honor." He called upon all that he could remember of the good manners his mother had imparted. The elder repeated his words to the men in the dwelling in their tongue, but it was apparent that the two languages were close enough that he had been understood. It was the right thing; the armed men seemed to relax at this response, and spears were set aside, not far from reach but no longer in hand.

"Still, you have brought us meat that we did not bring to ourselves, so we thank you and wish to speak awhile to you," the older man told him, indicating the seat to his right once again.

Again, Amaoke refused, adding respectfully, "I must know the man whose place I would take, and it is likely that I would find myself wanting." He'd searched his memory carefully for the words he wanted and was rewarded when the second elder stepped forward, smiling.

He placed a hand on the first elder's shoulder and said, "This one understands the old ways and follows the path. Brother, do you still wish to give him your place?" He looked around at the others, his gaze resting for a long time on the youngest present there as if highlighting a lesson to be learned.

"I welcome him to it," the first elder replied, giving up his place to the second man. Amaoke could now see the family resemblance, and would not have been able to discern which brother was eldest until he came forward. Amaoke thought the tactic was wise: protect the highest-ranking elder by not revealing him until the possibility of danger had been more fully assessed. The irony of the situation saddened him; he knew that he was still a very significant threat to these people should he decide to be; the wolf inside remained hungry and was surrounded by meat he would have gladly eaten were it not for the man with whom it shared an existence. If he were hungry enough, Amaoke was not sure that his human reason would win that argument.

When the seat was offered the third time, Amaoke accepted it, and once he was seated, all the others took their rightful places along the other walls.

"I am Usugan; my brother is Quuran," the eldest brother said softly. "He will speak for me today." He gestured quickly at his brother, who pushed down the mantle of his parka and stood before Amaoke, who had displaced him from his seat. His long hair pooled in the dome of his hood, white as the driven snow, striking against the mahogany skin that was windburned and softened by long years. His skin appeared fragile, with thousands of tiny lines extending from the outer part of his eyes and mouth, which told Amaoke that he had smiled long and often in his life. His eyes were a vibrant brown color, lighter than those of his brother, and they spoke of intelligence, and the witness to many winters, perhaps even a few as terrible as this one. Amaoke already had the sense that this man could see much more than he would reveal, and he seemed to carry some magic about him, a charismatic presence that Amaoke had recognized right away when he'd first encountered him at the entrance to the village. He smelled of wild celery and *ayuq*, and other aromatic plants, and there was a subtle scent of illness on his clothing, but his scent was that of a still-vital man, so the sickness was that of another. Amaoke suspected he was a ritual healer, a medicine man, one sensitive to the spirits.

Quuran examined Amaoke's face with interest and open curiosity. He paid particular attention to his eyes and his facial hair, keeping his face devoid of other emotions, and finally asked, "Your village?"

Amaoke shook his head, never taking his eyes from Quuran. "Gone, long gone. My mother raised me here, next to the river. Her people lived closer to the mouth of the river, nearer the sea."

"Your father?"

"Dead before my birth. I never knew him."

"A hunter?" Quuran's delicate eyebrows moved together; he was predicting more than he was asking. "A hunter who passed his gifts to you, perhaps?"

"I —" Amaoke faltered, unsure what to say. He stayed as honest as he could. "I do not know."

"I wonder what your heart says." The older man breathed the words softly, gently. Amaoke guessed he could sense the pain associated with thoughts of his father. More clearly, so others could hear, he said, "And your mother?"

"Dead for many years. Dead before I was fully a man," Amaoke replied, his heart aching to say those words aloud. The loss was still raw despite the intervening centuries, as her death marked a distinct boundary in his life: before it, he had been carefree, and happiness was always nearby; after it, he'd descended into a dual life, a life dominated by a beastly companion for whom he had never asked.

"You have survived on this river alone all that time?" Quuran could not hide his surprise, and his sharp eyes looked into Amaoke's with newfound respect, as he realized that Amaoke had been on his own for many years, even if there was no way he could imagine exactly how many years had passed since that fateful event.

"All the caribou had gone, none were there to be found," Quuran observed wisely, watching for Amaoke's reaction.

"She woke me from a dream," Amaoke replied, finding that he was unable to turn his own gaze away from the older man's. "She called to me, and I answered. She was left behind as a warning. I had seen the hunger in your children's eyes, and it was a gift I was compelled to share."

"There is truth in what you say, but there is something that you do not say," the old man surmised, and it was Amaoke's turn to be surprised.

"She is the last, for a very long time, I fear," Amaoke admitted. "The animals have gone south, into the warmer places by the sea, and beyond. They are trying to tell us how to survive. We must follow them, or the cold and the hunger will take us, and many, if not all, will perish. This is what the signs have said to me, because it is no longer the same as it was before. What was abundant here is now scarce. Summers have disappeared; last year, there were no new berries. The river remained too cold for many of the fish to return, the ice persisted too long, and it was impassable. There may be no thaw this year." It all came out of him, all that he needed to tell them, and it was the longest speech he had ever made.

Quuran looked at his brother. Usugan nodded slowly, then spoke. "You are speaking aloud what my brother has predicted to me privately. But still, there is nothing we have to give you in return for this gift of meat and life."

"I ask nothing in return, good fathers. Your fellowship is gift enough," Amaoke replied.

Just then, his nostrils flared as the scent of fresh meat reached him. Moments later, the young mother appeared in the entrance with a bowl of food carved from the caribou. Her eyes remained cast downward as she carried it forward and handed it to Usugan, greeting him reverently. "Grandfather."

Amaoke put his own eyes on the floor, not wanting to inadvertently disrespect these men by looking directly at one of their women, but he knew she was beautiful from observing her from across the river. Her parka was belted with an ornate beaded elkskin strip that encircled her waist twice, and her hood remained up, obscuring her hair. Her eyes were large and dark, bottomless pools, and she had given those lovely eyes to her child.

He had thought the child was sleeping against her breast, and was surprised when its small hand reached out from the front of her parka and touched his cheek, right on his skin beneath the eye, above where his beard began. He heard the audible gasps of those in the room, and although he too was surprised, he made no sound or movement.

Out of the corner of his eye, he saw Usugan dismiss the girl with a small smile and a gentle flick of his hand. Amaoke waited until she was gone from the dwelling to lift his eyes to his hosts.

Usugan picked up the first piece, a chunk of meat from the choicest part of the back, and offered it to Amaoke. He accepted it, and stepped forward, waving it over the fire for two passes and whispering a prayer of thanks before turning back to the elder and handing it to him. Usugan, and everyone else in the dwelling, was surprised, but the elder accepted the meat graciously, and ate it. Amaoke stepped back and purposefully avoided resuming Quuran's seat. He waited until all the men, to the very least and youngest boy, had eaten before he would accept any of the meat for himself.

The atmosphere was bewildering for Amaoke, and the sounds and smells of so many others in such a small space began to overwhelm him, particularly because it was associated with the scent of raw, bloody flesh, and he didn't trust his control. He waited until the men were engrossed in the telling of personal stories, and he slipped out of the dwelling. He followed the central path to the edge of the camp and headed off upriver, crossing on an ice bridge many inches thick, where the water's flow had slowed, and the river was too narrow to resist the freeze. He stepped into a stand of trees that sheltered the bend of the river before he looked back.

There was a figure near the edge of the camp. Quuran had come to the water's edge, and was standing motionless, watching Amaoke's departure, the fur trim on the hood of his parka dancing in the wind. Amaoke stopped, and turned to face him, acknowledging his presence there, before stepping into the woods and returning to the world he knew.

16

AMAOKE AWAKENED SUDDENLY A FEW mornings later because he sensed something unusual. It was a sound, or a feeling that he could not put a name to, and he wondered if he had been dreaming, but he could recall no dreams. His sleep of late had improved in spite of his continued lean diet, and he had long since stopped being concerned that anything in these woods would disturb his rest, even when he remained in human form, as now.

He approached the entrance to the cave and caught the scent of man, medicinal plants, and smoke. He spoke through the bright opening as he emerged. "Good father."

Quuran started in surprise at the sound of Amaoke's voice, but responded with one word, "*Noatak.*" He inclined his head toward Amaoke, conveying the name to him. The word meant "river which provides food for our people," and Amaoke was grateful for the nickname, which was respectful of him as a source of succor. He knew Quuran was too polite to directly ask his name, and Amaoke shared that superstition; besides, his own name was revealing of what he truly was.

"You will walk with an old man?" Quuran invited.

Amaoke inclined his own head in agreement, and they strolled together among the trees. He knew that Quuran's appearance was no random event; the elder was a very proficient tracker to have found Amaoke at all. His scrutiny was intense, and Amaoke felt that he was seen in a way he had never been seen before. It was as uncomfortable as anything he had known.

"You are of the people, but not of the people," he observed after they had walked hundreds of paces in silence. A rare day of sunshine was beginning, but aside from a cold, remote light, it would contribute no warmth to the day. But Quuran was wise, and many years of life had given him excellent instincts, and he touched on nothing that stung too severely as he made his observations.

"We come from the north. All of what you have observed here, we lived through there. We hoped we would not have to come this far for food, but it appears we must go farther."

Amaoke nodded slightly, saying nothing, knowing no answer was expected of him. Quuran continued, after a time, saying, "Your beard is gone. Your face is smooth."

Amaoke remained silent, but the older man must have sensed his distress, because he waved his hand slowly at his side in reassurance, and continued. "When I was no more than a child, I saw men with such beards as yours, and such blue eyes as well. They came across the frozen sea with the Aleut, the Kerek, and the Chukchi to trade with our father and his father before him. So pale they were! So strange and different from us, and yet, I can tell that you are not of them. You are of the people, but I would guess that you do not look much like your mother's people, for there was no other reason to raise you here.

"A woman trying to raise a child alone goes away from the path, against the path. It is a terrible and courageous thing to do. It is what a woman would do if her child were born with features she could not explain," Quuran concluded wisely. "It is what a mother would do to protect such a child from certain terrible harms."

Amaoke could neither confirm nor deny Quuran's suspicions, but he knew he did not have to do so. The man had a sense of things. Despite his insight, he assumed nothing supernatural; at least Amaoke didn't think so. And he knew what his mother had feared about his safety even though she avoided directly discussing his differences with him. As he had matured and grown into some wisdom as a man, he suspected that she wanted him to believe he was perfectly normal, to ease his transition into a world in which he would always be different. She had just never known to what extent that would be true, and his differences now were far more significant than what she had attempted to prepare him for.

"Usugan is my older brother," Quuran explained. "We shared the womb. He came into the world headfirst, strong, robust, and I followed after, feet first, and barely alive. Our mother did not survive our birth, and I suspect her sacrifice was what allowed me to survive.

"We have been like two parts of a whole ever since, even though the world has tried many times to divide us. Our father taught Usugan to hunt but refused to show me, as I was born with the unfortunate luck. The elders were concerned about my entry into the world, and felt I would be unlucky as a hunter, and unlucky out on a hunt with others.

"I had other talents, and turned my attention to the spiritual, trying to reverse my own bad luck within my universe by helping to heal others who were struggling with mightier spiritual problems, such as illness.

"We even loved the same maiden, and she chose me over my brother, but my father refused to offer for her on my behalf; he offered for her on behalf of Usugan, and I know he loved her enough. Her parents were relieved, I think, when the offer came from him. He gave her children, and she lived to see a few of their grandchildren, but did not survive the first harsh winter's famine, choosing to feed her children and grandchildren ahead of herself.

"We have even spoken our own language with one another, one that no one else speaks, from the time we could form words with our mouths. It has always been my role to take risks for him, to protect him as our elder; it was ever expected of me, and never did we speak on it.

"Nothing has ever come between us, until now. We have never had a disagreement about what must be done, until now."

Quuran stopped walking, his final step into the frozen snow the last sound he made. The silence that followed it grew and spread around them in the sunshine as Amaoke waited.

"We must travel further south, as a united people. We do this to survive. I have insisted that we must now travel with another, a stranger to us in looks, custom, and language. I have dreamt of this. You are the first sign," Quuran explained.

"I have told my brother that as we go south, we will become more than one people, and yet, of the many who join us, we will become one together, despite our differences, and that is the only way for all of us to become strong enough to survive.

"He rejects this idea, because he fears that our people will be lost, our ways will be gone, our families will be adulterated by outsiders. He does not accept that we will perish if we cannot accept change. He could order your death as a threat to our way of being, but he owes you fealty for the food you provided. Even he cannot answer peace with violence, because it would lessen him in the eyes of our people. But he could banish me, his own brother, and continue on without me, and suffer no ill effects other than the loss of my counsel and my medicine, and none would question this because they know of my defiance.

"But Usugan tolerated my argument because he can save face by asking you to join us. You are the *Noatak*, so the people will accept you. He can repay your gift by according you a better chance to survive, among our group. But if you come with us, I fear you will always remain separate in the many minds of our people, which may be a hard way to live. Harder than to be alone," he warned, but it would be many years before Amaoke would be able to understand that statement fully.

"I cannot come between you and your brother," Amaoke said softly, shaking his head. "It upsets the balance of things."

"It is already decided, whether you come with us or not. What has changed between us cannot be unchanged. It is just the new reality, different from the old. It has been coming our entire lives, and there was no way for us to avoid it. The universe asks of us what we must do to survive, and we ignore the signs at our peril."

With that, he turned and walked away through the forest, leaving Amaoke to watch as he grew smaller and smaller in the distance, until his figure blended with the young trees, and he was lost to sight in the forest.

. . . . .

Amaoke knew that his mother had intended him to be ready for society, and he had a blueprint for acceptable behavior. He had achieved enough wisdom in the intervening years to understand that being in touch with his own humanity meant more than knowing how to survive in human form. True understanding of his human nature would come from interactions that could only occur in the society of other humans. His life as a man would become both a part of himself as a whole and a reflection of what he could only be exposed to in relationships with others. Good or bad, these were lessons worth learning. So with a little regret for what he was leaving behind, but much longing for the self-knowledge he was lacking, he joined the tribe of Usugan and migrated away from the only home he had ever known.

Game and people became more abundant as the villagers traveled south, and Usugan and Quuran reflected much on their predictions. Amaoke was not the only outsider who joined with them in the name of survival, but although there were now small separations among the larger group by language and fundamental belief, no one was more distinct within the society than Amaoke himself.

At first, it was only his appearance that set him apart, and some of the travelers that the tribe encountered refused to join with them, mistrustful of this strange creature that appeared to be so allied with the elders. Eventually, his unusual and unique abilities kept him aloof, not by his own doing, but out of necessity as he correctly surmised that his dual nature must be kept a secret. This duality necessitated that he absent himself for the days surrounding the full moon, but this act was viewed with no greater suspicion than any other habit he had that the people may have found unusual.

In wolf form, he easily shadowed and tracked the group's movements, which created no difficulty in returning to the village camp at the end of his self-imposed exiles. This behavior, in particular, caused some mythical power to be attributed to him, but the whispers and the concern were allayed by the fact that he always returned with game to share with the hungry. He kept the nickname given him by Quuran, and the *Noatak* came to be known outside of the village, among other peoples who kept their permanent homes in this part of the river delta. He often wondered which of them had been his mother's tribe, but Amaoke was comforted when he realized that he was learning about them even if he had not returned to them.

It was when the group neared the seacoast that he began to hear legends from the local people about a maiden whose lost husband had returned from the spirit world to get her with child. He so loved her that the spirits could not hold him, and the *ellam yua* allowed him to return for one last visit. The maiden grew heavy with child, but before her delivery, she vanished, and her footsteps left a short path before they disappeared at the edge of the frozen river, where it was believed that she had passed into the spirit world, taking her child with her so that the family could be together in that realm. They suggested that the child would return to the world a great warrior chief, following an education by the spirits, and lead the people to prosperity.

Amaoke knew the truth, but he thought it a fitting tribute to his lovely mother, who had always followed the path until she could do so no longer. He knew that her love for his father, Uqii, had eclipsed all things, and he knew how desperately the childhood friends had wanted a child, and a life together. Overall, it was an imaginative story and likely had been born out of the grief of her loss from the tribe. He was proud to be her son, and knew that with this story, she was well-remembered; she had passed into legend a symbol of the power of love.

If he felt outside the structure of society in some ways, among the hunters, he was included and embraced. He kept quiet in the community house, and listened and learned as they made plans and preparations for seal, walrus, and whale hunting, activities for which he had no background or experience.

But out on the ice, or riding with the other men in the *umiaq*, he discovered that his sense of smell was nearly as keen as on land, once he learned to put aside the many distracting scents that came from the sea. He knew when a large mammal was nearby by smell, and this aided the men, who in turn taught him the signs of their approach, and their behaviors, so he knew where to look for them and what to avoid.

His skill with a spear was indispensable to him. Although spearfishing was very different than hunting these more massive beasts, the accuracy he'd learned in order to spear a small target made spearing a large target less difficult. But pulling a fish out of the river was a modest success compared to the effort required to get a whale to the shore, or a walrus to the women, or a seal onto the ice. But he was not alone, and he learned about the beauty of several men working toward a common goal, and his contributions were valued within the whole. In the closeness of the hunt and the necessity for mutual communication to succeed, the other men learned to ignore Amaoke's appearance as they understood and appreciated the many ways in which he was just like them. When that occurred, he could see himself from their perspective, and a part of him became whole, even if the respect was only fully realized in his role as the hunter and provider, the life-giving river, the *Noatak*.

Because in ceremonial life, in private life, he was still excluded in many ways by these same men who embraced him as a brother on the hunt. Amaoke could not fully understand this, and it caused him to hold himself even further apart, ascribing prejudice and superstition to humans as a whole, still unable to differentiate them as individuals, as so much of what they did was within a society that had to function cooperatively to survive. The only allowance he made in categorizing any observable difference was born of his relationship with Quuran, but he, too, despite his ties with Usugan, was both essential to and outside of the tribe hierarchy, much like Amaoke himself.

Quuran did much to explain away the behavior of his people without excusing it at all. "You are respected for the resources you provide, and your observation of ritual is perfectly nuanced – your mother was an outstanding teacher of the expectations of society, and any eccentricities you still possess are related to your complete lack of exposure to the mentoring of elder men. Your hunting prowess earns you a position within the societal hierarchy, but your skills are both a blessing and a curse.

"The people are thankful for your contributions to our food stores, but other hunters are threatened by your abilities. That is partly because they would rather that the most skilled among them was from our Koyukuk family, not an outsider. The younger ones also worry that their potential brides could be offered to you.

"Finally, they fear you. They might not even be able to put the reasons for such a fear into words. It goes beyond your appearance, but it certainly starts there. It is probably something as simple as your lifestyle, and the fact that you hold yourself apart. They do not see, as I do, that this is done out of respect. It is your acknowledgement, I think, that you recognize your position as an outsider, one who will never be fully accepted into the people as family, and that you wish only to coexist in harmony with the others here," Quuran observed. Amaoke had to admit that Quuran was wise, and saw much more than people thought he did. He listened, and watched, and seemed to be carefully guided by the spirits. Amaoke suspected Quuran felt spirit energies as he himself did, and he wondered what kind of energy Quuran could detect from him.

"I do not expect them to accept me as one of them," Amaoke protested, but Quuran only put up a hand, and frowned.

"Not quite a lie," he mused. "Expectation is related to what you have concluded about the likelihood of an event. But what if I asked you what you truly *wanted* from them, in here –" Quuran placed an open hand over Amaoke's heart, and continued, shaking his head when Amaoke started to answer. "The worst lies are the ones we tell ourselves. Every man wants to be known and accepted for who he really is, whether he believes it is possible or not.

"You and I are not so different, my son. You are also a twin, with a darker brother whom you are afraid you cannot control. This the spirits have shared with me." Quuran spoke kindly and did not bother to gauge Amaoke's reaction. "I am the darker twin in my own life, not because I believe that I am any unluckier or less skilled than Usugan, but rather because the world reflects that belief back to me with its judgments. I have been measured this way my entire life, denied the education in specific skills, denied a wife, but upheld for my particular talents. Those talents actually contribute to my relative exile-in-arms. Yet, unlike you, I still look for my people to behave better, to accept me fully, even though I have no good reason to expect it to happen in this life.

"So the young hunters should not worry about you – they should accept what they have been taught, that the natural world has room for many different points of view and room for many different talents. You are here and no less important to the *ellam iinga*, the great eye that watches over us, or you would not be here. Your appearance as it differs from them should not matter, because you are, generally, the same as they are underneath, and no less valuable to the circle of life."

"But they will not allow me to take a wife, that I already know, so I cannot understand the continued concern about the possibility of my intermarriage into the people," Amaoke protested.

"You are trying not to see what could be there, whether you are looking or not," Quuran pointed out. "It is natural for young women to recognize that a successful hunter not only makes a prestigious mate but is likely to father sons who are successful hunters and providers for the people. Our society is built upon our ability to subsist on the land and sea, and that is a powerful attraction."

"But I have never encouraged —" Amaoke started to argue, which was unlike him. Quuran stimulated him, pushed him, wanted him to think, but sometimes it was exhausting. The wolf was tired of so much talking.

Quuran waved gently with his hands, smoothing the air in a gesture meant to clear whatever was upsetting Amaoke. "You have been an example of propriety, indeed. But I exhort you to open your eyes to what happens around you, as it will further expand your understanding of others. One young woman, in particular, makes her desire for you obvious, and because of who she is, the village is full of speculation. And there are, naturally, others who are curious about the *Noatak*, but gender separation circumscribes much of our behavior, and our women are taught to exercise special care in their interactions with any hunter to avoid adversely affecting his ability to provide meat and hides to the people.

"More importantly, you should seek deeper relationships with people, no matter your reasons for caution. You are no less deserving of closeness to another human being, no less deserving of your own family, and your expectations of others should remain elevated, wanting the best of them as you give the best of yourself," Quuran explained. "This should be your way forward, even when others disappoint you, which will be often."

Amaoke was always grateful for Quuran's friendship, which appeared genuine, and his mentoring, which was invaluable to a grown man who had never known the society of others. He knew that Quuran also struggled with the mystery of Amaoke that he could not unravel, but Amaoke would not, could not, reveal himself to anyone. He sensed it would be unwise, if only to draw the attention of ill spirits. He knew enough of the Morningstar's capability for destruction.

So he kept his head up when in society, and listened, and watched, and learned. He learned that Usugan's granddaughter, Iniẍ, had been widowed when her own husband, a very accomplished hunter, had drowned in a storm at sea when on a whaling expedition, before her child was born. As she was still young, and from a respected family, she was a desirable wife because she knew the ways of her people. She had some freedom in deciding whether to accept another husband; it appeared she had more extensive choices than other young unmarried girls. He learned that she had turned down offers from acceptable suitors, and it appeared that Usugan thought it was due to her mourning for her dead husband. Quuran's words and her behavior gave Amaoke an alternative explanation.

Iniẍ had frequently sought him out at community gatherings, and he had assumed this was because her child had a fondness for Amaoke that was utterly perplexing. The baby had always wanted to touch him, and would even coo out soft sounds only for him, and the attention was uncomfortable, but he liked the child. The baby was inquisitive and beautiful, and the plight of the young widow was similar to that of his own mother and himself.

She often brought him his meals in the men's house, which was not wholly unusual, because he was considered a guest of Usugan, so it was the women of Usugan's family group that tended to his meals and repaired or made his clothing. But once Quuran opened his eyes to the situation, he noticed that many of the women in the family stepped aside in favor of allowing Iniẍ to interact with him. He wondered how he had missed it.

By the time the group reached the sea and established a permanent village site for the group, the child was walking, and if he escaped his keepers, he would show up suddenly at Amaoke's side, and would follow Amaoke until his mother or one of the other young women intervened. He had a precocious interest in Amaoke's tools and weapons, and Amaoke spoke to the child about these and many other things, never confident the child could understand him and never having any indication that the boy could not. The boy watched and listened with those lovely dark eyes, the eyes of his mother, appearing to absorb all that was said.

Time passed, and Amaoke's nose made him aware that Iniẍ was willing to share the comfort of her bed with him, but still, he was unable to lower the barriers that he felt kept others safe from the unpredictable part of his nature. So while he spent time with her fatherless son, assuaging something in himself, providing something for her child that he had gone without, he was unable to give her what she wanted and needed.

It was not that Amaoke did not find her physically attractive; something in him was closed off, and he could not work it open. He suspected that time would change him if their polite but celibate companionship were meant to be more, but he didn't trust his stronger emotions when it came to maintaining control. Also, he suspected that he was drawn to her plight, in its similarity with that of his mother, rather than having an independent, fully formed attraction to her as a mate, and because Amaoke could tell that her emotions in that regard were stronger than his, he did not want to hurt her feelings.

So he did not rebuff her, nor did he encourage her, and she must have concluded that he or her grandfather had deemed such a relationship improper, and she seemed to gain an acceptance of this. She continued to bring him special foods, and present him with gifts that were more appropriate for a husband than a respected mentor of her son, including *mukluqs* of beautiful craftsmanship and warmth.

Amaoke knew that Usugan and the other men and women of the village, without ever saying as much, were relieved at his circumspect behavior. Quuran's knowing eye saw it all, and suggested to Amaoke once that after so much time had passed, with his relationship to the boy, the people would have had difficulty refusing any suit he had offered for Iniẍ.

One early winter night, nearing festival time and the anniversary of Amaoke's birth, Usugan fell ill. In spite of the best efforts of Quuran, his health continued to decline, and he did not survive another moon. Quuran and the extended family were still in their initial period of mourning when the moon grew full enough that

Amaoke was compelled to leave, despite the prohibitions on much of the village. He did not see Quuran before he left, and by the time he returned, the older man, too, was failing.

"It has always been my job to follow Usugan and protect him. This is my legacy; it is the price I must pay for gaining life with our mother's death. He will need me in the spirit realm, at his side, as he cannot fully cross the river of tears alone. Born together, we must travel together to the land of the dead," Quuran explained.

Amaoke had never known Quuran to have suffered any illness, and his nose told him now that Quuran had ingested something that would influence his passage on to the next world, and he was deeply saddened.

Over the next days, Quuran faded further, saying only to Amaoke before he died, "I hope that you will embrace all that is within you, for I feel in you a power to do much good, no matter the darkness you have felt inside yourself." Amaoke was surprised at this, and again wondered how much Quuran had noticed, or had guessed, but before he could say anything, Quuran gave him the most knowing look of all, and concluded, "I have been blessed with you, my *Tiquana*, son who is not my son but is my family. You are a good man, and you must believe in that goodness. It can set you free from whatever darkness tries to claim you. Your goodness is more powerful than you know, and your mother's love is strong in you. Hold close to it, and you will always find your path."

He did not speak again, imparting no more wisdom to Amaoke or any other, passing on out of the world, to join his brother so they could finish their journey together. Amaoke wished him all speed, and when the days of mourning had ended, he knew that his time there had also come to an end. The village was prospering, there were ample resources to be had, and something in him knew that in order to find what he was looking for, to learn what he had not yet learned, he had far to go, and much to seek.

17

FOR SOME TIME AFTER QUURAN'S death, Amaoke migrated east and inland from the Western seas. He traveled from village to village, at times migrating in the company of large mixed-family groups in search of warmer climes and more abundant food sources, or an escape from enemy villages.

As he had with the wolves, he learned to assimilate among the various peoples he lived and worked with, learning their languages and their ways while remaining observant of the universal laws of his mother's traditions. Despite the accumulation of many tongues, including some of those spoken by the *Kass'aq* traders that were increasingly encountered in the eastern lands, his mind processed and thought in his mother's language whether he was on two legs or four.

He maintained his four-day absence with each full moon, just as he had done when living with the Koyukon families of Usugan's village, and this was little remarked upon over time. Those with him supposed him to be undertaking a careful religious observance; since he was ever and always an outsider, it was accepted unquestioningly.

Of course, his prowess as a hunter meant he was almost always welcome to return and live among a diverse array of families, all of whom had their own observances, many of which were startlingly similar. He was allowed participation in some of these celebrations and excepted from others; only rarely was he expressly excluded.

He attended with the other men the community houses, rarely speaking or showing any strong emotion; it was not so secretly believed that his stoicism was a favorable trait for a hunter so blessed with abundant game of all kinds. Yet, in spite of his significant contributions, or perhaps because of them, he was still viewed with suspicion. His appearance was undoubtedly prejudicial, and some justified excluding him from full society based on that alone.

Traditionally proscribed from marrying, he had ultimately disdained all offered unions in more receptive villages as a matter of course. He did so mostly in an effort to avoid offending families whose sons sought brides among their own people. He had practiced how to present his refusals through the elders to help avoid giving offense. But he also did it out of a stubborn practicality, because he did not want to burden an unsuspecting young girl with such a husband as he. The final reason was related to something he told himself often enough that he had long since believed it to be true: there was to be no love for him in this world, no one who would readily choose him as husband.

At times, he was whispered about and confronted as though he were a spiritual hybrid, like the legendary *ircenrrat* of his mother's teachings. He did nothing to discourage this thinking; neither did he disarm what he knew to be fundamentally untrue. In some places, this thinking even improved his treatment.

After long travels, he settled with and was provisionally accepted among the Innu people that populated the coastal areas of the Eastern seas. His whaling prowess and his appearance were suggestive of an unnatural spiritual connection to the animals, and the Innu, like the Yupiaq, descended from his mother's people, had a rich mythology to support such beliefs.

Thus his presence among them accorded him some honor, unlike the usual sufferance he was given. He was wary of such a designation, because people fear mythical beings, and in his experience, that kind of fear could breed unpleasantness. He was viewed as a shaman, a powerful protector, and provider-guardian with connections to the spirit world that were stronger than those of other humans.

The elders of the village answered to Mitshishu, the closest thing to a chief that Amaoke had encountered among the indigenous Northern tribes he had traveled alongside. Mitshishu had many sons, but his treasure and his burden was his only daughter Minu-Natutam, and she was attentive to much that happened around her, as her name suggested. But what she saw, and learned, and noticed, could never be enough for her, because she had some emptiness inside her that nothing seemed to fill.

Had she been other than Mitshishu's daughter, or had she been less stunningly beautiful, her path would likely have become difficult early in life, as she made herself hard to love. She did not try to fit in among her many cousins and follow the way of her people, and worst of all, refused to listen to her mother, who was trying to prepare her for all of womanhood. She was impatient with the boundaries of her culture, and Amaoke suspected that Mitshishu had indulged her overmuch.

She was a legendary beauty, and warriors from distant coastal tribes had traveled from afar to offer for her hand. Her appearance was considered a gift bestowed by the spirits, and the strength of Mitshishu's allegiance was also a desirable honor for the potential suitors' families.

Minu, meanwhile, had fixed her attentions on Atuya, a respected and decorated hunter, one of the most reliable providers of the tribe. His family had never offered for Minu, undoubtedly because she did not show proper respect for ritual observance and custom, which could negatively affect a hunter's ability to attract animals. The family had offered for another young woman, and Atuya had married. This threw Minu into a rage. It was this step from the path that set in motion a dangerous spiritual disturbance.

Complicating matters was the fact that a rival suitor within the tribe, a young man named Tuktu, wanted Minu for himself. His parents refused him his suit, and would not offer for Minu on his behalf. Minu continued to show outward favor for Atuya, despite his betrothal. This planted seeds of jealousy and resentment in Tuktu's heart, and he refused to consider taking any other wife.

Into the unrest caused by this serial disobedience came Amaoke, and because he earned the early approval and trust of Mitshishu, he also garnered the enmity of Tuktu, who viewed him as a potential rival for Minu's affection and, possibly, her hand. Atuya, too, was threatened by Amaoke's prowess as a hunter, and because he was secretly proud of Minu's fixation upon him, became obsessed with his status as the ultimate provider for his people. This created a common grievance for Atuya and Tuktu.

As she was called "she who pays attention," Minu saw all of this and began to petition her father to nullify Atuya's marriage and free him to marry her.

Unlike he had before, Mitshishu resisted and did not indulge her, knowing that Minu suffered from wrong-thinking, and that it was unwise for him to fail to uphold certain sacred principles. Atuya's parents were the rightful determiners of a suitable wife, and they had passed over his Minu, which caused him no pain, as it upheld the proper way of living.

So Minu began to whisper here and there that she had a new affection for Amaoke, intending this news to reach the ears of other young men who would surely tell it to Atuya and Tuktu.

The turmoil upset a spiritual balance, and Amaoke sensed it, although word of Minu's latest stunt reached neither his ears nor those of the chieftain he had come to respect.

The ripples in the spirit world were like the disturbance of the calm surface of a pond. They spread ever outward, carrying that disturbance to the darker denizens, one of whom was quite fearful and powerful. This one turned to the Morningstar for permission to intervene, and the Morningstar loosened the bonds that held it to the spiritual realm in anticipation of chaos.

Amaoke began to notice ill omens, such as small schools of dead fish, where there was no cause for their demise. Sudden storms over the Eastern seas stole skin boats full of men at the calmest part of the year, and small game, once abundant, began to disappear, and the signs of sickness as the cause of the animals' demise did not reassure him.

Moons passed, and autumn withdrew in order that winter could return. The cold was harsh, and food stores were more meager than in years past. Amaoke remained successful on his solitary forays inland, capturing several fat migrating game birds and a healthy bull moose. His disappearance and murder were plotted with equal enthusiasm by Atuya and Tuktu, who as yet had not shared their plans with one another. Neither man was courageous enough to challenge Amaoke directly, and they admitted in their secret hearts that they were afraid of him.

But minor mischievous spirits carried these thoughts abroad, and it was this that brought forth the attentions of the *Ungalek*.

Amaoke was valuable to the Morningstar, but the *Ungalek* had permission to intervene where ill thoughts were objectified. The Morningstar found it a useful tool for influencing a recalcitrant will, and it believed Amaoke still harbored too much of his mother's teachings, still lived too close to human society, still strove to uphold fragile social ideals. The Morningstar yet despised Raven's children; it was the oldest grudge he carried.

Unified hatred, then, provided the portal for the *Ungalek* to begin his journey into the natural world. Armed with only nameless suspicion, Amaoke was powerless to stop what had been set in motion.

Despite the relatively thin stores of food, Mitshishu approved the winter festival celebrations, relying on Amaoke's daily hunting trips to supplement the provisions available for the ritual sharing and yearly wedding celebrations of newly married couples. In addition to the dancing and singing, all new brides would toast their new husbands by publicly making food offerings to them while the rest of the villagers acted as witnesses to these unions.

The full moon arrived some days prior to the festival, and Amaoke took his ritual leave from the community house. He fed well in his solitude, on hares and an unlucky beaver, and cached his larger prey, which consisted of a pair of juvenile deer, to take back for the feast. He remained human in the days following the full moon, but delayed his return until his facial and body hair had been shed once more.

He pulled his sled with the deer into the village in the early morning of the first feast day and presented them to Mitshishu's wife for preparation. He bathed and attended his own prayers, acknowledging his gratefulness to the universe for another birth anniversary. He estimated that another century and more had passed since the Morningstar's fateful visitation.

He reopened his ice-fishing holes and made a required appearance to the chief before the festival. Mitshishu accorded him a place of honor with the other hunters who were seated near the center of the communal space.

As was his custom, he allowed others to partake of food offered the men. He was well-fed, as he always tried to be when he anticipated close quarters with many people. It helped with his control, and it was best if he did not mix eating and the smell of prey with human fellowship in general. He kept his seat and watched the celebrations, his face devoid of emotion. He spoke to no one.

Several of the other men passed on the initial food offerings as well; these were the newly married hunters who awaited the ceremonial feeding by their nervous new wives.

Eyes cast respectfully downward until she was sure she would only make eye contact with her betrothed, each bride approached her respective mate in turn. Adorned with new clothing provided by her husband's family, each of their faces glowed with pride and love, an expression that Amaoke privately thought rendered even the homeliest of them beautiful. It was, after all, one of the most important days of their young lives. He didn't quite dare wonder whether someday, one such expression might be for him alone. He denied himself the hope.

As the final young woman finished the public ritual of recognizing her new husband, there was a minor commotion at the back of the assembly.

Minu pushed her way forward with a ceremonial bowl of food, and Amaoke paid this no special attention. He had already turned to watch the dancers, young children that were preparing to begin the next entertainment.

He was jolted back to the commotion when Minu placed herself directly in his line of vision and offered the bowl of food to him. The collective gasp of disapproval from her people and her father was immediate and condemning in the otherwise silent space, but she was not deterred. He had known of tribes where tradition could be set aside for young widows to choose a second husband in such a manner, but had never known it to be appropriate for an unmarried woman who had fit parents to make a match for her and who had borne no children for which to provide.

When it became clear that everyone was waiting for Amaoke to respond, he did so, carefully pushing the bowl to the side, taking pains to neither touch Minu's hand nor make eye contact with her. She made a sharp noise of irritation and placed the bowl of food right back in front of him. Both Atuya and Tuktu had come swiftly to their feet, and Amaoke noticed that several other young men seated near him had followed suit.

"You disgrace your father," one admonished her.

"You disrespect your people," another called out; Amaoke thought it was Tuktu.

Still refusing to acknowledge Minu in any way, Amaoke carefully took the bowl from her outstretched hands and set it down away from himself, clearly rejecting it, and her. She was not in any imaginable way interested in him; this was a terrible misdirection intended to distress and manipulate Mitshishu, and Amaoke was angry and ashamed to be used in such a way.

The silence was awful and absolute. Mitshishu finally spoke. "Daughter, you will remove yourself from my sight. Return to your mother, and we will not speak of this again."

Something in his face was so terrible and so telling that she took a small step backward in response to what she saw there. Then her mother and her aunts stepped forward to collect her.

The air of celebration in the room was gone, and no one moved until all eyes could no longer see Minu's retreating form, followed by her maternal escort. The chief signaled for the children to begin their dance, and they complied reluctantly. Their earlier enthusiasm was gone, and they saw nothing in the stony faces of the adults that encouraged it to return.

The stench of male hostility was profound, and Amaoke struggled internally for control; outwardly, his posture and expression had not changed. At that moment, Mitshishu reached out with a reassuring hand and briefly touched Amaoke's shoulder, signaling that he absolved him of any offense, but the gesture was not well-received by the other young men, and the scents of their aggression and their jealousy surged.

It pushed Amaoke's emotions past the point of comfortable control, and the full moon was not long behind him. He requested to take his leave of the gathering, sensing rather than waiting to see Mitshishu's nod of permission.

The initial bite of the cold outside air did much to start restoring his equilibrium. He set out to walk for a bit and use the opportunity to tend his ice-fishing holes once again.

He had reached the outer perimeter of the camp, shaking his head at the sled dogs who growled at him and withdrew instinctively from his path. It was then that he heard and smelled his many followers.

He slowed his step deliberately, leaning back into the rough hands that grabbed at him. Several young men worked to restrain him, and with some difficulty, they managed to lift him off the ground. Among them were Atuya and Tuktu, as well as a small number of their contemporaries. The group carried him forward, shaking him and handling him roughly, trying to force him to cry out. They did not pay attention to his unusual silence that did not signal his stubborn acquiescence but rather the crossing of a boundary. Amaoke was unable to speak or cry out due to his significant efforts to deny the change that threatened his control.

Once they realized that they were struggling to hold on to him despite their overwhelming force, the men were out on the ice with a snarling, snapping half-beast with Amaoke's form and dripping fangs that grew from a face that was suspended in its journey to becoming something else, and they stopped with their hands held out in supplication, quietly pleading for mercy. They had realized that the tales of the elders were true, and then it was too late for words. It was too late for all of them, because Amaoke was not the worst thing out there with them on the ice.

18

THE WOLF COULD NOT CHANGE and then catch and kill them all, and some part of Amaoke didn't want to, leaving him suspended between man and beast.

The figure that materialized next to him was as fearsome as Noki's stories had promised. It wore a shaman's mask, but the countenance upon it was so horrific that it swiftly brought terror to the hearts of the young men, whose eyes roamed back and forth, from one horror to the other, from Amaoke to the demon that could only be called by their directed hatred.

The *Ungalek*'s terrible power was as death-bringer, and the young hunters fell where they stood, struck down with fear, and powerless. The inland lake ice was not fully matured this early in winter, and it was thin in places. The water below was deep, dark, and frigid. One by one, the *Ungalek* sent them through the ice, using evil force to slide them beneath the surface until they could not find a way out. As it walked its path over the ice, their bodies were dragged beneath its feet, and it bent over and peered at them through the thick scrim as they died.

Amaoke roared in anger at the wasteful cruelty, but found he was unable to complete the transformation to wolf; neither could he reverse the partial changes that he had already experienced. In this weakened frontier between man and beast, he could only watch helplessly as the Morningstar's reckoning began, brought in the form of this demon, until finally, it turned its evil attention to the task it had been assigned.

Its scent was similar to the Morningstar's, sulfur, blood, and spent fire, and as it approached him Amaoke could see that it appeared to be in some sort of ecstasy, and it came to his mind that the creature was savoring what it had done, eating the fear that now permeated this place. There was a subtle surge of energy, as if it could directly steal Amaoke's strength, and he felt weakened. His breath was labored, drool running from a mouth he could not close over too-large teeth, and he was hunched over with a partially transformed spine, his hands shapeless lumps arrested mid-change, heels drawn up, forcing him to his toes. He was off-balance and effectively neutralized, unable to fight.

The mask it wore was grotesque, but Amaoke was suddenly certain that the true countenance behind it would be worse, and he found he was newly susceptible to the fear provided by what his imagination could not confirm.

"Your turn," it said inside his head, and he felt the rush and screams of multiple beings swirling around him, their pain and agony on his skin; this new torment on top of the interrupted change was unbearable. But then the ice opened beneath his feet, and he, too, plunged into the frigid water and found himself trapped beneath it, as his form was dragged along the underside, his sensitive face scraping on the rough undersurface of the frozen lake. The *Ungalek* was a darker shadow on the other side, in a world that his lungs now screamed for as he realized he would drown. His sharp teeth were shredding his still human lips as he tried to clamp his mouth closed, but he could not keep the cold water from entering his mouth and pouring into him. His lungs began to feel like they were on fire, and he was shaken violently by the other lesser spirits who had apparently accompanied him into the water.

He closed his eyes, needing to find some respite within himself, knowing it would be worse if he were to continue to panic. He could no longer see what was happening. He shut out the voices and the violent shivering, and thought he could accept this death, and the water around him could instead be embraced, so he pushed himself away from solidity of the surface and allowed himself to sink. He could no longer feel the stinging pain of the ice pressed upon him. He was pleased with the control he was able to impose upon his fear, and he thought it could be a good death, here, under the lake, on the anniversary of his birth.

Then he heard a sharp sound from the surface, a harsh crack followed by excruciating pain as his thigh was pierced with a sharp spear. He opened his eyes as several more such pikestaffs were sent through the ice with spectacular force, each one piercing his form in a different place, consuming him with new and unrelenting agony. Gone was his regained control, and now he wished for death as a respite from this further torture. It was then he realized that he would not be allowed to die anytime soon.

He was pulled to the surface, impaled like a fish, and flipped onto the thicker ice where he spit up lake water and blood as he coughed violently and just as vigorously tried to fill his injured lungs with air. There was now a second figure on the ice, its heavy feet hooved and split like a caribou, its black body wingless, and grotesque in some new presentation that maintained a blind torso with the legs of a beast, its own face a mask of knowing eyes and cruel satisfaction, teeth bared with excitement, its long tongue traveling over them, writhing like a serpent—the Morningstar.

It approached him where he lay on the ice, its step heavy and fear-inducing. Amaoke refused to look at it, refused to give it any of the satisfaction of his agony, but the *Ungalek* took firm hold of one of the pikes and twisted and pulled it around in Amaoke's flesh until he screamed for his soul.

The Morningstar nodded in satisfaction, and Amaoke's blood ran cold when it said, "This is only a taste of your training. You will acknowledge us, bow to us, follow us."

Amaoke let himself think that such a thing would never happen, that he would rather die.

As if reading these thoughts, the Morningstar added, "There will be no death for you. Don't think in terms of never, because it will only prolong your debasement. We are enjoying ourselves," it whispered as it crouched next to Amaoke on the ice, and he flinched away as the tip of its tongue found the blood on his shredded lips and tasted it. Amaoke, in turn, could taste the foul death and feel the suffering of thousands, it seemed, and hear their unending screams, and this did not cease until the vile contact ended.

Then the unrelenting torture of the smaller spirits returned, pushing at his ruined flesh, jarring him and bouncing him on the pikes, and as he mercifully lost consciousness, he heard the *Ungalek*'s voice inside his mind. "Take him to the pit."

. . . . .

When consciousness returned, it was because he was suspended by ropes that were tied to the pikestaffs that still impaled his form. He hung over a dark abyss, with what was apparently sky above and the unseen bottom of the pit below him. The ropes put pressure on the staffs that broke through him, jarring their positions, ripping his flesh where his body weight shifted and twisted in suspension.

He floated in and out of a consciousness that left him whenever his flooded senses could no longer handle the ever-present, constantly renewed agony of his wounds. He could smell his own blood and pain and was unable to take a deep breath; one of the staffs had pierced his lung.

There were subtle alterations in the depth of the darkness. He twisted his head as much as he could, trying to ignore the searing agony that such a motion caused, but it was a wasted effort; he was unable to see the bottom. The walls of the hole sometimes smelled of simple earth and appeared to be such, and other times there appeared to be inlaid smooth stones, as the walls of a well.

His lips were crusted with blood, their torn flesh attempting to heal with his regenerative power, and his tongue was dry and had swollen enough to gag him. He could smell his own waste, and gradually he resigned himself to his new circumstance, his own exhaustion allowing him brief moments of respite.

When the cacophony of the spirit familiars rose again in his ears, he was unable to see anything – instead, he felt them like hundreds of hands grasping his flesh, covering him like a putrid infestation. Their energy rocked and bounced him on the end of the ropes, and too late, he realized that they were tearing him loose, and he was suddenly weightless, a short relief from the pull of his flesh against the spikes that penetrated him. He bounced off the walls in his descent, the pikestaffs striking sparks off the stones, before he was slammed into the depths, the force of his fall driving him down onto the spikes.

He screamed for a long time, a piteous muffled sound that had no air to power it past his swollen tongue and mouth. The darkness was too long in coming; it arrived when his shattered mind could take no more of the ceaseless agony.

He awoke fully human; whatever energy required to hold him in the limbo between forms was spent, and one of his hands flexed involuntarily. Despite his brain screaming at him not to do it, he grasped each of the pikestaffs in turn, and with all the strength he could recruit, he slowly forced them out of his body, feeling his blood well out of the wounds, weakening him further. Once he finished, he tried to examine the pikes by feel, thinking that just one of them would provide him with a good weapon, but as the idea occurred to him, utter exhaustion overrode the possibility of further movement, and his body slumped down onto the dirt floor, and he passed out once more.

Amaoke felt a great deal of malign spiritual energy when he awoke, and the pikestaffs were gone. He was still unable to fully characterize the quality of the light, and he suspected that his perceptions were being manipulated. The walls now had the appearance of rectangular stones, and when he reached out to touch one of them, its edges crumbled, showering a sandy residue down onto the ground.

What he could see at the top of the pit appeared to be the sky, but there were no natural cues such as birdsong or the smell of water or trees to suggest he was in the ground. He feared that in his weakened state, they had pulled him through to the spirit world, an underworld, a place of dark hidden things. The Morningstar had allowed the *Ungalek* to steal him away, and he could be kept, out of nature, with none who would notice his absence.

Repeatedly, the *Ungalek*'s familiars, howling in their damned voices, crawled over his skin in the darkness, pulling and twisting his hair, making it hard for him to breathe, invading his every sense. The sensation was enough to push him inexorably toward madness, and the worst were the screaming and tortured voices – and the sound of otherworldly laughter – that chilled him to the bone, as if they were born of homicidal frenzy, and he longed for surcease of this torment. It robbed him of any ability to reason.

Sometimes the voices sobbed and screamed for days, driving him in fits of stress and emotion to change; his sharpened wolf hearing only amplified the torture. During his change, he looked up to see the masked visage of the *Ungalek*, and then he was crawling with fleas, who left no part of him unbitten, unleashing a new madness as he writhed and itched, unable to resume a human form. He curled on the ground, inflicted with whatever sickness they carried, unable to master the crescendo of the itch, and once again, he was shifting back into human form.

Covered with bites and swollen, he was half-crazed and half-relieved to have recovered human hands with which to scratch, but this became yet another torture, because he scratched himself until he bled and still the itch would not relent. The bites coalesced and festered, scabbing over and then reopening with the desperate scratching that he could not curtail even as his exhausted mind slept.

Storms filled the pit like a cistern, water falling out of a grey sky lit by flashes of lightning that illuminated walls that now appeared to be shored up by thousands of skulls, the long-dead relics all that remained of the souls that screamed in his brain. The water began to rise, and his form would at first float upward with the rising water level, and then he would feel the scaly appendage of some terrible creature wrap itself around him, the smell of the *Ungalek* in his nose, and he was frightened into the change. The wolf was not so buoyant and struggled to capture breaths at the surface, and the exact form of the *Ungalek* was revealed, a water serpent of frightful features, and he fought with fang and claw as the water closed over his head and he lost consciousness. They never let him drown; they only let him believe he would.

The water at the bottom of the pit persisted, keeping him wet and miserable and unable to sit or lie down. But once, when on two legs, with it slopping to his waist, he tried to recall his mother's face, tried in desperation to remember the words to songs and prayers she had taught him, especially when the screams started. It was during one of the attacks of the familiars, when, focused on his mother, that he felt something hard materialize in his hand.

It was Noki's *ulu*, which he'd thought lost to him, and he used it to slash out blindly at the voices, and the blade made a tearing sound as though it sliced into substantial matter, and the screams pulled upward and away, sent elsewhere by its magic. There were other moments when it came to him with thoughts of his mother, and he believed it endowed with mystical power, like an *ünruq*, or spiritual totem, created from the power of his mother's kind spirit. How it was called and where it returned to, he did not know.

He found it effective against the *Ungalek*; Amaoke surprised it by severing its tail during a watery struggle, and the sounds it made as the blade went through its flesh were gratifying, and his reward was that it abandoned its physical attacks altogether. After that, the *ulu* did not return, and he was tortured in other ways.

He dreamed the Morningstar was nearby, hearing the sound of great wings beating the air as it hovered above the pit, casting its cold shadow on him. The fiend seemed to know Amaoke's mind, manipulating his form to fit the torture. At times, a sun appeared to blaze down on his naked flesh, blistering his skin as it seemed endlessly suspended at the center of the opening above him, cooking the parts of him that extended above the surface of the perpetual standing water. Without warning, the wolf would come through, a billion needlelike hairs pushing through his blistered skin like lances, the agonies complicated by his dual nature.

He slowly began to lose all sense of reality and was eventually unable to grasp any method by which to assess the passage of time. His memories had become disjointed and fragmented even further, making it a struggle to recall his existence before the pit.

The heat parched him, and he would drink the rain that fell into the pit, but it did not satisfy his thirst, and he suspected it wasn't really water in the sense of what he had known in the natural world. He was left to starve until he was unable to leave his wolf form, and the heat boiled away more of the water from the pit, leaving a ravening beast who paced in the brackish, muddy bottom of his prison.

Interminable intervals would pass before a skinned kid goat or pig was tossed down, perpetuating the torture. Just when he believed he must surely starve, and that he had been truly abandoned in the hole, new meat was offered to him, like a sacrifice. His mind slipped, and he was a slave to his hunger.

More hot days suffocated him, the steam rising from his wet fur without relief. The few inches of remaining water evaporated away, freeing the stench of rotting marrow bones from his meals in the deep, sticky mud. He lay in the wet earth in an effort to keep cool as long as possible, but something about the stench was familiar, and he pulled himself back to his feet, feeling the pull of the mud as it slowly released its hold on his thick fur. He let out a plaintive whine.

The wolf was not much bothered, but the man was not yet buried, and these were not the bones of the quadrupeds he'd thought he was feeding upon; there was no mistaking that the bones were human. He looked in disbelief at them, but was unable to convince himself otherwise. The worst part of the tableau was that the smallest of them were the most obvious, confirming the damning truth of what he had become, an eater of pureflesh.

The man trapped inside the wolf was unable to scream, but the howls of sorrow and anger soon became howls of madness, which then became part of the chorus of the damned. The demons returned when they realized he had broken, swarming over the wolf, as something vital broke loose from him.

The locomotive breathing of the wolf became louder, and the howling stopped, as the demons listened with satisfaction. The wolf ascended, embracing its lunatic mind, and Amaoke was no more.

Rage consumed him until it was all he was, and he forgot enough that it became all he had ever been. When the Morningstar finally freed his body, and unleashed him on the world, it was all that was left.

19

LEGEND TOLD THAT THE BOW-and-arrow wars among the people had been set in motion over a misunderstanding. One tribe, attacked in the night, suffered the loss of some of its women and children, finding them mutilated and murdered as they slept.

This tribe, suspicious of a second tribe to which they ascribed this atrocity, the excuse for which was the breakdown of a trade agreement, sent along their warriors to retaliate. Members of the offending tribe were attacked and killed as they slept.

But after the attack on the second tribe was undertaken, a hunting party that returned to the village found the carnage. They suspected it was retaliation by another tribe, whose chieftain's son had been denied the daughter of one of their own elders as a bride.

Thus, in sequence, tribe turned against tribe, one people divided by contrived boundaries. They were so divided when the true enemy came in the form of explorers and traders from other lands; it was not long after they arrived that the people succumbed to colonization, and the ravages of new diseases brought from faraway shores.

But some elders of the first tribe had visions of displeased spirits, and shamans suggested that the women and children were *eaten*, something that warriors of the people had never done before.

Some feared that the hatred and fear that had resulted in the wars of mistrust had been started by the senseless attack of a beast, unleashed upon the world by monstrous spirits, and that other men had taken the blame for its bloody feast. The Morningstar was pleased and rewarded the *Ungalek* for the successful cultivation of a monster.

Man blamed man and perpetuated the violence and chaos on a scale even the Morningstar had not anticipated. So they two, the Morningstar and its familiar, withdrew again from the human realm, having unleashed the Death-bringer's pet among the pureflesh.

. . . . .

It was dark in the forest, under the trees, and unnaturally quiet. Typically, small fauna would have spent their lives in that stretch of the woods, where food was once again abundant, and the life-giving river meandered nearby.

But the stench of death and fear had settled there, and even the fleetest of foot and swiftest of wing dared not penetrate that dark cathedral. For the thing that stalked that forest did not hunt to survive, did not kill for food; it did not even attack other living creatures for pleasure. It killed for the sake of killing, as if the sound of birdsong or the heartbeat of the hare offended it.

And other creatures who stumbled upon that place, where their noses told them they should not be, discovered it was already too late to escape. The beast harvested all.

It lay at the mouth of its cave, a sleeping curse, awakening at the slightest sound, the smallest movement, the merest disturbance. Such insults were met with violent death, and its appetite for bloody flesh was insatiable.

Yet it did not confine itself to those woods, where surely it would have succumbed to its hunger, having driven out all the game. Madness drove it to roam for days, following scents undetectable to other animals, tracking down other quarry, seeking other kills.

If a bramble scratched the leg of a sled dog, it would track the injured animal to its home and destroy all that it encountered there. Nothing was safe; it would take first the sled team, one by one, and then every human denizen of the hunting camp or village, swallowing their fear with their flesh.

If it was met with weapons and force, it ate that aggression just the same, seemingly impervious to even the most grievous injuries. It might return to its den nursing new wounds, and woe to the predator that came looking for the wounded prey that had put down a blood scent; by the time such a predator arrived, the beast was again healthy and ready to feed.

In time, other wolves arrived in the forest and correctly read the signs that one most dominant among them ruled the forest. They recognized the beast as alpha, and presented themselves, offering to follow it, seeking protection for their packs.

They offered throats and bellies in submission, and the beast tore them open one by one. None escaped, none survived. It left their carcasses half-eaten and rotting at the entrance to the cave, whether as an abject warning to others or because it pleased the beast to do so.

If the scent of blood or fear reached its nose, it followed these to their source and dispatched whatever it found with extreme violence. If its world was devoid of those scents, the beast went looking for them, and invariably it found them, and satisfaction.

Its baleful, empty eyes looked out on a world seen only through the lens of feral madness. The beast was comprised solely of appetites to be sated; it was ignorant of the fact that it had once had a name, had once walked on two legs, had once sat peacefully in the sunshine. The beast no longer knew that it was also a man, because that man was locked away in a prison, its walls his human conscience, and the door was sealed by the horror of what he had become.

The years ticked by, and Amaoke started his seventh century unaware.

20

THE WOLF WAS THE ONLY one who awakened each day; the man inside slumbered on; not even a flicker of the animal's memory recalled him. The spring breeze had carried to him the scent of prey, and he rose to his feet in one fluid motion. His tongue lolled out, and he huffed, tasting the breeze, waiting for it to show him the direction of his victim.

His senses led him down to the steep riverbank, where he briefly lost the trail, but with a growl of frustration, he snuffled in circles until he picked it up again. He set off through the trees, trotting downriver, following the gentle slopes that marked the boundary lands between the foothills at the base of the mountains and the tundra opposite.

He followed the scent through a stand of pines that acted as a natural barrier beside the river, and set himself down on his belly in the damp soil of a familiar, stunted tree. There was a generous clearing here by the river, and some of the scents were familiar to him in a way that made him shiver with excitement and impatience. He shook his head, focused on a sound he heard, up in the long grass ahead.

He tilted one ear toward the sound; it was too big to be made by a snake, and the scent marker told him that what he was tracking was a human, but he should have seen it standing in the field. He smelled no evidence of injury or pain, but it had to be on the ground somewhere in the clearing.

His mouth watered, and he stifled a growl, not ready to advertise his presence. He enjoyed the element of surprise and the heady scent of their fear and terror. And the humans almost always ran from him, which added to his excitement. If they ran, their flesh even tasted of fear.

He slunk forward through the grass, following scent and sound until he could see what was making the noise.

A female human sat in the grass ahead, pulling nervously at the stalks in front of her. She faced away from him, and he was ready to pounce when she stiffened slightly and became still; then, her head turned, and she looked directly into his eyes.

Her own eyes were as blue as the sky, as blue as his, large, sad, and depthless. They were remarkably expressive, ringed with long dark lashes like those of a child, but she was fully matured, based on what a part of her scent told him. Her black hair was striking against her pale, pale skin, and it was remarkably short; on the top, it stuck straight up in the air.

She did not drop her gaze from his, and he could see her eyes widen slightly in surprise as she recognized what he was, and she said a single word in a language the wolf did not know, but he guessed it was "wolf." She wrinkled her nose, and he realized that she could smell him; it probably was less than pleasant.

He smelled absolutely no fear on her, only sadness, and resignation. It was a smell he knew; he had noticed it when stalking a small bird with a broken wing. There was no need for fear; it had known it was caught, and there was no alternative. In its suffering, it had welcomed death.

The lack of fear was unusual, but the rest of what his nose told him was also puzzling. Weaved into the complexity of her scent was the scent of a male human, and it was not transferred by a companion onto her skin or clothing. Something about her called to him and disarmed the aggression that had lived under his skin for so long.

She turned more fully toward him, leaning on an outstretched hand for balance, and he saw the gentle swell of her belly, not large, just exaggerated under the simple, lightweight garment she wore. He realized that she carried a male child, early. She noticed his eyes upon her belly and put a protective hand over it, probably subconsciously, and pulled her too-thin shawl more closely about her torso.

Just then, a sharp voice carried on the wind from somewhere across the river. It was a male voice, speaking in a foreign tongue, perhaps hers, because her response was swift. She flinched and ducked slightly down, although there was no way she could be seen in the tall grass. He tested the air; now, she was afraid.

That scent broke through his new reverie, and he growled, low and prolonged, but she turned that resigned look on him again, refusing to be afraid, and he realized that she welcomed death. He could not trust what was happening somehow; her willingness for his attack put another check on his aggression, but because the scent of her fear brought on by the other voice was still present, and as he was inflamed by it, he was dangerously close to attack.

He backed away from her slowly, still growling a warning for her to stay away, and only when he breached the stand of trees, and she was utterly lost to sight did he turn away from the promise of meat; for the first time in over a century, he denied himself a kill. But he was not ready to return to his den.

He looped north through the trees, following the river to its natural bend. The course of the riverbed had changed slightly in the intervening years, but there was still a natural silt deposit where the flow slowed that built up the riverbed and left a point on the bend where it was shallow enough to cross. He peered across to the other side but saw nothing. He scented the air, but some brackish standing water near the bank flooded his nose momentarily, and when he regained his ability to smell, he could only pick up the woman's scent, and faintly, because the wind had changed direction.

From that spot, he climbed to higher ground for a better vantage point of the river crossing and burrowed into some wet leaves between two small aspen trees. His white coat was filthy enough that he felt camouflaged, and he settled down to wait and watch.

Enough time passed that he felt she was not going to cross over to the opposite bank, even though he knew that was where the voice had originated. Soon enough, he heard it again, still distant, but insistent. He was about to abandon his vigil when he saw her making her way along the near bank, and when she reached the shallow sandbar, she hopped across in three graceful steps, minimizing the amount of water she had to navigate, and shook off her feet before swiftly disappearing downriver on the opposite bank.

He didn't trust himself to follow, so he returned to his den. Something stirred within him, but he couldn't know what it was. He was curious about a creature who did not fear him, but perhaps he could teach her to fear him. A part of him was drawn after her, wanting to follow and solve the riddle. He was restless and frustrated, but as usual, he was well-fed, so he shrugged off the encounter, rolled over, and slept more soundly than he had in years.

Over the next week, he watched for her, but she never returned to his side of the river. Finally, after a night hunt for hares, with a full belly, he set out one morning to look for her.

He didn't have to go far; he splashed across the river where it slowed and turned downstream on the far side, picking up her scent almost immediately. The sun was bright and warmed the earth, and he encountered her some ways downriver, washing clothing on the rocks. She still wore the same thin frock, and her wet hands were red from the cold water, but she seemed to be singing as she worked the materials through the water. Her cheeks were rosy with effort, and a small apron covered her belly, obscuring her condition.

He stopped several feet upstream of her and forced himself to sit down. He tasted the air again; the only change he detected was twofold. The clothes she washed carried the stink of a male, and he also noticed the smell of dried fish.

She sat back on her legs, pulling the clothing from the water and arranging it on the ground to dry in the sun. She lay back among the scattered garments and closed her eyes; she had not even noticed him. He let out a short whine.

She opened her eyes, sitting up and looking around, and she appeared to give him a small smile when she saw him. He approached her warily, not sure why he was suddenly so cautious when she should be afraid, but she was not. Not one bit.

In fact, at that moment, she reached into the pocket of her apron and pulled out a piece of dried fish. She ate a bit and then held the remainder out to him, but he refused to come any nearer. She nodded, as if she understood something he didn't, and spoke to him again, but this time there was something familiar about the words. Her tone sounded like she was laughing. Then she lay back down in the sunshine and closed her eyes, seeming to forget about him entirely.

When he realized she had fallen *asleep* (some monster *he* was), he huffed indignantly and went home.

Days passed, and although he was not yet operating on any higher level of consciousness, he was subtly changed. He began to notice birdsong without needing to eradicate it. He saw the moon from the entrance of his cave as it climbed into the sky, feeling it sing to him as it grew larger.

He crossed the river often, once following her some distance downriver, where, in a false clearing ringed by small stands of stunted trees, there was a cabin made of new logs that had been built a short distance uphill from the river. Smoke from a hearth fire escaped the top, and although the structure was small, he noticed it was similar to something he had once seen near this river, but these thoughts confused him.

The first several times he went there, she was alone, but she seemed to manage her plight without difficulty. He watched her chop wood, set fish traps in the shallow water on the river, and pull wild onions and asparagus from where they grew along the riverbank. He followed her when she set a few traps in the woods and was successful at catching food for herself. The squirrels and hares she caught provided meat and furs. He would set himself off at a remove, watching her but never hiding from her, listening to her sing, and feeling in his bones that he did know the language from somewhere, and his mind flashed to water, waves crashing on land and the smell of the sea.

She spoke to him, and each day he understood more of it, until one day, when he refused her offer of fish again, she distinctly said, "Okay, handsome, have it your way." Then he knew it was the language of the mixed Aleut traders he had encountered at the Western seas, but still, his wolf brain could not completely decipher that bit of understanding. Nor did he consciously know where the words came from.

Her belly grew slowly, and near the end of the summer, she seemed to disappear. The fire burned at the cabin, and she was no longer alone. The stink of male human, aggression, and fear were on the air, but though he waited several hours, no one emerged. Darkness came down, and he saw flickering light coming from the small skin-covered windows, and then heard shouting, and cries of pain that could only be hers.

His hair stood on end, and he growled deep in his chest, pacing outside the dwelling and not seeing a place where he could breach it. The scents of aggression and fear were ultimately too strong for him to maintain control, and he feared that if he had an opportunity, the wolf would attack, and she could be a casualty of his violence, so he removed himself from the area, crossing back over the river, moving away until he could no longer hear her sobs.

When he set out to visit the cabin the next day, he picked up her scent before he could cross the river, and realized she was again on the near side. He tracked her back to the clearing where he had first encountered her, and found her hiding in the long grass, her tears falling silently, rolling off the tip of her nose and dropping onto her skirt.

He closed the distance between them, unmindful of the consequences, and settled down just next to her, his back against her feet, letting her feel the rumble of his lungs rattle out a comforting rhythm, as he tried to relax. He waited as she cried, noticing new marks on her face, dark and ugly near one eye that was swollen closed. Her lip was puffy, and there were marks where she had been grabbed on her arm. Finally, he put his head down on his paws and tried to be perfectly still.

"I'm sorry I have no fish for you today," she said softly, and the sound of her voice startled him so much that he lifted his head. He was poised to move away but controlled the impulse. She placed a light hand on the ruff of his neck and closed her fingers into it. It pleased him, and he leaned into her touch. She petted him gently. "You are a lovely boy, but you really do smell terrible." He could hear the smile in her statement. He half-rolled against her legs, and then they both became still when the shouting started on the other side of the river.

She shook her head sadly as she reluctantly got to her feet. "You stay here," she said, holding out her hand to keep him from following. "He would try to kill you if he knew you were here. And you stay out of his traps," she admonished, shaking her finger at him. Then she was off through the grass, limping slightly, and he could hear someone shouting for her for a long time, and then he heard the change when the voice was suddenly shouting *at* her because she had reached the other side of the river. The last thing he heard was the shriek of her pain, and he felt his answering surge of anger. Still, he would not act, because, in his rage, he was liable to attack her as well. But a part of him was waiting for something, even if he did not know what it was.

He found her a few days later on the opposite bank. "What are you doing over here?" she scolded, looking warily over her shoulder in the direction of the cabin. In the distance, he could hear the ringing of an axe as it split logs, and he slipped past her outstretched hand as water flows over rocks, remaining just out of reach.

"Silly wolf!" she hissed urgently, but he left her behind and went to investigate. By the time he reached the little cabin in the clearing, the axe had been abandoned, stuck in a tree stump. The wood was stacked against the wall of the dwelling, and a large man was pulling a jug out of the river, where it was secured on a leather thong. He was taller than local Inuit men, very pale, and his hair was dark like the woman's. But his blue eyes were as cold as their color, and bloodshot, and his mouth had a cruel twist.

The man took a drink of the pungent-smelling contents, freed the jug from its mooring, and carried it inside the cabin. The scent of the alcohol oozed from his pores, and he stank of unwashed male, and the small animal skins he trapped and likely traded. The wolf disliked his scent but tasted the air, the better to remember. Then the woman returned and chased him off upriver before carrying her laundry burden inside. He could not stay to hear her pitiful cries, but he let his anger bank deep inside, like the embers of a dying fire that were still hot enough to burn.

The next day she was again in the clearing on his side of the river, and he sat with her for a time, and she shared her dried fish and berries with him, feeding him out of her hand. He had splashed carefully in the river the afternoon before, and rolled in wild celery, and she admired his lovely coat. Her nose didn't wrinkle when he came near.

"I wonder if what they say is true," she began. "I heard of a large white wolf that lived in these woods, a berserker that the local elders along this river call *The Widowmaker*. I had hoped to find it, wishing it would take my life, but that was before…" she paused, thoughtfully running her hand over her expanding belly. "There is only one who needs rescuing now." She spoke directly to her womb, and several tears slid down her face.

Summer and fall slipped by them, and her many various hurts would heal when the man left to go trapping, only to return when he did. The wolf thought, incorrectly, that when the man saw that she was with child, he would stop, but the abuse only worsened as their unborn child grew, and soon her belly was big enough that the wolf worried that the baby could be seriously hurt.

An early snow fell that autumn, and the man returned from downriver with money and jugs of drink he had received in exchange for the pelts. The wolf waited outside the cabin and watched him settle the flasks in the snow before he went inside. He could smell their dinner cooking on the fire, and hear the low tones of the man's voice, and her softer, sad replies.

The night was dark and mostly silent, in the way that the world can be after snow. There was no moon. Eventually, he heard the man shouting at her, and the sound of flesh hitting flesh. Her sobs were cut short by more shouting, and then the man emerged, and retrieved a jug from the snow, drinking deeply from it before carrying it back inside.

Rage rose up inside the wolf. He knew what a widowmaker was; this was vengeance, swift, and sure, but in this case, there would be redemption over sorrow. The wolf stalked forward from the trees and stopped next to the axe, looking at it curiously. Something inside it knew it needed no weapon, but it also knew that the man would not let it inside.

The wolf began walking toward the cabin with purpose, and under the new moon, it shed its fur as it went, and time spooled backward. Halfway there, it walked hunched over on two legs, almost upright, remembering the rhythm. A few steps further, and he knew his name.

Amaoke knew this was something he had to do as a man. Another cry of pain reached his ears, and he smiled a terrible smile. By the time he reached the door and banged on it, his claws had incompletely retracted and left deep gouges in the wood, but he was fully human when it was yanked open.

The man's expression was fixed with rage and the effects of his drink as he peered out at Amaoke, and Amaoke could see the woman where she had fallen near the hearth. Her eyes widened in surprise to see the naked, bearded stranger at the door, and flashed with something else – shock mixed with recognition.

Before the man could register what he was seeing, Amaoke delivered a smashing blow to the man's face with his fist, knocking him backward into the room. The man cried out in fear and pain, and the animal inside of Amaoke fed on that, following him, willing him to fight.

The man did not disappoint him, and he fought for his life against a threat he had never seen coming, but he never had a chance. Amaoke's only regret was that the beating did not last long enough to fully soothe the beast.

When the man was near death, Amaoke dragged him out into the snow and down to the river, not wanting the woman to have to see it. He walked into the icy water and held the man under the surface until there was no reason to continue, then he let go, letting the river carry the man away toward the distant sea.

Amaoke stood with his back turned to the cabin, summoning his composure. When he felt that he, the man, was in ascendance once more, he climbed out of the river and stopped short when he saw her standing a few feet up the hill. She held a stack of warm clothing out in shaky hands, and finally, he smelled fear; now, she was afraid of him, too.

When he reached for the clothing she offered, she backed up the hill slowly, and he followed. She refused to relinquish the items to him until she had led him back into the house, one step at a time, where he could warm himself at the hearth.

Neither of them spoke as he dressed. Then he helped himself to several small animal skins from a bundle near the door, wrapping his feet before he took his leave, disappearing into the dark. Once he was back across the river, his nose told him that she had tucked dried fish into the pockets of the parka, and he smiled.

nanatha

21

AMAOKE HAD COME DOWN FROM a logging expedition to the small town by the river. Several small fishing boats bobbed in a small inlet that led out to the lake, which had formed by natural damming of the river hundreds of years before. The lake itself was long and narrow, extending along the same axis as the river, widening it enough to be useful as a logging station. There was a large mill that processed logs on the side nearest the river and wheat and corn on the landward side, and its owner was the richest man in town. There were a small general store and a modest church house that also served as the local school.

He was with three other men from his crew, including the foreman. The plan was to replenish some supplies, flints, food, and water. They also planned to meet with another logger coming on for the summer months.

Amaoke's attention was captured by a heavenly creature who descended the school steps with a purpose. It was her scent that reached him first, as sweet as day – earth, paper, and sunshine. She was graceful, hardly minding her skirts, and awkwardly tall for a girl, but he noticed that she did not try to change her bearing, as some tall girls did, in order to lessen her stature. She was lithe and lissome but had supple curves. Her skin was bronzed as though she lived in the sunshine, and freckles scattered across a remarkable face. Her eyes were grey, bright against her skin, and her dark brown hair, which was braided and twisted up behind her head.

The beast inside him shuddered and whimpered as she came near, and it took every ounce of control he had acquired to keep from changing right there, in the light of midday on a moon day far from the full moon. Any strong emotion could threaten the change, but he had never before had such a strong reaction to any human being.

As she passed, he dropped his eyes in respect, but not before he noticed the corner of her mouth turn up and a flash of white teeth before she turned down toward the mill. He wondered if the smile had really been for him or if it was just a polite acknowledgement of the four men together. He wondered if she was aware of their eyes on her departing form.

His reverie was broken by the scent of lust, anger, drink, and animal flesh that rose up then and caused his gorge to rise – he tasted bile in his throat. The scent was strong and unpleasant, practically an assault after the young woman's enticing scent, and Amaoke thought, not for the first time, that his sensitive nose was not always a blessing. He traced the smell across the main street down by the general store. The new member of their crew was watching the progress of Amaoke's young woman as well, but he noted with satisfaction that she did not cross the road until she was well clear of the newcomer.

The man was dirty and unkempt, with a rough beard. Amaoke's crew crossed over to approach the general store. The foreman greeted the man. Amaoke was generally suspicious about names but heard and remembered this one.

"I see you made it upriver, Audet," the foreman said.

Audet was quiet. Up close, his eyes were greedy, feral. Some of his clothing was made from the skins of small animals, and he smelled as though he had bathed in liquor but perhaps never in water. Tobacco juice stained his beard and clothing. He fixed a hard gaze on Amaoke.

Without looking at the foreman, Audet growled in a guttural voice heavily accented by his French heritage, "No 'un told me about ze Eskimo."

The foreman replied, "He's a half-breed. Best tree man I've ever seen."

"'S bad luck," Audet snarled. "Make him stop lookin' at me."

The foreman glanced at Amaoke and said nothing. He took Audet by the shoulder, and the two men walked some paces away. They spoke quietly, but Amaoke could still hear them. His sharp hearing could be even less a blessing, sometimes. He tried not to eavesdrop, but it was difficult with his extended senses.

Amaoke had experienced these prejudices before; he expected that the foreman would let him go. It had happened many times. So he tried not to hear the cruel words, concentrating on the sound of the water on the distant mill wheel, and the calls of the spring birds. He tried to conjure the pretty girl's smile in his mind.

He looked up as the two men approached, but the foreman merely gestured to Amaoke and the other crewmen to follow along to the general store. The men restocked supplies and headed back upriver to the logging post.

Amaoke didn't wait until the next full moon to change. For four nights in a row, he ran abroad as the wolf, down into the village and surrounding homesteads and farms to try to scent the girl again.

Once, he caught her complex familiar scent and tracked her to the river. The scent was lost at the shallow bank. He did not find enough of her scent to determine that she had been in and out, perhaps with laundry, nor was there another scent trail nearby as if she had gathered water or bathed there. No, she had waded in at that spot, but he could not find her scent anywhere else nearby.

He whined softly. Had she drowned? But he could sense no death here, so he kept searching.

He had to be careful with the change so as not to draw undue attention, and his work was consuming and strenuous, so it took Amaoke the better part of two moons to locate her again. He came up over a ridge one evening shortly after sunfall into a glorious purple twilight and saw the first glimmer of stars. Acrid cedar smoke from a new fire was coming from the chimney of a small stone house in the clearing below.

He caught a whiff of her unique scent, but just that. He rolled gratefully in some pine needles on the forest floor, letting the pine scent flood his nose and clear it of other small, distracting scents. Then he popped up to the top of the ridge again and tried to pinpoint her scent.

It flooded his nose this time when the wind changed, carrying the chimney smoke away from him. He climbed carefully down the slope and padded quietly around the perimeter of the clearing. Her scent was everywhere here; the relief was overpowering that he had finally found her again. Also, he felt a touch of satisfaction that hers was the only human scent strongly associated with the house.

Although he kept to the shadows because it was not yet dark enough for him to be fully concealed, his presence did not go unnoticed. Indeed, he was causing significant distress to the smaller inhabitants of the premises; there were four large rabbits in the hutch next to the back door. He could smell their fear, and one cried out a brief squawk of alarm.

Not interested in you, little brothers, he thought, moving slightly farther out so they would stay quiet. Amaoke didn't think it was sporting to catch hares in this form; he tried to do it in human guise – it evened the odds and decreased the chance that he could deplete them too quickly from an area in which he lived. It was doubly unfair if they were caged.

He backed into the space between three blackberry bushes, wincing as a bramble caught the side of his hindfoot. It was the best hiding place at the edge of the clearing, and he settled down onto his belly to wait and watch.

As soon as he stopped moving, the back door opened. She'd been alerted by the commotion in the rabbit hutch. And something else, perhaps. He could sense her curiosity about what had spooked them, but, interestingly, he could scent no fear on her.

She stood in the doorway, in a long white sleeping gown, her feet bare, with the long dark braid draped over one shoulder. Her hair was longer than he would have guessed; the end of the braid bumped against her hip, and it was as thick as her forearm. He could make out the silhouette of her body beneath her gown as she was backlit by the candles burning at her table, and the firelight from her hearth.

Amaoke's tail wagged fiercely, seemingly involuntarily, and he felt a mounting urge rise deep in his belly. He swallowed a whine and froze in place when he realized that she seemed to be looking right into his hiding place. Full dark had come down, and there was no way her human eyes could see him, but her piercing grey gaze seemed to find him in the shadows. It was as if she sensed him rather than saw him there.

She stood in the doorway for some time before slowly turning to go back inside. The rabbits had calmed. Amaoke stayed in his hiding place until the moon came up, which was long after she had banked her fire and put out the candles. The quiet from the house let him know she slept soundly. He backed out of his thicket and was gone over the ridge so quickly that even the rabbits slumbered on.

22

EVERY TIME THE LOGGING CREW had to come into town, he looked for her, but unlike that first time, Amaoke never saw her there. It was no matter – he never could have approached her, never would have done so in front of the others.

So through that spring and summer, he visited the house in the clearing, but always as a wolf, never as a man. He trailed behind her at a distance when she took clothes to the river to wash and waited just inside the shadow of the woods when she went into town. She visited the mill often and stayed for long periods on some occasions. He could scent a male human after her visits there, but the scent was similar to hers – her brother, perhaps. She did not regularly attend church but visited the building during school hours. She did some business at the general store. Occasionally she would leave the school or the store with a book; it was at these times that she appeared happiest.

To Amaoke's chagrin, and perhaps his amusement, she ate the rabbits in the hutch. She appeared to be breeding them selectively and eating the older ones. She grew most of her own vegetables in her garden and sold some in town. She carried flour from the mill and baked bread. She traded produce for milk and eggs from the dairyman's wife on a neighboring farm. She churned her own butter and made cheese.

Occasionally she was a successful fisherwoman, but he could scent her impatience with the waiting. She chopped her own firewood from parts of downed trees in the clearing and the nearby woods.

And, to his utter frustration, she bathed outside in one of two rain barrels she kept in the yard. She took drinking water from one and soaked in the other, partially emptying it when watering the garden to let it refill with clean water. Amaoke felt it was not proper for him to watch her; he had no husbandly claim and did not want to dishonor her virtue. At these times, he hid among the blackberries, the thorns a welcome distraction to the male agony he felt as he scented her naked flesh in the water, and his testicles tightened painfully. He put his head down with his paws across his muzzle so that they covered his eyes, until the clover and linen scent of her garments signaled that she was properly clothed.

Once, near the end of the summer, he topped the ridge next to the clearing, and she was in the tub, her naked back and shoulders clear of the water as she concentrated on unraveling her long braid. It was too close to the full moon for Amaoke to feel in control of such strong emotions, and that one glimpse of her smooth wet skin threatened to unleash the hungry Beast. The desire to assert any kind of dominance was too high, so he ran away from the house in the clearing. He marked every tree in that part of the woods that day; for the remainder of early fall he scented no game more substantial than a rabbit – the foxes and the deer stayed out.

Amaoke, the man, dreamt often of being a wolf, running through green woods and chasing rabbits and squirrels. Now Amaoke, the wolf, dreamt of grey eyes looking into his, and knowing him. He dreamt of her touching him, and imagined he could feel her dark hair loose on his skin.

23

BEFORE WINTER SET IN, WITH much regret, he collected his wages and traveled north and east to the seacoast. There, indigenous arctic peoples, the closest modern survivors of his own lost tribe, lived and hunted in a shaky peace with European settlers. He found a family willing to hire him for the season. He kept to himself and kept busy with the work of his mother's people, taught to him centuries before. Each task was deserving of his mindfulness, but he was not the same man he had been in years before. The months passed as they had so many, many times before, but it was as if she was with him every day.

In the spring, he could have stayed on, building and repairing moose fences, fishing, and trapping. But he took up his axe again and traveled gradually south and west with groups of men returning to the logging camps. Every year there were more men; every year, the foreman called for more trees. Conserving forests was becoming less common with the higher demand for lumber in the cities to the south. It hurt Amaoke's heart when he thought that someday the wolf would have no forest to run in. But he respected his foreman, who still seemed to care about preserving forest lands in spite of steeper demand. He had also never seemed to care that Amaoke was a half-breed. For that matter, he never seemed to notice.

Amaoke felt fresh disappointment when Audet returned to the logging camp. This time he brought two new men with him, men who smelled like him and apparently thought like him. The three of them had been trapping and fur trading over the winter. Amaoke liked the new men even less than Audet, and he was disinclined to trust any of them. He never turned his back on any of them, and he climbed high up into one of the tall trees away from the logging camp to sleep when he was in human form. In mid-spring, he heard one of Audet's companions remark that he'd seen wolf tracks, and that put Amaoke on his guard.

Amaoke knew that the three of them were discussing setting traps in the area at night. He was extra careful when hunting and avoided areas where he could scent them, aware of the potential complications of his own capture.

24

ONE SUNDAY MORNING, AMAOKE TRAVELED on foot down to the river, to the spot where he had seen her fishing on many occasions. He had fashioned a crude fishing pole for himself and settled in, hoping he would see her there.

Amaoke waited for five Sundays before she appeared. She was visibly surprised to find another person at her fishing spot. She recovered quickly and smiled openly at him. Amaoke realized he was holding his breath, and he huffed out a long, slow sigh.

He frowned slightly, thinking she should be afraid of a strange man in this isolated place, but just as quickly tried to smile so she wouldn't believe he was frowning at her. It was as if she sensed his discomfort, because she stopped staring and turned slightly away from him to slip off her shoes and socks. She turned her face up to the sun and closed her eyes, clearly enjoying the moment. She gathered her skirts, pulling them up between her legs and knotting them to form crude trousers. Then, without hesitation, she took up her fishing pole and waded into the water.

"It was only a matter of time before someone else discovered this spot," she sighed, glancing at him over her shoulder. "Have you caught anything?"

Amaoke shook his head. He was a poor fisherman, both as a man and as a wolf. The wolf usually relied on blind providence for fish, like during salmon runs when bears caught more fish than they could eat, and partially eaten carcasses could be had. The wolf was wary of the water. Amaoke, as a boy, had taken great pleasure in fishing, preferring a spear to the net fishing that he had learned over many years helping his mother. Amaoke, the man, had suffered from the diminishing skill and patience required to spearfish, and he would have looked ridiculous trying to recover the ability at his age. He was an adequate swimmer but viewed it more a necessity than a pleasure; after overcoming years of torture, he doubted that the appeal it had held for him as a child would ever return.

Her voice was deeper and more vibrant than he expected, but she spoke with confidence. He wondered about her age; he suspected she was not yet twenty, but she had the practical manner of someone older.

They fished in silence for a while. She stood so still that she would have seemed calm to any other observer; this belied her scent, which was marked with frustration and impatience. Again he scented no fear on her.

Over the next few hours, she caught three fish. He caught none. Eventually, she glanced over her shoulder and openly studied him.

"It's hopeless for you to try to catch a fish in your state," she remarked.

Amaoke raised an eyebrow, questioning silently.

"It's obvious that you're nervous. Somehow the fish sense it." She shook her head, gesturing broadly at the inlet. "My father taught me that fish could sense a predator, so calm and patience are needed to catch them." She paused, then stood a bit taller, pleased with something, and said, "He told me I would never be successful at fishing because I am not patient, but I have fifteen — no, sixteen years of practice. I can be calm enough, patient enough now to catch them."

Amaoke smiled at her, aware that she had not only just let him know her age, but that she had been looking for an opportunity to do so. It was endearing, in keeping with her apparent openness, this forthright manner. His smile encouraged her, and she waded out of the water, setting down her pole and untying her skirts, letting them drop around her feet. Without bothering to address her missing shoes and socks, she came and sat right next to Amaoke on the bank, so close to him that part of her overskirt touched his pant leg.

She curled her hands in her lap and said nothing, just looked out at the water. Since it didn't seem as though she expected him to speak, Amaoke said nothing. They sat amicably in silence for some time. The sun dipped over the water.

Finally, she sighed contentedly and then stood up reluctantly. She gathered her shoes and the small basket she'd brought for fish. Then, putting her pole over one shoulder, she turned to him and said, hurriedly as if it took all her courage, "After we're married, I'll do the fishing."

She turned and darted up the path so quickly that she missed Amaoke's shocked expression. He had no trouble believing that she had been reading his mind the entire afternoon. He knew such persons existed; there were those with a very keen sense of the emotions and motivations of others.

He stayed on the bank until dusk, listening to the cicadas and bullfrogs singing the evening chorus. Dragonflies danced over the water; occasionally, a fish surfaced to make a quick meal of one of them. Then he changed form and trotted out to the clearing where she lived.

The little house was bright with candlelight. The front and back doors were open, as well as the windows, to let in the soft night air. The smells of summer were beginning: lilac, primrose, and wild onion. Amaoke could smell the last of the spring flowers in the garden, their too-sharp perfume foretelling their decline, and the honey bread she was preparing for her dinner, and the briny smell of the salt cellar in which she had packed the fish. He watched her feed the rabbits in the hutch and pick some flowers that she arranged in a teacup.

He was so content that he fell asleep under the blackberry bush and awoke to a late moon. He padded on four feet back down to the river to retrieve his clothes and fishing pole, and walked on two legs slowly back up to the logging camp.

25

THE FOLLOWING SUNDAY, AMAOKE RETURNED to the fishing hole, though he was in doubt she would return so soon. It gave him something to do, and was the only place other than her house where he could successfully look for her.

Amaoke didn't feel comfortable going to her house; it would be too difficult to explain how he had found it. He didn't want to scare her; such a young woman living alone was unusual – he assumed she could do so because she felt safe there. Her sense of security was worth preserving.

No matter if it would be a five-week wait, in Amaoke's long years, five weeks was a short time. But he was surprisingly restless, intrigued about how much he was drawn to her. He had almost stopped questioning what was happening; in all his years, he had never been in a courting situation with a human woman.

He knew how to assimilate into a wolf pack and had done so many times over the centuries. Amaoke was dominant enough to avoid being run off; since he had no desire to be alpha, he willingly made himself submissive to the alphas in order to be accepted, even in situations where he was the more dominant wolf. His dominance meant he had no shortage of willing females with which to mate. As a young wolf, he was wary of mating, unsure about perpetuating his aberrance on the natural world. But the Earth Mother never allowed him any progeny; she kept balance and order. He had learned that when he lived within his first pack because he stayed around to be sure there were no pups. After a few seasons, Amaoke's mates would typically disdain him for his inability to give them young, although wolves generally mate for life. Often it was the reason Amaoke would leave a pack and go out on his own.

So he sat on the riverbank quietly, with his pole beside him, not bothering to fish, and waited. He forced himself to be still, to be part of the day as his mother had taught him. He listened to the bees' song, and the wind pushing the water, and the small animals in the undergrowth. He closed his eyes and concentrated his senses.

And then he caught her scent several moments before he heard her footsteps approaching on the path. The wind direction helped. He heard her stop abruptly on the track and laugh.

"You will never catch a fish if you don't even put the pole into the water," she teased. He could tell she was smiling by the tone of her voice.

He opened his eyes. He was pleased and surprised that she had come back so soon. Then he noticed she had no fishing pole, and his heart gave a funny little jump.

"I don't think you really want to fish," she observed, grinning so widely that her gray eyes narrowed with delight, and some mischief, he thought. Amaoke had to smile in return.

"How about a walk instead?" she offered, beckoning with her hand.

Amaoke stood up slowly and, with a small look of dismissal, left his fishing pole behind.

"Oh, no, no, no," she exclaimed, brushing past him to retrieve it. "It's a very functional fishing pole. You made it, didn't you? It's very nice." She admired it, and he could see she was earnest. He accepted it when she handed it to him and followed her up the path.

She glanced up at him briefly. "You're very tall. I'm taller than my father, which is unusual, and you are...tall." She finished her statement abruptly, obviously leaving something unsaid. They walked some distance in silence before she stopped suddenly and asked,

"Did you remember me from town – that time, before? You were with some other men, from the logging camp, right?"

He nodded, not ready to speak aloud, wanting to hear her talk, enjoying the sun on the bright green fields. They walked along an overgrown wagon trail between two small farms, staying together, one of them on each side of the left-hand wheel path. There were short silences punctuated by her observations and reminiscences.

She was visibly pleased to be remembered. It flattered him because he sensed that her pleasure was not at being remarkable in general, rather that she had been personally memorable to him.

Her long strides nearly matched his. Her enthusiasm made her seem especially energized, charged with life, zeal, and youth. It pleased Amaoke, and yet brought to him the strangest bittersweet sadness, because he knew he could not carry the joy she brought him into the centuries to come. That thought came to him early, but he scolded himself, remembering to be thankful for any bounty he had when he had it.

She stopped abruptly once more, and gazing up at him, asked, "What is your name?"

He did not hesitate to tell her, knowing that the belief of his mother's people was that names should not always be freely spoken so as to avoid giving another some undue power. Nicknames were often used. Sometimes the day of the week you were born, and your family affiliation were given. But she knew none of this, and every single member of his mother's tribe other than himself was lost to time. Besides, Amaoke knew that this one already had considerable power over him.

He watched as she repeated the name, sounding it, then saying it confidently. "Ah-mah-o-kee."

When she started to respond in kind, and give her name, he gently, briefly, put a finger on her soft mouth and shook his head, just once from side to side, to stop her. Her name, he knew, was magic, and he would not take the chance of putting it into his head where mischievous spirits or evil forces could get to it. He was all too aware that his magic was not really his own, and he did not want to own anything that would give the Morningstar any more power. He did not want to know her name, or even think it, for fear that the monster would come for her with its usual malign intent.

26

IN HIS MIND, HE HAD already given her a name, Na-na-tha, beloved woman, a derivative of an old indigenous word for mother. He gave her this name from his heart, as a tribute because she was the first human woman for whom he had felt love of this kind, and the only woman who'd made him feel human since his mother.

But he did not tell her this, not now, because it was not time. He actually feared she would eventually wholly understand and accept him, and he was not ready for those grey eyes to see even more deeply into his soul.

"Oh, you're superstitious." She nodded sensibly, walked ahead a few paces, and then turned back to look at him. To his surprise, she was not judging or questioning his response. It was Amaoke's experience that in the province of youth, endless questioning was the hallmark, and that quiet acceptance came to temper it after many, many moons.

"My mother was Iroquois," she told him. "I think they have similar beliefs, but I never learned enough to be sure. My father told me he was never certain that the name he used for her was actually her own."

Nanatha told Amaoke many things about her life as they walked along. Her mother had been an Iroquois woman working as a cook for a group of trappers that came through the area. Her father had seen that the woman was being mistreated and suspected that she had been stolen from her family, forced to work, and do other things for a very rough group of men.

So her father had hidden her mother, chancing retaliation if the trappers found out. But the trappers moved on, and apparently never returned to the area, nor discovered their stolen Indian maiden. Nanatha's father eventually took the woman to wife. She had died at childbirth, shortly after successfully delivering her healthy daughter.

Nanatha had been raised by her father, who owned the mill in town. Amaoke made the connection regarding the male he scented following her visits to the mill — it was her father, rather than a brother. Her father had remarried a local farm widow when Nanatha was very young; the widow had been kind to Nanatha but had also died when Nanatha was nine or ten years old.

Nanatha's father had taken to drinking in his grief and rarely left the mill in those days. Young Nanatha kept up the house her birth mother had lived in and tended the garden. The widow's property passed to her grown sons. Eventually, her father recovered from his grief, but kept the habit of living as a bachelor in his rooms at the mill.

Nanatha occasionally cooked for him and mended his clothes, but she continued to live independently. Being a half-breed had both limited and expanded her opportunities.

She had not been allowed to attend school formally, and there were some in the community who didn't want her at church services. Her father had stopped attending church as well, in protest. Her father had warned her that she was unlikely to marry, as there were no families with which he could arrange a match.

For all that these constrictions cost her, she had gained considerable freedom. She did not have to conform to accepted social standards, and any of her personal idiosyncrasies of speech, dress, and behavior could not affect her standing in the community. She went about as she pleased and was allowed to live alone, unchaperoned.

The current friar at the church was young, no more than thirty, and he was kind to Nanatha. He had been surprised to learn that she was able to read and write; her stepmother had taught Nanatha at home with the help of a few old childhood primers. Borrowed books had helped her improve. The friar was willing to lend books from his small library; the wolf suspected that this extraordinary arrangement meant that the friar was sweet on Nanatha but unable to risk his reputation by acting on such feelings. Amaoke ignored the twinges of jealousy he felt at the thought of her with another man; it was far from the full moon, and the man was in ascendance over the beast.

It helped that she was also the only child of the richest and most influential man in the village. Although her father had no strong political leanings, as the mill owner, his endorsement of her eccentricities meant that others would be willing to overlook them, too.

Amaoke listened, watched, and learned her body language. He became familiar with the cadence of her voice, the confident tempo of her stride, and the array of complex scents that contributed to the glorious signature smell he had used to find her. Despite her stature, her collarbones appeared fragile. Her bronze color was less a product of sunshine than heredity. Her freckles were like a fine sprinkling of cinnamon spice over her nose and cheeks.

But what did she see when she looked at him? The odd eyes and sharp teeth, the extreme stature, the old-fashioned if not downright strange clothing he wore, a mixture of indigenous and modern? None of that seemed to put her off; instead, she seemed determined to know him in spite of these things. He was used to other people moving away from him, rather than toward him, and he savored this new experience, although he did not fully understand it.

But perhaps understanding it was a part of understanding this amazing girl, who seemed to Amaoke so much older than her handful of years. Nanatha had lived as an adult for almost half of her life, had endured and rejected prejudice, and had accepted her own place in the universe without ever feeling sorry for herself. He marveled at the ways in which her life story paralleled his own. He could feel his own pain diminish with every step she took beside him, feel his usual unrest melt away as she spoke and gestured animatedly about the things she wanted him to know.

27

AFTER IMPARTING THE GIFT OF her life story, Nanatha became silent. She veered off the path and led him up the now-familiar hill up to the ridge that rose up next to the clearing on the far side where she lived. She stopped short of the rise and sat down under a gnarled ancient crabapple tree. He sat down some feet away from her and leaned his back against the trunk of the tree.

She asked him about logging, and Amaoke told her the story of trees as he had been told it. He spoke of their sacrifice, and their importance in nature. He talked to her about how to plant trees and how to conserve forests, cutting down no more than a certain number of trees in an area to ensure that the woods would survive. He told her of his fear that the demand for more and more lumber could mean the end of forests, and could mean that many animals would no longer have a home.

Amaoke surprised himself; he had not said this many words aloud to another person for centuries. For her part, she listened intently, and seemed genuinely interested in what he had to say. But she was astute enough to notice that he was not talking about himself, and her questions immediately became more personal.

"But where do you go in the winter?" she inquired. "You weren't working with the ice crews on the river."

Amaoke was unsurprised that she had noticed his absence. Even if she hadn't been fully conscious of the fact, he now knew that she had been looking for him, too. He explained his travels north to work among the indigenous people there, how he lived and worked within and beside an Innu family and as part of the tribe.

"Innu?" Nanatha asked. She was considering the word.

"The name for the Indigenous families there," Amaoke explained. He did not tell her that they were, among other groups in the area, descended from earlier Inuit families like his mother's people who had, over the course of centuries, migrated across what was now known as Canada and into Greenland. Amaoke had spent much of his long life following the migration or participating in it, and he had observed the evolution of the parent culture and language into four or five distinct groups with their own words and dialects that he had spent the time to learn so that he could continue to travel among them.

"Whaling?" she asked. Nanatha was clearly trying to decide what to say. "So, you are an…an Eskimo?"

He couldn't stop the small frown when he heard the word, and he considered how to explain. He wasn't sure how to convey it without making her feel as though she had done something wrong.

"Winter is the wrong time of year for whaling," he explained gently, then continued. "Yes and no. That word, Eskimo, is probably not specific enough." He gestured with his hands to reassure her when he could see she wanted to apologize. For the second time that day, his finger rested gently on her mouth to quiet her. He hoped it wouldn't make her believe he wanted to silence her, so to console her, Amaoke told her the story as best he understood it.

"It is a vague name given us by other people and may be considered somewhat insulting, although it is widely used," he explained.

Nanatha was quiet. He could see that she was bothered by something. "But it is the only word —"

"That is used," Amaoke finished for her. "When Russian settlers came across the Western sea, the word for us became the only one in popular use. European settlers adopted the term Eskimo as well."

"Terrible," Nanatha said, seeming to sense some sadness within him. Amaoke could not think of that word without thinking about what the arrival of settlers had cost the Inuit people, the disease, the relocation, the genocide. "So, what word do you use?"

He smiled at her thoughtfulness. He was still unsure how to fully explain it to her, but then discovered he did know how to proceed. "My mother's people were an ancient family on the western coast, far from here. Each family village had a specific name. Among ourselves, we still refer directly to the family names, but some of the names cover larger populations that may include more than one village within a region. I guess the name for most of the Arctic indigenous people is Inuit, but even that is limited to certain areas now and probably not specific enough. There are hundreds of family groups. My mother's people are probably all gone now, disappeared through famine, migration, or intermarriage. The name for their closest descendants is *Yup'Ik;* the language they use is still pretty close to what she taught me."

"And your father…?" Nanatha paused, truly awkward for the first time. "I'm sorry if I am being too forward. My father says I don't have to ask every question I have in my mind." She blushed, and it was so endearing that Amaoke smiled again.

"I never knew him," Amaoke answered as honestly as he knew how. "He died before I was born."

They sat again in silence, watching blue damselflies flit here and there, sometimes seeming to hover before shooting off over the top of the grass. Nanatha appeared to be thinking about all he'd had to say, and it wasn't long before the interrogation resumed.

"How old are you?" she asked suddenly, peering at him with open curiosity.

"If I told you, you wouldn't believe me." He smiled, fueling her speculation.

"Well, you are obviously older than I am, so I will guess, based on your apparent youth, that you must be in your twenties," she pronounced, with a pleased but expectant expression that told Amaoke she was confident in her guess.

He shook his head slowly, giving her another indulgent smile. How easy this was, how happy it seemed to make her, and he had never believed that being a half-breed would someday make such a difference to another person. Amaoke could see that she was delighted to finally know someone like herself, not just in the abstract, and he finally understood why she believed him to be the ideal suitor. She had held on to what her father told her and had assumed that to marry, she would need to find another person that the world held separate for no other reason than their mixed race.

Amaoke had lived much longer and seen much more of the world, and had known other persons of mixed heritage. But in his experience, their lives were harder, people were crueler, persecution and violence were commonalities of their existence, and he himself had never found comfort from his own experiences in being with any of their number. He had to admit that for the very first time, there were possibilities that he had not considered, had not sought in his life, and much of his loneliness was diminished just in knowing her.

"Older than thirty!" she exclaimed. "As old as that?!" Nanatha's surprise was a typical response of the very young, who seemed to view life beyond thirty years as some unfathomable frontier. Her reaction delighted him; ironically, it kept them away from the subject of his exact age.

He threw his head back and laughed for the first time in five hundred years.

28

WITHOUT ALERTING NANATHA TO HIS plans, Amaoke paid her father a visit at the mill on his next errand into town. It was extraordinary that she believed him to be the perfect suitor, but she was young, and despite her apparent cleverness was also naïve, and Amaoke wondered just how her father might view a stranger courting his daughter.

He had spent a great deal of time thinking about the many reasons why he was not an ideal husband for anyone, a list which included his dual nature and the inherent danger of loving anyone or anything that the Morningstar could reach. He knew he should leave the area, find work elsewhere, and keep her as safe as he could. But he already knew, deep within his heart, that something in him had changed. He was feeling selfish for the first time he could remember. He also knew that no matter where he was, the Morningstar could read his thoughts and sense his feelings, and that if he was with her, perhaps she could be protected. That was the only true lie he told himself, even if he knew better than to believe it.

It was a primarily selfish decision to stay and see where the relationship could go with Nanatha, because she was pureflesh that the Morningstar would not hesitate to use against him, which put her in mortal danger already. His absolute refusal to know her name meant he could not directly identify her in his thoughts, and maybe he could hide her from the Monster for a time, until Amaoke found some way of preserving her. He was superstitious, but he comforted himself in this way, and there were periods in his life when the Morningstar was puzzlingly absent.

Amaoke discovered the man loading sacks of milled flour onto a wagon. Amaoke introduced himself and was not surprised when the man took his hand and introduced himself as Nathan Guinness. Amaoke inclined his head to the flour sacks to indicate that he didn't want to interrupt the man's work, and started helping to load the bags side by side with Guinness.

He was as forthright with Nanatha's father as he could be, and started by telling him that she had predicted she would wed Amaoke. He shared his admiration for her many remarkable qualities with her father, and waited to hear what the man had to say.

To Amaoke's relief, the man knew his daughter well, and appeared to encourage her to make decisions about her own happiness. "She told me about you," Guinness told Amaoke, shaking his head. "This was last summer, after she had seen you in the road out yonder. She was fascinated by you and felt a kinship with you. Lately, she tells me you are kind. She knows I put a premium on kindness."

Amaoke remained silent, hoping Guinness would say more, and he was rewarded when the man continued, "She's a bit funny in some of her ideas, but I suppose it's her right to see the world in her own way. She is also…" He paused, as if searching for the right word, then continued, "Well, she has that thing that my grandmother called intuition, but it seems even keener than that in the girl. Like some sort of special insight. I can't really explain it, but if she says you're special, then you must be different enough from other men, or she wouldn't mention it at all."

Amaoke acknowledged the observation. The two men continued to work in silence for a bit, before Guinness remarked, "Just because she said she was determined to marry you doesn't make it a foregone conclusion, of course. Perhaps you're here to have me call her off?"

Amaoke was a man of very few words, and found it even more difficult to speak when his emotions were strong, so he shook his head and told Guinness that he was inclined to court Nanatha, with her father's permission.

"Very kind. But I reckon that decision is hers, and all hers," Guinness replied, placing the last sack of flour onto the wagon and brushing off his hands. He reached once more for Amaoke's hand, and nodded in the direction of the cart. "Much obliged for the help. I just want her to be happy."

29

SUMMER WENT ON, AND AMAOKE spent more and more time with Nanatha, traveling down to their fishing spot to meet her on several occasions each week. He actually stowed a change of clothing in his hiding place among the blackberries in case he needed them. If he ever had to change from wolf to man at her end of the journey, he could clothe himself. His nudity would be inconvenient at the very least and certainly was not something that would go unremarked upon. He had been in that unfortunate situation before – it was difficult to explain to others. And often cold.

He worked on a small bracelet for her, plaiting soft strips of doeskin dyed a deep red with the juice of berries he had gathered in the forest. His own mother had had such a bracelet; it had encircled her wrist twice and had been a gift from his true father. He planned to offer it as a token of his devotion to Nanatha.

Slowly, they began to learn about each other. He realized that his initial impression about her reading his emotions and her father's observation about her intuition were not far from correct.

"I can sense feelings, not really thoughts," she admitted, when he told her that sometimes he thought she knew what he was thinking. "It is difficult for me to get much from you, don't worry," she reassured him. "Most people are not very complex. From you, I get two predominant characteristics: kindness and sadness."

Her astuteness was astonishing to Amaoke. He changed the subject by asking her why she had told him they would marry.

"I dreamed of you," she responded without hesitation. "That is, I dreamed I was getting married to a man with long black hair. I had no other details, no specific face in the dream, but when I saw you on the road that day last summer, I knew you were the man from my dream."

"Are you sure?" he teased her. "How many men with long black hair have you seen other than me?"

"None," she admitted, but continued triumphantly, "I just knew you were the right one!"

Amaoke laughed, an event that was becoming alarmingly common. Her conviction explained the utter lack of formality or wariness she displayed around him. And he learned that she wasn't really that forward in her dealings with others. When they encountered other townsfolk that she knew, even those she was comfortable with, Nanatha was respectful and proper, to the point that it made her seem reserved when compared with her early friendliness toward Amaoke.

One week, she invited him formally for supper at her home the following Sunday, and he pretended to politely listen to her instructions on how to find the house from town.

Sunday's weather was clear, so he remained on two legs to make the afternoon walk into town. He ducked into the general store and picked out two shiny apples to take to Nanatha as a gift. He knew she loved them; she often smelled of apples, she ate them so much.

He approached the house from the overgrown wagon track and climbed the hill beyond the crabapple tree where they had sat together in the spring. From the top of the rise, he could see the side of the house, and his nose told him that she had bathed in her rainwater barrel recently. The scent of freshly cut wildflowers was also coming to him on the breeze, with the additional smells of baked bread and chicken. He smiled. Feeding him today had not cost any rabbits their lives.

Amaoke called out to Nanatha once he was halfway down the hill, and she came to the back door. She was wearing a light-green dress that he had not seen before. It was embroidered with tiny flowers, and he suspected she had made it herself. The fresh scent of her soap was strongest in her hair, which she had braided but left swinging free down her back.

Amaoke paused at the bottom of the hill just to look at her. He wanted to remember her at this moment, with the sunshine slanting through the leaves, her evident happiness, and all the radiant hopefulness of her youth. He held the apples in one hand behind his back and remarked as he approached her, "You look so lovely."

Her cheeks flushed with pleasure, and she dropped her eyes from his. He stepped close to her and put his fingers gently under her chin and pulled her face up so he could look into her eyes. He brushed her forehead briefly with his lips and presented her with the apples.

She nearly bounced with delight as she thanked him and led him inside the house. He could see she had been packing a basket with food, planning to eat somewhere outdoors.

The house was cozy and saturated with her scent, commingled with that of flowers, tea, honey, and bread. The fireplace took up most of one wall, with a door and windows at the front, a bigger back door, and two larger windows opposite the fireplace. Her bed was nearer the front door, which looked like it got less use as a means of entry or egress than the back door. There were homemade quilts on the bed and unmatched calico curtains at every window. The wildflowers filled a porcelain water pitcher on the small table under the window and sat in scattered teacups on shelves and windowsills.

Nanatha produced a small sharp knife and sliced one of the apples expertly before tucking it into the basket. While she was finishing up and gathering everything they would need, Amaoke wandered out the back door, trying not to draw her attention to the distress he was causing the rabbits in the hutch.

There were three adults this time, with a partitioned area holding four juveniles. *Hello, pitiful morsels,* he thought, shaking his head. Eating rabbits he could heartily endorse, but keeping them caged still struck him as unfair.

In the uncanny way she had of reading a situation, Nanatha came to the door at just that moment, and asked, "Do you want to know their names?"

He put a finger over his own mouth and pressed firmly, as if he was concentrating on what she was saying so that he could hide his amusement. He pretended to listen to what she told him but was really trying to avoid being on a first-name basis with any of his future food.

Then she did something extraordinary – she opened the hutch and began taking each one out and stroking it lovingly, saying a few words and snuggling it close.

Amaoke took a step back to decrease the likelihood that any of them would panic, as he could smell their fear. He watched as she took her time with them. They were well-loved and cared for.

Then she put the last one back and closed the latch. She went back inside and retrieved the things she had prepared for their meal. Leaving the back door open, she led him a few steps from the house before whispering, "I do eat them, eventually. I just want them to have happy lives."

He glanced over his shoulder and then back at her. "Why are you whispering? Do they speak English?" Amaoke smiled at her to show he was teasing before he reached out to take the basket and a small blanket she was holding, so he could carry them for her.

Nanatha gave a small shrug. "I think they can sense our intentions," she stated wisely, looking at him with a slightly puzzled expression. "They're afraid of you."

He nodded, then said in an exaggerated whisper, "They can see I'm hungry."

"Come on, then," she laughed, taking his arm and leading him away from the ridge, through a small wooded area, to an open field beyond. She chose a partially shaded spot and took the blanket back to spread it on the ground. They sat down and shared chicken, bread, and butter with honey and cheese, sweet peas in the pod, and the apple.

Afterward, Amaoke lay on his back and watched a few high clouds drift across the sky. Nanatha sat nearby, uncharacteristically quiet, and gently ran her fingers through the ends of his long hair.

"What's this?" she asked, unable to hide her curiosity about the tiny braid he kept concealed behind his left ear.

He explained to her that when he was a very young boy, his mother had woven the tiny braid behind his ear, telling him that she placed some of her love into it. She had also said to him that she hid it there to protect the totem from ill spirits. Amaoke knew the evil that had been part of his life for centuries was not deterred by it, but he had survived the long dark years of torture. He did not share with Nanatha that when his mother died, he had added some of her hair to the braid, keeping some of her spirit close to him. It brought him comfort, especially when the loneliness settled into him like a weight from which he could never fully free himself.

Nanatha spanned a length of the braid across her slim hands. Then she brought it to her lips and kissed it, saying, "I will add my love, too."

Amaoke's heart was very tight, and he knew what he felt for Nanatha he had never experienced before and might never feel again. Time was so fleeting, and she was so precious, and he was grateful to have this opportunity to be close to another human being. It was an unexpected and rare gift for him, and he was determined to endeavor to be deserving of her love. He knew her happiness was the most important thing he could imagine, and he wanted to please her, always.

He sat up and untied the red bracelet he had made for her from the fringe of his buckskins. "I made this for you," he told her. "I offer it to you as my marriage promise, if you will have me." He looped it over her wrist twice and tied it in place, then turned her hand over and kissed her palm.

She leaned over and placed her forehead against his. "It's beautiful. I accept it." She closed her eyes, and he rubbed his nose against hers as he remembered his mother doing to him, all those centuries ago.

30

MIDSUMMER CAME, WITH ITS LONG workdays and short nights.

Even Amaoke's arms ached from swinging the axe those long hours, and after dark, he often wandered away from the camp to change and enjoy the summer nights on four feet. Occasionally he remained a man and walked upriver some distance to cool off with short swims in a small, shallow beaver pond. In either form, when he returned to the camp, he stayed away from the fire, in the shadows where the firelight didn't reach, and kept to himself.

One evening about a week after the full moon, Amaoke returned to the camp very late after hunting rabbits on two legs. Most of the men had gone to sleep, but there were still three men sitting by the campfire, drinking whiskey from the smell that Amaoke picked up. As was his habit, he skirted the fire from well back in the shadows, finally seeing that it was Audet and his two companions sitting there, discussing new traps they had set, and their success collecting furs for side money.

Then Amaoke caught the scent of something wild, and a hot, bitter, metallic stench that he recognized immediately. There was a dark void near the campfire, and as he watched, it gradually resolved into the form of a man. The firelight illuminated the familiar, despised face of the Morningstar and was reflected back from the depths of those inhuman eyes that caught and held the glow of the fire like shiny coins. Then the figure seemed to shimmer, waver, and disperse like dark smoke into the trees.

Amaoke followed the vision into the trees, but a few steps into the woods and the scent was gone. He looked up and could see the stars through the treetops. There was no further trace of the Morningstar. Amaoke turned in circles, trying to follow the scent instead, but it flooded his nose and then disappeared. He was frustrated. It was bad enough when the Morningstar presented itself, and Amaoke knew the reason for it; it was worse to feel as if he were only having a vision for which he had no explanation. The appearance of the Morningstar could only be an ill omen. The typical night sounds of the small creatures and insects had fallen silent.

Amaoke picked up the welcome scent of the pines, baked earth, and the campfire. Nighttime noises slowly crept back in, and he could hear the thumping bass song of a bullfrog. He took a look around the camp, but nothing appeared out of order. He climbed high into his sleeping tree. He leaned into the trunk, but it took him a long time to go to sleep.

Amaoke woke to the sound of voices below him and recognized the accented speech of Audet and his companions. They were probably going off to check their traps, and they smelled like they had been up all night drinking, but they stumbled off in the direction of town.

Following instincts that had been developed over centuries, he came down from the tree and followed them. He crossed behind them and went into the woods to change and then crept as close as he could to them, keeping under cover of the trees at the side of the track. Their laughter echoed off the trees, and their stench made him want to sneeze, but he repressed it and continued to follow.

He finally caught on to their conversation and realized in horror that while tracking him, his wolf, they had come across the little house in the clearing. They were on their way to town to find Nanatha.

"Since 'ze girl is not a fit wife for anyone, why not we see if she like us?" Audet laughed.

"Even if she no like us, we like she," replied another, malice clear in his voice and his intent.

"We show her our friendship, no?" Laughter from all of them as they continued on their evil errand.

Amaoke did not venture any closer to where they walked along the road. He assumed they were too drunk to take the shorter path to the clearing through the woods, so he turned down away from the track, crossed a small creek, and began to run through the trees, down the slope toward the river and the town.

In his distress and his haste, he failed to pay enough attention to his nose, and he missed the spot where the diminished scent of the trappers and oiled metal on the path should have broadcast a warning. He heard the ping of the release as he tripped it, and then the heavy metal jaws of the trap closed on his left foreleg.

His yelping shriek reached the heavens, and he stifled the whines and whimpers that followed. The pain was excruciating, but he didn't want his cries to alert the trappers, who were still close enough to come and investigate. If they found him in the trap, they would surely try to kill him.

He felt bile rising in his throat and was dizzy and sick, but he forced himself to focus. The leg was broken, and the jaws had broken the skin. Amaoke put his head down and panted roughly for several seconds, trying to clear his head. He forced himself to listen for any sign that Audet and his companions had heard him, and after several agonizing minutes, he felt sure that they weren't coming. Yet each minute brought them nearer to Nanatha, and he was trapped.

He seriously considered changing back into a man, but for all the advantage having the use of his other hand might bring him, the disadvantages were many. There was a chance he would be discovered by another logger, and it would be difficult to explain a naked man in a wolf trap. Also, the pain was so terrible that it was fraying his control, and he wasn't sure if he could complete the change. Finally, if he did finish the shift, his emotions were so strong that they would likely trigger the wolf once again.

He struggled mightily for a few minutes but recognized that he was futilely wasting his strength. So he tried to clear his mind and remember the words of the prayers his mother had taught him to use to call out to the *ellam yua*, but it was no use. He was unable to concentrate. The pain was so intense that he shuddered and shook in his distress. He felt his consciousness waning.

He shook his head to clear it, and then coldly eyed his left forepaw, contemplating life without it. There was one way out of this trap, and it meant he had to free his leg at all costs. He closed his mouth over the leg, wetting the fur and trying to gauge how much force he would need to chew through it. He shuddered but was resolute.

And then Amaoke imagined he could hear a strange voice whispering his name, over and over, in a language he did not know, but somehow understood. He looked around, and the forest had disappeared, and he was in a barren place so alien it was like nothing he had ever seen. The ground was a near-endless expanse of dust, and the sun was unbearably intense. In the distance, through a shimmering haze, he perceived strange trees, tall and bare save for irregular foliage at the top. His dizziness increased and then subsided as the vision faded. He felt, rather than heard, a strange hum, and the air around him began to crackle and sizzle as if it were charged, like the tension one could feel in the air during a lightning storm, although there was not a single cloud in the sky. The forest coalesced around him, and the strange voice said his name one final, emphatic time. The air felt white-hot and electrified. His fur stood on end, and suddenly the trap's jaws sprung open so violently that the hinge broke.

Amaoke looked around but could neither see, nor smell, nor sense, another soul nearby. It was not the work of the Morningstar; he felt sure of that somehow. He knew that the power was not of his ability, either. He wasted no further time trying to resolve the question. When he tried to stand, he found that his left foreleg could not bear weight.

He made his way through the woods on three legs, paying better attention to his nose and the ground ahead of him. He reached the clearing, panting and still half-hopping with a three-legged gait that he was not used to, and caught the unpleasant scents of Audet and the other men nearby. But Nanatha's scent was no stronger there than the usual background that existed around the house, so he hoped they had not found her at home.

Then he heard voices on the ridge and crept upward. The unmistakable scent of fear and panic flooded his nose, and he hoped he was not too late.

The three men had cornered Nanatha at the top of the ridge and were teasing her, grabbing her and trying to force embraces and kisses on her. She was fighting back as hard as she could, scratching their faces, trying to kick them, all while screaming for help.

Suddenly, one of them pinned her arms to her sides and shook her roughly, then threw her down the far side of the hill. Her screams abruptly stopped, replaced by moans of pain. The men started down toward her.

Amaoke hopped up to the top of the ridge in time to see the men reach her where she lay on the ground near the bottom of the hill. She was shaking with fear and obviously hurt. She put her hands up to protect herself as one of the men brought the stock of his rifle down on her head. The savage blow opened a gash on her forehead and rendered her unconscious.

Audet laughed, and one of the other men said to his companions, "She talked too much for my taste."

The other one was kneeling over her, reaching for the top of her bodice and groping her roughly.

Amaoke felt an all-consuming rage that swelled inside of him until something snapped within him. Whether it was control or restraint, he could not tell. Suddenly his form began to shift yet again, but not back to man, instead into something even more feral, even more beastly. His torso reared upward, and his forelegs lengthened and thickened into something more like arms. His snout elongated even further, and widened, fangs growing so fast they split his gums, and bloody drool spilled from his mouth. His claws grew and sharpened, and he stumbled forward two steps before he realized that he was walking upright on much sturdier hind legs. His chest swelled outward, and his head was thrust out in front of him. He was no longer just a wolf; he was a true Beast, retribution, damnation, and death in one form.

The roar that came from his throat spiraled deeper and deeper as he leapt down the hill, briefly seeing their horror at his grotesque appearance.

Then his jaws were snapping into unwashed flesh, crushing bones and marrow, penetrating to soft innards, the taste gagging him, the blood in his throat and in his snout and his eyes, but he was unable to stop. His claws tore and slashed, and he didn't stop ripping and biting at them; he could not stop until long after the screams subsided. And then the blackness came down over his eyes, and he was overtaken by it.

When Amaoke regained consciousness, he was naked and human. His skin was slick with blood and gore. It took him a moment to realize where he was. He had somehow crawled back up to the top of the ridge.

He tried to push himself up with his left arm and nearly screamed with agony. He looked at it briefly and could see that his entire hand hung uselessly from the end of it.

He peered down the hill and felt ill. The three men were torn apart. Nanatha was lying where she had fallen, moaning softly.

He climbed slowly to his feet, and half walked, half slid down the other side of the hill to the house. Both rain barrels were full of water. He climbed into the one she bathed in and ducked under the water several times before climbing out. His left wrist throbbed painfully, but he was concerned about the hand, which was becoming strangely numb.

He pushed the rain barrel over on its side to drain the foul water and retrieved his clothes bundle from the blackberry bushes. He dressed as hurriedly as he was able with one working hand and climbed back over the hill to Nanatha.

She was struggling to wake up, her eyes fluttering but not focusing on anything. Her hands were moving weakly, and when he touched her, she tried to push him away and gave a frightened moan.

"Shhh," he tried to quiet her. "I'm here."

He looked her over. The gash on her forehead was ugly, the skin split roughly in a jagged tear, but it had stopped bleeding. Her right leg was turned out awkwardly, and he gently pressed along the length of it until she gasped in pain when he reached her hip, which was apparently broken.

He lifted her legs over his left arm, ignoring the pain it caused him, and put his right arm under her shoulders. She cried out when he lifted her.

"I'm so sorry, beloved one," he murmured to her in the language of his childhood as he started the long walk into town.

31

HE TOOK HER TO THE mill, figuring that the doctor might respond more quickly to Nathan Guinness. He carried her into the large load doors that faced the main road. Two young men were loading wagons, and one hurried over to them when he saw Nanatha. He looked suspiciously at Amaoke, then remembered his manners, and said, "Her pa is out on a delivery."

"She needs the doctor," Amaoke said. "Can you fetch him? I think her leg is broken, and she took a blow to the head."

"I'll fetch him now," the young man replied. "Jake!"

The other young man looked up from his work and hurried over. The first one said, "Show him up to Guinness's quarters right away. I'm goin' for the doc."

It was clear that Jake, too, was curious about Amaoke, but he wasted no time in getting him to the steps leading up to a vast closed attic above the mill floor that crossed from the front to the back of the ample space. There was a door from the workspace into this loft. Jake hesitated for a moment, then asked, "Would you like some help? You don't mind my sayin' so, mister, but you don't look too good."

Amaoke closed his eyes briefly. The thought of anyone touching Nanatha right now threatened his fragile control. But he realized the boy was being kind, so he sighed and said, "Show me where to get her settled. I'm obliged to you."

Jake nodded and led the way up the steps and opened the door, stepping back so Amaoke could take Nanatha inside. The loft was a mixed-use space, with a large desk nearly buried in papers that took up one end of the area, and at the other end a wood stove, table and chairs, and a bed by the windows overlooking the river. The space had a lot of light from large windows on three sides that also revealed the road and the central part of the town. Amaoke took Nanatha to the bed and set her gently down on the coverlet, propping her head upon the pillows. She moaned weakly, and tried to talk, but he placed a finger on her mouth, and said to her, "You just stay quiet now. Stay quiet." Thankfully, when she heard this, she settled down and closed her eyes. He knew she was in too much pain to sleep. He tried to move away, but she held tight to his good hand.

"Where's Guinness?" he asked Jake.

"Mister Guinness is out with a delivery of lumber for a cattle fence," Jake replied. "If I thought I could get to him faster, I'd try to ride out with a message for him, but he should be back in an hour. He's out to the west of town, no more'n a few miles."

Amaoke nodded, and at that moment, the first young man returned with the doctor and a young woman that Amaoke had never seen before. She was primly but expensively dressed, somewhat older than Nanatha, and he could see that her face was kind, although, at the moment, she appeared distressed.

The doctor appeared to be in his later fifties, with reddish hair graying slowly and thick long sideburns but no beard. His face had the look of youth that many redheads maintain well into middle age, and despite his profession, he appeared good-humored, more accustomed to smiling than the alternative. He was wearing twill pants, and a tweed vest with a watch pocket over a broadcloth shirt with the sleeves rolled to his elbows, and he carried a leather satchel and a broad-brimmed hat, which he set by the bed. "I'm Dr. Riggins," he told Amaoke. "Can you tell me what happened?" He was already leaning over to take Nanatha's free hand, taking the pulse there.

Amaoke looked around the room. He felt it was a delicate situation for Nanatha's reputation and was uncomfortable telling the story in front of so many witnesses. Guinness's two young apprentices apparently understood the situation, and they nodded to the room and excused themselves, heading back down the stairs.

"She was attacked by three men," Amaoke explained. "She was pushed down a hill and struck in the head with a rifle stock. I think her hip is injured. She's been confused, trying to wake up, trying to talk."

"A robbery?" the doctor inquired, looking curiously at Amaoke. Amaoke could see that the doctor also noticed his injury, but had not yet remarked upon it.

Amaoke looked at the young woman and back at the doctor. He was reluctant to say the words in front of her. "I think their intent was somewhat more malign. They had designs on her virtue. Pardon me, ma'am," he said to the young woman.

"Was she —?" the young woman stepped toward Nanatha protectively.

"No," Amaoke said quickly, then more softly, "no, ma'am."

"I'll need to take a look at her," the doctor said gently. "Miss Williams is the local schoolteacher. She knows the girl well, and often helps me with my work as an unofficial nurse here in town."

Miss Williams came up beside Amaoke, and to his surprise, gently put her hand on his arm. "We need to get her undressed and examine her."

Amaoke nodded, and, releasing Nanatha's hand, he went out the door and down the stairs to the street. He crossed the road and went up the farm lane a short distance until he found a fallen tree branch about the size of his wrist. He carried it back to the mill.

The two young men had resumed their work, but looked up when he broke the branch into pieces, using his uninjured hand and the rear edge of the bed of an empty wagon, choosing a length that spanned his forearm, and a smaller one that he curled the fingers of his left hand around. He then tore a burlap sack into strips with his teeth and used the strips to splint the wrist and secure his fingers in position around the second piece of branch. With the arm and hand in alignment, the flesh of his hand and fingers looked better, and some of the numbness began to resolve.

Picking up a few more burlap sacks, he said to the young men, "Tell Guinness I've gone back to her house." Then he set back out onto the road.

When he reached the overgrown wagon track, the sky darkened as if by a large cloud or shadow falling on the ground around him, and the smell of scorched bitter metal and blood filled his nose. He heard the loud beating of wings and a cacophony of screams in his ears that was so loud it felt like it was coming from inside his head. There was loud crashing and cracking as large branches were destroyed, and then a thunderous boom as a massive creature descended like a meteor into the forest and landed with a force that shook the earth on the track where Amaoke stood waiting. Then the shadow moved over and around him as the Morningstar stepped out of the woods, folding its enormous black wings behind him. Its cloven feet changed as it walked and it appeared human-like, still formidable, with the shiny coin-like eyes that were dead of emotion, and a smile full of razor teeth stained with what appeared to be old blood. It approached Amaoke, who gagged at the carrion stench of the Monster's breath as it spoke.

"*Firstborn, wolf-born, child of moon,*" its standard greeting echoed in Amaoke's brain. It spoke in a language that Amaoke had never learned but somehow understood. "It has been too long. I see you have discovered a more…" It paused as if searching for the right word. "…fruitful and beautiful form of expression for your wild brother."

Amaoke remained silent. From long experience, he knew that the Morningstar loved to hear itself talk, and he also knew that anything he said might give away something that the Monster would invariably use to hurt him.

"We have tortured you for centuries," it said, and its voice split and deepened into that plurality that meant it was accompanied by a legion of demons, the sound almost a hiss, and so painful it threatened to bring Amaoke to his knees. "We never saw this before…and all it took was love." The last word was spat out in contempt. "Love for *her* summoned the Beast. We could use her to control you, then?" it suggested archly.

The Morningstar changed shape again, taking on the visage of a tall, handsome, dark-haired man. It wore simple trousers and a broadcloth shirt that would have allowed it to pass as a local farmhand.

"Perhaps a rival suitor. I could win her and take centuries debasing and destroying her." It seemed to give this statement consideration, and its demeanor showed a little too much pleasure for Amaoke to stomach. Then it smiled a terrible smile, awful in its evil, a foul idea forming.

Abruptly, its form shifted again, and it didn't bother to cover the grotesque process of metamorphosis. When it finished, Amaoke was looking at his own doppelganger, and he shivered.

"Or…I could show her who you really are – would she love you then, I wonder? Really, did you think you could keep her from me? I am a part of you, and I will know you always, my son. What belongs to you is really mine."

Amaoke turned back toward town, desperately calculating how he could get to her in time, somehow beat this awful creature, and knowing it was impossible. Finally, the Morningstar spoke again. "We are not interested, for now," it allowed. "We think it will be much more interesting to leave you alone. It will hurt you much more to watch her live and die, and you will learn that it is better to embrace your inhuman nature and take your rightful place as a general over my armies. You will suffer as she suffers over this human lifetime, and we think that is a fit punishment for you."

"What do you want?" Amaoke couldn't keep himself from asking. If the Morningstar was abandoning Nanatha to her human fate, Amaoke knew it was because there was something it wanted more.

"We came to inform you of an interesting development." The Morningstar gave up his human pretense in favor of black wings and unnatural height. The feral, shiny eyes and needle-like teeth were back, showcased in an open-mouthed grimace. Amaoke could sense its satisfaction. Amaoke was also inwardly relieved to see the Monster no longer wearing his own face.

"Your new form comes with added benefits," the Morningstar hissed. "Let's just say it appears that you can pass on your gifts, under the right circumstances." Its laugh spiraled up over the trees, and came with a multitude of screaming voices, unnaturally shrill and chilling Amaoke to the bone. Then it was gone, completely, leaving only the stench of burnt metal and rotting flesh to fade in the summer air.

Amaoke had no idea what was meant by that last statement, but whatever had happened was a delight to the evil one, so the chill he felt persisted. He began to hurry along the wagon track and slowed only when the crabapple tree and the hill came into view. The carnage was still on display, and from a short distance, he could see dark smears on the slope where great swaths of grass were pushed over and covered in blood that had blackened as it dried. He scented death, blood, and remnants of the musk that was exuded when humans felt fear. The buzzing sound of carrion flies was already present, and he could make out several separate bloody fragments of the men's bodies.

It wasn't until he was much nearer that he saw the grotesquerie to which the Morningstar had alluded. The bodies were partially…changed. It was bad enough that there was evidence of predation; it was too early for other animals to have fed on the corpses, so it told Amaoke that he had eaten part of his victims, possibly for pleasure in his bestial state. The thought so overwhelmed him that he turned slightly away and was violently ill, regurgitating chunks of bloody flesh and bile at his own feet, the damning evidence to support his grisly suspicion. He had no memory of the events after the initial attack, which was overwhelmingly frightening. He stood hunched over for several moments more, retching and dry heaving until he recovered a bit of control.

He moved among the remains of the men and forced himself to look at the bodies. There was evidence of transformation, but it was incomplete. Here, a paw with dark bloodied fur at the end of a human arm; there, a disarticulated leg with a partial torso that had a tail. One of the heads, probably Audet's, was partially transformed, with an elongated snout and unnaturally sharp canine teeth, with ears that had grown fur and were beginning to triangulate at the top, more wolf than human.

Amaoke silently questioned the scene, and he didn't like the conclusions he reached. Something about this super-bestial transformation had made him something other, something more, something much, much worse than he had ever been. His attack had passed on the ability to change to his victims; thankfully, their injuries were mortal. He imagined the three men in wolf form and shuddered; it would be a plague on humanity. It was no wonder, then, that the Morningstar was so delighted. Was he becoming what the demon meant him to become? He thought back on his long, long life. He had bitten humans before, but rarely, and only in his pure wolf form. Admittedly, most of them had died. He had never known such effects could be possible, but before that day, Amaoke had not known that there was a more terrible Beast within him, and he was afraid. It had taken him centuries to reach a level of control over the wolf, but it was clear that he had no control over the other being, the Beast, and the Beast had power that Amaoke did not want for himself. It was aberrant to nature in a way he could not begin to comprehend.

Thankful that his stomach was empty, he shrugged off these dark thoughts and began to gather the body parts into the burlap sacks he had taken from the mill. He tried not to see the carnage, or smell the terror, or feel the alternately slick and sticky nature of the pieces as they disappeared into the bags.

Once the bags were closed, he wiped off his hand on the burlap and dragged them into the woods beyond the clearing where he and Nanatha had eaten their picnic. That day seemed so long ago, even though it had been only a few weeks.

He gathered kindling and used his flint to start a small fire. He carried logs from Nanatha's firewood pile to build it up, and soon it was burning fiercely, the heat of it stinging his face and the backs of his hands. He placed the bags on the fire and discovered he was relieved when they began to burn. There would be nothing left for anyone to see; nothing left to remind Nanatha or himself.

It took several hours for the bags to burn down, and Amaoke ensured there was steady heat by continuously adding dry kindling and firewood. He finally went back to the house to retrieve a shovel, and broke up the cinders, burying them with dirt, ensuring that the fire was entirely out, covering any remnant bones that had resisted the fire. Strangely, there weren't many.

He was bone-weary, and his left arm was throbbing, but he pulled a bucket of water from the second rain barrel and washed his forearms and his face, finally pouring the cold water over his head. He removed his shirt and hung it over a branch in Nanatha's yard to dry. The heat was already drying his long hair. He wanted to take this day away, somehow, didn't want there to be any reminder for her when she came home, so he used the remaining daylight to replace her firewood stores, lifting the axe with one arm and bringing it down on the wood, over and over. The labor was cathartic, the wood splitting violently under his effort, as if it were being punished.

The sun was low in the sky when Amaoke sensed that someone was approaching over the hill. He could smell Guinness, so he deliberately continued stacking firewood, even though he noticed the man looking behind him at the bloody grass when he reached the top of the ridge. Guinness didn't say a word to Amaoke for several minutes, looking at the woodpile and wandering over to the woods and examining the disrupted ground. Amaoke realized he was a keen observer; the smell of the fire and of burning flesh still permeated the air.

Amaoke finished his stacking and resumed splitting wood, feeling strangely calm swinging the axe, in spite of the temporary awkwardness of doing it with one hand. Presently, Guinness returned to the yard and leaned up against the house, a respectful distance away. He waited for Amaoke to interrupt his own task, and he said nothing until Amaoke set down the axe.

"Doc told me what happened to her," Guinness said, brave enough to meet Amaoke's eyes for a moment before looking at his injured arm. "He also said he'd like to take a look at your arm when you're ready. Do you want to tell me what happened?"

Amaoke said nothing, just looked at the axe, and out to the clearing, and back into Guinness's eyes, where he discovered understanding, mixed with anger, sorrow, and relief.

"No less than I would have done," Guinness grunted, and turned to walk back up the ridge. He paused at the top, looking back at Amaoke, who gathered his shirt and followed him back to town.

32

THE DOCTOR HAD TO ADMIT that Amaoke's splint was pretty skillful, but he cleaned the wounds with antiseptic and dressed them before replacing Amaoke's makeshift bandage and wrapping the entire arm in clean gauze. He puzzled over the pattern the trap's jaws had made on Amaoke's arm, but to his credit, he did not mention the strangeness of the injury. Amaoke wanted to like him.

"It should be kept immobile," Riggins advised. "The wrist is broken but should heal in several weeks. You'll keep use of the hand, I think, but it might give you problems with stiffness over time." He fashioned a makeshift shoulder sling for Amaoke's arm.

Amaoke nodded his thanks, knowing that he was unlikely to take that long to heal or to have ill effects. He knew that by the next full moon, the arm would be nearly healed, and he was grateful to know it because changing with an injury could be very painful.

The three men were huddled in a storage room on the ground floor of the mill, on the street side. Ms. Williams had long gone home, and Nanatha was resting soundly upstairs. Guinness had set up a bedroll on the floor near his desk before joining Amaoke and the doctor downstairs.

"She will be on bed rest for the better part of two months. If she resists infection, she should completely recover," Riggins told them. "She'll have a bad headache for a week, I expect, but her skull is intact as far as I can tell." He looked at each of the other men in turn.

"She won't ever walk the same, but I think she will make do. Thank God you were there, or she'd have injuries that might never heal." This last was for Amaoke, and then the doctor put on his hat and took his leave by the street door.

Over the next few weeks, the foreman had Amaoke stripping branches from felled trees and marking target trees to avoid worsening his injury. Amaoke was grateful; many foremen would have let him go, half-breed or not; the work had to go on. But Amaoke was a skillful and fast tree man, and the foreman didn't want to lose his experience.

True to prediction, when the next full moon called his wolf, Amaoke was mostly healed, even the silvery smooth scars from the jaws of the trap fading fast, and he ran again on four legs, feeling strong. He began to resume his regular duties at the logging camp. The missing men were not long discussed. It was assumed that they had decided trapping was the more lucrative endeavor and had taken their leave of the logging camp.

He traveled into town every evening, staying a few hours with Nanatha, watching her body heal, and worrying about her mind. She just wasn't the girl he had met and courted, and he hoped that one day she would be able to talk to him about what had happened to her.

When the time was right, and Doc Riggins permitted it, he helped her get out of bed for the first time. Initially, she just sat in a chair for short periods of time, but pretty soon she was standing, and of an evening, with his help, she would walk about the loft on unsteady legs.

"What are you smiling about?" she asked him one evening as she leaned against him. "This can't be fun for you, dragging me about." There was despair in her voice, and his heart hurt a little to hear it.

"I don't know," he said, allowing the smile to take over his face. "It's a bit like we're dancing."

She had to smile, too, then, in spite of herself. "Like two drunks dancing," she grumbled.

"I wouldn't know the difference," he said, trying and failing to keep his face solemn.

It was the first time he'd heard her laugh in a long time. But still, she didn't get better; her previous demeanor seemed lost, and it made him sad.

After three months, she was mostly back on her feet, with just a little residual weakness, and a bright scar over her forehead that did not mar her beauty in the slightest. She had lost some weight and some color spending the summer indoors, and she had a limp that would persist for her lifetime.

One evening, she appeared more agitated than usual when he came to visit. Her father was out, delivering flour to a shop owner two towns away, and this was the first time she had been left alone in the loft. It was the first time she had been utterly alone since the day she was attacked.

When he handed her the apple he had brought to cheer her up, she started to cry. Amaoke had no idea what to do or what to say, so he put his hands over one of hers and waited. When she didn't stop crying, he kneeled in front of the chair she was sitting in and pulled her into his arms, feeling her shake and shudder as the sobs grew louder and eventually subsided altogether. He stroked the back of her head and placed his lips gently on her forehead before he released her.

He decided the direct approach was best, which was ironic, because he talked much less than he ought, and asked, "Do you want to talk about it?"

Her short laugh was more a bark of frustration than amusement. She held her arms up as if to shrug, and then dropped her hands back into her lap. "I'm afraid you won't want me anymore, now that I'm lame, now that —" But then she stopped, as if there was something more she could not say.

Amaoke waited silently, willing her to continue in her own words. Finally, she did.

"I want you to know that I fought them. I didn't want to let them touch me." She couldn't look him in the eye.

Immediately, he understood what had been bothering her. She assumed that they had violated her. No wonder she was so blunted, so sad.

"Beloved, what do you remember of that day?" he asked her gently.

"I remember…they were saying awful things, and I was so afraid, but I knew I had to fight, because I wanted to belong to you, but they were too strong. They hit me, and I can't remember anything else!" Her voice broke as a new sob came through.

"I was there just in time, and I saw some of it, but they never touched you. Not that way," he promised her, hearing the anger in his voice and hoping she knew it was not for her, never for her. He realized that this was the thing that had darkened her heart, robbed her of her voice, and changed her.

She nodded as she realized what he was telling her, still unable to look at him, and unable to speak.

He placed his hand beneath her chin and lifted her face to his. "Nothing that happened that day could ever change my mind. A limp and a scar do not make you less beautiful to me; those things represent events that happened but did not take you away from me. My tradition celebrates such things," he told her.

After that night, more and more of Nanatha's distinct personality returned, and he found himself being teased and entertained by her wit once more. She was talking again, wanting to return to her little house in the clearing, but unwilling to admit she was afraid.

Later that fall, she was ready to try, and Amaoke began cleaning out the cobwebs and the dust that had accumulated. On the day she was to return home, he went ahead and cut wildflowers for her table and her windows. Her rabbits were fat and well-cared for since he had assumed the responsibility for their care. Her garden was grown over, but he knew she would restore it to order easily. The two rain barrels were clean and full of water, and her firewood was stocked for the winter.

When she arrived on her father's wagon, he helped her get settled, assisting her with placing new linens on her bed and trying not to imagine her in it. He should have been more alarmed at her delight that the rabbits were well; ultimately, she sacrificed one for the two of them to eat that night.

He slept on a bedroll outside her house until it got too cold, and then he took his bedroll to the mill and slept in the storage area so that he would be closer to her. By then, she had regained some of her former confidence, and Amaoke thought it would help her further if he did leave her alone a bit more. This seemed to have no ill effects, but he decided he would be unable to leave her for the whole winter work season, so he stayed on, joining the ice crews that broke up the ice over the river and lake.

She was still worried that someone could approach the house without her knowing, and was visibly startled every time Amaoke came to the door. He was her most frequent and virtually her only visitor, as she went out to others to gather the things she needed. Even Guinness stayed away, letting her resume her former lifestyle as best she possibly could, waiting for her to come to him at the mill when she was ready to visit.

So Amaoke taught her a very old song that his mother had taught him, and he trained himself to hum or sing a bit of it every time he returned to the house. He made a conscious effort to make a great deal of noise with his feet, stepping on dry branches and leaves rather than avoiding them, as was his habit as a hunter. This ritual comforted her; sometimes, she was moved to sing back to him so that he would know she expected him.

And every month, over a period of four days preceding and following the full moon, he would disappear into the woods with his axe. He explained away his absence with hunting, returning to her with whatever game animals the season provided, or berries and mushrooms he had gathered in the remote forests.

Eventually, the weather started to warm, and he prepared to begin sleeping outdoors again. Nanatha took him on a picnic in the field on the first warm spring day, and he could finally see that she was as recovered as he had hoped. She was talkative and robust, her skin was browning from the spring sun, and best of all, she was relaxed. She fell asleep on the blanket in the shade where he lay next to her, watching her face across the sea of his hair spread between them.

When she awoke, she did so by opening one eye to check that he was still there, and then she closed her eyes again and smiled. She leaned up on one elbow and looked around sleepily, shaking the nap from her head. "Beautiful day."

"Beautiful girl," he responded, looking at the sky, enjoying the warmth of a new year. "Shall I bring my bedroll back out here?" he asked.

She sighed softly and turned to pick some clover next to the blanket. "I'd prefer that when you come back out here to sleep, you do it inside the house, in my bed," she said frankly, giving him a look that burned through him like phosphor. "I'm ready to get married," she declared, holding her clover bouquet to her nose and inhaling deeply.

"Let's not keep you waiting," he laughed.

33

THEY MARRIED ON A SUNNY day later that spring, beneath an enormous oak tree outside the church. The young friar was happy to bless the union, which meant more to Nanatha than to Amaoke, whose ancient beliefs were somewhat different. Good spirits and love and family were good omens, and he knew he had all three. He barely heard the words of the friar's ritual but responded when he knew it was expected of him. Guinness was happily present as a witness.

Nanatha was radiant in a white gown that she had made for the occasion, heartbreakingly beautiful and bursting with happiness. He could see the woman she was to become, although the dress accentuated her youth. Her chestnut hair was braided into a thick crown that encircled her head and that she had decorated with seemingly hundreds of small flowers of a multitude of colors. Amaoke wore beaded buckskins and a new embroidered broadcloth shirt that she had made for him and presented to him the week before. It was implicit in the gift that she expected him to wear it on their wedding day, which he did, happily.

The only shadow was his own uncertainty about his past, and the malign spirit, the Morningstar. Amaoke never knew what would provoke its appearance, but could be sure that his happiness had been a cause of it in the past. He needn't have worried; all was silent, and the day remained bright and clear.

Guinness offered one of his wagons, but Nanatha insisted on walking home by Amaoke's side. She twined her fingers through his, and although smiling to herself, said very little on the long walk to the house in the clearing. Her limp had been incorporated into her determined stride, like a pause in momentum at every other step, but she was not ungraceful. The soft material of her gown made her seem to float along the wagon track, and its movement was like the whisper of the breeze through the highest leaves in the trees.

It was a perfect spring day, neither too hot nor too cool, and she opened the windows in the cottage when they returned home, and propped open the doors. The sounds of the birds in the trees and the smell of sunshine on new flowers surrounded them.

When she turned her attention back to him, Amaoke could smell her desire, and it inflamed him. His emotions were at war inside of him; he knew what he wanted to do to her, with her, but was acutely aware that he had never been intimate in human form before.

Nanatha stood before him and slowly unwound the braid on the top of her head, releasing a small shower of blossoms that floated gently to the ground. Some of the smaller ones landed on her dress, and on his shirt, and a few caught in his hair. Her eyes never left his, so he reached out for her face and held it as he kissed her open mouth for the first time. Her scent flooded his nose, so strong that it became part of the sensory experience of the kiss, enhancing her taste as her tongue gently touched his, then became more insistent as the kiss deepened.

He was rapidly aroused by her kiss, overwhelmed by his mounting passion, spurred on by the scent of her desire and another fragrance beneath it, her ready womanhood. He pulled her against him and held her so tightly he was afraid he was crushing her. But he felt her smiling into the kiss, and then she gently extricated herself from his arms and turned around, lifting her braid over one shoulder and letting her eyes invite him to help her remove the dress.

Amaoke had noticed every detail of the lovely gown, including the tiny row of buttons that ran down her spine, but he had not anticipated the difficulty he would have in removing it. His emotions were so strong that as he started to unfasten the first tiny button at her neck, his hands began to change, and his claws sprang from the ends of his clumsy fingers, clicking uselessly at the buttons. He closed his eyes and moaned, and she said, "Take your time, my love," not knowing that the passion and raw emotion in her voice incapacitated him further. He put his palms on either side of the row of buttons, careful to keep his claws up off of her body, and bowed his head, taking deep breaths and asking the *ellam yua* for strength, and after a few seconds, his claws retracted slowly, leaving in their place the clumsy fingers of a man who has had little to no experience with the ladylike buttons of his bride's wedding gown. He wasn't sure it was an improvement, but he took his time, unfastening one button after another, feeling his legs weakening as he exposed more and more of her beautiful smooth skin, finally reaching the last few, unable to stop himself from stroking his fingers into the cleft in her back, feeling the wolf's hungriness riding his reason, shaking with a lack of control.

She stood patiently, trembling slightly at his touch. He put his forehead on one of her shoulders, then turned his head and began to kiss and gently bite the side of her neck, making her moan and roll her head back onto his shoulder, which pushed her hips and her backside toward him. His hands slid down to her hips, and she pulled her arms from the dress, letting the top half slide off, arching her back as he moved his hands up and around her body to take the weight of her breasts into his hands.

He forced himself to take his time, knowing that she deserved his patience and care in his loving. It was a first for both of them, and her pleasure was to be his prize.

He reluctantly removed his hands from her skin, and turned his attention to her hair, gently taking the long braid and unraveling it, freeing her hair, seeing it wild and loose, flowing over her skin for the very first time. This maneuver released more of her scent, and he felt his arousal cresting again. He buried his face in her hair, and kissed her shoulders, back, and neck through the soft veil before returning his attention to her breasts and belly, which he stroked with his hands until she was moaning with pleasure and desire. He could scent her readiness, so he pushed the gown off her waist and downward, letting it slide to the floor. She stepped out of it and turned into his embrace.

He removed his shirt and leaned his face toward hers for another kiss. Their hair flowed around them, strands of each mixing with the other, like a flowing blanket, wrapping them together and hiding their faces from the outside world. Her body pressed against him, and his need became a living thing, but still he caressed and kissed her, until she moaned, "Ama, please," pulling him tighter against her. He helped her onto the bed, removed his remaining clothing, and climbed into bed with her.

Amaoke, the man, was unsure of himself, but the wolf was experienced, and so he relied on instinct when he reached for her. She looked over her shoulder at him, those grey eyes seeing into him, and trusting him, and his lust would not allow him to take any more time. He pulled her against him, claiming her as she had already claimed him. He was patient and gentle with her, hearing her first soft cries come before increasing his tempo and his force to match his need, holding on to her as they both shook with pleasure, consummating their union.

34

THEIR EARLY YEARS BROUGHT WITH them the typical bliss that accompanies two people who genuinely love one another. They learned about each other as no couple can before they wed and live together.

Nanatha learned that what she fed him was of little importance, as he was mostly interested in the meat. She wanted to make new jams and jellies, or put different herbs or fruits in the breads she made, and Amaoke could see she was doing it for him, to please her new husband, so he indulged her, but he had little interest in much beyond the meat or fish that she served him, occasional vegetables, and seasonal berries. To her credit, she could discern his disinterest, and loved him even more for continuing to encourage creativity in her cooking.

She also learned his true inner feelings about her rabbits. He explained to her that he was unable to eat anything with which he had formed a personal relationship and offered to teach her how to hunt them. She was game enough to accompany him once, but could not stop laughing at the sight of him chasing them down, his hair flying as he ran and dodged, gracefully trying to guess the animal's next evasive tactic. Her amusement distracted him enough that most of his quarry that day escaped him, as he could not make himself one with his prey, and observe the appropriate ritual relationship with them, as his mother had taught him was necessary. Nanatha capitulated anyway, agreeing that she would prepare rabbits he caught and abandon "farming" them.

Nanatha learned that he was indeed kind, and sad, as she had intuited from the beginning. He worked very hard to please her, weeding her garden, bringing fresh flowers to her nearly every day, and anticipating which of her many chores she liked the least and performing them before she could ask.

He planted an entire crop of sunflowers in their picnic meadow when he learned how much she loved them. He was an attentive lover, ensuring her pleasure always, rarely rushing or selfish in his attentions.

The sadness that surrounded him was not as easy to characterize, although she felt she knew him more and better the longer they were married. He appeared to be weighed down by matters that he never discussed, and sometimes he seemed much older than the few decades she assigned to him.

He disappeared into the woods for four days out of every month; after the first year of their marriage, she realized that it was always around the time that the moon became full. She never asked him, but his reverence in observing the days in each season suggested to her that the practice had a religious underpinning. She knew that many indigenous people had moon-related festivals, but was ignorant enough of her own culture that it became less something she had in common with her husband than otherwise. Even if she had developed a working knowledge of Iroquois custom, his background was different enough from hers that she felt it would not help in understanding him. The comfort she took was in their shared isolation because they were not full-bloods, but other than rare oblique references to his mother, which was clearly one source of his sadness, he did not speak of his background.

Nanatha also sensed that there was something more complex about these sojourns, as he seemed even more distant for a few days after he returned. And there was something almost mystical about those four days, when her normally smooth-faced husband would show up wearing a significant beard growth and sometimes body hair, most impressive during the winter months. She did not think he was unaware of her keen intuition, so it conveyed a sense of trust for him to come home with the beard on display, and shave it in her presence, although neither of them remarked upon it. For the rest of the month, his face and body were mostly hairless, which was to her understanding typical of most of the indigenous. She often wondered what would happen if he did not shave it, and she suspected that it would go away on its own, but her suspicion was never confirmed because it was always one of his first tasks.

At the end of the year, her curiosity got the best of her, and on a particularly idyllic day, after which they had shared an outdoor lunch and made love among the sunflowers, she asked him, "Are you some sort of medicine man?" She glanced over at him as they lay together, still entwined, with the nodding heads of the enormous flowers surrounding them like a swaying, silent audience.

Amaoke's quick laugh was neither cruel nor condescending. "Not to my knowledge, Beloved, why do you ask?"

"Because there is something…something…I don't know. I think you have some magic about you," she concluded.

"If I do, it isn't of my making," he reassured her. "There is nothing that I am able to do that I have any special control over." This was not quite the whole truth, but it was the truth of his overall circumstances, so he was comfortable with the omission inherent in his statement. Nanatha did not know it, but it was the closest he would ever come to telling her about his great secret. And because she felt it was a secret, and it was his, she decided to trust him with it and believe that he would tell her whatever she needed to know to keep safe. This, she felt, was the actual well of his sadness, and there was a darkness there that she did not want to make him touch, and did not want to see for herself; she only wanted to be a comfort to him, and provide a safe place to come home. So Nanatha kept her own counsel about what she suspected, what she felt, and what she already knew.

35

AMAOKE LEARNED THAT HIS WIFE was superstitious about many things, which he felt supported her intuition and warred with her otherwise Christian upbringing. She wasn't fooled by his subterfuge and knew that there was more to his "hunting trips" than he let on. To her credit, she took life with him in stride, and did not push him for information, for which he was grateful. He did have persistent guilt about the essential omission of a significant circumstance of his life. He believed that he had selfishly decided that it might change the way she saw him, that it might have interfered with his courtship and subsequently with their life together. Ultimately, some part of him realized that she was aware of the omission, loved him in total disregard of it, and discarded what was probably her very keen need to know more about it. After her initial shy questioning about whether he was a magical shaman early in their marriage, she let her intuition guide her to a settled acceptance of their unique circumstances.

For his part, he tried to make the trips as fruitful as possible, returning with braces of rabbits, or deer, elk, nuts, berries, flowers that she didn't have in her own garden, wild onions, and occasionally a stolen honeycomb wrapped in cheesecloth as presents for her. He wanted her to know that for him, it was not about leaving; rather, it was the return to home, and to her, that was his grounding force, more significant an occasion than what took him away from her.

He also learned that he had been correct in his assessment of the poor friar's heartsick love for her, and that she was oblivious of it, which made him secretly pleased. Amaoke would watch the poor man observing Nanatha as they did errands about the town, and even the wolf in him could not be angry about such a wretched creature, whose feelings were as understandable to him as his own. Apparently, her father had also reached such a conclusion, but it gave Guinness no end of private amusement. He said to Amaoke in a low voice one day as they watched the friar frozen in place at the sight of Nanatha crossing over to the general store, "Serves him right. If he were half the man you are, he would have offered for her hand before you ever came to town, and shown these folks that proper has nothing to do with the color of your skin."

"He won't find another like her," Amaoke agreed, glad not for the first time that Guinness was the man he was.

Amaoke had to teach her about chivalry, as she had been independent nearly to a fault. He could see that there were tasks she despaired of yet would never ask him to help with, so he had to take them over in spite of her protests. Then there were other tasks that he could easily claim as his own, like chopping firewood, which she apparently enjoyed doing so much that she challenged him one day while pointedly holding the axe, saying, "Don't you get to have enough of this kind of fun at the logging camp?"

The mischief in her eyes and her aggressive pose with the axe made him hold up his hands and laugh. She was so appealing, standing there in friendly opposition to his attempt to be gentlemanly, that he had more than half a mind on toppling her over and lifting up her skirts, but he behaved, knowing she needed her independence like living things need air.

In spite of that outward spirited enthusiasm for life, one thing that remained unchanged was her general mistrust of strangers and a continued shadowing fear of a repeat attack. Those first few years of their marriage, he suspected that she hardly slept when he was away, making him wonder if he should shift forms and circle back to the little house. Yet he knew that such an approach would surely bring them face to face with what he preferred to keep away from her, better ensuring her safety in more than one way. Surely the Morningstar would consider its moratorium on interfering with Nanatha's life void if Amaoke conferred real knowledge of his dual existence to her. Notwithstanding that, there was the real risk of another breakthrough of the true Beast due to the heightened emotions created out of his love for her.

With the logging efforts in the region steadily growing, there were increasing numbers of crews of strange men, both in the summer, for logging and fishing, and in the remainder of the year, when there were trappers, and new workers on the ice crews. The town would sometimes seem full of strange men, inquiring at the mill for her father and doing business at the general store, so in those early years, Amaoke found himself squiring her into town to alleviate her anxieties.

At night, especially as the weather warmed, the cacophony of night sounds would jar her awake at strange hours. She seemed hyperaware of any possible new sounds while somewhat alarmed that the natural noises might mask an approaching attacker. Eventually, she learned to trust that his entire being was employed in her protection while supporting and applauding her every effort to maintain near-total independence.

When he had to be away, he spent a great deal of time contemplating whether an explicit knowledge of his nature would help or hurt this residual fear, this dark and unwelcome gift of her attack. He was unable to decide whether the presence of a real monster would be a comfort to her or a source of further distress.

It was the essential dilemma of his own existence, as he struggled to discern his place in humanity, in nature. He could not reconcile himself with the Beast, could never find commonality with the Morningstar, even though the Monster itself suggested that the Beast had been created to further its evil designs. Was he indeed a tool of destruction, destined to harvest lives and breed fear among people?

Before finding Nanatha, he had become increasingly concerned that he felt no particular bond to humanity and could find no lasting connection between himself and them. He was always other, separate, and content to be so. He had found ways to exact a sort of justice without fully participating in their lives, without wanting to connect. The Morningstar had fostered this separation; Amaoke suspected he was to view other people at a remove so that he could carry out some frightful legacy that was foretold only to the Monster.

But Nanatha, and both his love for her and her love for him, had changed something in him. He could more clearly see the ways in which he was truly human – Amaoke was flawed as they were flawed, but he could love, and through that lens, he had learned that there were some outstanding people in the world, who sincerely desired to help each other and foster understanding despite differences. Guinness was one of them, his foreman, another. Both men were viewed differently by Amaoke than he would have had he not known Nanatha's love.

Amaoke now understood that tolerance alone did not explain the behavior of either man, that there was inherent good in men, a generality that Amaoke had previously been able to see, but unable to believe. If it could be seen in individuals, at some point, it had to be appreciable in more substantial groups, and this realization gave him a great deal of hope, which forever changed him.

36

AFTER A FEW YEARS, AMAOKE recognized another growing sadness in his lovely wife. She was waiting for something, he felt, expecting something, and he spent some time trying to figure out what it was before he realized that she was going through all the behaviors of a woman looking for signs she was with child.

His nose finally told him that she smelled most of despair after the onset of her womanly cycle each month, and he understood what was happening. The concern about getting her with child was never an active consideration for him; he assumed what had happened as a wolf would occur as a man and so he had no expectations. He felt even more guilty that he had not considered that she likely had hopes and dreams of a baby.

One hot afternoon, after returning to the house in the clearing, he dipped himself into the rain barrel and then sat in the sun to dry, enjoying the fall warmth and the changing afternoon light as the year crept around to winter. The leaves were changing, desiccating, falling to the ground, and the remainder of the harvested plants had a scent all its own that reminded him of dry grass and aging fruit, and the end of something. He realized he must have fallen asleep when he was awakened by the feel of Nanatha's light touch on his hair as she combed it. He smiled, and put his head back to enjoy it, but then smelled her sadness and felt her shaking with silent sobs.

Amaoke turned to her and took the comb from her shaking hands and held her. When she quieted, he took her hand and led her into the sunflowers. It was their haven, their safe place, the closest thing they had to a church, and he brought her among the flowers she loved to whisper softly to her in his own ancient language, comforting her even though he knew she had no way to understand what he told her.

Eventually, she admitted her despair that her body had failed him, her despair that she could not give him a child, her despair that such an admission might cost her his love. Amaoke knew enough of the time, and the prevailing culture, to understand how a young woman might blame herself for such an outcome, because many men were ignorant of their own failings or did not want to admit them out of a fear of appearing weak.

He shocked her by suggesting that he might be the problem, not her. He forestalled any argument from her with a silencing finger on her mouth, imploring her to consider that there was no real way of knowing and no real reason for assigning blame, either to oneself or to another.

"I would not have expected you to marry —" she began, but again he stopped her.

"There were no conditions on my love for you," he stated firmly. "None. I loved you because you are you, not because I expected sons or daughters. These decisions are made by the Spirits. If we are meant only to have each other, so be it. I find no fault in you at all."

Acceptance of this particular reality only strengthened them, and Nanatha seemed to heal and become stronger and more confident of his love. Amaoke had comforted her in her sadness, both keenly disappointed for her and acutely relieved that he was unable to give her a child, out of uncertainty of what such a child could become. There was too much to be thankful for to carry the disappointment, so he focused on the blessings he had that he had never expected to know, and little by little, life had new meaning in every sunrise, in every moment, in every way.

37

YEARS PASSED, AND NANATHA'S BEAUTY of fifteen matured into something truly spectacular by the time she was forty. There were knowledge and temperance in those grey eyes, and a sensual expression would animate them that stripped Amaoke of all ability to stay on task, bringing him to worship at her feet, reminding him how much of himself was entirely devoted to her every whim.

One hot summer, Nathan Guinness died, leaving to his daughter a large inheritance that included his bank account and the deed to the mill. With her characteristic kindness, she passed the mill directly to his two employees, Peter and Jake, who had long since formally joined the business following their apprenticeships. Now both middle-aged men with families to feed, they were grateful for the gesture, offering to buy the mill outright. But she refused to take any money for it, so they struck a bargain with Nanatha to repay her generosity by helping others who needed their services but might not always be able to pay. She had no idea what to do with the money in the bank; she and Amaoke had everything they needed, and her father's account held a goodly sum. Amaoke had no advice to give; he had little use for money and had always turned over his wages to Nanatha for safekeeping. Even the large amount he had amassed prior to meeting her sat untouched in a bank in Quebec, and he was unsure it *could* be reclaimed.

She possessed a timeless handsomeness by sixty; indeed, she was almost regal in appearance, after which her face softened and became more translucent so that at eighty, she remained unusually youthful-appearing, with rosy cheeks and preserved high, angular cheekbones.

She still laughed often, but her limp was worsening, and her gait slowed terribly, although she persisted in performing her daily household tasks. Eventually, they had to abandon sexual congress due to her frailty. He had stopped pursuit of it once he realized he was hurting her. He also realized that if he hadn't, she was too dutiful and kind to refuse him.

Amaoke, in contrast, was much the same man he had been when they married. As with the other "magical" things she had long ago observed, his wife appeared mostly to ignore this fact, or perhaps to her, it was less evident since she looked upon him nearly every day. He suspected that it was her usual forbearance with him, that she avoided the subject as a kindness rather than due to any real ignorance of it.

The winter of her eighty-fifth year was a hard one, in which they were snowed in from early October to May. Amaoke noticed that she began to decline more rapidly, starting with a loss of appetite and weight, and progressing to a kindly forgetfulness.

Late spring into early summer was wet and cold, and one day, pneumonia caught hold in her, and he could smell the sickness on her breath. She took a fever, and when he held her through fits of coughing, her skin was so dry and hot, it reminded Amaoke of being too close to a banked campfire. Despite his efforts to nurse her through it, she pushed away his attempts to feed her and refused to drink.

On the second night, Amaoke awakened beside her, disturbed by her restlessness. She was moaning and trying to talk to him about fishing, and her father, until her words made no sense. This delirium gave way to an even more striking lucidity, in which she clutched him tightly, looking deep into him, it seemed, as she searched for the words she needed to remember.

He tried to hush her, and settle her down to sleep, but her grip and her manner were insistent, so he waited, holding her now-frail frame, in this bed where they had once been young and carefree newlyweds, where there had been a beginning, where now he would bear witness to an ending. Finally, she managed between gasping breaths to say to him, "I saw the Beast that day…the day…the men came for me. I know what you did. I know who you are."

Amaoke remained silent, realizing her understanding was more profound than he had ever imagined.

Nanatha reached up to touch his face and whispered, "I know you, beloved husband." And with that final declaration, she drifted down into death, away from sickness and pain, forever out of his reach.

Amaoke left her there, in repose, and ran out of the house on four legs. His howls of sorrow and grief echoed through the trees, across the ridge, throughout the forest for weeks.

On a warm day in midsummer, he returned to the small house in the clearing, wrapping his wife in the sheets where she lay. He walked around the house in circles that followed the path of the sun for four days, fasting and avoiding those activities that would block her way to the afterlife. He dug a grave for her in the dormant field where they had spent so many hours together. He placed her into it, unwrapping her shroud long enough to remove a length of her hair, and then covered her with earth, knowing that each year, in the late summer, the sunflowers would return to keep her company, and she would be happy. He prayed, thanking the spirits and Nanatha for the gift of this life, his prayers inviting her soul to come back to earth again, to be reborn and rejoin the cycle of life.

Back inside the house, Amaoke sat at her table and slowly unraveled the tiny braid behind his left ear, twisting Nanatha's hair with that of his mother before braiding the small bundle back into his own hair. He sat there, silently, for a very long time. Finally, he stood, ageless and ancient, took up his axe, and walked out of the house, and out of the clearing, neither pausing to reflect nor looking back.

38

AMAOKE SETTLED HIS WELL-WORN messenger bag more securely onto his shoulder as he turned off of Magazine Street and followed a small footpath that divided two large yards. The path was overgrown with leafy vines that threatened to choke the entrance, and that nearly obscured it from casual passersby. It led to the side gate of a stately colonial-era home constructed of planked cedar and now painted brick red, which had wrought-iron frippery at the windows and along the fence facing the main street.

It was mostly quiet here in the western Garden District, but he could hear the homeowners' two ancient mutts. He knew they could smell him, and more particularly, the fish he had just bought for his dinner at the Whole Foods Market at Arabella Station.

On cue, when he opened the gate, they were waiting, neither in her prime, one arthritic, bowed, and slow-moving, her spotty coat and bobbing head making her appearance approximate a molting horizontal emu rather than an aged Labrador mix. Her cohort was a dark grey-bearded lady with a dreadlocked tail and severe cataracts in both eyes who frequently (yet unsurprisingly) crashed into Amaoke's legs. For all that they were nuisances, Amaoke could sympathize with the plight of old dogs; after all, he himself was one of them.

When he had first come to live in the carriage house, the homeowners had warned him that their pets were free to roam the entire property, so if he had an allergy…? It was amusing to Amaoke; no allergies to animals, he'd readily reassured them.

He had wondered at the time just how much privacy he would have from this clearly lonely middle-aged couple, but as it turned out, the humans left him alone. The pets did not.

Surprisingly, despite the fact that domestic canids usually knew what he was immediately and gave him a wide berth, these two had always been curious, swarming him coming and going and "visiting" his patio door when he cooked or ate outside. These two were clearly into bad boys.

And this bad boy typically carried food, preparing, as he did, his own fresh meals every evening. He still made his own jerky as well. So this evening, like every other, the dogs were probably more interested in the whole salmon tucked in with the other groceries in his bag than they were in him.

He made it to the carriage house unscathed, and the landlords' cat, who was sunning himself on the patio, screeched out a protest and ran off through the garden toward the main house. He was prudent enough to dislike and distrust Amaoke's scent, and his reaction was unvaried from that of any other cat Amaoke had ever known.

He and the cat had formed an uneasy truce, though. When Amaoke had first moved in, he hadn't paid attention to what his nose told him – the cat believed he owned the patch of sun at the western end of the patio. Amaoke had set up a grill at that spot initially, and the cat had started using the patio surrounds as a litter box in protest. So Amaoke, in a mixed display of submission and dominance, had moved the grill to the east end of the patio, but during the first full moon that he inhabited it, the wolf defiantly scent-marked the boundaries of the carriage house.

The cat had its sunning spot but was put in its place, and the dogs remained undeterred.

He shed the dogs at the patio door, securing the screen across the opening and stepping out of his work boots. He pulled the two small carrier bags of food out of the top of his pouch and then slid the messenger bag to the floor near the door. His tools clanked in the bottom as it settled with a small puff of road grit and stone dust.

He shed his dirty clothing, putting it directly into the open washer that stood next to the mini-fridge in the kitchenette. He deposited the groceries on the counter before heading off to the shower to rid himself of the day's grime.

Once out of the shower, he pulled on cotton chinos and returned to the kitchen, barefoot, his long damp hair cooling his skin as it draped down his back. He washed strawberries and blueberries, still missing the wonderful salmonberries of his childhood that grow best in Arctic regions, but weren't readily available to him in this country except on the West Coast. He hard-boiled two dozen eggs — his lunches for the next week. Although he liked eating them raw, they were easier to handle when boiled, and invited fewer questions and speculation from the others on his work crew.

Finally, he removed his mother's *ulu* from its pouch and fileted and quartered the salmon. It still had the walrus ivory handle, but he had replaced the blade many times over the centuries. It now boasted a ceramic blade as a matter of best preserving its many functions. He found that the *ulu* maintained its special abilities no matter its edge, but he had never well understood the phenomenon, so this fact was of no great concern.

He simply knew that the knife had defended him from the tortures of minor mischievous and ill spirits, and its power had once chased away an ugly demon familiar of the Morningstar. Over the centuries, if it was ever put aside or abandoned during times when he had been lost to the world, whether physically or spiritually, he always knew where to find it. Somehow, it would return to a small rock shelf in a cave he'd inhabited for a time, near enough to his childhood home that he presumed that the spiritual force that lived within it was tied to that place, and to him.

A Sardinian knife smith on the West Coast had replaced the steel blade that had reached the end of its useful life. He had admired the handle and suggested a ceramic replacement blade. "You won't be sorry, my friend, but you do have to be careful, it is wicked sharp, might be overkill for cutting pizza, you know?" He had given Amaoke a knowing look, and added, "Don't get in trouble with this thing, and don't forget you have it – it will get through a metal detector, but if you got caught…"

Amaoke had been confused by the pizza reference until he had seen a similar implement being used to cut a pizza when passing by one of the local storefronts where they prepared the food right in front of you. The irony was not lost on him; he appreciated such small amusements. At some point, the simple and effective design of the *ulu* knife had been put to work as a chef's tool by some enterprising individual. Fancy pizza cutter. Right.

He ate the raw pink flesh of the salmon directly off the skin and crunched into the tiny spinal bones, saving the head, his favorite, for last. He smiled; in his mother's culture, fish heads were often the food of the dead, and any good hunter was admonished to steer clear of them to avoid the misfortunes of disrupting the boundaries of the universe. He recalled her indignation when he snuck pieces of rabbit meat from her as a boy – it was another food that she believed could ruin his hunting prowess. Unfortunately, it had always been irresistible to him, and didn't appear to have adversely affected him as a hunter. To be fair, given his dual nature, he was not sure that much could.

While commercial fish still did not compare to fresh catch, Amaoke had to admit that one of his favorite modern luxuries was the ability to obtain awesomely fresh fish nearly anywhere on the North American continent. Since he had no time to fish, and no longer had any inclination to do his own fishing anyway, finding it so fresh at market was a more than acceptable substitute.

Amaoke had never gotten used to television, but he recognized the value of keeping up with current events in this, the information age. His compromise was an hour or two of NPR each evening, and occasionally as background noise during his morning preparations. In this way, he obtained basic knowledge about local and world news, popular culture, weather, and his favorites, those special-interest stories that often catered to or focused on fringe interests or oddities. Such programs made Amaoke feel slightly more mainstream, if that was even a word that could be applied to werewolves.

He especially enjoyed *The Moth Radio Hour*, and *This American Life*, despite an occasionally strong urge to bite Ira Glass. The personal insights of misfits appealed to him, for obvious reasons, and made him feel less alone in the world.

What an interesting time to live, where the population was becoming ever more diverse despite the preserved amount of divisiveness among some groups. Amaoke's name was no longer universally remarked upon as being so unusual. In fact, there was a very popular and famous movie actor named Keanu.

Even Amaoke's appearance, which had always marked him as a half-breed and which had been a source of derision, scorn, and prejudicial hatred, now garnered mostly curious glances, if even a second look was hazarded at all. In many cases, he experienced outright admiring looks from women and men, and that never failed to surprise him. The historically narrow Western standards of attractiveness had certainly broadened a great deal in the past half-century. He was no longer a half-breed, either, as the term had been softened to biracial. It was of no matter to him; words were words, and both were only labels that had never really applied to him anyway.

It had been a shock to him when he started working on the road crews how many women in passing cars would call out to him suggestively, or throw out scraps of paper with telephone numbers, or even, occasionally, their undergarments. Once, when he'd been the newest member of the crew and had gotten stuck with traffic-flagging duty, a beautiful and well-groomed young woman had bared her breasts and fondled them suggestively while he had the traffic stopped for a one-lane relay. The entire time she had maintained eye contact with him, or at least had tried, as even he with all his long years was unable to meet that frank, open gaze. The same woman had driven by the worksite every day for a week, so demonstrative in her interest in Amaoke that he was still ribbed about it by his crew.

Women wore next to nothing, from a historical perspective, at all hours of the day and night when the weather was warmer, and he was unsure how his stunted and old-fashioned courtship ideas would fare. It seemed that relationships were not all that private anymore. The values he had been taught by his mother and while living among the migrating Arctic societies were not particularly prudish regarding sexuality because these things were part of the natural order where consenting adults were concerned. But Amaoke still could not see how he would even begin to conduct such a relationship in this society. It all seemed pretty fast and informal.

Also, there was so much of himself that remained devoted utterly to Nanatha that in spite of the intervening centuries, he knew in his deepest heart that he was still a married man. Indeed, he had avoided sexual congress as man or beast since that time, probably not wanting to dilute the closeness he had shared with the only woman who had really known him. He also had a profound sense of fear that he would be betraying her memory.

These thoughts made him involuntarily reach for the tiny braid behind his left ear. He tried to remind himself about not allowing the past to wrap its arms about him too tightly, for he especially could become mired in it, which would prevent him from participating in life, now and in the future, as he was clearly meant to do. If he were not intended to be a part of this time, he would not have lived so long; such was the logic of the ancient elders' teachings.

As appealing as that young woman may have been, Amaoke had lacked some essential temptation to pursue her. There was something like dread in him in these latter days; it was as if some endpoint were approaching him more rapidly than ever before, and the Morningstar was everywhere and nowhere.

39

NEW ORLEANS WAS A PLACE charged with energy. Not only the spark of the humans who lived in and visited the city, but spiritual strength as well was heightened, Amaoke noticed. It was something his animal senses could feel and almost smell. And there were dark rituals performed here, by the Candomble priests and the voodooiennes.

There was solid religious faith, anchored mostly by the Catholic church, but certainly bolstered by the Baptists and further out, in the bayous, by Revivalists. The city hummed with spiritual power, much of it very dark.

Amaoke could feel and almost see the spirits in the moving shadows of the trees where Tchoupitoulas Street met Napoleon Avenue, and it was powerfully concentrated near the Lafayette cemetery on Prytania, but that didn't surprise him. Spirits gathered near the dead in any culture, not all of them bad. Some were probably the souls of the newly dead, some may have been conjured for some dark purpose by ritual, usually involving blood or sacrifice, and these spirits typically darkened the shadows or depressed the temperature in the air surrounding them, expending a shade-like energy that was probably depleted just to create the effect. Some were likely to be spirit guides or totems, receiving prayers or tributes, flowers mostly, he noticed in this culture, although people wrote letters and left burning candles as well. The energy of these spirits was brighter, benign, and altogether more positive, probably due to the love and respect showed them. The problem was that the balance was off; it was darker here, quieter, colder, and smelled often of fear.

There was also a concentration of this darker energy about three blocks away from the raised section of I-10, where his road crew was based—the corner of Ursulines Avenue, at Roman Street. Amaoke had been walking the neighborhood, one afternoon when he finished work, simply exploring, as he had always done. It was his habit to walk in overlapping squares on a grid, and learn the rhythms of the places he lived. How different it was than his long-ago youth, when trees, marsh plains, and mountains dominated the landscape, and there was not another human being within many days' travel. Cities such as had not been imagined were now commonplace, and New Orleans was one of the older cities on the continent, an aging, dusty Southern belle with plenty of enduring charm and beauty.

There was a Catholic church within the block, on the southwest end, St. Constantine, with a grand façade of crumbling red brick and large round stained-glass windows in the tower arch. The doors were banded oak, the legacy of some thousand-year-old tree, probably brought over from France when the city was barely rising from the swamps of Louisiana. It was a magnificent structure, in some decay, but there were very dark spirits concentrating around the church, which didn't make much sense to Amaoke. He assumed the rituals there would drive these beings away. He was drawn back to the place often, almost expecting the Morningstar to present itself, since the burnt metallic smell and ozone-like odors that permeated the area were reminiscent of the Monster. But the Morningstar never appeared.

He thought it was unusually cold in the shadow of the church, and there was more than a single presence there. Amaoke felt watched, but not by any human eye. He persisted in his habit of exploring other parts of the city, but he found himself back in front of the church often. Sometimes on weekends, he would wander into that part of town, trying to sense whether he could pick up the same nerve-jangling feeling in other parts of the neighborhood, but the other blocks were spiritually silent.

He took a chance and went there one evening in wolf form. He felt it was a balanced risk; while animal-control practices were more stringently followed than ever before, this particular neighborhood was somewhat downtrodden, so he suspected that enforcement of dog leash laws was looser in favor of other types of patrols. He had figured out how to get into a collar once in wolf form; it took several attempts, but he had adjusted it repeatedly until he could wiggle into it. Domestic dogs were used to them, he supposed, but to him, it always felt like a noose, and his instinct was to panic.

Without a collar, he was more likely to be reported and targeted by the local authorities. He had had a close call some years prior when, lost in Los Angeles, hungry and down on his luck, he had decided to check the dumpsters in an alley for discarded food. One was promising, smelling of the remains of several sumptuous dinners, but on closer inspection, the food was splattered about and not easily gathered by hand. Amaoke, the man, could be fastidious about how his food was presented, but the wolf was too hungry and worn-out to care. So he had changed, jumped into the dumpster, and licked all he could from the side of the container that had captured most of the splatter. He had crawled out, too tired to do much more than curl up between the dumpsters and fall into an exhausted sleep. So tired was he that his nose hadn't even alerted him to the presence of others. He had been awakened with the animal control officer's loop around his neck, and he was so undernourished and weak that when faced with a team of animal-control officers rather than a single person, he had been unable to avoid capture. He tried not to use his preternatural powers to harm humans unless he was in some mortal danger or was trying to protect someone, and the precious control he had gained over his wolf instincts over the centuries was worth preserving.

Amaoke had spent several days in quarantine at the local humane society, listening to the whispers about stupid rich people and their exotic pets, didn't they know a wolf was a wild animal?

Because of course, they knew he was a wolf; in Los Angeles, people make pets of all kinds of animals, the wilder, the better. The veterinarians there practically had to be zookeepers. His escape was unnecessarily complicated and painful, and he vowed to avoid such difficulties in the future.

He tried to wander aimlessly but in a consistent direction, pretending to be distracted by smells, with his head down, behaving like any domesticated animal would act. Most people didn't look closely enough to notice that he was actually a wolf, because in a neighborhood where they expected to see a dog, most of the time they would see just that, a large white dog, and they would assume it was a Siberian husky or a malamute. Arriving there in wolf form would actually attract less attention than walking there as a man and trying to remain unobtrusive while making the change.

Luck was on his side apparently, because the abandoned building across the street had a ground-level fire escape that led up to the roof, and which was really more like a staircase than a ladder, allowing him to climb it handily on four legs. At three stories high, it gave an excellent view of the church entrance on the street side. It was a better vantage point than he had expected, and he settled down to watch and wait.

The lights were on inside the sanctuary because an early evening mass was being given. Amaoke could pick up parts of a long monologue, presumably the priest's homily, and some occasional organ music and group singing. He could smell incense, beeswax candles, some decaying flowers, dust and paper, and the commingled smells of less than a hundred humans. Still predominant were the aromas of burnt metal and sulfur. And the deepening shadows seemed alive with energy, the source of which he again couldn't place. The hairs on his ruff stood on end as if electrified. There was no wind, but it felt as if several hands were stroking his fur, and he suppressed a whine because the sensation brought with it the smells of fear and death.

He lay down next to the brick ledge at the front of the building and tried to calm himself. He stayed crouched low until he heard the last of the parishioners making their way home, and then dared to stand up. There were a few remaining stragglers at the front door of the church, the light from within spilling out onto the sidewalk but still not seeming to touch the shadows. These few finally dispersed, but the door to the outside remained open.

After several minutes, an elderly woman emerged, either the organist or a parishioner who had stayed for confession following the mass. She made her way slowly to an ancient gold Buick, got into it, and a full five minutes later, the car pulled tentatively away from the curb, as if reluctant to join the nonexistent traffic. The glow from her red brake lights had just dimmed as she turned west at the next block, and then the really interesting events occurred.

The priest emerged from the doors of the church, holding a broom in his hands. He was startlingly young, likely fresh from seminary, surprisingly tall and muscular, with unusually long dark hair that reached his shoulders in waves and extremely thick glasses with black frames that were so old-fashioned it made the man seem as if he were from another era. He wore traditional if old-fashioned priestly garb, a black cassock with multiple buttons that was fitted to his upper torso and flared out like a gown and flowed from his hips down to his feet. His white collar seemed to glow in the gathering dusk, and he wore an elaborate silver cross on a chain that hung from his waist. It looked brutally heavy, and it made Amaoke think of a weapon.

Amaoke could not really make out any details of the priest's face, as the man had his back to the light coming from the church doors, and he ultimately turned his face to the ground as he swept the steps and sidewalk with brisk, economical motions. As he moved, the shadows around him began to move, and Amaoke could see vague shapes of darkness on darkness. A deep shadow at the peak of the steeple began to creep downward, past the stained-glass rounds, until it perched just above the doors. It appeared to reach out to the priest, and to the other shadows, but the man paid no heed to what was happening around him; he just kept on with his task.

Amaoke could smell no fear coming from the priest, but the bitter metallic smell was much stronger, and Amaoke identified the priest as the source of it, which was also interesting. And once again the shadows were moving, this time slowly crossing the street, and Amaoke realized too late that their inexorable approach was going to give him away because he could see that the rhythmic, calm sweeping was part of the act, and the priest was about to look right up and see him watching over the ledge.

Amaoke ducked down again, quickly, but had the strangest feeling that the priest was looking up at the roof, and seeing him despite the brick ledge that concealed him. All at once, as in a terrible wind, his fur was pushed and pulled around as if by a thousand insistent hands, and the shadows were upon him, but they had no substance, and he could not close his mouth on them or shake them off. The scent of fear and rotting flesh saturated his nose, and he let out a low whine, because it was too much like before, too much like the pit, and the other Beast was threatening to emerge, and he was running to the fire escape at the opposite corner of the roof, running headlong into a plumbing vent in his attempts to shake the demons. He finally got there and down to the ground, and he ran and ran, away from the church, not looking back, until he arrived in the Garden District and could not remember when the spirits had left him.

40

LISTENING TO NPR ONE EVENING in late spring, Amaoke came across another program about outcasts, and this time he was drawn in when he heard the word *werewolf.* Apparently, a local psychiatrist, Dr. Madison, was a specialist in rare disorders of psychosis. One of these disorders was apparently called lycanthropy, which dealt specifically with patients who exhibited wolf-like behaviors, for all intents and purposes, werewolf-ism on a spectrum, from wild behavior to biting to homicidal ideation of a predatory nature.

The public-radio journalist was appropriately skeptical, as anyone would expect, but Dr. Madison was very convincing in her articulation of the data she had gathered from her unique subgroup of patients, and admitted that she was not dealing with actual old-world monsters, but rather men who believed that they turned into beasts and could not control their behavior. Some of them had mild manifestations, and some were criminally insane, having committed heinous crimes. Listening to her, Amaoke realized that she believed in what she was describing, and had studied the issue extensively, even if he was too distracted to hold on to many of the finer details. The most disturbing thing she said came at the end of the interview when she told the journalist that this particular patient population was growing, rapidly becoming the focus of her practice.

Amaoke lost sleep over the program for three days, wondering what Dr. Madison's final observation might mean. Were there others, like himself, out in the world, only now coming to the attention of medical experts and law-enforcement authorities? Was this the work of the Morningstar? He felt he had a responsibility to get some answers to such questions, and he had to admit, a part of him wanted to know how Dr. Madison was treating these patients. He knew there was no cure for his condition, but he wondered not just what the extent of her knowledge might be, but what the extent of her *understanding* might become if there were true beasts among them.

That evening, when he returned from work, he went up to his landlords' home, escorted, as always, by the dogs. He used the trip to both pay his rent and inquire whether they had a telephone book that he could borrow. While this resulted in a brief look of confusion from his landlady (probably because she assumed he was a "Millennial" and therefore would get any and all necessary information, worthless or valuable, from a smartphone – which he didn't have), without another word, she and her husband cast about for it for the next several minutes, finding one that was relatively recent, only the better part of two years old. This let Amaoke know that the two of them were probably pretty reliant on the internet for information as well, as the book appeared to have been stowed away by habit, unused.

"You're in luck," the husband exclaimed, bringing it over to Amaoke with a smile. "I suspect they will stop printing these altogether any day now."

"May I take it with me?" Amaoke asked, politely adding, "I will return it in the morning."

"Of course, you can take it, dear, no rush to return it." The wife smiled at his earnestness. She touched his arm, briefly, seemingly for no reason at all, perhaps only to make a connection. Amaoke wondered, not for the first time, if they had ever had children. They had done some traveling while he lived on the property, and he had fed their pets and collected their mail, but they didn't have many visitors. They would be about the right age to be his parents if he had been a twenty-something human, and he sensed their loneliness when in their company.

Amaoke looked up the clinic with which Dr. Madison was affiliated, and the following afternoon, when his workday ended, he traveled into New Orleans to locate the clinic address, which was part of a complex of buildings at Galvez and Canal, on the campus of the University Medical Center New Orleans. The outpatient mental health center was one of several small charming outbuildings that stood apart from one another on beautifully manicured lawns, which did not look anything like a medical facility, which Amaoke suspected was the point.

A severe-looking older receptionist assisted him in making an appointment, which required the production of a surprising amount of identification and supplementary paperwork. Such processes had long since lost any of the intimidation they had once presented for Amaoke; he had been smart about obtaining and building a verifiable human identity over the past several decades.

In the 1950s, when he had first learned that the United States was going to grant statehood to the arctic region of Alaska, he had traveled back to his childhood home, back in time, to the spot where he had lived on the banks of the Kuskokwim River with his mother all those centuries ago.

He reconstructed a sod house near the site where they had lived, and smiled at the natural signs around him that told him that the path of the river had changed many times over the last thousand years. The reclining maiden was also gone, the victim of a change in the river's flow or a flash flood; the entire stand of trees that he remembered from his long-ago childhood was much changed. He could also tell that the area had become far more populous; in his wanderings along the river, there was a significant increase in the evidence of temporary fish camps and permanent settlements. He had much nearer neighbors, although he rarely saw another human being. He set up a semi-permanent hunting camp there and lived much as he had as a child, off the land, netting fish, gathering plants and berries, and trapping for meat and furs.

The wolf hunted for larger game, and a stroke of luck just after the first hard freeze had brought him an aging caribou and its mate, weakened by hunger. Amaoke was meticulous in his prayer rituals, thanking the animals for their sacrifice and their great gift. He dried the meat that he was unable to cook over the fire that first meal, and knew he would have enough protein to survive the winter, even if times got very lean. He tried to avoid going hungry, as that threatened what precious control he had over the beast.

He settled back into the rhythms of Arctic life and prepared himself for the drastic changes in the weather. In February, it was probably ninety degrees below zero (or worse) with the wind and snow roaring down from the mountains, and he only went out in wolf form, and sometimes stayed inside in wolf form because it was the best way to keep warm enough to sleep. In contrast, there were several days in July that topped seventy degrees, which helped with hunting, and meant that there would be more berries to harvest in late fall.

The berries were a double bounty that year. As there were too many to pick at summer's end and in the fall, Amaoke enjoyed the ones that had been preserved by the cold over the winter, gathering them at the first break from the freeze that following spring.

And he waited for the inevitable visitors that he knew would come. Change and time would bring them. He waited several years before they arrived, and he recognized them for what they were — surveyors from the United States government. There were three men, one obviously uncomfortable, giving himself away as the government agent, which his whiteness would have predicted anyway, and two translators, one of mixed Russian and Inuit descent, and one of *Yup'Ik* heritage.

As he had known it would, the new state of Alaska was taking stock of its citizens, categorizing them, cataloguing the numbers of various tribespersons, and providing them with the necessary documents with which to prove their identities. Amaoke had self-identified as a Russian-*Yup'Ik* half-breed, which was what most of the modern locals assumed he was, and which was convincing since he could speak both the Central *Yup'Ik* and Russian languages. He provided them his given name, adding the surname of Severnoj because it secretly amused him. The other individual of mixed race also understood Russian, of course, and looked puzzled, because the word meant *north*, making his name roughly mean wolf-of-the-north.

But it was then a simple process to obtain formal identification; the men gave him some official-looking papers which identified his place of dwelling and his assigned name, and he was expected to present himself at Bethel where he could formally obtain vital records through a mail program with Anchorage, such as an estimated birth certificate and state identification once he was photographed. He was also counted among the many Alaskans whose indigenous group affiliations were recorded. They told him that he was expected to complete the process as soon as possible, as he was now a citizen of the United States, congratulations, etc.

Citizenship was a formality; it was much more vital for Amaoke to have a verifiable identity. It had been increasingly difficult to obtain employment without some form of vital record, and he expected it would become compulsory in the future. He had also lost much of his money from banks in areas that he had needed to abandon for long periods of time, and with proof of identity, he hoped he would have recourse for recovery of deposited funds in the future, provided he could figure out a way to deal with the persistent problem of his lack of aging. He had enjoyed centuries of anonymity, and it had its benefits for one such as him, but the world was changing rapidly, and he felt it would be irresponsible to ignore those changes that could so negatively affect him. His mother's people had instructed their children to pay attention to the world around them, noting changes and learning what those changes might mean for the future, and Amaoke intended to continue the practice of mindful participation in the world, even though bureaucrats from the new government were probably not as cognizant of the effects of their interventions on the local indigenous population.

Using the original paperwork he had been given from the state of Alaska, he had been able to obtain identification in the other places he had since lived. With very minor occasional forgeries to his birth year on that first-issued birth certificate, he was able to appear a rightful age according to the document. He had a social security number and had even obtained his first passport after September 11, 2001, unsure how he was going to keep renewing it if his picture didn't reveal any aging, but he relegated that concern to the future.

Thus he was ultimately able to give the medical receptionist all the verification she needed to register him as a patient. Then came endless additional questions from a medical assistant, who took him into a private room to do an intake questionnaire. Most of the questions did not really apply to him, but he answered them as best he could, trying to remain as honest as possible. No, he had no specific referral from another physician; he was self-referred. Although the question made him squirm a bit, he denied ever having been the victim of abuse. No, he had no suicidal ideation, and no active homicidal ideation (mostly true). Yes, he did have a firm belief he was a werewolf. No, he could not be more specific; he was very eager to discuss his problems with Dr. Madison, and he left it at that. He was counseled that medical insurance did not always cover this type of care, and that he could be responsible for all or part of his medical bill.

Amaoke realized that this screening was meant to weed out individual patients who were not a fit for the profile of the practice, and probably to flush out the more dangerous of them, in an effort to protect the doctor, and determine which patients would be better served in the hospital psychiatric ward. He wasn't sure he had passed the test, but at the end of the intake procedure, he was left in the waiting room. After several minutes had passed, the original receptionist called him back up to the desk and gave him an appointment at the end of July, nearly three months away. She told him it was a standard scheduling delay for new patients, as Dr. Madison had a very busy practice.

So Amaoke put that investigation on hold for the present and tried to decide what to do about St. Constantine and its unusual priest, with his demon familiars.

41

AMAOKE MAINTAINED A LESS-THAN-discreet surveillance on the church, but not much was happening there. He always approached in human form, and had been bold enough to enter the church on several occasions, but the sour scent of metal and sulfur he had noticed on prior visits was lessened the first few times he came, and gone entirely after a few weeks.

He avoided times when the Mass was spoken, preferring to come when the place was nearly empty. The mysterious priest was not present, and Amaoke suspected that was the reason that his scent had disappeared.

There was another priest performing Mass, and Amaoke saw him taking confessions at different times during the week, but this one was middle-aged and rotund, and he smelled only of wine and ivory soap beneath the incense that clung to his surplice. The shadows were darkest in the nave, but none of them were moving, and most of the dark spirit energy Amaoke had sensed was gone.

One evening, after Mass, he entered the nave and discovered the aged organist waiting there. She must have been waiting for a ride home, as he had not noticed the old Buick on the street. She seemed sad, and said to him, "You missed it, the Mass ended about twenty minutes ago."

"Oh," Amaoke responded, acting bewildered. "I can't seem to get the schedule right."

"It's been hit or miss these days," she told him. "Father James is splitting his time here with his duties at St. Cyril's, and the Masses have been cut back significantly. I think the church still publishes the available times on its website. The confession schedule is there, too. And they post the times on the bulletin there." She pointed to a spot just inside the doors.

Amaoke wandered over to look at the schedule. No daily Masses, only a handful of random Mass celebrations during the week; the only consistent celebration was a single Sunday Mass at 8:30 in the morning. Likewise, there were precious few time slots for confession. "This doesn't seem like much," he observed, wondering if she would give him any more information.

"There are rumors that this parish is going to be suppressed by the bishop," she whispered, although Amaoke's ears and nose confirmed that there was no one in hearing distance. He could hear Father James moving about in the rectory, but they were otherwise alone.

"Suppressed?" Amaoke asked, unsure what it meant. He assumed that his appearance told the woman that he was probably not traditionally Catholic, and hoped she would explain.

"It is the way the Church closes the doors of a parish that is failing," she told him, unable to hold back the single tear that ran from one eye. She sighed. "If that happens, our congregation could be accepted into another parish, and all of the church belongings could transfer there, and this church could close. The Church could even decide to reduce the church to profane use –" She stopped talking because Amaoke jumped when she spoke that term.

"Profane?" Amaoke prompted, holding his breath.

"It simply means that the church building can be sold and used for non-religious purposes," she clarified, eyeing him warily.

Amaoke tried to act as if his inquiries were casual. "But why is the church failing?"

"Because our parish priest, Father Weston, is called away a lot. He is doing some vital work for the Vatican," she replied, looking down at her feet. "Without him, the church has declined. He is very popular with the congregation, and many of our parishioners prefer coming to confession with him as our confessor. He has quite the way about him, and he loves St. Constantine. He is also a local boy, which is unusual among our other priests. He grew up here, and he understands us," she told Amaoke. "The church comes alive when he is here, which is less and less often these days," she lamented.

Then the ancient gold Buick pulled up to the curb, and she said, "My ride is here. Will you be all right? I can get Father James, if you like."

But Amaoke shook his head and smiled at her a little, and even though he could see she was a bit startled by his teeth, she placed a gnarled hand on his arm and gave him a little pat. "Thank you, young man, for listening to this old lady."

Amaoke put his hand briefly over her own, and to her surprise, helped her out to the waiting car, giving her a hand into the passenger seat, its low-slung positioning, and her arthritis obviously created challenges for her. The young woman in the driver's seat smiled at him before helping the woman, who was probably her grandmother, fasten her seatbelt. He closed the door gently, and the car pulled away, leaving him alone on the curb.

He turned to look up at the church behind him, the gathering gloom darkening the shadows, but he felt no significant energy, and the darkness was still. He stood there for some time, until the lights went out in the sanctuary, and then started the long walk home.

His canine escorts were asleep in the house when he arrived, and a lonely quarter moon was about to set. He took his time in the shower, letting the hot water warm the chill he felt in his bones.

What interest did the Vatican have in a young Louisiana priest that was so important it threatened the viability of his parish? What made the young man so popular with parishioners who couldn't have known him more than a couple of years, since it appeared he was newly ordained? And the older woman's statement about how *alive* the church seemed when Father Weston was in residence — wasn't that detail in keeping with the energy that Amaoke had observed congregating around the church in his initial wanderings? Was it likely that humans, who now mostly ignored any residual animal instincts they had once relied on, could actually sense those spirits and had attributed that energy to their charismatic priest?

He puzzled over these answerless questions until the cold water made him yelp in surprise. He toweled off and pulled on cotton pants and a thermal top, marveling at the incredible softness of modern clothing, as comfortable as his old buckskins and available in an abundance that had once been unthinkable. Even the denim in the blue jeans he used for work was not the stiff, thick construct that it had been a century before, when it could take years to break in a pair of pants to satisfactory softness. These had been irresistibly comfortable from the time he brought them home and put them on, as though they had already been washed and worn a thousand times before. It amused him that some young people had brought into fashion the wearing of the tattered rags of blue jeans that appeared to have been destroyed in some war; the garment could be bought in such a condition for exorbitant prices in the downtown boutiques.

He finally retired to his bed, fearing that sleep would elude him once again. He drifted down into nothingness, but not before the thought occurred to him that all of these strange happenings had to have something to do with the Morningstar.

42

SUMMERS WERE HOT AND HUMID in Louisiana, and the highway construction project saw multiple days with approved overtime hours for Amaoke's work crew. Everyone on the full-time team was performing critical tasks while the weather held, since part-time summer help from college and high-school students provided ample traffic-flow workers and flaggers. As he always had, Amaoke volunteered for weekend and evening overtime; he had learned to concentrate his work hours in such a way that when the full moon approached, his absences were expected and did not affect his employment.

Since he lacked the inclination to be out in the heat with an Arctic winter coat and could mostly control the change except on the nights nearest the full moon, he walked the streets, circling back to St. Constantine to search for any new developments or signs of Father Weston's return. He sat through Mass one day, not really listening to Father Peter's words but using it as an excuse to wander around the sanctuary after the ritual, to pick up scents and explore the small chapels that surrounded the main worship space. Nothing exceptional appeared to be happening, but he did enjoy the old organist's music. The instrument was larger than he had expected, and sitting among the scattered parishioners in the pews, he could feel the transmitted vibrations in his breastbone.

He wandered the streets of the French Quarter after dark, and as he was crossing Jackson Square one evening, he glimpsed a familiar figure sitting alone among the tourists at the Café du Monde. Wearing an expensively cut three-piece suit with a matching shirt, silk tie, and pocket square in a shade of burgundy that would have looked ridiculous on anyone else, the Morningstar appeared in human form, sitting gracefully among the pureflesh with a newspaper balanced on one knee, and a cup of black coffee at hand. It could not mask enough of its appearance to fool Amaoke, so its eyes were the eyes of a wild animal, shiny, metallic, reflecting redly under the lights, even though to the humans nearby, they probably looked perfectly normal. It seemed just eccentric enough to be a local Southern gentleman, its wavy hair fashionably cut, its manner urbane. It called to mind the deadly spider sitting in the center of a web, surrounded by the hapless insects on which it was about to feed.

As it often disappeared once he identified it, allowing its sighting to be an omen of future events, Amaoke knew that its persistent presence and deceptively casual demeanor meant that he was supposed to find it here and that it wanted something. He jaywalked across Decatur Street on the diagonal and weaved through the outer tables to where it was sitting.

"*Firstborn, wolf-born, child of moon,*" it began, then paused, as if reflecting. "Speaking of the moon, isn't it awfully close to the full moon for you to be about?" it asked, looking around at the pureflesh seated nearby and deliberately putting out a grotesquely long tongue to lick a sharp-nailed finger and turn a page of the paper. "It would be a shame to lose control here," it added, sounding bored. The scent of the chicory coffee in combination with its carrion breath was almost too much to bear, and the fact that it spoke in a conversational Southern drawl rather than the usual ancient cacophony added to Amaoke's distress. The drawl was still composed of several different voices of varying pitch and tone, setting his hair on end. "Do sit down; certainly we have much to discuss with you."

The Morningstar always referred to itself in the plural; it was part of the theatrics it regularly employed as a show of power and to encourage confusion, as if its power could not solely be concentrated within the habitus of this single being. Amaoke suspected that it was a singular being, but there were always powerful dark spirits about when it traveled abroad, probably to be called upon as it saw fit. And Amaoke knew better than to believe that the Morningstar needed any of them to be awesomely destructive; alone, he knew, it could lay waste to civilization. But these minions hung about to be deployed as distractions, supporting and creating superstition, fear, and chaos. Some of them had engineered his own centuries of torture at this Monster's bidding, and while he was better able to master it, his fear at what he knew he had done on their behalf had a life of its own.

But this was playing into the Morningstar's hands. It wanted him to realize that it could unleash the Beast on this unsuspecting crowd of goth teenagers and newlyweds, and it would sit right there in that suit and sip its coffee in the center of the bloody rampage. His power to resist such a loss of control was considerably more reliable than it had been in his earliest years, but he did not have any delusions that he could ultimately prevent the worst. It was more important to sit here, knowing that the Morningstar knew about his fear, and could see that Amaoke was conquering it.

He refused to ask it what it wanted, and after a few minutes of silence, it sighed, as though put upon, and bared its long, needle-like teeth. "We're here because of you. Thinking of us, assigning blame, curious – are you ready to join us? All the answers you think you can obtain by sniffing about will gladly be provided. You can't keep up this endless quest and look for a way out of your predicament if you do not know what the true nature of that predicament is."

"Tell me why your demons have taken up residence at St. Constantine," Amaoke responded, finally taking the offered chair and turning it around, straddling it because he knew it would annoy the

Morningstar, who hated the idiosyncrasies of humans almost as much as it hated the humans themselves.

"Not specific enough," it replied, turning another page of the paper and finishing its coffee in a single gulp. It waited for Amaoke to contemplate its answer while fussing with the cuff on its left pant leg, the only outward sign that Amaoke's behavior was annoying it.

"Who, exactly, is Father Weston?" Amaoke responded, suddenly confident that this query was at the heart of the Morningstar's audience with him. It tried to remain nonchalant, but something flashed in the depths of those inhuman eyes, and Amaoke knew the priest was the key to what was happening at St. Constantine and whatever was causing the spiritual disturbance he had felt.

"Aahhh, yes, the *good* Father Weston," the Morningstar sneered, emphasizing his word choice carefully. "We think you would find that you have a lot in common with Father Weston."

"Who is he?" Amaoke was more insistent this time, uninterested in engaging in its games.

"A lost soul who believes he is saved, just like every other wretched person on this planet," the Morningstar explained. "He, like you, fails to realize that his power lies in embracing the beast, in accepting the dark place from which his special abilities are forged and setting himself apart from others. He is, by far, the most gifted of all of you. Now that we think on it, he probably would have a very dim view of you and your particular abilities, so best not get you together to compare notes, hmmm?"

The Morningstar started to say more, but its attention suddenly shifted to the sidewalk just beyond the awning of the café. A voluptuous young woman in a scrap of an evening dress wobbled toward them on impossibly high heels, her focus entirely upon the Morningstar. As she approached, not a single eye was not upon her, as her dress barely covered large, perfectly rounded breasts and skimmed the very top of her thighs, nominally covering what were sure to be attractive assets. Her face was flawlessly sculpted, with full lips and wide-set brown eyes. Her blonde hair was fashionably cut short and lay in wisps against her cheekbones.

Amaoke could smell her unbridled lust, and something else, an acrid odor that he could not place, and decay, like the scent of dying roses, coming from her skin. The Morningstar stood to greet her, and she pressed the length of her body up against it, and Amaoke watched with horror as it kissed her, exploring her mouth with that long tongue and catching her bottom lip in those sharp teeth. He watched her lips slacken and turn grayish, deathlike, but when the kiss ended, her mouth appeared full and pink, the picture of health, and he wondered if it were the Morningstar playing tricks on his mind.

The Morningstar resumed its seat, and she quickly sat upon its lap, crossing her legs, but not before Amaoke and half the patrons in the café could see the thin red lace between her thighs that failed to conceal her sex. Amaoke was plagued by lust that came on him from nowhere, and with it his own disgust that he could not resist such feelings, and that this was yet another of the Morningstar's petty tortures.

The woman appeared to be writhing with desire, as the Morningstar stroked her hips, and when she turned her gaze to Amaoke, it was the blasted, dead look of a burned-out addict, damned, derelict, lost. And then the Morningstar's voice, again that head-splitting cacophony of a thousand screaming voices in some lost demonic language, saying to him, "You might like Agape, she is truly insatiable."

And then she was reaching out to Amaoke, stroking his face, and though his skin burned where she touched him, he shook with lust, smelling her readiness, and the Beast was too close, too close for this bright place. Amaoke stood up so quickly that he knocked over the chair he'd been sitting on and backed out of the café, noticing that several patrons were staring and pointing at him, whispering to each other, because the table he had been sitting at was empty, save for an upset cup of chicory coffee that was dripping onto the pavement. He realized that the only performance that any of them would remember had been his, even though he could still hear the laughter of the Morningstar inside his head, hissing that single word over and over, *insatiable.*

He made it to the carriage house before he doubled over with the change, and he forced himself to remain inside, lying next to the window beneath the air conditioning unit, shivering in spite of the fire raging inside him. He remained there for two days, shaking and ill, imagining himself mounting her, having her, ripping her flesh from her bones and dining on it, delirious with such visions, his mouth watering uncontrollably, until the full moon set, and he could mercifully dispatch the wolf once more. He checked himself over carefully and had no evidence of destruction under his nails or in his teeth. He crawled into the shower on all fours and washed away tears of relief that he had maintained his control, and tears of grief that he could still be manipulated.

When he passed the newsstand near the streetcar stop on St. Charles at Third Street on his way to work the next morning, he saw the headline *Popular Exotic Dancer Latest to Succumb to Heroin Overdose,* and the photograph was unmistakable. Agape had never had a chance.

43

AFTER A FEW DAYS, WHEN the horror had subsided somewhat, Amaoke contemplated one of the Morningstar's cryptic statements until it made his head hurt. It had told Amaoke that the priest was the most gifted *of all of you*…and he couldn't make sense of the statement without having to believe that he was not a lone creature fashioned by the Morningstar to deliver on some diabolical plan. Was the priest like him? Were there really others? The Morningstar was a deceiver, but Amaoke knew that it couldn't always keep him away from what was real. He was even more curious to learn what Dr. Madison could tell him, if anything, but that appointment was still weeks away.

The only other place he could search for answers was back at St. Constantine. Expecting to be frustrated yet again, he wandered by after work the next chance he got, coming up to the church at dusk when Mass was ending. The spirits were back in force, and the damp, metallic, rotten smell that he associated with the Morningstar, and now Father Weston, was present once more.

He stepped into the nave and consulted the schedule, which was more developed than it had been the last time he had been there. It appeared that Father Weston was back for at least the next several weeks. Several parishioners passed him on their way outside, some glancing at him with curiosity. He supposed his orange highway vest and dusty appearance were unexpected, and he probably didn't smell very good after a day spreading tar and sweating away under the hot sun.

The day's entries on the schedule included time for confession following the Mass, and it appeared that there were several people who had remained following the service to give it. Amaoke was curious, so he waited in the last pew and observed the ritual carefully. One person would leave the curtained enclosure, and after several seconds, someone else would go in. Some people were in there for quite a while; others took only minutes. He waited almost two hours until the last remaining person entered the confessional. It was long after the time set aside on the schedule for confession; he suspected the priest planned to stay until he had heard the last of them.

While he was making this observation, the final parishioner left the enclosure, and his footfalls were loud in the empty sanctuary. Amaoke waited a few seconds, contemplating what would happen when the priest emerged. He got up quickly and crossed the worship space, his own footsteps in his heavy work boots louder than any of the faithful's. After a moment's hesitation, he entered the confessional, pulling the curtain behind him.

In the small space, the bitter metallic odor was strong again, and it mingled with the integral scents of the church. He smelled old wood, the beeswax of the hundreds of candles, both burning and dormant, as the smells were different, and incense that had impregnated every soft surface in the building. But there was another smell, and it was familiar, but Amaoke could not immediately identify why he knew it. The scent was definitely male, and so subtle that it was too quickly eclipsed by the stronger scents of metal and blood, making it impossible for him to pinpoint it further. He decided that the smell was likely part of Father Weston's full scent signature, inappreciable until Amaoke was in close proximity to him.

Also unusual was the absolute silence that presided over the spot. Amaoke sensed no spirit activity here; in fact, if he thought about it, the spirit activity he felt outside the church had ceased when he entered the sanctuary.

There was a delicate mesh screen between the compartments, and the dark partition was suddenly pulled back, and the scent of the priest momentarily strengthened. Amaoke could just make out his profile, but his wavy hair and the outline of his spectacles along with the shadows here obscured the details of his face. The priest's breathing was measured and even, almost meditative, and he seemed to be waiting. Amaoke realized there was something he was supposed to do to initiate this ritual, but, not being familiar with the fine details of Christianity, he had no idea what it was.

"May I help you, my child?" Father Weston finally asked, his voice deep and rich, and again familiar in a way that Amaoke couldn't place, and he felt he could hear in that voice that the man was inherently kind. The tone conveyed a sense that the priest cared deeply about what a person was about to say to him. Just those few words seemed to work a little magic on Amaoke, and he immediately understood why the parishioners at St. Constantine were so fond of this man.

"I'm not Catholic, Father," Amaoke said, though whether it was an admission or an explanation he did not know. He was feeling a bit guilty about being there, especially knowing what he suspected about this man, and he hadn't expected to find goodness. He hadn't expected to find someone he could like.

"What is important is what is in your heart, my son —" Father Weston replied, but stopped himself before continuing. Amaoke waited, his senses sharpening as his nose told him that the priest was in some distress, and there was a new scent of fear, but his other feelings told him it was unaccompanied by some of the other hallmarks of anxiety, like a rapid heartbeat and heavy breathing.

Instead, curiously, Father Weston was still breathing calmly, and deeply, so profoundly that Amaoke realized that the priest was breathing this way to pick up a scent, and he was considering the information his nose had given him. Something in Amaoke's scent was frightening the other man. Then a new scent reached Amaoke's nose – male aggression. He stood abruptly, pulling the curtain and leaving the confessional in haste, pulling his messenger bag tight against his side as he strode quickly toward the doors. He heard the priest step out into the sanctuary, but Amaoke did not look back, and Father Weston neither spoke to nor pursued him.

When Amaoke reached the nave, he crossed it in two steps, suddenly desperate to be free of the place, but the doors did not open when he first attempted to get out. It was as if a strong wind had come up outdoors and was making it more challenging to move them on their hinges. He put his shoulder to the door and had to use considerable force to get it to move, but once he got it open, he realized that it wasn't the wind that was impeding him. The spirit energy had reached a crescendo and had concentrated at the entrance to the church. The force of that energy blasted Amaoke as he stepped onto the sidewalk.

He was jostled as if he moved through a large crowd, and then the legion of voices, whispering and hissing to him, that one word, the same word, a new torment, *insatiable…insatiable.* It was the mischief of beings that were of one mind with the Morningstar, and had probably had a role in Agape's downfall.

He tried to pay attention this time, decided not to panic, and he noticed that he had to travel less than two blocks before the assault ended. He crossed the street and turned around at the far corner to look back, watching the shadows retreat and settle in corners and recesses near the church. Father Weston stood outside the doors, the skirts of his cassock moving in response to the disturbances created by the spirits, face still in shadow, clutching the heavy silver cross in his left hand. His posture was that of a prizefighter, not a priest, and Amaoke finally turned his back on it all, because he had no quarrel with Father Weston as yet, and he began to make his way home.

44

AS HE NEARED THE STARBUCKS on Magazine Street, he saw the familiar figure of the Monster once more, under the dim lights just beyond the seats in the windows facing Washington Street. The Morningstar's suit was an emerald green, a near duplicate of the burgundy one, but instead of a pocket square and a tie, it wore an emerald lapel pin and had casually undone the top buttons of its shirt. Its appearance was so pristine, at that moment, it was the very antithesis of Amaoke's, with his dusty braid, filthy clothes, and spattered work boots.

It was entertaining another young woman, this one expensively groomed and wearing a sleeveless summer tweed dress with a fur collar despite the outdoor temperature, which was still in the nineties. Her dark hair was pulled back into a fashionable chignon that was so severely tight that it made her appear much older than she was. She was laughing at something the Monster was saying, and her crimson lipstick had stained the paper cup on the table in front of her, the exact shade of fresh blood.

The Morningstar turned those shining eyes toward Amaoke, giving a small shake of its head and a dismissive gesture, signaling that he should stay away. Amaoke was suddenly angry. That such a being should disdain him should have made him thankful, and although he knew some of the anger was manufactured by its presence alone, he stepped off the curb to cross the street and go into the café. It was not lost on him that there had to be some meaning to the fact that now the Morningstar was just casually hanging around the neighborhood, and besides, he still wanted answers. He suspected it was here waiting for him, that it knew about his previous encounter with Father Weston, that it desired to take his measure and learn whether there had been any confrontation.

But that wasn't right, was it? The Morningstar would know precisely what had happened, as it had likely engineered the drama as Amaoke left the church. Its diabolical powers brought information unbidden, Amaoke knew.

But when he reached the glass doors, they were locked. It was then that he noticed it was well past closing time, and even though the Monster had a table, there were no other patrons about, and not even a lonely barista remained to finish his or her chores. The Morningstar looked over at him, and shrugged, as if to say, *what can you do?* Then it and the woman shared a laugh as she looked pointedly at her watch. And then, they ignored him altogether and resumed whatever private discussion they had been having.

Amaoke banged both fists on the glass in frustration, and the booming sound startled the woman, who jerked her head up and turned to look. And Amaoke knew those piercing grey eyes, that beautiful face; even though the hairstyle was wrong, the clothes were wrong, the time was wrong, and she was long gone, he could recognize his own wife. He was seeing her again for the first time, but she was not seeing him, as these eyes did not know him, and he could hear her heartbeat accelerating, and smell her fear from where he stood, a natural response to his anger, but not the response of his Nanatha.

And that thing, smiling as it placed its hand on her arm as if to reassure her, and Amaoke could no longer feel the ground beneath his feet, because he was falling, changing, the wolf emerging unbidden, and he was all too aware of the traffic cameras at the intersection, and the howl of the legions in Morningstar's laughter. Barely holding on to his control, he looked again, willing her to see him, but it was too late when he realized that the woman was not Nanatha, merely the Morningstar's trickery, finding a susceptibility with which to manipulate his mind. But it was too late for him to stop the imminent change, and as a growl rose up from his throat, he ran away, deeper into the Garden District, but not before he noticed the cassocked figure that had been watching from the shadows across the street.

. . .

He was awakened by a cold, wet tongue on his face, naked under the magnolia tree in the corner of the yard. He looked around, confused for a moment, but he recognized that the dogs were just dogs and thankfully were not his landlords. "Hey, no tongue kissing until we know each other better," Amaoke said, and both tails wagged enthusiastically. Grateful for the doggy alarm clock, he made his way quickly to the carriage house and let himself in through the patio doors as the first rays of morning sunshine pierced through the trees.

He showered away the previous twenty-four hours, feeling as though he was washing away years of filth, grateful that there was no evidence of any predatory activities. Possibly he imagined it, but the Morningstar's stench was still in his nose, and he could not seem to shake it. His stomach rebelled at the thought of breakfast, and he wondered what he had done during those lost hours. It had been a long time since he had lost control and wandered mindlessly as the wolf.

He searched the yard, but his messenger bag was nowhere to be found. He retraced the route he would have taken as a man back to Magazine Street, knowing that in wolf form, his path back to the house was likely to have been much more circuitous. It was still early, but he knew from observation that Starbucks was generally open early every morning regardless of whatever arbitrary hour it closed.

Opening the door and going inside at this hour, Amaoke was threatened by sensory overload. People jockeyed for position to accept their morning stimulant, and his ears were overwhelmed with input, phones pinging, shrill laughter, the espresso machine, the overly cheerful exhortations of the baristas, and the curated music playing discreetly in the background. Personal music was piped through dozens of different headphones, which he could still hear with his sensitive ears, as well as the sounds of two hundred thumbs pecking away, sending text messages, and answering emails. His nose got the worst of it; humans were most artificially fragrant after their morning showers, and he was assaulted by so much perfume, cologne, and fabric softener that he could barely smell the coffee.

When he finally reached the counter, a young man with pierced eyebrows and an enormous shock of wheat-blond hair pointed at Amaoke with both index fingers like they were guns and said, "Dude, what'll it be?" He picked up a paper cup and stood there, poised with a marker he had produced seemingly from nowhere, ready to shorthand whatever complexity his customer could create in five seconds or less.

Amaoke inquired whether anyone had found an old messenger bag and turned it in that morning, feeling reasonably certain that whoever found it would take whatever they wanted and then abandon it somewhere. But the kid's eyes lit up, and he said, "Your lucky day, man." He ducked between his coworkers and went into the back room, emerging with the dusty article. By the way he carried it, it was still full of tools and Amaoke's other belongings.

As he handed it across the counter, he said, "Some dude in a bright-green suit brought it in."

Amaoke thanked him out of habit, stunned by the statement, since he doubted such attire was so commonplace that there was any chance it had not been the Morningstar. He fought an urge to search among the faces in the café, knowing that the Monster would be long gone. He forced himself to turn away from the counter to leave when he noticed a display full of the morning's newspapers. *Evidence at the Scene of Socialite's Disappearance Suspicious for Homicide, According to Law Enforcement Officials* was just above the fold on the first page of the *Times-Picayune*. Even though half the photograph was below the fold,

Amaoke saw enough of her face to identify it as belonging to the woman who had been sitting right here in this room only hours before. He shivered in horror, wondering if what he had seen was another manipulation, since she had probably been dead for some time before the tableau he had witnessed the night before. Unfortunately, Amaoke knew all too well that the Morningstar could easily manipulate the dead.

45

ALTHOUGH HE CAUGHT GLIMPSES OF the Morningstar more and more frequently, stepping off the streetcar on St. Charles or strolling through the Quarter, it made no contact with him; indeed, it would vanish if he attempted any pursuit. Once, it even drove past Amaoke's worksite in a midnight-blue Jaguar, wearing sunglasses and driving gloves, giving the work crew an ironic little salute.

Contained with the expected contents of the messenger bag, he had discovered something else, something that disturbed him deeply. It had taken him several days to find it, as it had slipped down between the larger items in the bag and settled into one of the bottom corners. It was the bracelet that he had given Nanatha as his betrothal promise, or an extremely expert facsimile of it. It made his heart hurt when he examined it; the red color from its natural dye was nearly gone, and the hide strips in the braid were furred and soft, as they had become from a lifetime on her wrist. There was also some deep-seated grime that had the scent of the loamy soil in which he had buried her. He was aware that the Morningstar wanted him to feel the volatile anger that would come with the thought that his beloved's remains had been violated. But he swallowed as much of the pain as he could, not allowing it to manipulate him. He carried the bracelet on his person, as a physical tribute, turning the insult away. Nanatha's memory gave him the strength he needed to do it.

Amaoke had never known the Monster to present itself so frequently, and it appeared to be immersing itself in human concerns to a degree that was unprecedented. When he contemplated the meaning of these strange developments, he could not separate them from the unexplained happenings at St. Constantine, or Father Weston, or even himself. The escalating spirit energy, and the calculated efforts of the Morningstar to have him bear witness to its torment of the pureflesh, made him believe that whatever role he was intended to assume was near at hand. Amaoke just hoped he had the strength to avoid allowing the Morningstar to cultivate whatever destructive potential it had created within him.

He thought about the circumstances that had brought him to New Orleans, his search for work, how the ample construction jobs during the recovery after Hurricane Katrina had drawn him here like many others. Perhaps his actions had been subtly influenced somehow, even though he couldn't see it. Amaoke was wondering now whether his presence here was part of an elaborate manipulation, and he had the feeling that he was one piece on a chessboard, and like that chess piece, he worried that he was ignorant of some larger diabolical plan being set in motion. As ever, he remembered that there was a purpose for everything, and if he was here, it was where he was supposed to be, and he would accept and face whatever was coming.

He started to concentrate on mindful acts, and pray as his mother had instructed him long, long ago. He had become somewhat lax in his ritual practices, even privately, over the course of his life, believing himself to be utterly damned for the acts he had committed in madness over half a millennium before, and others that he had committed out of his own sense of justice. He knew he would have to answer for those acts someday, and often wondered if Raven had lengthened his path as a punishment, denying him the peace and privilege of death and rebirth, removing him from the cycle of life.

And as he increased his attention to these neglected prayers, it became readily apparent that there was additional spirit energy about, very positive energy, and that he could identify it in separation from the dark powers that had claimed so much of his focus. The Lafayette cemetery was a very different place with this new outlook, and the energies appeared to be more balanced than before. But he could tell that the darkness still had a foothold, and the advantage was to the darker spirits in many places.

He had been avoiding a return to St. Constantine, dreading a confrontation with the priest that the Morningstar was probably welcoming. There was no point in escalating a situation that he did not understand. His next task was to follow the priest and try to learn what he could about Father Weston's activities, but he put it off to focus on an attempt to better understand himself. There were rituals he could use for self-discovery and meditation, and he needed to more closely reflect upon the natural order and his place in it.

On a scorching July afternoon, some seventy-two hours before the full moon, he boarded a bus north, getting off in Hattiesburg, Mississippi, and hitching a ride into the Desoto National Forest, where he set up camp off the southern end of Ashe Lake, away from the recreation area on the northern side of the water. Although there was a small town nearby, there were also thousands of square miles of woodland for the wolf to run. Even though it was a poor substitute for the forests of his home, and the heat was going to be somewhat uncomfortable with his thick coat, he felt at ease in these natural surroundings, where he could pretend for a few days that he was the only one around. He also knew, from previous trips to this spot, that there was a great deal of spiritual energy in this place, and this energy had always welcomed him, and he believed it originated in the trees. They were old, and there were strong spirit totems in many ancient forests like this one. Once he'd had a vision of Nanatha here, and he was grateful to the spirits for allowing him to see her.

He hiked as a man that first evening, listening to the sounds of the animals and the water, and he slept under the stars. The next day he fasted, sitting in the sun, sweating, and praying for spiritual guidance; he rubbed his skin with ashes to open the pathway between his world and that of the spirits, praying for guidance and the knowledge to defeat the controlling malevolence that he had inherited at birth. As the full moon approached, he was rewarded with visions.

Amaoke walked with his mother, through the snowy woods near the sod house by the river. But he walked next to her as a man, the man she had not lived to know, not as the boy to whom she had taught the old teachings. They walked along in companionable silence, and he waited for her to speak, when a beautiful white wolf with gray-tipped ears appeared in the trees up ahead.

Noki went ahead of Amaoke, and the wolf seemed happy to see her. It rolled in the snow and playfully jumped about her as she walked on through the forest. The wolf led them further and further from the river, hurtling ahead into the trees before circling back to make sure they were following him. Its blue eyes seemed knowing, not feral. Then it disappeared over a ridge and did not return.

Noki turned back, walking straight toward Amaoke, and she seemed sad. "Mother, is the wolf my totem?" he heard himself asking her, but she only shook her head, still very sad.

She turned slowly in a complete circle, arms held out from her body, and turned her face up to the sky, letting the snow fall onto her upturned cheeks. "Amaoke, the wolf is not a totem; the wolf is part of you. Until you embrace him and accept him, he cannot fully be controlled."

Then she called out, in a clear voice that carried on the wind, "Ah-mah-o-kee, ah-mah-o-kee, ah-mah-o-kee!" Through the swirling snow, the wolf answered in a lonely howl that pulled a plaintive answering cry from Amaoke, the two songs in discord, achieving no harmony.

Amaoke woke suddenly, lying on his side on the ground. He was incredibly thirsty, and when he tried to sit up, he felt dizzy and saw spots before his eyes. The sun was high in the sky. He managed to wander into the shade and allowed himself a mouthful of water before he resumed his vigil in the sunlight, sitting cross-legged, singing more of the old prayers, willing his mother to return.

When he dreamed again, he was running through the forest, running as the wolf, through the snow, hearing his mother call his name. When he saw her standing in the clearing, his ears lifted, and his tail wagged vigorously. She looked strangely satisfied, as if she recognized him in his four-legged form, and knew him, even though in life she had died before he had ever made that first change. It filled his heart with gladness to be seen by her, and he pranced a bit for her, letting his large pink tongue loll out of his mouth. Then he rolled in the snow at her feet before letting out two or three joyous yips.

"When you give thanks to the spirits, I can see you. Love opens the portal," she explained. "My son, you have turned your back on faith; you have failed to recognize that the rules govern all beings, whether human, animal, or spirit." She placed a hand atop his head, scratching him lovingly behind one ear before running her hand over his thick neck ruff.

She rested her hand on his shoulder, settling her fingers deep in his fur, and walked beside him through the forest, silent for a time. He let out a small whine because he wanted to hear her voice; he desperately needed her counsel.

"Patience, my son," she admonished him, letting go of his fur. She pulled the hood of her parka up over her head and lay down out of the snow, on a bed of pine boughs sheltered by a downed tree. He climbed into the enclosure next to her, stretching out with his back to her, and putting his head down on his paws. He closed his eyes as she stroked his fur, and sang the ancient songs to him, explaining that the Wolf was here before Raven made the Man, and knew the rules and rituals as humans do. As her hand moved over him with her prayers, he felt a growing energy around them both, but he could not resist the soothing tones of her voice, and he drifted off to sleep.

He awoke within the dream, and stepped out of the enclosure to approach Noki, where she sat next to a smokeless fire. Her beautiful face was just as he remembered it, youthful and smooth, but her long hair was now as white as snow. Amaoke, the man, emerged from the wolf to sit at her right hand, while the wolf sat to her left. She reached out and placed a hand on each of the two heads, and contemplated the fire.

Finally, she spoke. "Amaoke, my son, the Wolf understands the *alerquutet* and the *inerquutet* that allow it to live correctly. The laws and instructions of living, and the prohibitions, are known to it and followed as they are known to humans and followed. You have been following your own mind for too long, letting fear proscribe your behavior. If you do not recognize and respect that the wolf will also know what must be done and what must be avoided as well as the man does, there will be no further control because there is no unity between your two persons.

"We cannot know or see all of the reasons for your duality, but the wolf requires respect, and must be embraced, not excluded from your totality. He is part of you, and any belief within you that separates the beast from the man will leave both of you vulnerable to manipulation. It is by accepting all of whom and what you are that you will gain the strength you need to protect that which is most important."

Noki released them both and stepped away from the fire to the edge of the clearing. "Now you must sing as one, my sons. That is your salvation." Then she made a pulling gesture and said a prayer that Amaoke could barely hear, and the song was pulled from him, rising into the sky, mingling with that of his wolf brother, of himself, and there was harmony.

He sang himself awake under a glorious full moon and was astonished to find that he was still in human form. Although Moon's call was powerful in his bones, and in his blood, for the first time since he had crossed into manhood, he ignored the pull of brother *Iraluk*, and walked as a man on the earth below him, strengthened immeasurably by faith.

46

THE DAY OF HIS APPOINTMENT with Dr. Madison was overcast and humid, and that afternoon he left work on schedule for the first time that summer. His crew was working on the overpass near the Superdome, so he only had to walk a few blocks to make his appointment. The gentleman in him would have preferred to clean up before the meeting, but the timing was too close for him to make it home from work and back to the clinic in time, even if he didn't eschew public transportation.

The potential information he could gain from this meeting overrode any concerns he had about his appearance, and Amaoke relied on the impeccable social manners that his mother had raised him with to represent the best of who he was, so he let go of other social imperatives regarding his immediate lack of grooming. Even though he had not lived among other people until he was entirely an adult, she had stressed that respectful behavior was more important than anything else when interacting with others, and he relied on her wisdom in this instance as he had in others. He hoped, as always, that who he was superseded *what* he was.

He arrived fifteen minutes early, signed himself in with the receptionist, and resigned himself to wait, having heard that doctors were rarely on time. But just prior to his scheduled appointment time, the medical assistant who had performed his intake interview appeared, and she led him down the hall to a room that was more like a living room than an examination room. He wasn't sure what he should have expected; there were an ebony desk and a credenza at one end of the room and large windows with privacy blinds that let in a surprising amount of light even though the day was overcast. There were two plush modern sofas set at right angles to one another, and two large armchairs across from the first sofa, creating a loose U-shaped seating area that was clearly the focus of the room. The colors were muted but tasteful, with modern accent pillows and brushed-nickel table lamps placed at intervals. Exquisite and probably expensive watercolors in shades of grey and light green decorated the walls, and they appeared to be part of a cohesive collection, the work of a single artist. There was an air-freshening device stowed discreetly out of sight, but he could smell the citrus and sandalwood scents it emitted.

Amaoke was almost afraid to sit down, suddenly aware of the amount of road dust on his jeans, but he lowered himself into one of the chairs and set his messenger bag down with a clanking thud next to it. The chair was extremely comfortable, which surprised him. Someone had clearly put a great deal of thought into the use of the room, ensuring that it felt like a sanctuary. The light was soothing, it was private, and the surroundings were also calming.

Less than five minutes after he sat down, there was a light knock on the door, and then it was opened by one of the most beautiful women Amaoke had ever seen. Her cocoa-colored skin seemed to glow, enhancing the loveliness of startling green eyes with lush eyelashes that peered at him through fashionable tortoiseshell eyeglass frames. Her brown hair corkscrewed out from her face in ordered spirals, and she was taller than average, slim but athletically built. She wore a pristine white coat, and used forearm crutches to navigate over to the desk efficiently.

She propped the crutches against the desk long enough to remove her lab coat, revealing a light-green sleeveless sheath dress that skimmed her body, ending just above her knees. The color highlighted her eyes and her lovely skin. Her bare shoulders and arms were shapely and muscular. He stood up, finally remembering his manners, trying not to appear as if he were staring at her.

"Oh, please, Mr. Severnoj, don't get up," she protested, smiling slightly. He was shocked that she pronounced the name perfectly without asking for help with it, and he watched her check her watch and open the drawer to retrieve something before taking up her crutches again and coming around to the seating area to hand it to him. It was her card, and he glanced at it as he sat back down.

ALETA MADISON, MD, PhD
Forensic Psychiatry

Her scent drifted over him as she came near, an enticing spicy scent that was complemented by the other fragrances in the room. He noticed as well that he did not smell any injury or bandaging from her person, and concluded that her crutches might be a permanent part of her life, which made sense considering the graceful way that she managed them.

She settled onto the sofa opposite him, skillfully stowing her crutches against its end, and said, "I'm Aleta Madison, and I apologize for being late. Are you comfortable sitting there? Is it all right if I sit here?"

He nodded, still not sure whether he trusted himself to speak, but while she got settled, he took the opportunity to observe additional small details about her. She was probably in her middle thirties, had delicate gold earrings in both ears, and wore a dainty necklace with a Mobius loop charm. Her dusky skin was flawless, not a blemish anywhere. She had no rings on her fingers, her hands were neatly manicured, and she wore a slim gold watch on her right wrist.

She fixed him with a direct look, placed her hands on her lap, and assumed a relaxed pose that he felt was genuine. She asked, "Are you comfortable telling me why you wanted to see me?"

"I heard your program on public radio," he admitted, in the interest of full disclosure. If she thought that was unusual, nothing about her posture gave it away, but there was a slight lift to one eyebrow that he could not decipher as anything other than curiosity. "I wondered if you could tell me a bit more about what you are studying, what you do relative to this…this…lycanthropy." He cast about a bit trying to think of what to say, and finally settled on using her word for the condition.

She didn't seem put off by his request and obliged him by describing the tenets of her work. "Lycanthropy as such was felt to be a historical diagnosis," she explained. "In less enlightened times, persons, usually men, would be suspected of the disorder because they exhibited certain behaviors that were considered wolfish. Biting, wildness, predatory acts. Such persons were, without exception, institutionalized, and probably their conditions did not improve.

"These behaviors were later attributed to a number of causes as scientific knowledge developed, such as medical diseases that caused abnormal amounts of specific metabolic, or otherwise naturally produced, substances in the body that had an effect on a person's ability to reason. For example, diseases like porphyria and rabies, the symptoms of which explained the urge to bite, were associated with lycanthropy. Other disorders such as manias, and psychoses, especially those of an episodic nature, which were sometimes associated with criminal acts, usually involving violence toward others, were also implicated as causes of monstrous behavior. There is also a rare condition called hypertrichosis, which is associated with an overabundance of body hair; in some manifestations, it makes the faces of those suffering from it appear wolf-like.

"Many of those felt to be 'werewolves' were, in fact, no such thing; instead, they had untreated medical or psychological issues that were poorly understood, and the explanations for their behavior was rooted in superstition. Most of the classic legends about werewolves come to us from people of Indo-European background."

"Indo-European?" Amaoke asked.

"Persons from language groups originating in Europe and western Asia," Dr. Madison clarified. "There are several legends about wolves from that genealogical subgroup. The word *lycanthropy* is derived from the Greek myth about Lycaon, whom Zeus turned into a wolf. Lycaon ritually murdered a child and apparently tried to feed its flesh to Zeus as a test to see whether Zeus was truly a god. So as punishment for murder, cannibalism, and impiety, Zeus made Lycaon into a beast. In Scandinavian lore, you have the *Ulfhednar*, fighters who wore the hides of wolves to frighten and overcome their more superstitious enemies. Even the medieval Catholic church got into the act, suggesting that a devotion to St. Hubert could cure a lycanthrope, which probably contributed to the superstition.

"Of interest, almost all of the patients said to suffer from lycanthropy appear to be from Indo-European backgrounds," Dr. Madison said. Looking closely at Amaoke, she added, "Although Native Americans also have legends about shapechangers and skinwalkers that have the forms of both human and animal, including wolves, those beings are not exclusively wolves, nor do they seem to affect the sensibilities of the people who believe in them as much as the classic European werewolf stories.

"Our beliefs suggest that it is part of the natural order that animals or their spirits can sometimes appear in human form," Amaoke agreed, not telling her that in his mother's tradition, there were spirits that were half-human and half-beast, some of them wolves. "Do you have any patients who are Indigenous?"

"Apparently, I do now," she said, studying him. "But I have never heard of one with such a disorder before. The study of the psychology of the disorder developed to a point where it was fairly universally recognized that the sufferer or his family had some extraordinary belief in werewolves from a superstitious or religious perspective, and that it was those untrained beliefs that led to the conclusion that the sufferer was a werewolf. As you just said, for Native American people, the phenomenon was usually a natural one, and no cause to have someone's head examined, or to have them committed for care."

"But if this is a historical diagnosis," Amaoke protested, "why did you indicate during your radio interview that it is becoming a focus of your practice, and the population of this type of patient is growing?"

"Ah. For the very reason we have just discussed," Dr. Madison replied. "Disease, finally, is about susceptibility. That is, of course, a gross oversimplification. Diabetes is about susceptibility to sugar. The inability to properly metabolize sugar causes a host of medical problems that, if untreated, can ultimately be fatal. Mental illness, too, is about susceptibility. Persons who suffer from psychosis are particularly susceptible to suggestion. They hear voices, and sometimes those inner voices are telling them to do things, often unpleasant things, such as harm themselves or others. Over the past several decades, there has been a significant increase in literary fantasy, especially in which the role of the monster, the typical dark antihero, has been romanticized such that he becomes the hero, often with romantic appeal and redeeming qualities. These ideas become modern legends, glorified in print, in song, and certainly in movies.

"The dialogue of a psychotic's inner voice is probably influenced by that person's own world view, cultural background, and a number of social factors. Now that the werewolf has a place in popular culture, the fact that there are higher numbers of psychotic patients who believe they may be werewolves is not that surprising. And when such persons are criminally violent in conjunction with such delusions, they exhibit predatory behaviors such as biting, rape, ritual animal sacrifice, and even murder. Unfortunately, many of my patients are referred to me from prison, after a psychotic break in which their belief in their own werewolf-ism has been acted upon in violent fashion.

"There are less extreme manifestations of the disorder, and as with any disease, patients can exhibit a spectrum of behaviors, such as an isolated and inappropriate desire to bite, which can be affected by behavioral therapy and medication, to public exhibitions of nakedness or public urination, which may or may not be unrelated to psychosis but rather can be a mixture of narcissism and other personality disorders that could also respond to medication and counseling.

"Your questions are compelling, Mr. Severnoj, but you don't seem to be a journalist, which I feared you might be when we started talking, unless you are a journalist moonlighting in construction?" she inquired, and Amaoke marveled at her easy manner and the way in which she remained entirely non-confrontational.

"Most journalists are not patient enough to wait three months for an interview," he conceded and was surprised and delighted when she laughed. He would expect a psychiatrist to blunt their own emotions in consultation, but to him, she read as authentic in her responses. "I do have one more question, and then I promise I will get to myself since the hour is almost up. Have you ever had a patient who you felt was different from the others, whom you couldn't get a measure of, who remained a mystery, or who made you think that the myth could be real?"

"I think I see where you are going with this." She nodded, then paused for a few moments, and he suspected she was choosing her words carefully. "There was one patient who still haunts me, a man who believed he was a werewolf. He was exceptionally gifted, exceptionally talented, and I have an ongoing argument with my colleagues about whether he had psychosis at all. He was exceedingly difficult to categorize from a forensic standpoint, but despite what some psychiatrists would have you believe, it isn't the most exact science, you understand. I could never convince myself that I was seeing everything that contributed to his disease, his mental makeup, if you will. He was the most creatively violent person I have ever been in the company of, a remorseless killer. He died by lethal injection some years ago, which was unfortunate, but certifying him insane was difficult, given the details of his acts. There was evidence of some deliberateness and sophisticated calculation that suggested rationality, and the court overturned an insanity defense on appeal. But he was entirely human, at least as we categorize ourselves among the other animals. There are no true werewolves, but there are beasts among us."

She shivered as she described the man, and Amaoke noticed how her hands crept to her upper arms, gripping them reflexively. She had broken out in gooseflesh, and he could smell her fear. Which made him feel particularly guilty about what he had come to confront her with.

Dr. Madison was clearly well-read and took a reasoned approach to the challenge that her patients presented. It was evident that she cared about their welfare. Which, on balance, made her the best person to recruit to help him better understand his own physiology. She had, in a very short time, earned his respect and a measure of trust. Amaoke felt she deserved to know the truth, and could probably handle it. On the other hand, her scientific mind would either reject the information he had for her, or try too hard to explain it away, which meant he had to be convincing.

If he was reading the clock on the wall correctly, they only had about ten minutes left in the session. It was now or never, and she was looking at him expectantly, waiting for him to make good on his promise to discuss his own concerns with her.

"Now tell me a bit about what has been happening with you," she prompted, recovered entirely from the discomfort she had felt only moments before.

Amaoke let the change come over him, speaking through it so she could hear the plunge in the register of his voice. "Better if I just *show you, Doctor…*" The last few words were barely more than a growl as his teeth lengthened, and his midface elongated, becoming a snout. He could feel the hair sprouting from his face, and he held up his hands so she could witness their transformation, letting the claws spring from the tips of his fingers.

As quickly as he had let it start, he pulled it back, exerting extraordinary control over the process, refusing to let it get away from him. He made his facial features settle back to normal, and felt the changes in his hands resolving.

And the whole time, she watched, her eyes getting bigger and seeming to take over her face as she pushed herself back violently into the sofa cushions, unable to look away, her hands coming up to her face, screaming a soundless scream. Then her eyes rolled upward, and she slumped forward, losing consciousness as her body slid off the couch.

He finished the transformation in time to pitch forward and catch her weight in his arms. She felt very light to him, and he lowered her gently to the floor, letting go of her almost reluctantly. Looking around, he grabbed a couple of the accent pillows from the sofa and propped her legs up on them. Her glasses had fallen when she passed out, and he retrieved them from beneath the couch and folded them neatly before setting them on the arm of the sofa next to her crutches. He tilted his head and listened to her heartbeat; it was rapid but steady. She was breathing just fine, but the shock had short-circuited her consciousness.

He forced himself to walk calmly to the door and down the hall to the reception desk, where he got them all moving by telling them that they needed to come quickly, Dr. Madison had passed out in the office. In the ensuing chaos, he retrieved his messenger bag and slipped out before the paramedics arrived.

47

AMAOKE SPENT THE NEXT SEVERAL days looking over his shoulder, unsure when or if the authorities were likely to arrive to question him about the events leading up to the good doctor's incapacity during their session, but no one came.

He realized that most of his concern was related to the unfairness of what he had done and his own guilty conscience. In a way, he had behaved disgracefully; among his people, it was not right to draw too much attention to oneself, and he could have just explained to her what he wanted. But the stubborn rational part of her would not have accepted it, and she probably would have tried to medicate him, the side effects of which could have been disastrous. There had really been no other choice.

But a part of him had to admit that after listening to her, seeing her, he had wanted her to know the truth. So he justified his behavior as the most appropriate way for him to be completely honest with her. He wanted her to know him; wasn't that the real reason?

It was that last thought that pierced him to his core, making him admit that he was attracted to her, not only physically, but also because of her sensibility and her strength. Yet he felt that he was doing Nanatha an injustice because he had never given her the chance to see him fully. Even though at the end of her life he had learned that she really did know the fundamental truth of his existence, he had never been forthcoming and honest about who and what he truly was. He sighed, knowing that that time had been a different time, and he had been a different man. Amaoke had had too many years in which to count the many ways in which he felt he'd failed his wife, despite knowing in his heart if she were still around she would forgive each and every one of them.

He continued with his prayers, and mindful practices, and he spent a second full moon without the change. The Morningstar had absented itself, and the settled spirits at St. Constantine told Amaoke that Father Weston was away again.

Several weeks passed, and the work on the I-10 overpass was completed in September. His work crew was assigned to state highway maintenance out by Ardoyne, so Amaoke accepted rides to and from work from his foreman, who lived in Central City. He would walk up Josephine Street, where the man lived, each morning, and walk back to the Garden District from there every evening. He contributed gas money and was grateful for the transportation. Without it, he would have had to quit his job, and he knew it was more convenient for someone to drive directly to and from their own home, and he didn't want to present anyone with any inconvenience.

It had the unfortunate side effect of curtailing his wanderings through the city, but that couldn't be helped. Since Father Weston was gone, and Amaoke had not figured out what to do about Dr. Madison, he was content to keep residence off Magazine Street, becoming a homebody once again, a revenant who dodged aging canines and listened to NPR.

About three weeks into the new assignment, he arrived at the patio door to find a scribbled note on pink paper taped to the glass. Curious, he pulled it off and took it inside to read it. He stepped out of his work boots as he read the short note: *For AS, Telephone call from Aleta Madison, return call at earliest convenience, c504.929.2992.* It was scribbled in a neat hand; probably his landlady's as indicated by the pink paper. He dug briefly through the paperwork he had been given at the clinic and saw that the hospital's area code was 702, and that little *c* meant cellular, so Amaoke wondered if this was her private number, which he thought was extraordinarily courageous of her.

Someone turns into a monster right before your eyes, and you give them your personal cellphone number only seven weeks later. Amaoke was impressed; she had quite a backbone.

He stripped out of his dusty work clothes and stepped into the shower, thinking about the note. She had provided her given name; it did not say *Dr.* Madison, but then he remembered that it was the way she had referred to herself in the office, by way of introduction. He turned off the water and shook his head vigorously, then thumped himself on the chest with an open hand. Here he was acting like a lovesick teenager trying to decipher what a girl was thinking from a note, when he was really a very old man, ancient, actually, who had well learned that understanding what a girl was thinking was nearly impossible even if she was trying to tell you what she was thinking.

And what to do about the note? It was impolite not to return the call, but he had no telephone of his own. A return call would mean one of two unpleasant options, find a working payphone or ask to borrow the house phone at his landlords' residence, neither option offering privacy or the opportunity for a meaningful conversation. Use of a payphone these days would probably result in enduring telephone surveillance for her, since to his understanding, only racketeers and drug dealers used them anymore. Besides, there were so few to be found, since every person on the planet seemed to have their own personal cellphone, and many of the ones that were still in place did not function, as they were inconsistently serviced or had been abandoned by the big telecommunications companies. They had even disappeared from diners and airports. And what, exactly, did etiquette dictate once he got her on the phone? A heartfelt apology for shapeshifting in her office? While he was intrigued, this was a conversation best had in person, if she would even see him. At the moment, he certainly didn't think it was the best idea to make a follow-up appointment with her.

He was going to have to resort to that other standby employed by unsavory characters and werewolves alike: namely, stalking. So, once again, he abandoned NPR and resumed his nighttime forays.

He learned that she worked late that very first night, when he went by the medical center to see if he could locate her. She left the clinic after eight and got into a silver Audi and drove away. She looked gorgeous in a black tweed pantsuit, if a bit tired, but was apparently no worse off for her encounter with him. She appeared to be getting on with her life, and he admired her when he saw that she wasn't looking over her shoulder or studying the shadows of the dark parking lot. This was one tough lady.

Over the course of the next several days, he mapped her route to her house in pieces, following the scent signature of her car for a few blocks until other scents diluted it enough that he lost the trail, and then waiting in the spot where he had lost her the day before, killing time until the silver Audi drove past him to pick up the next leg of her journey. Of course, she didn't always go straight home, and after she led him to a dry cleaner with late evening hours, he had to backtrack through three days of locations to locate the adjustment in the route, but by early October he knew where she lived. Then he lay low for several days, not wanting to be caught hanging around her neighborhood. He had a much better way to do the close surveillance, anyway.

Aleta's home was in a quiet neighborhood in Lakeview; a sprawling stucco ranch style painted a muted grey. It was very modern in design, but had an open backyard with magnolia trees and a double row of hedges instead of a fence at the back of the property. The rear of the house had a glass wall between the kitchen and the yard, with a sliding glass door that led out to a tiled patio under an overhang. It was decorated like an outdoor room, with sectional seating, a cedar dining table, and a fire pit. She spent a great deal of time on the patio, eating some of her evening meals, reading, and watching Monday Night Football on an outdoor TV that was mounted in the protected corner of the space. Occasionally, another woman joined her, and by her scents and mannerisms, Amaoke deduced that this was her sister.

In his hiding place, crouched down in a gap in the hedges, he was transported back more than two hundred years to the time he spent under the blackberry bush when he had been courting Nanatha. But he still hadn't figured out what the proper approach should be, so he just watched and waited.

It appeared that she had some significant leg weakness, potentially a congenital disability, but it did not appear that she let her disability define her. She was often dressed in what he came to refer to as her uniform, old blue jeans that hugged her slim curves with a V-neck T-shirt. She was also on the telephone a great deal and appeared to be conducting some clinical interviews through a program on her computer. He was careful to avoid overhearing these exchanges, usually abandoning his surveillance to maintain the privacy of these other persons, whether they were her colleagues or her patients he never knew.

For her part, she continued to leave messages at his landlords' house, and when he'd gone up to pay his rent, his landlady had given him a shy smile and passed him yet another message, as if she thought he'd found a girlfriend who was repeatedly calling every number she had for her new boyfriend. He had been unable to hide his pleasure at receiving another message, which made her smile even more.

Once, Aleta left a message for him while he was positioned only several feet away from her, under the hedges. She said all the same things, but by now it was in shorthand: *yes, this is Aleta, would you please ask Amaoke to call me,* and *I appreciate you taking all these messages, I know he works very hard,* and his landlady telling her, *of course, dear, I will make sure he gets this right away.*

Something stirred deep within him, hearing that rich voice speak his name, the way he imagined she would perhaps say it directly to him someday. There was absolutely no indication that Aleta's interest in him extended beyond her fascination with his condition, which made his presence here an even greater invasion of her privacy. But if her interest in him was merely professional, so be it. He was confident that she would do everything she could to understand him and provide insight, and maybe scientific theory would help. Maybe there was a medical way to control his change, although he was wary of that option, both because there were sure to be untoward side-effects and also because it went against the natural order, against his mother's most recent guidance. He would welcome any solution that would render him useless to the Morningstar, even if it meant his death. He was ready for any eventuality, as he suspected that whatever use the Morningstar had in mind for him would probably have the same result.

48

HALLOWE'EN NIGHT CELEBRATIONS IN NEW Orleans were second only to Mardi Gras, so Amaoke was determined to be a homebody, even though this was the one night when he should have gone out, awash in anonymity, and enjoyed the spectacle. He had to admit, he enjoyed seeing the outrageous costumes; it was human crowd misbehavior that he made it a rule to avoid.

So he settled down to a special Hallowe'en edition of *This American Life* on NPR, enjoying the mild Southern fall weather as he sat on the patio with his canine sidekicks. He could see the glow from the nearby Quarter and hear revelers in his own neighborhood. The main house was dark, and he assumed his landlords had retired early or were out at a function of their own. He wondered briefly what Aleta was doing and whether she was participating in the costume ritual or sitting on her own patio miles away from where he sat on his.

He must have dozed off, but was awakened to the smell of sulfur, blood, fear, and familiar bitter metal. He stood up, and as he did, the lights in the carriage house flickered and went dark. The silence with the loss of the radio chatter was abrupt and total, and he noticed that the usual night sounds of the bats and other creatures were eerily absent as well.

He looked around for the dogs, but they were gone; it was possible they had returned to the main house, but it was unusual for them to give up on him when he was sitting outside unless their owners called for them. He suspected they were spooked, as the air was newly charged with energy, and that stench was not pleasant. There was a deepening of the shadows that he did not like, and his instincts told him that whatever was happening was drawing on a more profound, darker energy than that which animated the spirits around the church, or in the cemeteries.

This energy was suddenly too familiar. Amaoke slid the patio door open and retrieved his shoes, putting them on carefully without sitting down or turning his back to the yard. If he wasn't mistaken, it belonged to the demon that had overseen his torture many centuries ago. If the Morningstar was the principal, this was its bloodiest general, and the only name it had was the one Amaoke used for it in his heart. It was taken from stories told him by his mother about a spirit that visited those who did not live properly, and its appearance could be fatal for the wayward. This was the *Ungalek,* a powerful being that was supposed to scare people straight.

Amaoke had learned that his *Ungalek* could scare them to death. He had seen it with his own eyes. His mother's people thought the *Ungalek* was another manifestation of Raven, sent to encourage them to do right. Amaoke never had believed that the *Ungalek* and Raven could be the same; as a child, the legends had been too frightening. Despite his mother's reassurances, he had refused to believe that Raven would cause his own people to drop down dead, because Raven loved them so much.

Centuries before, the *Ungalek* had found him, when he was weak-thinking and unbalanced in his power, and the Morningstar had used it to try to break him. It had set Amaoke loose on the world after unspeakable torture, and he had not seen it since. If the *Ungalek* was nearby, something terrible was disturbing the natural order. His first instinct was to lead it away from his home and try to keep it away from the large groups of pureflesh that were right now converging on the French Quarter.

He exited out the side gate and onto the path but went deeper between the two properties toward the alley rather than the street. He remained on two legs, not wanting any of his own spirit energy to alert the demon and its familiars of his exact location, although he knew if they were as close as he suspected that they already knew where to find him. By the time he reached the alley, he could hear them in his head, the howling legion of voices, and then the spirits were upon him, and he pitched forward onto his hands. He felt the wolf trying to break through, a reflex protective action, but he resisted the change, putting his hands over his ears as he struggled back to his feet.

He tried to control his direction and pace as he ran in what he thought were random directions through the streets, but the further Amaoke went, he realized that he was being herded toward some specific destination. No matter which way he ran, through the force of their energies or with noxious stimuli, they drove him onward, with the threat of the *Ungalek's* presence and the temporary madness caused by the cacophony of the dead enough of a deterrent to keep him from any real effort to resist them.

The crowds were nearly impassable when he arrived in the Quarter, and he was forced to walk the last agonizing few blocks, driven to near madness by the screeching din in his head, until he found himself standing on Bourbon Street, on the brick pavement in front of Galatoire's. Amaoke felt more than heard the throaty chuckle of the *Ungalek* at his back, although he knew that if he turned around, it would not be there, and then the voice of the Morningstar, a whisper in an ancient tongue that cut through the clamor in his brain, "*Firstborn, wolf-born, child of moon,* join us inside."

Galatoire's was synonymous with New Orleans, but it had an old-world beauty that attracted kings and peasants alike. Drunkenness seemed to be encouraged, and it had a dinner jacket requirement that normally would have kept Amaoke away, but on this night, it appeared to have been relaxed in deference to the Hallowe'en revelry. As soon as he opened the outer door, there was a blissful cessation of the voices in his head in exchange for the clatter of a busy dinner service, the respite a reward for obedience.

The maître-d was busily engaged with several patrons clamoring for his attention, and Amaoke relied on his senses as he stepped into the dining space. He followed the Morningstar's scent to one of the private dining rooms, where the Monster itself was entertaining among friends. There appeared to be a mix of mostly male forms and a few females, but none in the room were pureflesh, and he recognized their collaborative scents as profane, and their humanoid forms nothing but glamour.

They were gathered around their demagogue, the Morningstar, who on this evening was wearing a black sharkskin suit with a blood-red pocket square, a black silk shirt, and no tie. Its hair was loose and curling over its ears, and there was a porcelain demitasse on the table in front of it – one of its ubiquitous cups of coffee. Its shiny eyes were undisguised as they settled on Amaoke, and its lip curled in amusement. The other demons in the room had assumed the forms of various attractive young humans, but each had in its appearance a "tell," some feature that gave away its inhuman provenance. These details were probably undetectable by pureflesh, but Amaoke, being a true half-breed, could almost always see them, and at that moment, he wondered, not for the first time, if he had any such features that were hidden to human eyes but could be seen by this horde.

Their clothing had to be couture; one of the so-called females was wearing a constructed jacket that appeared to be made of the plumage of a nonexistent plum-colored bird – it alerted Amaoke that the feathers were not real, and their hairstyles were so over the top as to be ridiculous, but humans probably only saw them as very fashionable youngsters. Perhaps this was the way demons dressed on All Hallows Eve.

The slender youthful figure seated to Morningstar's right had the brooding presence of a male model, its chiseled cheekbones nearly eclipsed by the oversized opaque amber-tinted sunglasses it sported. Its suit was a light-brown tweed, with a proper multi-button vest, with which it had paired a grey shirt and black velvet bowtie. Its pocket square was a red paisley silk, and its exaggeratedly high haircut was very of-the-moment and would have cost a fortune to maintain had it been human. The plate in front of it was full of raw seasoned meat, and it fed itself chunks of the flesh with its left hand, displaying otherwise fastidious table manners. Its presence and scent identified it as the *Ungalek*.

The heat and hatred in its eyes as it regarded Amaoke made him want to growl, to force those dead orbs to look away, but it merely smiled, revealing a row of jagged teeth reminiscent of broken glass. It was a smile that confirmed its identity immediately, but he had a hard time reconciling this trim figure with the misshapen, lizard-like creature that he had learned to loathe all those centuries ago. Then it turned slightly in the light, and he could see the rows and rows of flesh-colored scales on its face, neck, and hands, their outlines subtle, but still unmistakable to Amaoke's keen eye.

"Clean up well, don't we?" the Morningstar observed, and Amaoke thought it was showing off, using a double entendre to refer to its bespoke companions, while delivering a back-handed insult to Amaoke, who stood among them in old blue jeans, a long-sleeved white Henley, and heavy work boots. The Morningstar indicated that Amaoke was welcome to sit down, which he declined, and then it said, "Forcas is having steak tartare. I think you would like it; it isn't on the menu, but they will make it as a favor to us, of course."

In response, Amaoke merely crossed his arms in disdain, to express his absolute refusal to break bread with these beasts. He tried to hide his astonishment that the Morningstar would assign one of his generals a name, and so casually was it spoken that Amaoke was certain that Forcas's power was even more terrible than he personally could attest from his own experience.

The whole meeting was a show of power, or the Morningstar would have come alone. Forcas was here because of its prior relationship with Amaoke, which meant that something was bothering the Monster. Forcas was the source of a great deal of humiliation and pain, and its presence was meant as a message, the kind not to be ignored. So Amaoke waited them out, prepared to stand there until they made their purpose known.

One of the females was circling him with a hungry look on its face, licking its lips with a forked tongue. It appeared to be fascinated with the tiny braid that fell over his left shoulder, separated from the loose strands that hung down his back. The creature reached out a manicured hand toward it, but before she could touch it, or him, she hissed in pain and recoiled as though he had struck her. Amaoke caught the look of confusion that came briefly to the Morningstar's face, and he watched the expression deteriorate to a more monstrous form before it recovered its urbane appearance and composure. It surprised him.

Then Amaoke smelled something he had never encountered when in the presence of the Morningstar or its legions. It was fear — not the musky human scent of fear, but an older smell, like a primitive dawning awareness, when there is a new reality as the predator recognizes too late that it has chosen dangerous prey. The thought made Amaoke want to smile, but he remained expressionless.

"The moon has called you two times without answer, our son," the Morningstar observed.

Amaoke was not surprised that this fact was known to the Morningstar; it was an unpleasant side-effect of its pseudo-paternity that it could know things about him that he would have preferred to keep to himself. He could never predict what it might know, or what information in his innermost being was sacred from its probing. The sense of fear increased among the occupants of the room, and this interested the wolf, instinctually. His predatory feelings were aroused by it, and the weaker ones grew even more fearful. Since the Monster had not asked any question, Amaoke remained silent; as a show of his own power, he licked his lips, liking the taste of their disappointment better than anything he had enjoyed for a long time. For the first time in his life, he had done something that the Morningstar did not understand, and it freed something inside of Amaoke to know that his prayers were providing a means of obscurity from it. He finally allowed himself the smallest of smiles, and the energy and temperature in the room plummeted.

"Perhaps another hundred years in the Pit will help you see things our way," Forcas suggested, earning a frown from the Morningstar, who clearly did not appreciate its underling speaking out. Forcas indicated its nearly empty plate, and the bloody residue from the meat still smelled enticing to Amaoke, but then it said, "This was just an appetizer; I still have plenty of appetite for pureflesh on this night of the year." The register of its voice dropped and split, and it held something in its hand, a small blue rosary, probably originally the belonging of a child. The demon's possession of such an item meant that it had long since lost any talismanic power, and Amaoke was suddenly angry that it had been taken from one of the innocent.

Something inside of Amaoke expanded and stretched, and his anger pushed itself out of him like a living thing, and then, rather than trying to control it, he heard his mother's words telling him that the wolf knew the rules, and he released his anger. The change was upon him, but he was no mere wolf tonight. He remained on two legs as the Beast came forward, and he stepped into its terrible and beautiful body, and he turned his intent upon the *Ungalek*, leaping upon it with the full force of his malice, feeling its power disperse in the face of his wrath, dispatching it back to the spirit plane in the presence of its Master. It was gone with a whiff of ozone and burnt meat, Amaoke observed with satisfaction, and as he calmly licked the blood from its plate, the other demons likewise retreated to some other place. He was doubly pleased that his control over the true

Beast seemed to have grown with the understanding he had gained from the visions of his mother.

He was left alone with the Morningstar, who sprouted its enormous wings rather than confront him, and Amaoke felt and heard their desperate beating amid the howling screams of thousands, and then the silence descended, and he was once again a man, utterly alone in a private dining room, satisfied that whatever ill purpose they had devised for him on this night he had avoided.

49

THE CONSTRUCTION COMPANY HAD A mobile office that was located in a trailer at the Ardoyne site, and although the team secretary was surprised when Amaoke requested the use of the telephone (probably because it was inconceivable to her that a person did not carry a cell phone) she passed it across her desk without comment and went back to whatever she was working on at her computer. A few moments later, she signed out of the spreadsheet she was working on, and, giving him a conspiratorial smile, she discreetly recovered her handbag from somewhere under the desk and left the trailer. He was grateful for the privacy.

He dug in his pocket for Aleta's card and pulled it out. It was bent, and the top edge was slightly furred from the friction generated by his movements and the heat, but the subtly raised print was still legible, and he dialed the office number, which connected him to the mental health clinic. He recognized the cultured tones of the older receptionist's voice, and he told her he needed to schedule another visit with Dr. Madison.

There was a slight pause, and she asked him whether he was able to hold for a moment, not bothering to wait for his response. He was suddenly listening to a muted jazz rendition of some popular tune, elevator music for the telephone.

Less than fifteen seconds later, the line was picked up, and Aleta herself was on the phone. "Amaoke, are you able to come on Friday afternoon, at about three o'clock?"

He was surprised that he had been connected directly to her, and so quickly that it had to have been prearranged. He was also surprised at her suggested appointment time since it was only two days away, and he had expected to wait at least a few weeks. He was stunned and didn't respond right away, so she spoke into the silence.

"I'm going to clear my schedule that afternoon in order for us to have a proper discussion," she told him, and admitted, "I had a criminal task force meeting, but I will schedule it out another month, which will break no one's heart, including mine. This is important."

Amaoke could barely register his surprise when she added, "*You* are important."

After a few moments, he realized that he still hadn't spoken, so he said, "I will be there, but can't make it until closer to four o'clock."

"See you then," she replied briskly, and the click in his ear told him she had hung up the phone.

When he finally arrived at the clinic that Friday afternoon, it was closer to four-thirty. When he checked in at the desk, rather than being asked to wait in the waiting room, the receptionist gave him a speculative look and escorted him to Dr. Madison's office herself. Her behavior suggested that this was not protocol.

Aleta was not there, but he assumed she was attending to other tasks and that she had asked to be notified when he arrived. He sat down in the same chair he had occupied on his previous visit, stowing the messenger bag beside it, and repeated his scent interrogation of the room, but nothing had changed. There was no telltale warm plastic scent or imperceptible electronic hum that accompanied recording equipment, and Amaoke smiled. She was according him serious respect and exhibiting significant courage, but he suspected that she had also taken to heart some moral oath about patient privacy. He liked her immensely, which made being there much more comfortable.

After a short wait, he heard her brisk knock at the door, and she swept into the room, shedding her lab coat and seating herself opposite him as she had on their previous visit. She was wearing a grey linen power suit, finely tailored, and it was the type of clothing intended to make others take her seriously, suggesting that she suffered as much as anyone from the curse of being highly attractive, female, and handicapped in a male-dominated field. It was also a departure from the more casual and feminine dress she had been wearing when he met her, and he wondered if it was a specific wardrobe choice with him in mind, subconscious or not.

She sat quietly for several moments, studying his appearance and his demeanor, and he calmly waited for her to reach whatever conclusions there were to be gained from this scrutiny.

Finally, he saw her reach some level of satisfaction with her visual survey, and she asked, "Are you well?"

He nodded slowly, trying to anticipate what was coming, but she surprised him when she said, "I'm sorry, but I have to ask, for my own conscience – do you believe you are a danger to yourself or others?"

"Immediately? No," he responded. "But to be completely honest, both possibilities exist at any given time in my existence. I rely on the control I have gained over time to minimize any danger that remains."

"Thank you for your honesty," Aleta said, sitting back on the sofa and visibly relaxing. She placed one elbow on the arm of the couch and waited for him to speak. "Now tell me why you really sought me out. It certainly was to learn what I knew, but I still cannot understand why you chose to reveal yourself to me. I have gone over our first meeting a thousand times in my head, and I cannot convince myself at what point you decided to show me what I didn't – what I couldn't know, and what you hoped to gain from it.

"I have also entertained the idea that I myself was suffering from some sort of delusional exhaustion, but my physician assures me that my health is excellent, and I have no other hallmarks of mental instability, so I have to conclude that the mild shock I suffered was due to witnessing an extraordinary and unexplainable, yet real, phenomenon."

"I wasn't entirely sure that I was going to reveal anything to you," Amaoke admitted. "I was impressed with your knowledge of the subject, your professional demeanor, and most importantly, I could tell that you really cared about your patients. All of those things convinced me that I could reveal my true nature; I felt that you deserved to know, and that to tell you without demonstrating the change would be wasting your time."

She nodded. "I would have credited you with a convincing delusion, and I would have medicated you," she told him, and then looked at him sharply. "But you knew that, didn't you?"

"I guessed it," he said. "I still have had no end of guilt about the way it was done, however."

"Well, now you have the chance to debrief me," she offered, looking at him expectantly.

"I'm not sure how much I have to offer by way of explanation," he began apologetically. "I believe that my...unique characteristics were purposefully created. I was meant to have some of these terrible abilities as part of a greater plan, devised by a being that even I cannot adequately understand, except to say that its aims are probably destructive."

"Purposefully created?" Aleta repeated his phrase as a question, and he realized that she was asking for clarification.

"According to my mother, there was some controversy about my paternity. It was unnaturally influenced," he responded.

"By a *being*, I think you said." Again she repeated his words. "I take from that statement that your father, for lack of a better term, was not human?" Her brows pushed together in concentration, creating a furrow between them, but it was not a gesture of skepticism; instead, she was concentrating, trying to put together the mystery by finding a place for each puzzle piece he gave her.

"That is not entirely accurate," he said softly. "To my best understanding, my father was my mother's new husband. When she became pregnant, it was under extraordinary circumstances, because he had been away on a hunting trip and had been mauled by a bear and killed, reportedly on the same day that he, or his spirit, had come to her, perhaps in a dream, perhaps in a sort of suspended reality. My mother always referred to her husband as my *true* father. But she also believed that there was some dark-spirit mischief involved, as if my father had been animated in that twilight between his death and entrance onto the spirit path. Whatever happened, a powerful and evil being, the Morningstar, contrived to block his passage to the next life, and in the process, stole and corrupted his procreative ability in order to create a child of an extranormal nature."

"Demonic paternity?" Aleta asked, and gave a small, ironic smile. "It is a widespread delusion, more common than most people would think. In any other case, such an observation would be written off as such, but in your case, it anchors your condition in reality by providing a foundation for your extraordinary existence. Did your mother give a reason for her belief that this Morningstar being was on the side of evil rather than good?"

"She had a visitation from the being just before my birth, in which it revealed itself to her. Additionally, it implicated itself in my father's death. She suspected something unusual, because she was having terrible dreams throughout her pregnancy, but when the Monster came to her, and showed her in visions what had happened to my father, my mother knew that whatever its purpose, it was not a divine being who had wanted her to bear a child out of the love she had felt for my father; rather it was of the other ilk, and ultimately, she never fully understood why it had chosen her.

"She was a very moral person; among her people, there are a set of rules and rituals that are supposed to be followed, and if a person is faithful to that way of life, they are fulfilling their purpose in the natural world, in the cycle of life. She had lived within the boundaries of those teachings, doing what was to be done, and avoiding what was prohibited or proscribed behavior. Then she married my true father, and although he did not survive the hunting trip that he took when they were very newly married, suddenly she was pregnant with me, and the elders from their village suspected the involvement of spirit magic. They deferred judgment as to whether that magic was of negative or positive origin, delaying any decision about her fate until I was born.

"Through no fault of her own, she was suddenly on the wrong side of the boundary, and then when I was born, she recognized that I was different, significantly different in appearance from her people, and it may be that she suspected such an outcome before I was born. She left her people in order to protect me, and though she raised me in the ways she had been taught, even that would have been considered an aberration, a corruption of her upbringing. She raised me on her own, when the teachings suggest that a whole village is needed to raise a child in accordance with the proper rituals. Also, there were some gender-based rules that according to routine she was not supposed to teach me, but she did what she could — mainly my mother taught me everything she knew about village life — how to be a boy and a girl, how to be a hunter and preparer of hides, how to gather berries, how to honor the spirit and animal worlds, how to bless food, how to honor the dead, how to build, how to respect the natural world.

"She kept me away from her people, because the details of my paternity were questionable, and my appearance was unusual, even as a child. But she made sure I knew about village life and had all the skills needed to take my place within such a family. She made sure that I knew the right ways to live, and she taught me how to perform the rituals. In her mind, someday I would be old enough to defend myself, and perhaps I could then rejoin society.

"She didn't survive my childhood. She never saw the change on me; it arrived with manhood. When I am at my loneliest, I wish she had been with me through the change; she would have accepted it, and I suspect she had foreseen it. Mostly I am grateful that she was already with the spirits, because I was very dangerous then, even to someone I loved that much."

"How did you find your way without her?" Aleta asked softly, so softly that he suspected she was trying to preserve the reverence with which he had spoken of his mother, as if she sensed just how meaningful his relationship with Noki had been in the context of his life.

"Not very well, I'm afraid," he admitted. "I was eventually accepted into a somewhat mixed group of families that were in transition, migrating in a large group during a period of relative famine near my homeland in what is now western Alaska. Over the course of several hundred years, these people migrated across the northern part of the continent, looking for better living conditions and renewable food sources.

"Because there were so many different people that came together as one group, my differences were allowed, even though I was still considered unclean, and an outsider. I was given work to do and proved myself an excellent provider because I was successful as a hunter. That will usually elevate someone within the group, but I was different enough that my prowess was viewed with suspicion, and I was prevented from marrying.

"I had to function well enough within the group that they would consider my contributions valuable and keep me around. At the same time, I had to absent myself regularly, because, in those days, the moon was an inflexible master whose call I could not ignore, and the change was on me for about a full week corresponding to the time the moon was waxing to fullness.

"Eventually, there was a period of relative warming, and food sources that had been scarce were more abundant, and the migrations stopped altogether as people settled in various areas on the eastern coast of what is now Canada. I stayed with the Innu for a time, as their philosophies were similar to those of my mother, and they tend to embrace those from dissimilar cultures. I have occasionally returned to them over the centuries as a seasonal work hand, but I have now been away for about two hundred years.

"After the migration, I lost track of time for a while to madness. I was tortured by dark and dangerous spirits, I was set loose on the unsuspecting, and I became the beast I never wanted to be. When I escaped, I spent a great deal of time in wolf form and lived among various Arctic wolf packs, staying away from humans for a very long time. But I didn't really belong among the wolves, either, and they have their own ways of making that clear.

"For a time I lived between the two worlds, allowing humans to suspect my dual nature, because in our culture such beings exist in legend, and although they are treated with wary respect, they are accepted as a part of the natural world. This was the closest I came to having meaningful human relationships, as a pseudo-spirit, a wise natural being who was the sought-after sage born of superstition, but I was far from benign and still in poor control of my strongest animal tendencies.

"Eventually, I began to live as a man again, hiding my true nature. I took work as a laborer, preferring to be outdoors, and watched the world change. It was easy to be an anonymous part of the workforce at the start of the industrial age, and again, I tried to be as useful to my employers as possible so as to overcome my less frequent but still regular absences. I started to really learn about the good in people, how I could be surprised to find kindness and understanding where before I had only encountered hatred or suspicion because of my physical human appearance. Some of the latter behavior still exists, of course, but there appears to be a societal embrace of differences, especially now."

"In some ways, that is true," Aleta agreed. "But prejudice persists, and it has a profound effect on the development of entire cultures."

They sat in silence for a while, and he noticed that full dark was established, and he realized that he had ceased to hear the background noises that meant other people were still working. The clock on the side table indicated that it was well after six o'clock. Concentrating more fully on the sounds coming from the rest of the building, he realized with surprise that everyone else had left.

"It's late," he observed. "Your staff has gone."

"I know," she replied, "I told them to go home when I came into the office."

Amaoke must have looked surprised, because she said, "They didn't like the idea of leaving me alone with a patient, but I assured them that another colleague knew I would be here, and stressed the importance of completing your intake interview, considering the embarrassing outcome of our first encounter. They are used to my particularities when it comes to putting patients first, so even though my staff tends to be protective of me, they agreed to honor my decision. And, it's Friday night, so I am not sure they needed much convincing, in the end." She smiled.

He could scent the slightest bit of fear coming from her; it had spiked when he had made the observation that she was alone here with him, but then had subsided somewhat. Again, he admired her courage. Whatever professional interest she had in him was also overriding her natural instincts to be afraid. He was a puzzle to solve, a tool to further understanding the human condition, a specimen. He could hardly blame her, his situation was unique, and she was a scientist.

"You spoke about what happened over the course of several centuries," she recalled, returning to their discussion. "How old *are* you?" she asked, so directly and in so interrogative a tone that it reminded him of being asked the same question by a young Nanatha all those years before, and he smiled.

"About a thousand years, give or take a few decades," he replied softly.

She was quiet as she tried to absorb what he was telling her. He could see her processing it, trying to fathom it, trying to imagine it. It was a very long time before she spoke again. Her bright eyes studied him from behind her glasses.

"That must create some emotional difficulties, dealing with your…condition, and the burden of immortality."

Her observation was so clinical, and so removed from everything they had been discussing, that he was unable to hide his disappointment. It triggered his doubts about seeking her advice and her help. Aleta must have seen something of his feelings in his expression, because hers softened, and she leaned back, and said, "I'm so sorry. Too much doctor, not enough empathy. That was far too clinical of me. Forgive me. I can't help myself sometimes." She laughed a little, but there was sadness in her demeanor, and he could not tell what was causing it. He had the uncanny feeling that she didn't want to let him down, though there was no way she could be expected to have all the answers even if he were just a "regular" patient; medicine was an inexact science.

Relieved, he took up where he wanted to, on the subject of immortality. "I have never believed myself immortal," he explained. "Despite being long-lived, I have always believed that I would eventually die, that it was my destiny to do so as it is the destiny of all living things. I don't really know the reason for my longevity, but I view it as a gift, and I am mostly thankful for it."

"Mostly?" she prompted.

"As I said, the mysteries of my origin created this duality, and my abilities could be subverted to the ultimate devastation," he replied, then provided more detail about this belief.

He explained the Morningstar's apparent plans for massive destruction, and its expectation that Amaoke would be a tool in that destruction. He alluded to the torture he had endured, which was intended to transform the beast into something even worse than its fundamental animal nature. He explained the evolution of the wolf into the true Beast, how it was occurring with higher frequency than before, which form was what the Morningstar intended to unleash upon humanity. Foremost, he was honest with her about his uncertainty that he could prevent that ultimate terrible change and control an outcome he wanted to avoid.

"If I am right, then I will eventually no longer be needed, and my life will end, as it rightfully should have centuries ago," Amaoke sighed, and shook his head in frustration, because he felt that despite all he had said, he was not adequately explaining anything to her.

"Is there any chance that you could avoid contributing to whatever destruction you say is coming?" Aleta asked, and for the first time, he wondered if the Morningstar's most recent reaction to his behavior suggested that she was right.

"I guess I have been trying to figure out how to do just that," he replied, unsurprised to hear himself saying it out loud. "Not just recently, but for a very long time. I have never had enough information about what is to come to prepare myself; I hope that when the time comes, I have at least a chance to make a choice."

Aleta raised her fine brows, silently asking a question, but she didn't say any more, so he continued, in an attempt to give her a fair representation of himself.

"I did some…pretty terrible things a very long time ago, before I learned for myself how much good there is in humanity. I know my mother tried to teach me about the proper ways of conducting myself in the world, and teach me about my place in it, but after she died, and I changed, I lost those things for a long time," he admitted, still not ready to discuss the centuries of torture and its effects. "I didn't want to be a monster, and I isolated myself for a long time. My long life has naturally brought me in contact with many different kinds of people, and some of them showed me what a gift life was in a purely mortal context, and I came to appreciate the gift of longevity, and the need to embrace change and be part of the time one is living in, while honoring enough of the past to maintain my identity. It was, finally, through the eyes of a few extraordinary people that I could see the good in myself and touch the human being that is as much a part of me as the wolf."

Aleta remained quiet when he had finished, as if waiting for him to say more. After what seemed like several minutes, she said, "I think that's enough for now. This has to be difficult, and intense. Self-examination is always a bit like torture, in my opinion, with the exception that self-examination is probably necessary."

She gathered her crutches and stood up, which solidified the decision to stop the conversation. He glanced at the clock again and noted with surprise that it was already eight o'clock. She walked around behind her desk and flipped over a couple of pages in a small book; most likely, it contained the record of her upcoming engagements. She frowned down at it and scratched behind one ear absentmindedly, and then took up a pencil and said, "Will you come back again?"

She looked up at him when he didn't answer immediately, but it was because he was again surprised by her behavior. It was considerate of her to make such a request, letting him decide if he wanted to continue their discussion, irrespective of her own desire to pursue it. She was respectful of self-determination, which he suspected endeared her to her patients.

She waited patiently while he composed himself enough to agree that he would very much like to meet again, and offered him a late-afternoon appointment nearly two weeks into the future. "It's the best I can do right now, but please call me if you need to. I believe I left my cell phone number with your landlady?"

He nodded, and she thanked him for coming. He could hear her sincerity, and it seemed there was also an element of relief in her voice.

Because it was clear that she had some work to attend to, he let himself out of the room but waited in the waiting area. He guessed, correctly, that she would leave from that side of the building, and it was more than an hour later when she appeared, visibly surprised to find him there. Her expression telegraphed a silent question, but he merely stood to escort her out, ensuring she made it safely to her car.

It was the least he could do, since he was unsure whether he was putting her in harm's way by being there.

He watched her drive away, then walked back to the Garden District, arriving at Delachaise in plenty of time for a meal. Their kitchen was open until midnight, and most of the Friday night dinner rush was over. He ordered two plates of the steak *frites*, having his meat rare, and grateful, as always, that the fries were cooked in goose fat, both because they were delicious and because he needed the energy.

50

AMAOKE WENT ABOUT OVER THE next several days expecting another visit from the Morningstar or one of the lesser demons, feeling that the frustrated purpose of their meeting would have to be revealed at the next opportune occasion, but all was strangely quiet.

Had the appearance of the ascendant Beast changed something? Surely the Morningstar had ongoing plans for Amaoke, and if so, what were they? He still did not know for what purpose he had been summoned on Hallowe'en night. Amaoke had plenty of unanswered questions, and as time passed, there were only more of them. Answers, on the other hand, were sorely lacking.

Amaoke went to the library and pored over the newspapers from the days following the confrontation at Galatoire's but did not find anything extraordinary; nor were there any unusual happenings, with one exception. If he believed, as he did, that there was any connection with recent diabolical activity and the priest, this exception was significant.

The local section of the *Times-Picayune* had a short feature on St. Constantine Church, and it was apparent that the organist's fears had not been unfounded. The bishop had ultimately decided to suppress the parish. The article went on to say that the parish's popular priest had revived the congregation but that special assignments on behalf of the church had interfered with his ability to fully rescue the troubled place, whose buildings had fallen into disrepair when its faithful had been scattered following the devastation of Hurricane Katrina. Despite Father Weston's success in achieving a resurgence in attendance, and restoring the church as a place of sanctuary within the community, a particular assignment from the Vatican had interrupted his efforts to work toward growing the parish community and restoring it to its former place within the New Orleans archdiocese. The bishop expressed his regrets at this outcome, but refused further comment on the possible fate of the property.

Amaoke went back to walking the streets at night and hit all the recent hotspots of activity, from Café du Monde to Galatoire's and back to the now dark and quiet St. Constantine. Apparently, there was no Mass being celebrated there since the bishop's announcement, but there was still a lonely light on in what Amaoke assumed was the rectory window at one of the rear corners of the building on occasion, and the presence of the light corresponded with times of increased spirit energy. Amaoke couldn't positively separate Father Weston's scent from the strong smells around the church property on one occasion, and he had stubbornly stood on the sidewalk out front for most of that night, but the deepest shadows at the peak of the steeple remained still despite the strong feeling he had of being watched, and the good friar never revealed himself.

On another occasion, the back doors of the church were open, and he could see down the steps into a meeting hall of sorts. It appeared that there was a gathering there, and from what he could hear, it was a support group of some kind, most likely Alcoholics Anonymous. Although Father Weston's scent was present, Amaoke could tell it was blunted enough that it was unlikely the priest was in residence or at the meeting.

It was an unusually mild night in late November, and he took a chance and went down the first two steps and could see that the space was a type of dining area that was used for multiple purposes. There were ancient green floor tiles with specks of white, yellow, and red that appeared to be a standard flooring choice for church kitchens and school cafeterias in the late twentieth century, and he could smell the remnant smells that lingered around such a kitchen long after it goes out of use. There was the scent of residual char from the ovens, metallic iron, sulfur, and copper oxidation from hard water, and dry rot, undoubtedly progressing in the stored, unused linens. There were scents of wood and floor polish, and the ghost scents from the comings and goings of thousands of people over the years, more sadness and grief, as they had gathered here for post-funeral meals more regularly than for celebrations, similar to many such gathering places.

The fluorescent lights were on in the far half of the room, and he could see about twenty people at the meeting, sitting in a circle. One of them was a nun, and she appeared to be providing the spiritual leadership for this gathering. Her scent was very clean, clover, and soap, with the dry-clean smell of starch coming from her white habit. She glanced up when he reached the bottom of the stairs, sensing him rather than seeing him there in the shadows, but directed her attention right back to the group.

Somehow her glance was inviting and made him feel welcomed, and that only served to make him feel even more like an intruder, so he retreated back to the alley. He walked out onto the far block, where there was a clean white late-model Dodge minivan parked parallel to the small church parking lot. It had Louisiana plates and looked very out of place in the neighborhood. Amaoke could smell the nun's scent when he neared the vehicle, and placed her as its most recent driver, potentially its only driver. There was a rosary hanging from the rearview mirror, with a white plastic rose entwined in it, and that made him think again of the rosary that had been stolen by Forcas.

He heard the minor commotion of the meeting breaking up, and wandered back to the mouth of the alley in time to see the lights go out at the back of the church. In her white habit, the nun practically glowed in the gathering dusk as she locked the doors and made her way toward the van. She paused for a moment before she stepped out onto the sidewalk, and Amaoke noticed something very interesting. The blunted scent of Father Weston was also coming from her, as if she had spent quite a bit of time with him, and Amaoke didn't know how to interpret this discovery. Why would such a scent cling to her? He knew little about such things but was reasonably sure that priests and nuns were not often in close proximity to one another, unless they worked together, so he wondered if she was also associated with St. Constantine, although he had never seen her there before that night.

She, too, was very young, probably in her early twenties, with a delicate build and a pixie's face. The most marked feature she had were her large eyes, which had a haunted look, as if she had known much suffering in her short life. Amaoke had the strangest urge to protect her, although he had no idea where such a strong desire could be coming from, making him suspect that it was artificially influenced. She did not appear to be exerting any spirit energy; indeed, her predominant demeanor was so calm as to be a counterpoint to the priest's apparent menace.

The cross that was suspended from the chain on her neck was a duplicate of the heavy silver one that hung from Father Weston's waist, and it seemed out of place against her snow-white gown, because it still brought to mind a weapon. It made her look like a fairy carrying a machete.

"We will keep having meetings here every Tuesday night at least until February," she said, assuming that he had come for the meeting. "Everyone is welcome. Come back anytime."

When he remained silent, she moved slowly past him, turning her back to him as she approached the minivan. He smelled no fear or apprehension, but she was agitated about something, and she turned back to him with a look of curiosity, tilting her head as if there were something familiar about him that she could not place.

"Is Father Weston coming back here?" he asked suddenly, confident that she knew exactly where the priest was.

She replied without hesitation, probably trusting that he was a misplaced parishioner. "He is on his way to Rome. I just dropped him at the airport this afternoon. He should be back at the end of next week, but he won't be celebrating Mass here anymore. I think he will be hearing confessions at Our Lady of the Blessed Sacrament until after the Nativity, and if you need to reach him, he will be staying at the rectory there once he returns."

Suddenly her eyes widened in surprise, and the hand holding her keys shook. She closed her eyes and shook her head from side to side as if she were trying to clear it. She said to Amaoke, "I have to go now. Please take care of yourself." Then, putting her hand on the cross around her neck and saying a whispered prayer, she quickly got into the car and drove away without another look back.

Amaoke glanced down the alley, but he already knew what he would see there. The shadows were moving along the walls of the church, and he felt the energy building like a wave, but he stood his ground at the mouth of the alley and they never even approached him, eventually seeming to melt back into a hundred dark crevices, never once breaking into the silence of the evening.

More questions. No answers.

51

WHEN NEXT HE VISITED THE church, St. Constantine's was dark, and there was new scaffolding at the front of the building. Workers had been contracted to nail heavy boards over the large round stained-glass windows above the heavy oak doors to prevent vandalism. There was a chain in place that crossed the space between the heavy handles of the doors, and it was secured by a stout padlock.

A second padlock, twin to the one on the front doors, had been put in place on the alley door, but there were no chains, which told Amaoke that the basement space was indeed still in use, as the nun had told him. On this night, although the padlock was secured, there was lamplight in the second-floor rectory window casting a glow into the gloom of the alley, and a long rectangle of light onto the sidewalk running perpendicular to it.

After several moments of observation, he noticed a disturbance in the bar of light on the sidewalk, an intermittent shadow cast from within the room. Periodically, the glow from the lamp dimmed as someone moved across the room between it and the window, and he suspected that the priest was pacing. He could very faintly hear the resonant tones of the voice speaking prayers in Latin and the rattling of what sounded like a rosary. With every passage, there was a soft thump, so rhythmic that it had to be a part of the ritual, so Amaoke pushed off the wall beneath the window to look up at it.

Father Weston was indeed pacing the room, and Amaoke could make out the priest's shadowed upper body as he passed from one side of the room to the other, and the thump was actually caused by Father Weston tapping on the cross-shaped window trim each time he went by, right at the crosspiece in the center of the four panes. Using the hand that was free of the rosary, he would reach out beside himself as he went one way, and across himself as he went the other way.

There was still something overly familiar about his carriage and his posture that Amaoke was as yet unable to pinpoint. He was not wearing the ceremonial cassock that he had worn for the Mass celebrations; instead, he was wearing a short-sleeved black shirt with the ubiquitous white collar, and that small tab seemed to stand out in the weak lamplight and shadow. He was a study of *chiaroscuro* as he went back and forth, endlessly pacing and praying, with that exclamatory thump each time he passed the window.

Amaoke's first impressions of the man's muscular build were confirmed; his arms were thick and roped with hard muscle, the kind only seen on men who were seriously disciplined in their gym time and usually vain about their efforts. He was still unable to make out any subtler features of the man's face, the long wavy hair and thick eyeglass frames obscuring further detail.

And during the pacing and the thumping, Amaoke noticed something else — the shadows were still. Once again, he could feel dark spirits collected here, and, of interest, they were now concentrated away from the front, congregating in the alley, as if to remain nearer the priest, which he still thought was odd. He did not know enough of the practices of Christianity to understand the prayers, but he felt certain that the words, the movement, and the ritual thumping were keeping the spirits quiet. This observation only raised more unanswered questions.

A telephone rang somewhere upstairs, perhaps on the floor where Father Weston was staying, but Amaoke could not be sure, as the tones bounced back and forth, echoing off the stone structures within the church and making it difficult for him to assess the exact point of their origination. The sound had the solid hardwired jingle that he associated with landlines, unlike the more ethereal tones he recognized as belonging to a cellular phone, and Father Weston disappeared from the window, probably to answer it.

Amaoke moved back into the shadow directly under the window and cocked his head, trying to pick up any conversation, but what he heard was oddly and artificially distorted, and he knew that he was being prevented from hearing it. The distortion was not subtle, a buzzing background with higher-frequency squeaks that were tailored to distract him, so when the sulfur and ozone scents flooded his nose, followed by a bitter metallic odor, he knew the distraction was deliberate.

There was a movement in the center of the alley, and a grotesque form emerged from the deepest shadows. There was no need for a thousand-dollar suit here, so the Morningstar dropped all human pretense. Amaoke suspected the grotesquerie was a reminder to him what it really was. The enormous black wings were missing, as even they carried an element of beauty, and in their place were ugly knobs of bone where a human would have shoulder blades. The upper torso was that of a human male, absent the umbilicus, and the lower body and legs that of a goat with matted hair, fly-spotted as the animal itself would be if ungroomed and left to its pen, neglected. The head was a hybrid of goat and human, with a twisted dark beard and the shiny, slit-like eyes that saw everything. The top of the head was smooth, lacking horns, and Amaoke felt that because he lacked a Judeo-Christian upbringing, the Morningstar did not bother with the full-blown cliché.

"Firstborn, wolf-born, child of moon," it crooned to him in its dead voice. "We think we won't let you eavesdrop on the good priest tonight. Such bad manners anyway. Father Weston is on a secure line to the Vatican receiving instructions that he won't bother to follow anyway, so you shouldn't be disappointed to miss out on the details.

"How troublesome you are! Why should you care about this priest and his doings? He belongs to me as do you, but perhaps in a more meaningful way, he will be the key to our ultimate ascension, and the disgrace of all that is divine."

It stopped suddenly and appeared to leisurely consider the state of its fingernails, which were clotted with filth, and Amaoke could smell the carrion scent like that of a small rodent that has died, out of sight but evocative of its own decay. And then it reached out and closed those same hands on Amaoke's shoulders, touching him for the first time that he could remember in several long centuries, digging those nails in under his clothing and into his skin, and he could feel the threat of the change upon him.

For the first time in his long life, Amaoke did not call for the wolf to come forward; he called the other. And it was the true Beast that came forward, snarling and snapping, as if summoned by death itself, but the Morningstar did not let go, and the Beast was dominated by its touch, unable to escape, unable to attack.

"You seem to misunderstand our roles," the Monster hissed up at him, then increased its own stature to match that of the Beast. "You will lead our armies, on our command. This is the beautiful form that was always intended for you, but for some reason, it is only called by *love*. So be it. We made the mistake of letting you keep your love in the past, thinking that the suffering its loss created would deform you further. Know this: we will destroy everything you love to force you to embrace this glorious monstrosity permanently, and we will own the destruction you unleash, and we will taste the death with your mouth."

It shook the Beast roughly and Amaoke, hearing the descants of its laughter, the thousand voices of the damned, finally felt free of the constraint of his conscience, and sank his teeth into its putrid flesh. The bite was satisfying, because the Morningstar had taken on flesh for this appearance, and his teeth ground into bone and gristle, and he shook his head to tear it before it released him, howling into the void, and it melted back into the shadows, gone.

Amaoke was left with a foul, dry mouthful of desiccated, tasteless flesh. He could feel the places where his own flesh remained broken, where those claws had retracted, beginning to fester, and for the first time, his own scent was tainted with the smell of the Monster. There was a moment of triumphant hope when he realized that his own reaction to the Morningstar had banished it, no matter how temporarily. He was so distracted that he nearly jumped out of his skin when he heard the thump at the window crosspiece above him. He abandoned the alley to its other spirits, and the sounds of Father Weston returning to his prayers.

52

BY THE TIME HE RETURNED home from work the next afternoon, his wounds were worsening, causing physical pain and oozing foul-smelling fluid. In the shower, he examined the ones that he could see on the front of his shoulders, and the skin was red, swollen, and blistered around each ragged puncture. He could see several more on the back of each shoulder by looking at them in the mirror as he stood with his back to it. They were equally ugly, and there was no evidence of his usual rapid healing taking place. Worse, the pain was accompanied by a strange heaviness that made him feel weaker than usual, and he knew that healing these wounds would require purging the contamination.

After he dressed, he sat on his bed, contemplating the shirt he had been wearing when it happened, examining once again the scorch marks where the Monster had touched him. Amaoke could think of only one person to ask for the type of help he needed. And he needed more help than his own prayers could give him, so he stuffed the ruined shirt into his bag and set out on the long walk into Lakeview.

It was far too early for her to be home when he finally arrived, but he looped around to the back of the house as casually as he could, behaving as though he had every right to be there. He was hoping that the neighbors were not as vigilant as the neighborhood warranted. He sat for a short time on the patio, listening and waiting for any sign that would suggest his presence had been noticed and reported, or that his arrest was imminent, but all remained quiet.

It had been dark for some time, but if Aleta kept to her usual schedule, she still wouldn't arrive for at least two hours more, so he prepared a small ritual fire in her outdoor fire pit, and sat next to it. After freeing his hair from the single long braid, he began to sing prayers, waving the smoke over his head. When the fire died down to embers, Amaoke fed the tainted shirt to it, watching the flames grow as he sang for the healing breath of the spirits. But his prayers were also for healing hands, and as the fire died away to ash and the last wisps of smoke rose out of the pit, he heard the unmistakable hum of the glass door opening on its track. He did not open his eyes or turn around, letting her scent reach him and comfort him.

He knew her eyes had not adjusted to the darkness, and she had no reason to expect anyone to be there. He said her name softly, adding, "It's me, Amaoke, don't be alarmed." Which, after all, was ridiculous, since she had no idea that he knew where she lived, and his voice alone startled her, and he heard one of her crutches clatter to the tiles. Thankfully, she did not scream, for which he was grateful, but he felt like the intruder he was. He had no right to be here, no reason to scare her this way.

"Amaoke?" she said tentatively, repeating his name as if to reassure herself. He could smell her distress and fear upon finding him at her home, where she had every reasonable expectation that she was safe, and the meekness of her tone further worsened his guilt about the trespass.

"Over here," he replied, letting her know where he was sitting.

He waited a few moments while she gathered up the fallen crutch and ventured further out onto the patio, moving slowly, because she was still unsure what he wanted. He could hear her heart pounding in her chest, and smelled panic, as if she were deciding whether to flee. In his vulnerable state, he did not want to risk her flight triggering the Beast, so he closed his hand on her arm to keep her from running, even though he was frightening her even more.

He stood up to face her, saying only, "I really need your help."

She stopped abruptly, her fear subsiding somewhat, apparently having decided he wasn't here to visit some destruction upon her, and just as suddenly asked, "Were you burning something out here?"

"It's a long story," he replied. "Come inside so you'll be warm, and I will try to explain."

He followed her back inside, paying attention to what his nose could alert him to in case there were dark spirits about. But there were no unusual scents, so he secured the sliding door behind him and walked to the center of her kitchen, anticipating that she would turn on the light. She did so, and came to him with a quizzical expression on her face.

"Amaoke, will you please tell me what is going on?" Now he could see the concern in her eyes, and he wondered what she was seeing. It was as if she could sense his distress, and could tell he was in pain. "You're hurt," she concluded. "I can see it in your face."

Rather than answer her, he pulled his shirt off over his head, gathering his hair in one hand to pull it off of his shoulders. Rather than explain, as he had promised he would, he turned around so she could see the worst of the damage to his shoulders.

"What in the world?! Amaoke, these are awful," she began, and he could hear the halted intake of her breath when the foul smell of the wounds reached her nose, and he knew she was trying not to gag. "Come with me," she ordered, leading him down the short hallway and into the master bedroom suite.

She crossed the room at an angle and went directly over to the dressing table and expertly balanced the stool next to it in one hand, allowing her to continue to maneuver with the crutches as she led him into the bathroom. It was a beautiful, serene space, with a vaulted ceiling and a large soaking tub that took up most of one corner. There were a large, double-sink vanity and a separate, tiled shower stall with a glass front. There was a substantial skylight, and she had suspended a few hanging plants above the bathtub.

Aleta placed the stool next to the vanity and indicated he should sit down. She was still wearing her overcoat and carrying her keys. She set the latter on the countertop, and he was glad to see that her overcoat belt was tied loosely about her, because it was one way to try to keep her out of sight of certain spirits, but he didn't tell her this. She leaned down and rummaged in one of the small drawers and pulled out a green hair tie.

"May I?" she said, but it was not really a question because she had already begun to gather his hair atop his head. She paused for a moment, noticing the tiny separate braid that ran behind his left ear, but did not stop to comment on it, arranging his hair up out of her way in a messy man-bun that reminded him of a samurai. It was endlessly amusing to him, but she was already on to her next task.

She pulled several bottles out of a small closet that he could see held linens and other bathroom supplies, and a plastic basket with what appeared to be first-aid items.

"Sorry," she said by way of apology before pouring copious amounts of liquid from a brown bottle onto the wounds. It caused minor stinging, but other than that, had little effect. After that torture, she selected a needleless syringe, which she repeatedly filled with saline from another bottle and used to flush each ragged wound clean. When the salt solution hit the open wounds, they began to foam, and the skin at the edges of the punctures peeled away, the flesh making a hissing sound that caused Aleta to flinch away from him as he cried out in agony.

"What is happening?" she cried, as she watched the flesh shrink back as if it were alive.

"Unnatural wounds." Amaoke managed to grunt the words out as he struggled to maintain control over his form. "Probably the salt."

The result was not very pretty, and the edges of each wound gaped wider than when she had started, the abraded skin darkening to an ugly grayish hue. Aleta bravely attended to them by taking a small pair of very sharp scissors, and, expertly balanced on one crutch, she began to trim the loose strips of broken skin, which made each hole slightly bigger but made the wounds look much less ugly, from what he could see reflected back in the mirror.

It was causing him no end of discomfort, and was occasionally quite painful, to the point that he was unable to concentrate enough for complete control, and could feel thousands of tiny hairs sprouting out along his spine, his jawline, and the backs of his arms. Aleta gasped and stopped her ministrations, lifting her arms away from him, but she did not move away, and he regained control, resuming his smooth-skinned form with the slightest shiver as the hairs retracted back into their follicles.

When she finished, she was sweating and shaking with the distress caused by what she had seen, and he was gasping with the effort of staying human. He knew his body was trying to shift to decrease some of the considerable stress the wounds caused, in response to the emotional toll that the pain caused, but he wanted to avoid creating further terror for her, because he could tell she was barely holding on to whatever mental strength was allowing her to continue. Her professional training was allowing her a bit of remove, but no doctor could fail to be affected by the burning, putrid smell of these wounds, the recoil of the defiled flesh, and the knowledge that the patient could turn into a snarling beast. The fact that she had come home to this, instead of the respite she must have been expecting, was probably adding to her difficulty. He was sorry he had brought the problem to her door instead of finding a way to get her to come to him, but there was no changing it now.

"Bring me the ashes from the fire pit," he directed, and his voice came out in a growl that neither of them expected, and she took up her other crutch and nearly fled from the room and from him. He wasn't entirely sure she would return, but he was pleasantly surprised both when he heard the tapping of her crutches in the outer room and at the speed at which she had fulfilled his request. She shook so much that her crutches rattled, but she had swept the ashes of the burned shirt and the remains of his ritual fire into a copper bowl that she balanced by wedging it between her upper arm and her side. She passed him the vessel with hands that shook violently, and he could hear the rapidness of her heartbeat, thumping away again like a scared rabbit.

"This isn't going to be pleasant," he warned, relieved that his voice was closer to normal than before. "I need you to spread the ashes into the wounds. You have to use your hands, and it will help if you pray while you do it."

She opened her mouth and looked as if she were about to protest; he assumed because he was asking her to soil the wounds that she had just cleaned, knowing it went against everything she had been taught. But then she squared her shoulders and made eye contact with him in the mirror. "Pray what?" she asked, and once again, he silently admired her fortitude. She was prepared to help him if she could, no matter the emotional toll it must have been costing her.

"The words don't matter as long as you believe in them," he reassured her and reached up to touch one of her hands. "The ashes allow spirits to move between worlds without getting caught, and putting them on the wounds will finish removing the contamination. It may also hide me from other spirits that would try to get to me while I am weakened. Your hands and your touch will complete the healing; your hands and your voice are critical to the observance of the ritual, since you are a healer."

She did as he asked, taking some of the ashes into her hands and placing them on the open areas in his skin. He saw her lips moving slowly, but she was otherwise silent, and he was grateful that she had instinctively closed her eyes. She did not see what he watched in the mirror as the ashes released whatever minor demons that the putrid flesh possessed, and the dark swirling shadows that expanded to fill the room slowly disintegrated into a million points of darkness and dispersed to nothingness.

He shook violently as the contamination was purged, pushed as if by invisible hands, and felt stung as if each dark point were a fiery spark landing on his skin, causing him to flinch and jump, but he refused to cry out. He prayed in his mother's ancient tongue, and it comforted him enough to fend off the change.

Aleta did not lift her hands from his shoulders, and he sat very still, waiting for her to move. It seemed a long time before she opened her eyes, and pulled in a long, deep breath, like a skin diver returning to the surface, grateful for air.

She lifted her fingers slowly from his skin, gazing in wonder at the small residual marks on his now-intact skin. She pushed the ash residue around, convincing herself that the wounds were actually gone. "I have never seen wounds like that before, and now they are completely closed." There was a dazed, childlike quality to her words, and he understood that even though she had witnessed the regeneration with her own eyes, her mind was still questioning everything she had seen. He was worried that it was the beginning of shock, so he stood up, offering her the stool, and she sank gratefully onto it, allowing her crutches to slide onto the tiles.

A violent shudder passed through her, and he crouched next to her, putting a hand on the small of her back when she put her head down and closed her eyes. She hiccupped out a few dry heaves and then regained her control. He waited, saying nothing, allowing her to recover.

She finally opened her eyes, then glanced over at him and paused, giving him a lopsided grin, perhaps as reassurance to him that the worst of her distress had passed. She reached for the hair tie she had placed in his hair. "That looks ridiculous," she said, pulling it out, freeing his hair and allowing it to cascade over his shoulders.

It made him smile, and he shrugged and stood up, stooping as he did so in order to gather up her crutches. He held them out to her, but to his surprise, she gripped his forearms to pull herself up, leaning forward into him, allowing her cheek to touch the center of his bare chest for a brief moment before she reclaimed her crutches and turned away to lead him back out of the room. He pulled his shirt over his head and took a bit of the remaining ashes from the bowl before he followed her.

When they reached the living room, she turned to him and said, "I can still expect to see you next week, in the office?"

Amaoke was surprised at how quickly she reestablished their emotional distance, and the step she took away from him reinforced a physical divide that could not entirely erase the intimacy of their recent physical contact. After the intensity of the events of the evening, he was concerned about her state of mind, but her next statement clarified what she was thinking.

"If we meet in my office, I can justify protecting what is said, and what happens, as doctor-patient privilege. I think that is going to become very important to maintain." Involuntarily her hand closed over the Mobius loop at her throat, and he suspected it represented her personal talisman. He also guessed that she realized there was more here that she needed protection from than him.

He stepped up close to her, saying nothing. He dabbed a small amount of ash onto her lips with the tip of his finger; even though she had tolerated everything that had happened until this moment, he felt it would be a step too far to ask her to swallow the ash. He hoped the ritual would come close enough to provide her some protection from the other monsters that were around.

She gave him a probing look, and started to say something, but he startled her into silence by reaching for the belt at her waist. She became very still, and her scent changed, ever so subtly. Under other circumstances, it would have made him smile. He grasped the ends of the belt and tightened it slightly, then added another loop to create a secure knot.

"Keep this coat on as long as you can," he instructed gently, releasing the ends. "Sleep in it tonight if possible," he added, seeing her confusion. "It is part of the ritual."

Amaoke also realized that she was going to have to work to regain a sense of safety within her own home, so he left her to start that journey, letting himself out into the night.

53

AMAOKE ARRIVED ON TIME FOR the previously arranged appointment with Aleta. He noticed that she had once again scheduled him at the end of the day, and he suspected that it was not just out of respect for his work schedule, but also so that she could again extend the appointment if needed. Despite the incident of a few nights before, she slipped into a professional remove once they were both seated. She avoided the subject of his wounds entirely, and did not ask him how he was doing. He suspected it was her way of protecting herself from events she could not fully understand, and reinforcing boundaries that had felt somewhat eroded in the personal exchange at her home.

She repeated her initial interrogation of their last meeting, inquiring whether he felt he was safe from self-harm, and whether he had any thought of harming others. He again answered in the negative, and then was unsure where to take the discussion, but she already had an agenda.

"When we last met," she prompted, "We were discussing your concerns about the possibility of being manipulated into contributing to some destructive end."

"Yes, my fear of becoming involved in some wanton destruction, and being manipulated to become a monster I never want to be." He allowed himself to share this, his most fundamental concern.

"Perhaps that fear can be overcome," Aleta reasoned hopefully. "There are many mechanisms that can be used to understand fear, and figuring out whether it is unfounded or warranted by the accumulation of information about the root causes of it can be helpful. If the causes can be understood, or even controlled, fear can ultimately be banished." She surprised him when she admitted, "I am still a bit afraid of you, and that demonstration from the other night…" She shuddered, briefly wrapping her arms tightly around herself, before returning her focus to him.

"I know you are, I can tell. But it requires a great deal of strength and courage to master fear, and it isn't always intuitive," he pointed out, adding, "fear can also be useful, especially if it keeps us away from harm."

"So, I have not seen you fully changed," Aleta said. "You have told me you change into a wolf, but you were explaining that you can also become something else. Do you want to show me the complete transformation?"

He smiled bitterly. "If you want to see an Arctic wolf, you can look up the image on any computer, or in any nature resource at the library. I would prefer to maintain a fully human interaction with you. The longer I live, the more I try to persist in human form unless there is some advantage in doing otherwise. As we discussed, your initial introduction to my nature was a matter of necessity, not something that I intended to be the focus of this relationship, whatever it is. You have my gratitude for your help with my injuries."

She looked at him with a great deal of tenderness, as if she was acknowledging something painful in what he was sharing with her. She raised her hands as if in surrender, patting the air in his direction, and said, "I understand. I don't need to see it, but can you help me understand what happens in those other, uncommon instances?"

"Something much worse." Amaoke shuddered involuntarily. "I look just like an enormous Arctic wolf under ordinary circumstances. But the first time the true Beast came through, it was called by extraordinary stress, and I was horribly destructive, even if my actions were justified. I had no recollection of all that I had done, and at the time, I was horrified, because I had no idea that I could even become such a thing. And such a transfiguration did not happen again for a very long time, much to my great relief.

"In the past year, this ghastly form has been called from me twice, once a product of my own rage, and once, two nights ago, when it was forced from me by the Morningstar's touch, which surprised and distressed me greatly, because I temporarily lost control of my ability to defend myself. This provides the greatest concern that I am vulnerable to manipulation when at my most dangerous."

"Transfiguration is traditionally a term of divinity," Aleta interjected, as if she were trying to get him to see the positive aspects of such powerful abilities. "Perhaps it is an extension of something that you can use to protect yourself from the Morningstar, and prevent the outcome you wish to avoid?"

"As a wolf, I have done terrible things. In both human and animal forms, I have exacted revenge, made myself judge, jury, and executioner, and even tasted innocent blood. But I had no procreative power to pass on this curse in either form," Amaoke responded, shaking his head, unwilling to see any advantages. "In this case, the change is as profane as it could possibly be; the Beast can pass its characteristics to its victims. I could create an army of such terrible power and destruction that humankind could never recover."

"But you alluded to the fact that you had gained some control over the change," she said. "I witnessed you start it and stop it of your own accord, right here in this room."

"It has taken most of my life for me to gain control over the wolf, and it was ultimately accomplished by acknowledging and embracing my dual nature," he sighed. He shook his head, exhausted with speculation, unwilling to say more. He was afraid to say out loud what he believed in his heart: that to gain control of the true Beast, he would have to achieve unity with it, but at what cost to his conscience? Would all of the characteristics that he had worked so hard to cultivate, the principles of right living, be subverted by the Morningstar's directive?

"I am seeking your help to see if there may be other ways to control my nature, beyond the physical, and apparently incomplete, control I have gained over time," he told her.

"Scientifically, you mean?" she asked, studying him carefully. "One would have to understand the cause of your nature on a cellular level, which would probably require focused genetic testing, taking your DNA, which is perhaps not advisable. If it gave us, the scientific community, *any* indication of the existence of a supernormal genetic code, you would likely be locked up somewhere and studied, and you, Amaoke, the individual with self-determination and freedom, would cease to exist.

"And mapping out your genetic makeup really wouldn't be the end of it," she surmised. "A directed therapy would have to be devised to control only those parts of your genetic code that were responsible for your transformation into the wolf."

"But in addition to my own control, couldn't that treatment work as an antidote to unleashing the Beast?" he asked her.

"Interestingly, both in theory and in practice, maybe not," she told him. "Trying to control the function of one gene could change the function of another. There are subtle complexities, all of which are not well understood and may never be fully understood, although the technological advances in the field are incredible and rapid. In theory, the sound science behind gene therapy could be used to control your change, arrest you in human form, but at the same time, other processes that you need to survive could be, at the same time, negatively affected. In simple terms, there could be untoward side effects.

"Not to mention the exorbitant costs, both in money and other resources, needed to investigate such a possibility. These kinds of endeavors are selectively undertaken in situations where hundreds of thousands of people are affected; to get your hands on the type of money necessary to direct that kind of focus for a single individual, you would have to be of interest to the military, as a weapon, which would be worse for you than just the run-of-the-mill scientific curiosity that would justify your ongoing captivity. I am sure that if certain people knew about your nature, you wouldn't be allowed to walk around unfettered."

Amaoke considered all that she had told him very carefully before he spoke again. He admired that the root consideration behind her response was his welfare, and he was thankful yet again that he had chosen to reveal himself to her. She was smart, she was brave, and she was very protective of her patients.

"Would you know where to send my blood for testing? Is there a way for you to request a private evaluation?" he asked her.

Her expression gave away her surprise at his persistence, but she sighed. "I can make inquiries," she assented. "But I fear that the type of place that would perform such testing would be staffed by the most intelligent as well as the most curious minds, and an extraordinary result would raise questions that neither of us can answer without inviting further scrutiny."

"The other night, you mentioned physician-patient privilege," he pointed out. "I assume that signifies that you have the means of keeping what happens here private?"

"To an extent, that is exactly what it means, with some limited exceptions," she warned. "Psychiatry can be especially sticky, because if the physician has any knowledge that the patient is a danger to self, or others, especially to others, the physician has an obligation to report such knowledge to the proper authorities." She tilted her head slightly and gave him a look that he easily interpreted.

"You already have such knowledge," he whispered softly.

"In one way, I do," she acknowledged. "In another way, I don't necessarily see an immediate threat, even if there is a plausible one that exists at any given time. That is what was behind the formality of the exercise of asking you the question at the beginning of each of our sessions. I can document your negative assertion and balance it with my clinical suspicion based on the tenor of our interaction. If I document that you deny having suicidal and homicidal thoughts, and my clinical concern is low to nonexistent, then I have satisfied my duty to protect society from a known source of harm."

"And is that concern low or nonexistent?" Amaoke asked, suspecting he knew the answer.

"Unfortunately, it is not," she replied with her usual candor. "And I am obligated to maintain records of our visits if I want to assert the privilege. However, your condition presents a difficulty that has created a bit of a loophole, albeit a false one."

"The proper authorities —?"

"Just so." She smiled at his acuity. "Who are the proper authorities? If I were to go to the police, my story would not appear credible, and I would be sitting across from one of my colleagues, trying to explain myself and my behavior, probably unsuccessfully. And whatever risk I was concerned about regarding the possible danger of harm would certainly not be mitigated because there would be insufficient investigation of it. So, for now, my conscience is clear about my current state of inaction, but it is precarious ground."

"So what could happen if a smart scientist started asking the wrong questions?" he asked.

"At first, I could hold off most of the intrusive inquiries by citing the privilege. But the smartest of them would work for private labs that are involved in some serious research and development, and they have equally serious lawyers who would probably wonder what I was hiding — if the results were really extraordinary. More serious inquiry could come in the form of subpoenas to produce files, with the suggestion to the court that because of the nature of my practice there would be enough in the way of protection of public interests to see the information, because of a not-so-nebulous threat to society from potentially dangerous patients."

"Could they do it?" he wondered aloud.

"Of course. We could fight it, but the bottom line is that we probably should avoid the scrutiny. Nobody would win." She shook her head sadly. "I think you would be taking a huge risk for perhaps no reward." He was pleased that she was referring to the two of them using the collective pronoun, but he was pretty sure that it was a subconscious change of thinking.

"What if your differences are catalogued, but there is no way to control the change in the way you are seeking? You have to consider that there may be more to lose here than there is to gain. Are you certain that there is no other way to proceed?" she asked, but he could see that she didn't expect him to answer. "Despite all the unanswered questions, and my recommendations, ultimately, you have to decide what is the best course to take. I am aware that you can seek other means to investigate this solution, and I don't want you to think that I am unwilling to help you, even if I have reservations about it."

Rather than comment on this, Amaoke changed the direction of their discussion by asking quietly, "Am I allowed to see my records?"

"In theory, a patient has a right to their medical records," she told him. "In psychiatry, we often use a caveat for certain patients, denying them access to certain sensitive psychiatric records if that information could cause distress or a deterioration of their condition."

"How often?"

"Almost always," Aleta admitted.

"Are you going to raise that exception with me?" he asked, mostly out of curiosity about her answer, because he was pretty sure he knew what she *wanted* to do.

Rather than reply, she pulled herself up onto her crutches with a sigh, and walked behind her desk to the credenza. He hadn't noticed it before, but the drawers had electronic locks, and she disarmed one of them, flipping through several folders before selecting one and pulling it from its place. She returned to her position in front of the couch opposite him, passing the dun-colored folder across with a slim hand, but she remained standing. Her fingers shook slightly as she released it to him; the only tell that she was concerned about him seeing it.

"The records cannot leave this office," she informed him. "Take as much time as you like to review them; I will step out until you are finished." Then she crossed back to the desk and picked up her laptop computer, secured it beneath one arm, and quietly left the room.

It was already well after eight o'clock, and he felt a bit guilty about keeping her there so long, but he knew she was very good at setting boundaries with him and would have said something if she had a conflict. He also suspected that she was encouraging his trust by letting him read the records at the same time he asked to see them; thus, Amaoke could not accuse her of altering them in some way as he could if she had raised cause for delay.

He read through her notes, which were organized, thorough, and well-considered, even the ones that she had, by necessity, dictated much after the fact owing to the events of their first meeting. Her observations were accurate, spare, and made use of very little conjecture. She sketched out his concerns, and made her own clinical remarks. There were some technical notations about function that he did not understand, and also some areas where she had written *deferred*, and he assumed it was because she hadn't finalized a clinical opinion on some point. He noticed that the term was used regarding psychosis, as if she needed more time to categorize his behavior.

What was clear to him was that she had reached a reasonably definitive conclusion on the question of his potential threat to others; her notes suggested that she believed he was of moderate to high risk of harmful behavior, but that it was significantly mitigated by a stable social attitude toward humanity, although possibly occasionally influenced by detrimental external actors. He took the last to mean that she was acknowledging his concern that his actions could be adversely affected by the Morningstar, but in her records, she made it sound as though he had some unsavory acquaintances, which he thought was very clever of her. Overall, she was hiding what he really was in plain sight, suggesting that she was in the process of deciding what elaborate psychiatric diagnosis to assign.

As he read, there was not only admiration for her, but also a growing concern. Aleta was putting herself way out on a limb, significantly risking not just her own credibility, but possibly her career. Not to mention that he still didn't know how much of this relationship that the Morningstar could somehow divine, either from Amaoke's thoughts or behaviors, or its own nefarious methods.

He went out of the room and down the darkened hallway, and he finally found her sitting in what appeared to be a small conference room, typing away at her computer, having engrossed herself in other work. He watched her for a moment from the doorway, thinking how ironic it was that one who appeared so fragile was really so strong. He inhaled her scent slowly, unwilling to admit how much it affected him.

She finally looked up, and did a sort of double-take, putting a hand to her neck involuntarily, and he knew he had startled her.

"Sorry, I didn't mean to startle you," he apologized, but she had already returned her attention to the laptop, waving him into the room. Her fingers clacked out a few more words before she shut it down and closed it.

"I am reaching out to a colleague who might be able to help us," she told him, placing both of her hands on the table, palms up. "I may ask you to have your blood drawn anonymously. Perhaps at the AIDS clinic, where you don't have to leave your name, you just get a number for results. From there, I can put in an order with instructions on what they should do with the specimen, and they should be able to send it on to whatever facility is requested and forward my orders for its handling and evaluation.

"This way, the results will be anonymous. They may agree to contact me directly, as the physician of record, or they may require that you show up in person to give a passcode that will release the results.

"I have a feeling that we may hear something ahead of those two responses if they discover anything unexpected, which I guess is what we are hoping for," she said. "Once the genetic evaluation is done, I will have to find out to whom to send it for answers about intervention, and at that point, we will have to revisit whether we persist in this mad course or not."

Amaoke said nothing, understanding perfectly that the next step she was referring to would probably require revealing his true nature to strangers in the hope that they could help him better control it. He stood up and gently slid the folder across the table, wedging one corner underneath the back of her upturned hand, before retreating to the hallway and the waiting room beyond, ready to escort her to her car whenever she finished her tasks.

54

AMAOKE'S ATTENTIONS TURNED TO UNRAVELING the mystery of the elusive priest as the holidays approached. The Morningstar stayed away, but Amaoke suspected, as much as he felt, that it was tracking his movements carefully. The timing of its recent appearances was not coincidental, and he was always on guard for it.

St. Constantine was now completely dark, and utterly silent of any spirit energy. When he arrived to pick up on Father Weston's whereabouts, there were no signs of human activity, and the rectory window remained dark. Amaoke returned a second time, on a Tuesday night, to see if the promised meetings were still occurring, but the church was silent, the basement door padlock solidly secure, and he could scent no recent human presence on its surface or in the alley approach to the door. He listened carefully, blocking out other intervening noises from the neighborhood, but was unable to pick up the low hum he associated with electricity as it moved through the wires. The power had been turned or shut off.

Amaoke thought that last detail strange; hadn't the Morningstar suggested that there was a secure telephone line to the Vatican within the building? Come to think of it, what was the purpose of such a thing in a suppressed parish?

What were these instructions that the priest was receiving from the highest authorities in the church? And why wouldn't a priest follow instructions from the Vatican? In Amaoke's limited knowledge, he thought such guidance would be as law to a man of the cloth, and as such, would be followed instinctively.

How did the Morningstar have knowledge of these things? Amaoke already understood that the line between the divine and the profane could be very fine indeed.

He shifted his attention to Our Lady of the Blessed Sacrament, a historic treasure in the heart of Bywater. The church itself was built of stone that was whitewashed regularly in its earlier days, and now likely owed its glowing white appearance to paint, making it a gleaming jewel in comparison to its poorer cousin, St. Constantine. It was a much larger structure, with multiple spires atop its sloping roofs. The rectory was a separate, smaller structure that lay adjacent to the church across a small courtyard, and the signage suggested that the nuns were cloistered in the dormitory-like structure with its own chapel that was set back into the next block. There was a wrought-iron fence along that part of the compound, and it enclosed the alley between the blocks and the side garden of a small private house. The house had probably originally belonged to a private citizen because of the unattached garage whose old wooden carriage door directly faced the street. The garage itself had likely originally housed both a grand carriage and the horses that pulled it.

Amaoke suspected it was a caretaker's residence, and he thought it strange that the fence ran up beside the garage rather than enclosing it, but the convenience of opening that door to the street was probably a necessary practicality that outweighed any genuine concern for security, since the grounds were open between the church and rectory at the front of the property anyway.

The place was made even grander because of the ongoing Nativity celebrations, and it was lit up like a birthday cake on most evenings, the glow from altar candles giving it life as the winter solstice approached. Mass was celebrated several times each day, with confession heard two evenings each week, and apparently also by appointment, if he was reading the calendar posted inside the main doors correctly.

Unlike St. Constantine, this church was scrubbed of any spirit activity that he could discern. The rectory was home to at least four different priests; trusting his nose he could separate four distinct scent signatures that were male, and one that was less pervasive and female that he assumed belonged to a housekeeper there.

On an unseasonably chilly Sunday morning, he wandered by the church, wanting to assess its energy during one of the times of highest human activity. It was cold enough that he could see his breath, and there had been a light frost that morning. Although the day was bright and sunny, there was a chilly wind off the Gulf that would keep any warming at bay for several hours.

Amaoke noticed that the parking lot was full, but a white Dodge Caravan stood out like a beacon among darker late-model sedans and brightly colored compact cars. When he got closer, he could see the white rosary and the rose through the front windshield. It was parked nose in, in the first row next to the church wall, the closest spot near a side door that probably led into the rooms behind the sanctuary. He identified the scent of the young nun that he had encountered at St. Constantine when he got near the driver's door.

This gave him information he had not gained on previous visits, as he had never seen the car in the parking lot before. It made him wonder if the nun herself were cloistered on the property, and a quick turn around the block gave him the answer. He positioned himself at the corner of the fence nearest the dormitory, letting the wind push the air towards him, and he could just separate her unique scent from that of several other women, all much older than she based on what his nose told him. He felt that her cell was probably on the lower floor just off the corner of the building, based on a concentration of her scent that he identified from that area.

She was the only person at the new church that he could identify as a known associate of Father Weston. Her presence here confirmed his; if Amaoke recalled what she had said to him at St. Constantine, the priest should have returned from Rome by now, and should have been hearing confession and staying in the rectory here.

Amaoke retraced his steps, passing by the front of the church and crossing the courtyard to the rectory, but his nose gave him no different information than it had before; of the four men living in the structure, none was Father Weston. There was likewise no evidence of his scent near the white Dodge, which Amaoke returned to after his fruitless nose work at the rectory. But this did not worry him; the car smelled as though it had recently been cleaned and detailed, which was also unusual.

Amaoke's observations of the church's properties led him to the conclusion that most of its automobiles were frightfully outdated, and though cared for, were not maintained to the degree of this vehicle. This, he thought, would be the type of car that was used to transport the bishop, not the youngest nun in the neighborhood cloister.

On his next pass, Amaoke strolled the perimeter of the entire property, focusing on the far side of the block that he had not visited, and he was rewarded for his efforts. As he approached the caretaker's house, he began to pick up the familiar scent that was nearly interchangeable between the Morningstar and the priest. There was a complete lack of spirit activity, which was odd. Every time he had picked up the priest's scent in the past, it had been positively associated with the presence of dark spirits, but here there were none. The small house was silent, its windows dark. But Amaoke's nose told him that the priest was staying there.

The scent concentrated and seemed to hang in the cold air outside the carriage door facing the street, and as he came closer to the short driveway that led out to the road, he could hear sounds coming from within the garage.

The street itself was quiet; anyone who had business here at the church was at Mass, and everyone else was likely to be taking advantage of that other place of Sunday morning worship at this hour, the church of St. Mattress. Though it was only a little after eight o'clock in the morning, Amaoke could hear the soft clanking of tools against metal, and the softer wisps of someone whispering to themselves as they solved a thorny problem. He stepped right up and put his ear to the door, and the scent flooded his nose. Although the whispered words did not coalesce into anything discernable, he could also smell the musk of sweat from exertion and some frustration. He identified the tool as likely a wrench, and from the scent of gasoline, oil, and upholstery cleaner, he knew that there was a car in the garage.

Suddenly, a long string of Latin was uttered, and although Amaoke did not understand the meaning, the sentiment was that of an oath. He was dumbfounded. In his experience, the typical cause of such an outburst comes from a garage when someone is trying to repair something on a car unsuccessfully.

Who was this priest who eschewed Mass on a Sunday morning to change his own motor oil? And since no priest really owns anything, the car had to have some significance for him to be dirtying his own hands with it. Why wasn't he housed with the other priests? Reconciling any of what he was learning with what he already knew was impossible; he remained in the dark, unearthing more questions, and still, there were no answers.

He put his hand up to knock on the door, but his ears told him that all sounds from inside the garage had ceased. Amaoke had that strange sensation that the person inside was listening for him, was hyperaware of him standing on the other side of the door, much like when he had entered the confessional booth. His instincts were good, and they were telling him to leave, which he was inclined to do, as he was on a public street, on sanctified ground, with a foe that he could neither see nor adequately defend against.

But he was not prepared to retreat very far anymore, knowing that answers would only come with persistence, so he went back to the corner and crossed the street. Amaoke went down just past the first house and cut through a few empty rear yards until he reached one behind a vacant house, his intended destination, as he remembered the *For Sale* sign he had seen in the front yard when he had been across the street. The outer cellar door was open, as if the house had recently been shown, and the agent had forgotten to secure it. The door at the bottom of the stairs was locked, but this wasn't important to Amaoke, who used the sheltered space to undress and change, grateful for the wolf's heavy coat after exposing himself to the cold morning.

Then he crept back up the steps to the yard, and slunk slowly around the side, pleased that he had a good view of the carriage door at an angle from the front right corner of the house. There was an evergreen shrub that conveniently wrapped around the side and across the front of the yard. He hunched down in the shadows, aware that his white fur would stand out on such a bright day, hoping that the greenery would camouflage him enough that he could watch without being seen.

It was still mostly quiet in the garage, but he heard a new sound, the heavy rustling of cloth, and he was rewarded by the grating sounds of a bolt being disengaged, which told him the occupant's curiosity was aroused. With an unexpectedly loud clatter, the door swung outward, so large that its path took the leading edge nearly into the street. The priest's back came into view as he folded the door out of the way, securing it to keep it open.

He wore a heavy, long-sleeved black T-shirt, no collar, and heavy brown canvas pants with work boots that were similar in construct to Amaoke's. Behind the priest, there was an ample open space that would have accommodated three cars, and assorted tools that Amaoke recognized as serious mechanic's equipment – it was similar to some of the gear that was in the motor pool for the construction company. There was a car inside, but it had been covered with a heavy tarp before the door had been opened.

Father Weston turned to the street, and Amaoke could see that his fingers were grimed with grease. The man looked up and down the road, as if looking for something. His wavy hair blew in the wind, and he was wearing safety goggles in place of his usual spectacles. These he pushed up onto his head and squinted across the road in Amaoke's direction, although Amaoke was reasonably sure he was not visible from the other side of the shrubbery.

For the very first time, Amaoke could see the man's face clearly, and it was a face he knew almost as well as his own. And the scent of the Morningstar was immediately explained, because that face was its own, its human guise, the handsome features it adopted to walk among the pureflesh. Incarnate in this priest, the Monster could do evil far more significant than Amaoke had allowed himself to imagine. And Amaoke felt a singular dread when he realized what else the Morningstar could gain access to in this form.

55

AMAOKE KNEW THAT ALETA WAS not safe, but he had to arm her with two things that might help protect her. The third involved presenting himself to the lab for testing, so that if anything happened to him, there was a possibility that having his DNA results on record and in her possession could give her leverage, to some advantage that he could not now see.

When they had parted after their last appointment, he had failed to schedule another, and he also needed her to provide an order for his blood to be drawn. When he showed up at the clinic, the receptionist gave him a strange look and said, "Dr. Madison is out for two weeks. She does have a colleague covering her practice, if you need something —?" He was sure his surprise showed on his face, but he recovered as best he could, and reported that Amaoke had failed to make his next appointment and that he hoped to do so now, if possible. He avoided asking about the blood draw because he was sure that Aleta was keeping that information very quiet.

He and the receptionist agreed on a time for his next appointment, and he could tell by her struggles as she hunted through the calendar that there were not many openings before the end of the year, but she put him in as the last appointment on Christmas Eve, and he had to smile to himself. It was probably his birthday, according to his mother's best reckoning using her people's moon calendar and her memories that he was born around the time of an essential annual festival. When in the Arctic, he could identify the day by the sun's position on the horizon at midday. He had later acquired an understanding of the Gregorian calendar, which allowed him to assign a probable date for the occasion. He accepted the appointment as a good omen that he would live to see at least one more birthday.

When the day arrived, he hung around the house, enjoying the sixty-degree weather. No matter how mild the climate, he doubted any construction crews were working on Christmas Eve, and his own was no exception. He even took a short nap after lunch, leaving all the windows open, before setting out across town to Aleta's office.

Her skin was even more radiant than usual, and it was apparent that she had gotten some sun – perhaps a well-deserved vacation in a tropical locale. But there were circles under her eyes that he didn't remember from before, a pronounced sign of stress that belied a recent return from a relaxing sojourn.

They did their ritual opening exchange, and Amaoke was feeling particularly guilty when he told her that no, he did not feel he was a danger to himself or others. But perhaps, if her notes had been any indication, she did not accept his assertion at face value after all, allowing that the background risk never really varied. Maybe she even thought he might be trying to convince himself that it was true, giving the thought power by saying it aloud, like a prayer to ward off the possibility he could hurt another.

He didn't want to lie to her or to himself, but he knew his next task was to face the priest, and as there was sure to be a confrontation, the potential for violence was significant enough that his unchanged response tasted like a lie. There was no guarantee that violence would occur, though Amaoke judged it all the more likely now that Father Weston's identity revealed him to be a creature of the Morningstar – his appearance confirmed it. All of the cryptic statements made about their possible meeting by the Morningstar suggested that a confrontation was an expected outcome.

"I found a lab that will process your specimen confidentially, but it is expensive," she told him. "The laboratory is owned by Rising Sun Industries, a Japanese research and development firm. They will arrange and pay for your blood to be transported by courier to their facilities in Nagayama, which they say is one of their conditions, in order to preserve the chain of custody, which ensures the integrity of their reporting. A colleague recommended them, as it appears they do a significant amount of forensic work as well as developing gene therapies. They are the most technologically advanced genetic research lab in the world, and this was begrudgingly and somewhat admiringly admitted by several people I spoke to in the course of my investigation."

"And the anonymous blood draw?" Amaoke asked.

"The order is sent. I filed it electronically with the public laboratory associated with the Urgent Care clinic on Orleans Avenue, and they have instructions on how to contact Rising Sun. Rising Sun will pay your lab fees for the blood draw, and rather than asking you to reappear as the lab normally would for other results like HIV testing, they will send the results directly to me, and I can then share them with you."

"What's the catch?" Amaoke asked, seeing her sad expression.

"You will have to wire them five thousand dollars in US currency before they will lift a finger," she responded, and he was certain that she was worried he wouldn't have the money and that such a situation would create some distress. "For that princely sum, you get the courier service as well as extensive gene mapping and comprehensive analysis of active genes and their products. Provided there is anything novel, as we suspect, the utmost privacy will be maintained, and, should gene-directed therapy be desired, they would quote you a price for developing a tailored intervention."

"How was your vacation?" he asked, abruptly changing the subject because he was concerned about her demeanor. "You don't seem rested." He was almost sure she wouldn't answer, that she would ignore this blunt intrusion into her privacy and maintain her professional reserve.

To his surprise, she answered him with equal directness. "I'm not. It was terrible. I really thought that if I could get away just for a short while, maybe get some rest, some sunshine, I could shake my stress. But as it turns out, I was unable to sleep much, and I couldn't stop thinking about everything I have learned since I met you. The world will never be the same. I will never be the same."

He remained quiet for several minutes, and she likewise did not appear in a hurry to rush in and say anything further. So Amaoke left her dilemma alone for a moment, returning to the subject of his DNA test. "You mentioned that they will look for not only uncharacterized genetic material but also what substances those genes produce which are unique?"

"In this case, yes, but it goes a bit beyond the standard analysis that you might get if you were trying to prove genealogy or confirm the presence of a known disease through overexpression of a certain gene, in which case there are known places to look. Also, it is possible that some of your genes are only in full expression as you are changing or once you are changed," she pointed out.

"Which is why you suggested that ultimately, to get the answer to my original question, I might have to reveal myself to these scientists," he said.

"That is a plausible eventuality," she replied. "It might be the only way to find a way to control what you want to control. I suspect the price they quote if they find something will be exorbitant. I think this is a company used to doing business with the richest people in the world."

"Crooks, in other words," Amaoke suggested, guessing at the reason for the disapproval in her tone.

"I'm trying to keep an open mind," she told him. "But who else has that kind of money and needs such absolute privacy?"

"Werewolves, apparently," he told her, pleased as ever when she barked out a spontaneous laugh.

"All right, all right," she said, still smiling, lifting her hands in her familiar gesture of surrender. She was too polite to ask him if he had the money, but she gave him a small leaf of paper torn from a notepad that had the name of the company and her brief notes about the wire transfer as well as the physical address of the clinic on Orleans Avenue.

"I'll take care of this tonight," he promised her, her puzzled expression probably due to the fact that it was Christmas Eve, which was no time to be trying to do any banking maneuvers.

"They warned me that it could take up to three months to get the results," she warned. "I think we should meet before then, and just keep up our schedule."

"There is something I want you to do for me," Amaoke told her, and he was surprised by the sudden seriousness in her expression.

"Why do I feel like I am not going to see you again?" she asked suddenly, her voice catching slightly at the end of the question, and he felt sorry for her, because he knew what it must cost her to betray so much emotion.

"How else will I get my results?" he asked, trying to be reassuring but suspecting that even she could hear the underlying uncertainty in his voice. Truthfully, at this point, the test really was a safeguard for her professional reputation, since he expected that whatever was to come of his encounter with Father Weston, it was likely to happen before the testing could reasonably be completed.

"I want you to write down a name," he continued, giving her something else to focus on other than her concerns. When she appeared poised and ready to write, he said, "Father Weston. He is a Catholic priest, used to be the parish priest at St. Constantine, and now he is at Our Lady of the Blessed Sacrament, over in Bywater."

She shook her head and looked questioningly at him. "A priest?"

"I'd prefer not to give you any details other than that. If you don't hear from me, keep him in mind, but be wary of him. If you have to ask for him, see if you can do it through the offices of the bishop? Promise me at least that much," he implored.

She appeared momentarily unable to speak, but she pressed a finger firmly against her upper lip and nodded.

He stood up, preparing to leave. He moved so quickly to her desk that she had no choice but to remain seated on the sofa. He opened the flap of his messenger bag and took out his mother's *ulu*. He had wrapped it in a new sealskin pouch, saved from his most recent seal hunt about five years earlier, and he set it down gently in the center of her blotter. "Use this if you need to. Keep it with you at all times. I like to think it has a magic of its own."

She remained silent, and he moved toward the door. "Can you make it to your car alone tonight?" he asked. She nodded mutely, but her face was drawn and sad. She gave up, dropping her eyes and looking down at her lap.

"Aleta," he whispered softly, and her head came back up. "I would hate to leave here believing that knowledge of my existence could take anything away from yours. Please remember to enjoy the little things like sunshine and sleep, and find joy wherever you can, because your life is so much more precious than you can understand."

Then he let himself out of her office, but not before he saw the first tear splash onto the back of her hand.

56

AMAOKE KNEW THERE WAS A Western Union at Canal and Broad, across from a Burger King, and said intersection was right up the road, so he went there to arrange the money transfer. Since he was sending it to a company rather than a person, he wondered aloud how useful the control number would be to him if there were a problem. It turned out that there were some failsafe questions in place since he was sending the money out of the country; apparently, Western Union was trying to keep regular folk from getting fleeced by foreign interests. Amaoke knew it also meant that the government was tracking this type of transaction irrespective of the amount, but since he wasn't trafficking anything, it was of little concern to him to answer the inquiries.

The agent looked at something on his computer screen and told Amaoke that Rising Sun Industries was listed as a direct notification entry; there was automatic notification of funds received at any hour of the day or night, and the company could verify the transfer immediately. This appeared to reassure the agent once he heard the sum to be transferred, and he looked at Amaoke as if surprised.

From there, it was a short walk to the clinic on Orleans; they, too, were open late because the facility operated as an urgent care after hours. The clinic was busier than he would have expected, with people in various states of repose, probably based upon the amount of time they had been waiting. He had witnessed the same phenomenon in waiting rooms before. Those who had just arrived were still inclined to be patient; those present longer had resorted to steadily deteriorating behaviors related to the amount of time they had been waiting, abandoning magazines and the television in favor of nervous tics and simmering anger.

In the time it had taken him to travel less than a mile on foot, two things had happened. When Amaoke checked in at the desk, telling the receptionist he was a coded draw; she did not ask him to sit down among the others. She pulled a folder from a rack just next to her desk, confirming that the number he gave matched the one associated with Aleta's request. It was marked *Urgent*; the word was stamped on the front in red capital letters. He smiled, remembering what he had read in his file, and wondered if Aleta had put in the request with that priority to prevent the frustration of a wait.

Second, Rising Sun must have confirmed the receipt of the funds he sent, because the second thing that the receptionist did was to make a call for a phlebotomist, and as she spoke into the phone, she reported that he had arrived and that the collecting courier was already waiting for the specimen.

Amaoke was surprised at the news, which suggested that someone was on standby, but that didn't seem possible. No matter how big the company or how lucrative its work, to have a person stationed in every city of consequence around the world made poor business sense. And if it was a private courier service based in New Orleans, it was the biggest holiday of the year, and notice was needed to get the proper travel arrangements made to go halfway around the globe. It was possible that they were aware of the case due to Aleta's initial inquiries, but they could not know when he would present himself for testing. Amaoke felt a slight chill and paid attention to his instincts, which made him immediately suspicious.

He did not have to produce identification or complete much paperwork; when he was called back to the phlebotomy lab, the tech apparently already knew just what to do. He admired her spiky purple hair and face piercings, which suited her personality, and the blood draw itself caused minimal discomfort. The whole process was so routine that his concerns faded.

As the technician led him back to the waiting area, he noticed a trim Asian gentleman standing just inside the clinic, near the door going back out to the waiting room. He hadn't been there only moments before, when Amaoke had come through from reception. He was dressed all in black, with a nylon windbreaker over meticulous dress pants, and his shoes and watch were costly items.

It was nearly ten o'clock at night, and the man wore sunglasses with lenses of a strange blue, almost violet, shade, and his eyes behind the glasses revealed impossibly large pupils, with a rim of grey irises. His lips were abnormally ruddy, as if he wore some type of lip stain. It was incongruous with the remainder of his appearance, an odd contrast to what seemed an otherwise fastidious presentation. He appeared at the same time bored and impatient, and his indifference to the happenings around him seemed contrived, because when Amaoke came abreast of him, he started abruptly, visibly spooked by something. Even this reaction he tried to deemphasize by checking his watch.

His scent was strangely absent until Amaoke was very close, and then he noticed the strong coppery smell of blood mixed with something that had such an acidic, acrid signature that it made Amaoke's eyes water. His clothing smelled of cold air, and snow, which was strange for New Orleans, even in December.

Amaoke turned to the side to pass him and went out the door to the reception area, feigning disaffection but not failing to see the pretty lab technician hand over the vial of his blood to the man. He produced a padded envelope from his jacket pocket, and without ever touching the vial, he captured it with the open end and sealed it away, placing it into a small case that Amaoke had initially failed to notice. There was a stylized logo etched on one side, the details of which Amaoke could not make out.

Before the door closed behind him, he saw the man set off toward the back of the clinic with so determined a step that he had passed several doorways in the interior corridor by the time Amaoke had fully registered his movement. Amaoke watched through the glass door a few moments more, and as casually as he could, strolled out of the front door and then sprinted around the side of the building.

He didn't immediately see the man, but his nose told him that the man was there, hesitating just outside the back door of the building, and then he turned and walked in the opposite direction, away from Amaoke, at such a rate of speed and purpose that Amaoke knew it was not possible for him to be human. He turned at the corner of the building and passed out of sight, and Amaoke had the strangest feeling that it had all been an elaborate set-up, and suddenly he wanted nothing more than to reclaim his blood specimen.

He backtracked, going back around to the front of the building, but the man had already crossed Orleans and was walking against the traffic flow on the far sidewalk. The headlights of a passing car reflected red in his eyes, and Amaoke growled, the Beast inside reacting to the unknown threat.

In response, the being turned its face to Amaoke and opened its mouth in a silent scream, showing needle-sharp lateral upper incisors, two on each side, and the smell of human blood was the predominant scent that came from it, so strong that Amaoke could smell it on its breath, in the way an alcoholic's breath is heavy with drink, from where it stood some hundreds of feet away. It tossed its glasses aside and fixed its gaze on Amaoke, apparently expecting a response it never got. Its pupils consumed all the color in the irises of its eyes, and the red reflected from its eyes by the passing traffic lights flashed its anger at him, a warning not to pursue.

Amaoke let the Beast out a bit, ignoring the intermittent traffic flow, bowing forward slightly and feeling his snout elongate enough to let the other see him for what he could become, and then he flexed his jaws to pull the change back, snapping upright to his full height, never losing eye contact with the thing.

It hissed in frustration and leaped into traffic, slamming its feet down on the hood of a passing car with such force that the car came to a halt, skidding sideways and coming to rest at the curb with a small thump. But the being itself was gone, using the momentum from the landing to launch itself up into the air. It ascended so quickly that it was lost to sight before the car was entirely at rest, the specimen within the case still in its possession and lost to Amaoke for good or ill.

57

INCREASED SPIRIT ACTIVITY, UNEXPLAINED INHUMAN creatures, and the persistent presence of the Morningstar all led Amaoke to believe that the decision he had long dreaded was near at hand. Gathering evil could only mean that at any time, the Monster would come and demand his fealty in whatever war was to come.

World events were also suggestive of the Morningstar's work in many places, as terrorism, homicide, human trafficking, and other crimes of inter-human hatred increased. People seemed to be looking for any minor difference that could be found to justify unspeakable acts against others, ignoring the common ground that must be discovered to generate justice or peace.

Amaoke knew that he had lost whatever capacity he had once had to disclaim humanity, understanding that the Morningstar was always perfectly willing to generate further power through terrible sacrifice and that his death would be the price of his refusal. He shuddered, remembering the torture of those long-lost centuries. His death would only be the end of a very long journey of pain and debasement; they could make it last years.

Would his loss to them be enough to avoid the greatest disaster he could imagine, the loss of true humanity in the world? He was not hopeful enough for such an outcome; the Morningstar had too many tools for destruction.

His dreams were more vivid than they had been in centuries, so lucid, and of such subject matter that he wondered if there were spiritual influences at work. He dreamed the dreams of a wolf, and in them he ran next to the Kuskokwim River of his childhood, seeing the little sod house on the tundra where he had spent such an oblivious and happy childhood. He searched for his mother in his dreams, but she never reappeared to him.

In his dreams, he also ran through the forests of the northeast, and into the sunflower field outside the little stone house where he had lived out a human lifetime as a husband and a logger, as close to a real human as he had ever been. In his dreams, his beautiful wife was alive, and she saw him as he really was, dancing in the sunshine with his coat of ivory fur, joyous to be in her presence once more.

Awake, he had to set himself to the task of pursuing whatever end there was to be. He needed to follow the priest and confront him. But he wasn't willing for that confrontation to come without gaining some information about what was happening between the man and the Vatican.

He considered all he had learned. Although the priest's scent signature was similar to the Morningstar's, it was not exact, and Amaoke recognized that it had real human underpinnings; the scent of pureflesh was also present in the man. His knowledge of Christianity was severely limited, and he surmised that possession of the flesh was possible. He was unsure that any human could survive such an invasion; further, how was the man functioning in his work? The Morningstar would be unable to keep its focus on anything sanctified for long.

He sat for hours, cross-legged on the floor of his room, praying and meditating for strength. He contemplated his axe, standing where he had stowed it in the clothes closet. He had put it there when he had moved in and had not had occasion to remove it. It was a modern version of previous axes, with a steel head and a hickory handle nearly four feet long, a custom instrument built in proportion to his height and with consideration to his grip stance, which was antiquated compared to logging men of modern times. He had been grateful to the engineer who had agreed to make it for him, since in his hands, it was a useful weapon in addition to being a functional tool.

Amaoke recalled his first inadvertent discovery that he had the ability to grant power to an implement he took in hand for use between the human and spirit world, but he had neglected to use that power, afraid of its corruptibility. He'd learned of it only when confronted by the demon familiars in the pit. The *ulu* caused their flesh to come apart, becoming insubstantial, or weakened, in response to only his desire to fight back. It had caused the *Ungalek* to cease direct physical torments, and he had a fleeting remembrance of the sense of some powerful spirit intervention, or an unusual, secure feeling that some overwhelming positive energy was being imparted to him. It had been an early version of what he had witnessed occur in his present interaction with the Morningstar's familiars at the restaurant, except in the latter encounter, his emotional fortitude and newfound control over the wolf had become the weapon. He kept it in mind at present, but rejected the idea of going about the streets with his axe, which would probably only get him arrested. It was a comfort only if they brought the fight to him.

And the *ulu*, which he could have concealed in his messenger bag, he had given to Aleta, hoping that its magic would work in her hands, knowing that she could better control it as a weapon. It had dispatched these demons in the past, and he hoped the walrus tusk handle would recall its magic if she ever had to use it.

It was both the worst and the best time of year to be hanging around Our Lady of the Blessed Sacrament. The church was busy with Nativity celebrations, and there was a great deal of activity to witness, but there were so many people coming and going that the possibility of detection during Amaoke's surveillance was also high.

He took advantage of the fact that the vacant house across from the caretaker's residence remained unsold, and would change at the bottom of the cellar steps and do his surveillance in wolf form. He had made a special trip to the local pet store, and using their automated machine, had made himself a new dog identification tag, which listed a fictional address in the Bywater neighborhood near the vacant house. He positioned himself in a different place each day, searching for the best spot to hear and smell the events unfolding across the street. Sometimes he wandered the block putting on the "I'm just a big dog" pretense, but he felt it was safest when he was stationary and out of sight.

He saw Father Weston on multiple occasions, putting together a rough schedule of his movements. The young nun was present as well, and she spent a significant amount of time with the priest.

In the mornings, the priest regularly attended Mass; Amaoke's talented ears told him that the person celebrating the Mass was not Father Weston. Yet each morning, he went into the sanctuary dressed in the flowing cassock in which Amaoke had first seen him, the silver cross swinging from his waist, carrying a small prayer book or Bible in his hands.

After Mass, the nun often accompanied him back to the caregiver's cottage, the two of them walking briskly side by side. Often, they were deep in discussion, voices so soft he was unable to make out any words, heads somewhat inclined to one another, which made him think they were very close. If not for the obvious vocational barriers, he could have assigned them the roles of young lovers, but their posture was likely only an indication of fondness, or deep mutual respect. Perhaps she thought Father Weston her friend.

They regularly took breakfast when they arrived at the house, based on what he was able to hear from inside. The clink of silverware on plates and the smell of food cemented the suspicion. Although they kept up a lively conversation at this meal, and he often heard her laughter, Amaoke avoided eavesdropping in keeping with previous habits. He was tempted to listen, especially since it seemed they were enjoying themselves, but he avoided invading even this unusual privacy.

When breakfast was over, he followed their scents as they moved into a different room, and the acoustic patterns of their voices changed enough to confirm that they had retired from the kitchen, which was nearer the street, to a place located on the side opposite the thoroughfare.

At this time of day, the cleaning woman from the rectory would come bustling along with a pinched look on her face and enter the dwelling without knocking. She was an austere gentlewoman of about sixty years, careworn but well-groomed, and she wore an elaborate gold cross on a chain around her neck. He could hear her moving about – doing the housework, from the sounds he could make out – and interestingly, this activity coincided with relative silence from the other two for the duration of the ninety minutes she stayed. When she left the house, he watched her retreat down the alley toward the rectory, and she never failed to look back, giving a disapproving look in the direction of the door from which she had just exited.

Based on her behavior, Amaoke deduced that she was a sort of assigned chaperone, and that her disapproval was due to an inability to rule out the possibility of an inappropriate relationship between the priest and the young nun. He imagined she had yet to confirm such a thing, since such a discovery would have likely been accompanied by righteous indignation rather than silent disapproval. He suspected she was not a woman who would hold her tongue.

Muffled conversation would resume in the interior of the house, but it did not have the lighthearted tones of the breakfast conversations. This was instead a quieter, more measured discussion, and no sounds of levity were heard.

Just before noon, the nun would reappear, habit virtually flying behind her as she rushed across the grounds to her cloister. It seemed she left the house later and later, and it was apparent that she had to be back in chambers with the sisters by the noon hour.

Sometimes Amaoke watched her retreating back from the street outside the fence, and sometimes he strolled around to the dormitory side of the block to watch her approach. Many days she appeared pleased, with a secret smile or laugh as she reached the stone building. On the days she was cutting it closer, these emotions were undercut with apparent distress, as if she knew she wasn't going to make it back on time, and on one occasion, he smelled her actual fear.

On that occasion, shortly after her arrival, which was apparently later than allowed, he heard two or three voices raised in anger from inside the structure, soon after which he distinctly heard the sounds of her sobs coming from the room he had identified as hers by scent on a previous visit.

The afternoon routine was more varied, and involved her return to the caregiver's cottage. The first day Amaoke was watching, she returned and came directly out to the street, pulling open the carriage door. The white van was parked inside, to the farthest left as he faced the door, and all of the auto-repair equipment was still present, along with the mysterious car under the tarp. She would unlock the van, climb in, and pull it out, parking it on the curb while she got out to close the carriage door.

Sometimes she drove out into the city with the other sisters in the white van, probably to perform service projects in the city, and on such occasions, he watched her drive it around the block in the direction of the cloister, pulling a wide U-turn in the street in front of him, which he found interesting. She never failed to park the van facing east when she left the garage, necessitating such a maneuver. Amaoke could see that it would have been just as easy to turn left out of the garage and park on the opposite curb, except that she would have had to cross the street twice more to close the carriage door and return to the vehicle. Or alternatively, she could have taken the long way around the block, rather than turn around in the street, but her routine never wavered, which made him suspect it was intentional, possibly even subconsciously so.

Very occasionally, she did not leave the cloister at all, which was the case on the afternoon when he had witnessed her sobbing. Even less often, she left alone in the white minivan that she had been driving when he had first encountered her at St. Constantine. Most commonly, she pulled out to the curb and did not get out, since the priest followed her out, closing the carriage door before joining her in the van.

The two never returned before full dark, and sometimes not until very late; once it was after two o'clock in the morning before they returned. In the latter cases, the priest dropped her at her dormitory and parked the van inside the garage himself. Amaoke noticed that he was entirely unwary when out at night, seemingly unaware of his surroundings, which he suspected was far from the truth. His scent did not change, and Amaoke waited to see if the Morningstar was about, or if the Morningstar was somehow in visitation with the man, but it only served to make him more suspicious that neither scenario could be confirmed.

After he had established the routine, he attempted to track their actual movements. Using scent markers, he followed the group of nuns in the van on two separate occasions. On the first occasion, he followed them on foot only a few blocks away, to the local food bank pantry, where they were volunteering with food cataloguing. On the second occasion, they went across town to volunteer at a blood drive; by the time he reached their destination, he recognized it by scent even though the women had already left.

He tracked the nun on three occasions when she was alone. Her trips all had a consistent destination: the offices of the Archdiocese of New Orleans on Howard Avenue. There was no variation in the amount of time she spent inside, and since it was nearly an hour each time, he suspected that her trips were scheduled meetings with someone inside.

But Amaoke was frustrated each time he tried to track the van when the two of them left together. He could only get so far when the scent of ammonia would flood his nose, obliterating the scent trail, and rendering his nose useless for long enough that he would lose their direction and become unable to reconstruct it when his ability to track returned. It was too regular an event and too irregular in location to be a natural happenstance, so he assumed that whatever caused it was a calculated precaution, taken by the pair to avoid the possibility that they could be trailed.

58

HE WAS REMAINING IN WOLF form so much that he had to shave every day. He had spent more on razors in two weeks than he had spent on them in the two years prior. That, as much as being frustrated in his efforts to learn much more, had him in a bad mood. That and the unprecedented soreness of his face.

After the first half of his life, Amaoke was wary of his time as a wolf for any extended period of time, because he noticed that his mood changed, and he could tell he was more volatile, more easily frustrated, more prone to anger. In contrast, as a man, he could maintain tolerance and patience for long periods of time, and he had always been slow to anger.

Provocation of the beast was always a possibility during times he spent in wolf form, and as he had achieved more significant control over the change, he preferred to remain human as much as possible. It was probably going against nature to do so, and certainly, it contradicted the advice of his mother from the dreams and visions he'd recently had, but the two parts of his nature were not alike in action. There were slightly different aspects of his character that each favored, like twins, one somewhat darker in thought and deed than his brother.

So, having catalogued the daytime routine of his subjects, he decided to watch at night as well, and for that, his two-legged form would do. He developed an irregular schedule by which he would wander the neighborhood, reducing the risk of being discovered spending too much time around the church grounds.

He had never seen any of the nuns out after their supper hour, so his quarry for nighttime surveillance was always Father Weston.

In the evening, the priest often shut himself up in the house, and although his lamps burned well into the night, he was occupied in some quiet study or contemplation, because Amaoke could hear nothing from inside. Occasionally, the man took a telephone call on the landline in the kitchen, and again, Amaoke caught a buzzing noise that interfered with making out any of what was said. He wondered if the secure landline had been relocated, and if its properties were such to prevent both supernatural and technological means of eavesdropping. He half expected the Morningstar to present itself, but it remained conspicuously absent; the nights remained spiritually quiet.

Invariably, the small hours of the morning would find the priest engaged in his prayers, keeping to the unusual ritual that Amaoke had witnessed from behind the rectory at St. Constantine. Pacing, praying, and thumping for at least an hour was not uncommon. Although Amaoke had no direct visual evidence that Father Weston was praying, what he could hear was so similar to what he had physically witnessed that it left no doubt that the prayer observance was the same.

On several occasions, Amaoke heard the sounds of serious car maintenance coming from the garage. The priest often hummed to himself as he worked, and there were the occasional expected sounds of frustration if the work wasn't going well.

Amaoke was nearly three weeks into his nighttime surveillance when, on a night marked with wispy high clouds and the dark of a new moon, the carriage door was opened well after midnight. The interior of the garage space remained dark, but Amaoke's night vision was excellent, and he could see the priest secure the door and duck back inside. He heard, more than saw, the tarp being removed from the other vehicle, as yet unseen.

He adjusted his position just in time to avoid being illuminated by two powerful vapor lamps as the car was started; its ignition climbed to a throaty roar that diminished to a heavy rolling burble coming from what he suspected were twin exhaust pipes. It rolled gently down the slope and into the street, and the priest returned to the carriage door to secure it.

The car was the color of the night, a gleaming black Dodge Charger, probably the latest model year, with the bright chrome cross like a beacon on the grill. It was equipped with racing tires, and from the sound of the engine as it idled, it had more aftermarket modifications than an actual racecar. *Who was this guy?* Amaoke wondered. What priest has a custom muscle car? Wasn't that a violation of a vow of poverty?

Father Weston settled himself in the low-slung seat and pulled away like he was launched from a slingshot, without squealing tires or any grandstanding. Not that any of that was necessary; the rumble of the car could be felt and heard for quite some time after he had gone.

Amaoke considered his options. He could try to track the priest, which would be simplified by the acoustics of the car, or wait to see what happened when he returned. A voice, suddenly at his ear, made him growl out a warning, but as he turned to identify the source, there was nothing there. It was the Morningstar, whispering in his head one word: "Constantine."

The Monster was nowhere to be found, and if it had provided the destination so readily, it was likely to be manipulating a confrontation between himself and the priest. Amaoke was out of time and patience, and he had decided that if the right opportunity presented itself, the time had long arrived for him to speak to Father Weston, but he would do it on his own terms. There was little reason for him to leave this spot, as the priest was bound to return. Secretly, he celebrated his own small rebellion against whatever small wish of the Morningstar he could deny.

It was another cold night, with temperatures dropping into the upper thirties in the wee hours. Amaoke remained still and silent in the shadowed doorway of the vacant house. He pushed his hands into the pockets of his jeans when they got cold, and felt a small card against his fingers. He pried it out; though it was folded and soft at the edges, the heavy laminate of Aleta's card had survived the washing machine, and he could still make out the print.

He pushed it into his back pocket and considered removing it and discarding it on the spot. His own fate was unpredictable, but he felt that if certain demon familiars got ahold of the information on the card, Aleta could be in peril. He closed his eyes and took a deep breath, pulling the cold air into his lungs while he thought. He was so quiet and still that someone observing him might think that he'd fallen asleep standing there.

A few moments later, he opened his eyes, and he'd made a decision. He would trust that if something happened to him, it was just as probable that a good citizen would contact her to deliver any news they had, and he felt that preserving such a possibility was better than assuming the worst.

He must have actually fallen asleep after that, or slipped into a doze brought on by inactivity and boredom, because he was awakened by the thumping rumble of the Charger returning to the carriage house. It was still many streets away, but the sound was unmistakable and unlikely to be anyone but the priest at such a dead hour of the night.

The priest pulled in at the curb, just past the carriage house door, with the front of the car facing east, as the nun had always done. This time, when he opened the carriage door, he went inside momentarily, and turned on the light, which spilled out into the street in a broad rectangle, and probably appeared brighter than it really was because there was no moon.

Amaoke didn't hesitate, and he was already crossing the street at an angle, coming from the rear of the car and the far side of the carriage house doors, by the time Father Weston reappeared, heading for the front passenger side of the vehicle. Amaoke adjusted his course, changing direction and keeping the car between them.

He thought that Father Weston might stop on the curbside when he realized that Amaoke was there, but his eyes narrowed behind his glasses, and he kept on coming. He was wearing standard priest garb on this night, but surprisingly was in a short-sleeved black shirt with his collar in place, and he seemed ignorant of the cold. His muscles were even more impressive in person, his forearms and biceps bulging as he increased his walking speed slightly, passing the side of the front bumper at full stride and turning toward the mesh opening of the grille as Amaoke approached the drivers-side door.

The priest paused to press firmly in the center of the space above the front fender; it glowed with a blue light, and there was a hydraulic click as the entire center of the Dodge cross was thrust outward into his hand. He disengaged it from the grill and continued around the front of the car, lifting it toward Amaoke.

Amaoke saw the cross, and the determined look on Father Weston's face, and he was suddenly amused. Was the priest trying to use the cross to ward him off?

With a small smile, he said, "I'm not – -" but never got to finish, because the priest was closing in on him.

"Catholic, I know," Father Weston finished without breaking stride.

"The cross doesn't care," he added, which Amaoke thought was a strange statement to make, but he didn't have time to consider it further, because two small wires shot out from the cross and lodged in his chest, and he felt the pain of the metal as it pierced his skin and then the involuntary awful jerk of a vigorous electric current. The implement was a powerful Taser, modified for terrible use, and the priest was correct: It was effective irrespective of the victim's religion.

Amaoke heard rather than felt his heart stop beating, and the world slid sideways and darkened as he lost consciousness, and the thump of the unyielding asphalt against his head was the last thing he felt.

Yet the night sounds around him persisted, and there was a scent in the air that he knew was the faint smell of his own burnt flesh. But it seemed only moments later that he could open his eyes, and discovered he was no longer lying in the middle of the street, he was lying in a field. It was her field, and the sunflowers were grown, their tops nodding and swaying between him and the sky.

Nanatha was there, on her knees beside him, and the wolf had broken through, his whines of pain increasing as she curled her fingers into his fur, gently trying to comfort him, and wherever she touched him, the pain and heaviness left him. It was replaced by a lightness, as if he were no longer attached to this body, and the feeling was not distressing, but at that moment, Nanatha stood up to leave him. She began to wander away through the field, and his whines were plaintive, then, full of pain and longing, the wolf wanting to follow, but unable to find his feet. Finally, she turned to him sadly and shook her head, saying, "Not yet, my love, not yet."

after

Text of report addressed to Dr. A. Madison, Dept. of Psychiatry, c/o University Medical Center New Orleans:

Result Completed   28 February 20XX
Result Reported 02 March 20XX

Specimen Taken 24 December 20XX
Specimen Received   28 December 20XX

Specimen Identification Number 1XXXXXX4
Specimen COC CONFIRMED

Subject Age   UNKNOWN
Subject Gender UNREPORTED;
      DNA   Result   presence   of   human   Y-chromosome,   MALE (UNCONFIRMED, see results)
Subject Race   UNREPORTED

Method
DNA extracted using proprietary protocol and expansion performed with PCR, subsequent STR, Y-chromosome, and mitochondrial analysis attempted as specified in original request

RESULT

Unable to generate clinical report based on specimen as submitted, analyses aborted

Decisions

D1. Cross-species contamination present
D2. Presence of animal DNA renders analysis impossible for disease mapping, genealogy, or paternity
D3. Genetic byproduct detection not performed

The report was the 51st of 137 pages of patient results scanned into an electronic notification system for review by Dr. Madison prior to e-filing within each individual patient's medical record. An automated audit by the Health Information Systems at University Medical Center New Orleans revealed that the report was acknowledged by Dr. Madison's electronic signature on March 5th, 20__.

report was acknowledged by Dr. Madison's electronic signature on March 5th, 20__.

*Text of the **original** report containing language redacted from clinical report results sent to Dr. Madison, but retained in the master file at Rising Sun Laboratories follows:*

REMAINDER OF PAGE INTENTIONALLY BLANK

Result Completed 28 February 20XX
Result Reported   02 March 20XX

Specimen Taken   24 December 20XX
Specimen Received   26 December 20XX

Specimen Identification Number   1XXXXXX4
Specimen COC   CONFIRMED

Subject Age   UNKNOWN
Subject Gender   UNREPORTED;
        DNA Result presence of human Y-chromosome, MALE
        <u>DNA Result presence of canid Y-chromosome, MALE</u>
[redacted]
Subject Race   UNREPORTED

Method
DNA extracted using proprietary protocol and expansion performed with PCR, subsequent STR, Y-chromosome, and mitochondrial (mt) analysis attempted as specified in original request

RESULT

Unable to generate clinical report based on specimen as submitted, analyses aborted *
<u>**Relevant findings follow**</u> [redacted]

Determinations

D1. Cross-species contamination present
D2. Presence of animal DNA renders analysis impossible for disease mapping, genealogy, or paternity *
D2. <u>Protocol AZ analysis initiated with incomplete analysis, responsive protocol modifications in progress</u> [redacted]
D3. Genetic byproduct detection not performed *

<u>Conclusions</u> [redacted]

C1. <u>Human male DNA present</u>
C2. <u>*Canis lupus arctos* male DNA present; when cross-referenced to Arctic wolf project autosomal microsatellite DNA and mitochondrial DNA (mtDNA) reveals unexpected unique haplotype which suggests member of previously unrecognized subspecies (supports new subtype in concordance with research hypothesis first published by Chambers, et al, 2012 and subsequent USFWS and NCEAS data from 2014)</u>
C3. <u>Unidentified genetic material found in sample, supernumerary unexplained STR segments present with unidentified chemical bases/unknown chemical bond structure; cross-reference to control specimen alpha</u>**
C4. <u>Lead project science team believes genetic material originated from a single bio-organism (UNABLE TO CONFIRM)</u> **
C5. <u>Potential cross-species/superhuman chimera (UNABLE TO CONFIRM)</u> **

*Reported to ordering clinician

**[1] Flagged alert to RSI Taskforce AZ Priority/Defense [redacted]
**[2] Material characterization project commenced as of report date [redacted]

These results were included in the agenda for RSI Taskforce meeting at an undisclosed location, electronically distributed to taskforce members in advance of the discussion. It was prioritized item 1, displacing the other items on the agenda for the meeting, which took place on March 1st, 20__.

Azuma Himura entered the conference room once she knew that all her people were in place. The conference room was a long, narrow rectangular space, with floor to ceiling windows on one side, and an enormous bamboo table custom crafted for the area, surrounded by 24 matching chairs of the most modern design. The décor was muted and minimalist. Azuma had chosen the exact shade of eggshell tint for the walls as a foil to the scarlet painting, which dominated the western wall and which was now worth so much money that it was electronically locked in place, by recommendation of her financial advisors. She was amused by the advice, but complied with it, mostly for insurance purposes; she doubted anyone would dare steal from her now.

She ignored the seat at the head of the conference table opposite the large monitor on the far wall, instead taking a place at the back of the room, leaning against the wall with the upper half of her body in shadow. The lights were kept low at all times, not just when a presentation was in progress, as now. Azuma preferred it, and despite the assumption that the light level might encourage less than perfect attentiveness, she found that it forced people to focus on the tasks at hand, rather than the others in the room that would otherwise have provided a distraction.

The windows faced east, slightly northeast to be specific, in the general direction of the rising sun, which for several more hours was not due to make an appearance. She looked out upon a darkness untouched by any moonlight, toward Kofuji, and the military base beyond, and Lake Yamanaka in the distance, beyond the Higashi-Fuji-Goko Road, all of which could be seen from here on a clear day.

The other 23 chairs were occupied, twelve by members of the scientific team and senior executives, who were unaware that the other eleven were members of Azuma's private elite guard and not company personnel. The eyes of all the occupants had followed her from the time she had entered the room. One could surmise that this was natural for her security detail as a matter of course. It would also be easy to assume that the remaining group would do so because she was the CEO of Rising Sun Industries, or because she was over six feet tall and possessive of the severe beauty of a supermodel, but whether they realized it or not, it was likely due to the fact that human beings, no matter how naïve, respond to the presence of a dangerous predator, no matter how subconscious that response may be.

Azuma had been the first to receive the priority results, but she forced the team to address the secondary items on the agenda before turning her attention to the foremost issue. She waited patiently while the scientists gave their presentation, only able to provide half of her attention. It took them the better part of an hour to complete their discussion on the unusual findings, but she didn't need the tutorial. Azuma herself was the source of control specimen alpha, the exceptional DNA exemplar to which this new sample had shown so many similarities, but no one in this room had any knowledge of that fact.

She was more excited, if that was actually what she was feeling, or perhaps more interested in the source of the new sample, and Azuma waited for an opportunity to ask the question she had been considering since the flagged result had pinged into her inbox.

When the presentation concluded, she remained silent, as was her custom. She was not disappointed in her team – the questions she would have posed were asked in succession. The sample had been specifically requested by a physician in active practice in the United States, but the specimen had been collected in an AIDS clinic, following anonymous payment through a global wire service. Since there was no evidence that the subject suffered from HIV infection or any other identifiable genetic illness, the collection method was supposed to have been undertaken in the interest of privacy. That hypothesis was now amply supported by the results of the testing.

When the initial excited furor died down, she asked quietly, "How do we propose to proceed? We must consider that the subject must have some suspicion of the differences in their DNA profile, but to our knowledge, this result has never been logged anywhere previously. Nothing in our network suggests that this is not a first evaluation of the individual.

"Is the doctor aware of the abnormality?" she asked, not expecting an answer, and impatiently waving away the attempts of the staff to reassure her that the results sent to the physician were a classic misdirection. Azuma privately thought that great intellect came with great blind spots; if the doctor had ordered the testing, she either knew or suspected there was information to be gained from it beyond what had been done before, and might even be appropriately skeptical of RSI's attempt at subterfuge.

"We have to operate as if Dr. Madison has some special knowledge that the individual in question is highly exceptional," she concluded, ignoring their protests. "It would be foolish to assume otherwise. What information do we have about the subject? Have we done diagnostics on the Western Union transaction?"

Her pointed question was met with silence. They hadn't considered any forensic financial intrusions, and she was somewhat surprised that this information was not forthcoming. There were at least three people in this room who should have already obtained this information and who should have been prepared to share their findings with this group. She refused to be the first to speak, which was her standard way of telegraphing her disapproval.

One of her most senior business advisors rushed to fill the silence. "Himura-san, the subject can be positively identified. The Collector saw the individual when securing the blood vial."

She remained silent. This was information that she should have already known, and should have been included with the conference materials. It was tantamount to incompetence to reveal this information to her in such a manner.

The same gentleman, recognizing the implication in her continued silence, squirmed a bit in his chair, cleared his throat, and continued, "The Collector reported the contact when he logged receipt of the specimen, but after he delivered it to the courier in Los

Angeles, he disappeared, so we have no other details. We have been unable to contact him since that night; it appears the courier was the last person at RSI to speak to him."

Seeing that this information was not improving the situation, a member of her executive board added, "We have been actively trying to locate the Collector, and wanted to better understand the situation, the reasons for his disappearance, before debriefing you without clear answers."

Azuma considered this carefully, not allowing her expression to give anything away. She turned toward the door, neither rebuking nor reassuring anyone, and said, "Then, as of now, we have nothing at all." She waved off the leader of her security detail when he rose silently to shadow her from the room.

She paced in the corridor for a moment, knowing that no one would leave the room until they were assured that she had gone. After a moment of indecision, she let herself through a doorway requiring voice signature recognition and took her private elevator to the top floor of the facility. When the doors opened into her private quarters, she crossed the great room and took the back door into her public office, unsurprised to find she had an uninvited visitor.

"Interfering with my business? There must be an important reason my Collector is missing," she said, failing to bother with the niceties of a formal greeting. "I should be thankful. Until now, I was wondering just how to appropriately categorize these results," she said bitterly, picking up the conference agenda from her desk, where it was apparent the monster had been reading from it and sending it kiting across the room toward her guest. "Now I *know* it's important if you have deigned to get involved, and that I should not expect my Collector to be seen again, since he must know something that you did not want him to tell me."

The Morningstar turned from its place at the windows, watching the pages drift in lazy arcs to the floor, and merely smiled at her.

Acknowledgements

I am exceedingly grateful to Professor Maria Shaa Tláa Williams of the University of Alaska, Anchorage, both for her writings and for her kind advice. She pointed me in the right direction for information that would assist me in building an authentic worldview and childhood for Amaoke. The writings of the late Angayuqaq Oscar Kawagley and anthropologist Ann Fienup-Riordan were indispensable resources in the creation of this story. Several historical and scholarly accounts of the Thule Migration were also studied as background in building a framework for the nomadic wanderings of Amaoke's middle adult life.

Any errors in reconstruction of the Alaskan Native cultural norms are entirely my own. In the interest of generating this fictional account, some liberties were necessarily taken in order to create certain characters whose behavior may have diverged from standard practices or where cultural situations were abbreviated or modified to facilitate the flow of the narrative. It is impossible to fully understand a cultural worldview when it is not one's own, much less by reading a few books, but I wanted my hero to have an indigenous Alaskan foundation, so I hope my shortcomings do not materially diminish the inherent beauty and spiritual underpinnings of his culture. In addition, I took an obvious liberty with the number of trees that exist on the southwestern Alaskan tundra, even along the Kuskokwim River and in the foothills of the Kilbuck Mountain range, for which I hope I may be forgiven.

Glossary of Terms

Akerta = *sun; from legend the sister of the moon god, Iraluk, who was said to be in love with her and continually chasing her across the sky*

Alerquutet = *expected behaviors of one who follows a rightful path, it suggests mindfulness in approach to all things, with a goal of maintaining order in the universe; best understood in concert with inerquutet*

Aana = *one word for mother, Amaoke's name for Noki*

Ayuq = *Labrador tea; along with wild celery, it was burned as a ceremonial plant, and the smoke was used for fumigation following deaths but also in preparation for a hunt; hunters would fumigate themselves and their hunting equipment, even their boats*

Ellam yua = *the all-knowing, all-seeing person or spirit of the universe; it rewards mindful behavior and observes transgressions and metes out punishment*

Iinruq = *the word literally translates to spirit; it can also be used to refer to an object with mystic power*

Iraluk = *moon; from legend the brother of the sun goddess, Akerta, who fled the earth rather than be captured by him*

Ircenrrat = *a type of extraordinary being that shared features with humans and animals and interacted among them, nonhuman persons (note that animals are also considered nonhuman persons). While Amaoke is regarded as this type of being in part of the story, his appearance does not correlate with traditional beliefs about the ircenrrat, and he would not actually be categorized in this way within the Yup'Ik tradition*

Inerquutet = *prohibitions and behaviors which are to be avoided to maintain balance in life, and among the human, natural and spiritual realms; best understood in relation to alerquutet*

Kass'aq = *white persons, broadly used to refer to non-native explorers, traders, and missionaries of various descent, most commonly European, Scandinavian, and Russian*

Nukalpiaq = *good hunter, provider; the literal translation of the word is boy*

Qasgiq = *men's dwelling or community house, a central place of gathering and male mentorship within a village, also the site of ceremonial events*

Qayaq = *the Yup'Ik version of the word kayak*

Tarvaq = *wild celery, similar in use to ayuq, or burned in conjunction with it as a ceremonial plant*

Tiquana = *adopted son; on his deathbed, Quuran bestows this honorific upon Amaoke*

Uluaq = *a curved knife most often used by women to butcher/prepare fish in the fish camps; the blade is also used by men as these duties can be shared tasks; also referred to as an ulu*

Umiaq = *a larger skin boat that carries multiple persons, used for fishing and sometimes for hunting larger sea mammals*

Ungalek = *legendary being; a name for Raven when he once appeared in bearded form among the people, but when people laughed at him they fell down dead — Raven was distressed to be the cause of death of his human descendants, so he is said to have departed and has not been seen since that time; for the purposes of this story, a curious and thoughtful Amaoke decides that the Ungalek must be a monster who is separate from Raven, since he cannot reconcile such terrible outcomes with Raven, the loving creator of the people*

Yup'Ik, Yupiaq = *two words that are the self-designated name of western Native Alaskans that populate the Kuskokwim river delta, Amaoke's provenance; the word means real or genuine person; the former term can be used as a singular or plural form, the latter is singular, and the word **Yupiit**, which is also used, is a plural form as well*

About the Author

LJ Farrow's childhood fear of the dark naturally led to a fascination with supernatural beings. Writing about them sometimes leads to sleepless nights, which frees up more time for writing. A Colorado native, she now lives and writes in rural Indiana. She is still afraid of the dark.

If you enjoyed **north**, look for **south**, the second book in the Morningstar series!

Kusini is a sorceress who wanders the Serengeti for centuries in search of the answer to an ancient question. Traveling alone through the wilderness, and through time, she avoids capture and dismemberment by witch doctors who would commit murder to obtain her limbs for their potions. She endures the ugliness of civil wars, and love allows her to restore a lost martyr who will accompany her to salvation. Within the cradle of life, she will prepare for what could be her final battle, and she must try to rescue the weak from the growing evil that had a hand in her own creation.

south is the second novel in the Morningstar series, which follows the lives of four supernatural beings, each of whom must overcome a specific challenge to their humanity as part of a personal journey toward redemption. The prevention of an apocalyptic war planned by the Morningstar will only be possible if they work together to harness the unique powers that each possesses.

www.ingramcontent.com/pod-product-compliance
Lightning Source LLC
Chambersburg PA
CBHW072004110726
47910CB00005B/1653

* 9 7 8 1 5 3 5 6 0 6 1 2 7 *